Journey to the Past

Holly Hunter

ARCHWAY
PUBLISHING

This is a work of fiction. All of the characters, names, incidents, organizations, and dialogue in this novel are either the products of the author's imagination or are used fictitiously.

Archway Publishing books may be ordered through booksellers or by contacting:

Archway Publishing
1663 Liberty Drive
Bloomington, IN 47403
www.archwaypublishing.com
1 (888) 242-5904

ISBN: 978-1-4808-8157-0 (sc)
ISBN: 978-1-4808-8156-3 (e)

Library of Congress Control Number: 2019911474

Print information available on the last page.

Archway Publishing rev. date: 08/21/2019

I dedicate this book to all the people who have given me joy.

Contents

Prologue

Grannyme speaks:

Allow me to explain my existence. I dwell on the other side of the veil. It is an ethereal place that few corporeal humans can see. It takes imagination to visualize me, for I am a frequency of energy. Those who do see me may find glimmering color that shifts its shape, much like a cloud. Most importantly, I am Aster Snowden's higher self, which means I am her go-between from heaven and earth. To be clear, I am not an angel. The exalted ones do, however, pop in on occasion, because they are my mentors. As a pupil, I strive to emulate them, to take the ascension route to the highest level. Roughly fifty thousand years ago, my council of teachers said that completing my mission entailed coming to terms with all aspects of compassion. They advised me to go to earth to experience a million lives to replace fear with love. Then, and only then, would my status rise.

A promising match for growth was to join with the body of Aster Snowden. Our body, mind, and soul connection challenged us both. A big chunk of the curriculum involved sending holographic images of me to Aster's dream state. Granted,

I took human form. She befriended me immediately and deep in her gut understood that we were a team.

Looking back, I often think of Aster's experience on earth as a flower going through various stages of life. I refer to her childhood on the Minnesota farm as the manure phase. Crappy, yes, but be that as it may, such beginnings provided a rich soil for the seed to germinate. Her cruel father beat her, and her vacant mother wreaked havoc on Aster's heart. On bad days, she prayed for mercy and sometimes wished to die. Life lessons such as these rarely seem fair. Hard as it was for both of us to endure the suffering, I knew she had to work through it. Not alone, though; I always came to her aid. I held space around her heart, imprinting an image of love and companionship in her unconscious mind. My intervention planted a glimmer of hope. I welcomed her into my dimension. I became the water bearer encouraging her primary leaves to sprout.

You see, I know her destiny. Therefore, as long as Aster lives, I am devoted to helping her blossom.

Chapter 1

Boulder Creek

Aster Snowden twisted her graying, ash-blond hair into a bun as she waited for the tub to fill. Standing naked in front of the mirror, she asked herself, *Who am I? I used to be so thin. Look at that belly. It muffin-tops over my jeans. I hate those pucker lines. No, not lines; more like trenches around my lips. Makes me look like an old hag! Aging gracefully is not my forte. At least my mind feels young.*

She added a few drops of lavender oil and a pint of Epsom salts before stepping in. The slant-back, extra-long tub allowed her body to stretch out fully.

Three months ago, in midwinter, when shoveling Colorado sidewalks grew tiresome and migrating to a warmer climate sounded great, fortune had blessed Aster. She had won the lottery. The numbers had come to her in a dream. A large blackboard framed in wood had appeared out of the mist. Written in bold, white chalk were the winning numbers. Printed below them were the words "Gamble with these, and the jackpot is yours."

A dream analyst would interpret the meaning as a symbolic message from the unconscious, but not Aster. She knew to take it literally.

Since childhood, her dreams had come true every week. The

nocturnal forecasts enabled her to finish sentences for people and win silly bets. Sore losers suspected foul play, thinking she was a cheat. In grammar school, classmates began to call her a *loco conejo* ("crazy rabbit"). Despite her awkward attempts to make friends, Aster could not erase the oddball stigma. She sat alone in the lunchroom and played alone on the playground. Worst of all, she was always the last one picked in gym class, even though she excelled in sports. From grammar school on, the gift of sight became part of her secret world.

Winning the money at age fifty-five retriggered her fear of being set apart from normal. Not wanting to draw attention to her fortune, she told no one.

She had bought a modest ranch home in Boulder, Colorado, a fixer-upper with musty shag carpeting, avocado bathroom fixtures, and chipped Formica counters. After remodeling and decorating, there was six million left over to retire comfortably. Gradually she reduced her workweek down to two days. Her private practice as a health coach and herbalist made it easy to set her own hours.

Now that the whirlwind task of customizing the home was finished, Aster had less to do. Life had kept her so busy that self-indulgent freedoms, such as taking a bath, felt like luxury. Excited about her new custom-fit tub, she promised to nurture herself with a bath every week. During today's soak, she tried something new, placing cucumber slices over her eyes. In no time at all, her muscles relaxed, and last night's dream consumed her.

In the dream, Aster sat cross-legged on a round cushion large enough to sleep on. Its purple velour fabric added a soft touch. A mist shrouded her vision, but she cleared her mind, rendering a serene yet attentive mood as she waited for the show to begin. Soon, an image came into focus. A wooden box the size of a bread box appeared, with the italicized words *Stumbling Block* carved into its side. The box replicated, and each one lined up behind the others like connected train cars. Suddenly they popped open, and manila folders floated out. All at once, the folders flew toward Aster, only to land on a newly arrived granite podium.

Aster reached for one of the folders.

"Stop," said a raspy female voice, ancient as the wind. As if speaking through a megaphone, the voice added, "You are not ready."

A wrinkled hand with manicured nails splayed over the folders.

"Grannyme, you crafty dream weaver, I should have known it was you."

Since Aster was five, this seemingly thousand-year-old woman had frequented her dreams, appearing as an older version of Aster. The resemblance was uncanny, like looking into a magical mirror. Grannyme lost teeth and grew them back when Aster did. Their eyes were the same shade of green. Whatever hairstyle Aster wore, so did Grannyme. More than once, Aster's mother insisted the old crone was an imaginary friend Aster would discard when she grew up. Strangely enough, Grannyme never left.

"What's up with the files?" Aster asked.

"Chapters of your life," Grannyme answered in a nonchalant manner.

"Oh dear, my life review! Am I gonna die?" Aster stammered.

"Eventually, my little bumpkin. Not today. These are personal contracts and vows your soul has made. Some have been completed, and others you'll finish later. Nothing to fret about."

A tress of wispy, shorter hairs loosened from the bun on top of Grannyme's head. Grannyme absently tucked the strands behind her ear.

Aster did the same with her own hair.

"Are these like destiny report cards?" Aster asked, glancing at the ominous files.

Dread crept into every nerve of Aster's body at the thought of a giant red check mark screaming, "Failure." Loneliness heaped plenty of burdens on her plate. Why add more crap? She wished the folders would disappear, yet she felt compelled to read the label of the top folder. As she bent down for a closer look, a strong hand lifted her chin.

"You made these vows before you were born, and you came into this life to work the kinks out. You chose to learn these lessons; the universe did not thrust any of this upon you."

"Can't I read them and get a head start? At least an overview?" asked Aster as her stomach tightened.

Usually Grannyme blurted out straight answers. Never before had her communication been so cryptic.

"I will hand them out to you when the time is right," Grannyme said as she picked up the folders and hugged them against her bosom.

"Patience, my dear. I'll say this: 'Thoughts are powerful.'"

And with these last words, Grannyme faded into the mist.

"Come back! What do you mean by that?" Aster raised her voice.

The temperature of the bathwater had remained warm, thanks to the heating coil on the underside of the tub. Unable to make sense of why Grannyme had suddenly become so mysterious, Aster dunked her head and let the delicious hot water melt away her worries. Sure as the sun came up every morning, the old crone would return.

After several dunks, Aster wished for a snorkel so that she could stay under longer. Nothingness prevailed until a worn-out mental tape invaded her quiet.

Widowhood sucks! she thought. *The thing I crave the most money can't buy. What a cruel joke. I miss the touch of flesh ... the nurture ... the sense of belonging. I'm queen of the lonely hearts' club.*

From out of nowhere, a violin played in the background, then became louder as it whined a screechy tune. In her mind's eye, Aster saw Grannyme working the bow across the strings of a Stradivarius. Her face was painted like that of a sad mime.

Aster suppressed a grin. She found it sobering that Grannyme had the nerve to invade her daydream, as if night dreams were not enough. She knew the only way to stop the wretched tune was to take the hint.

She thought, *Okay, enough pity pot. What gives me joy? Ah yes, the little things like chocolate on a rainy day or finding a parking spot. Cliché or not, I choose to see the pot half full.*

The ear-splitting tune continued.

Okay, I can do better that that. How about this: I won a jackpot; I'm thankful for the gift. There are countless options for me to pick from to make my life better. I want to be mindful of my choices. I need to just take it slow.

Grannyme lifted the bow from the strings. With a quick nod of her head, she vanished.

Aster drifted mentally from one subject to another, making a short bucket list of easily attainable pleasures: write more, do yoga, get a massage weekly, exercise, and be outdoors. For starters, run as many errands on my bike as the weather permits. And, yes, definitely buy a snorkel.

Boulder's spring weather was as erratic as ever—seventy degrees and sunny one day, and a foot of snow the next. The fickle pattern wreaked havoc on the local plants. Newly leafed trees acted like serving platters, catching flake after flake until the burdensome weight caused the branches to snap off. Early flowers sometimes withered from frostbite after their first day of bloom. Watching the natural process of the weight of the snow pruning the trees made sense to Aster. What bothered her was the sudden death of young flowers. Once again, something she loved disappeared abruptly.

As summer drew near, Aster explored every bicycle route in town. One morning, while pedaling down a street lined with Victorian houses, much to her delight, the lilacs were peaking.

Their fragrance brought her to a complete stop to inhale the nostalgic aroma.

She let out a pleasurable sigh. “Oh, I grew up with these. Mm, my favorite. I want some in my yard.”

Realizing she had spoken aloud; Aster suppressed a giggle. She loved how her life had slowed down. In a car she would have buzzed on by and missed the moment.

One of her frequent destinations was Boulder City Park. Sometimes she packed a meal, but she was never without her journal and favorite pen. Aster enjoyed a fruit salad under the shade of a cottonwood. She often wished for a cushion to soften the hard picnic bench, but her journal and the gentle roar of Boulder Creek made everything sweet.

A pair of mallard ducks climbed out of the water and waddled near. The vibrantly marked male stared expectantly at Aster as the plainer female shook her wings, sending droplets shooting in all directions.

Aster spoke to them as if they were children. “Hello, Hank, Irma; nice to see you. Just in time for breakfast.” She reached inside her backpack and tossed a handful of cracked corn kernels onto the ground.

Greedy beaks competed for the yellow morsels in the grass. Aster marveled at the sounds they made. Before long, she quacked gibberish to the adorable pair as they inched closer, eager for the opportunity to secure more grub in their gaping bills.

“You speak ‘duck.’ Well, do you have any idea what you are saying?” asked a man’s voice from behind her.

She turned to face a thickset man in a golf shirt and khaki shorts. He removed his straw fedora. His white, layered hair was carefully coifed down to the nape. A matching beard, white and closely trimmed, set off a handsome look.

“Patience, my fat friends,” Aster laughingly said to the ducks while directing her full attention to this interesting new visitor.

"My name is Jack. Jack McFadden," he said, his hazel eyes twinkling. "Once an animal caller, always an animal caller."

Jack laughed, fanning his face with his hat.

Aster placed a hand over her heart. "Aster Snowden. I love mimicking animal sounds, different dialects, and cartoon voices too. When I read children's books, I go way over the top."

She marveled at how easily the words flowed out of her mouth. *Where do I know him from?*

"Ever do it professionally?" he queried. When his thick lips stretched into a smile, he looked like a toothpaste model.

"No, but it was a childhood ambition of mine," Aster said, reminiscing.

"I got a hunch I can admit something and you will not judge me as a loony bird out on a stroll."

"These ears of mine are so well seasoned, I've got cooking oil oozing from them daily," said Aster, wondering if his inside was as interesting as his outside.

"I feel like we've shared many lives together," he said as he scratched the bridge of his roman nose.

Aster squinted at him, trying to decide what type of guy would blurt out "past lives" to a perfect stranger? At best, it was a topic discussed with close friends. Sizing him up as a bit odd, she thought it best to distance herself. But try as she might, there was something about him that lured her like a fish to a baited worm.

She said, "Wow, more candid than I expected. Now that you mention it, I keep wondering if you were a client of mine that I can't recall. Past life, you say. Hmm. Maybe."

Jack enthusiastically said, "The hair on the back of my arms stands up when intuition rings true. Let me check for some clarification." He held his forehead. "You were once part of my Navajo tribe. We shared other lives too."

Aster thought, *He's either a nut case who forgot to take his meds or a friendly neighborhood psychic.*

Curiosity had her ask, "Are you saying that because of

these?" Aster grabbed a braided pigtail, a hairstyle she wore occasionally. "Or are you a regular, born-again Navajo?"

"Born-again is a bit of a loaded word," said Jack.

"Is Navajo-heritage worshiper too harsh, then?" she asked.

Sensitive to the prospect of such posing, Aster kept her radar turned on.

"Ouch. I revere what my Navajo heritage has taught me," said Jack, taken aback.

"Sorry. I had a bad experience with a Native American wannabe." Aster crinkled her nose, remembering. "This guy, Eagle Elk-hyphen-Ganski, bragged of his one-eighth Cherokee lineage and then proceeded to steal the CDs from my car. The turkey justified his thievery as a raid."

Good-humored, Jack said, "I'm not that guy. My canoe paddles on much calmer waters." He settled the fedora back on his crown.

"I stand corrected. You're undoubtedly the type of guy who has a full library of CDs," Aster said smiling, deepening the lines around her green eyes.

"That I'll admit to be true," said Jack.

Peering deep into his eyes, she looked for answers. Trusting people was no small issue in Aster's world. She thought, *Jack is eccentric as hell. Why do I find him so compelling? Holy crap, I've got it! He's a loco conejo, just like me.*

Her lips relaxed around teeth that angled forward like the prow of a boat. Aster put on an aloof air to hide the growing intrigue and tossed more corn to the waiting ducks.

"I facilitate soul journeying into past lives. I teach classes at Discovery Center," Jack offered.

"I see. I'm an herbalist-slash-health coach," she said, relieved to measure him up as a friendly intuitive.

Jack looked at his watch and snapped his head back abruptly. "Well! I must be at the center in twenty minutes!" he exclaimed. "I come here to find solace in the water. I give my fears to the current before each lesson. It works like a charm."

"Gets rid of the jitters?"

"Definitely. You'd think, after all these years, I'd get over it," Jack said and pulled out a business card. He wrote something on the back and handed it to Aster.

"Thanks," she said meekly. Exchanging cards at this point was absolutely out of the question.

"Tell ya what, Ms. Snowden," he proposed. "Why don't you join the class as my guest and find out more about that past Navajo life?"

"Today?" Aster's eyes enlarged.

The back of the card read, "Guest Pass, Room 237, @ 10:00. Jack Mc."

"Sure. Are you free?" Jack asked.

"Well, umm. ... Yes, I suppose I am."

"No problem, then. Just go to the office, and reception will give you a name tag," he instructed and walked toward the creek.

"I'll think about it," she said casually.

Curiosity gnawed at her like an itching mosquito bite.

It was late spring, and the surging water from snowmelt had receded from the tree line. Aster watched as Jack took a moment to be quiet. He exhaled, and muttered some indistinguishable words. Turning toward her, with a knowing smile, he pointed at his watch, waved, and walked away.

Aster looked down at the female duck preening feathers with her bill. She asked, "Hey, Irma, whatcha think? The school is a safe location. Should I go to Jack's class?"

The duck lifted her bill high into the air, as if swallowing a bug whole. Then, she repeated the motion.

Aster laughed. "Okay, Irma. I'll take that as a yes. I'm going."

She scribbled a quick note in her journal, "Psychic Jack the Maniac. Navajo Indian; past life kin-ians!"

As she pedaled along the bike path to the center, large cottonwoods along the creek shaded her way. She mused, *Grannyme and I venture into the future. Jack's gonna send me into the past. I wonder what the heck I'll find. Am I crazy to let a duck show me the way?*

Aster had always wanted to explore the Discovery Center, but her frugal nature refused to pay the high tuition. Jack's class was an easy find on the second floor. Before entering, she popped into a restroom to verify she looked presentable. Her pinched nose and high cheekbones were pink from too much sun. Nevertheless, her blue capris were zipped, and most importantly, there wasn't any food lodged in her teeth. Her one last remnant of youth remained exposed to the world—something gravity and cellulite had yet to invade—tan, shapely calves, sleek and recently shaved.

Satisfied, Aster strode a short way down the hall and knocked on the door of room 237. Her stomach fluttered while she waited.

Jack opened the classroom door and extended his hand to greet Aster. He said enthusiastically, "Welcome! So glad you came. Come join our group."

The room had no furniture. Green carpeting stretched from wall to wall. Yoga mats were arranged in a circle, like rays extending from the sun. One mat was vacant.

Jack guided her to the group, saying, "Yo, everyone. This is Aster."

Like an AA group, all attendees chimed in unison, "Hello, Aster."

"Cheers," Aster said in a nervous tone.

Jack announced, "Aster will be our guest. I met her in the park, recognized her as part of my tribe, and invited her here. Aster, why don't you take a seat, and we'll get things rolling."

Jack pointed to the empty mat on the floor.

Aster settled in.

Next to her, a petite woman with light-blue eyes and a deeply lined face said, "Hi. I'm Galen Barlow." She pointed back and forth between Aster and herself, saying, "Yoga class, five or six years ago. Remember? You used to wear that purple outfit. Your hair was shorter."

"Oh right! Hi. Good memory," said Aster.

Here in a group of like minds, part of Aster felt less shy, without the usual high anxiety she experienced in a room full of strangers. To her relief, there was no time for further small talk.

Jack began instructing everyone to have journals ready to record the experience. "Okay, everyone, lie on your backs and get comfy. If necessary, close your eyes."

"A-a-ah," said Aster, enjoying the soft landing. Her closed eyes blacked out the new environment, providing an escape route into a calmer personal space.

Jack's words moved like smooth ocean currents flowing through seaweed. He was a maestro, conducting pauses just long enough for each wave to form. "On this shamanic journey ... you must set ... your intention. Choose the life ... you wish to see. Relax."

The room quieted. Jack paused for a drink of water. A faint smile graced his face as he watched Aster's abdomen rise and fall.

Aster set the intention to explore her past life as a Navajo Indian.

Jack's hypnotic voice carried on for another ten minutes. A snore from Galen had Jack walk over and press a thumb on her forehead.

At the end of the guided imagery, Jack said, "See ahead ... a golden light. Before you ... is an archway ... to the life ... you seek. Step through the archway."

The room was silent.

Since meditation was part of her daily routine, Aster found the instructions easy to navigate. Her mouth gaped as she began to float into timelessness. Golden rays of sunshine lit an archway of gray stone that hosted blue and pink blossoms of morning glory vines, beckoning Aster to venture across the threshold.

Chapter 2

The Fall

Aster stepped into the different surroundings and felt the arid air of the high desert permeate her nostrils. A cloudless blue sky carried no wind, and somehow the terrain felt like the landscape of New Mexico. Rugged grass plains with patches of yucca and prickly pear met the foothills of a mountain range dotted with pine trees. The dry soil was just rich enough to host prairie grass, fodder for the local sheep. To her left, cottonwood trees lined the narrow creek flowing down from the higher canyon. In the well-trodden location, a canopy of leaves gave welcome refuge from the relentless sun. Crowded between the trees thrived a lush display of sumac, chokecherry, and skullcap. Further from the water, the scenery became more desert-like.

A leather-clad teenaged boy, whose outgrown breeches reached halfway up his calves, climbed the rocky embankment. An ebony ponytail swished across his back with every move. He hopped effortlessly onto the lowest branches of a cottonwood and paused there to take joy in replicating the sassy croaking of a raven in the neighboring tree.

"Thank you for your greeting, old bird," he said, patting his heart.

Upward he climbed, striving to reach the highest overlook

of the plains. More than anything, he wished to prove his worthiness as a man at hunting. He and his father were searching for deer. Catching domestic sheep for meat was no challenge, for they grazed peacefully next to the village. Maneuvering fearlessly, much like a squirrel, he stepped out on a thin branch. In the far distance, a sienna-colored creature moved in the grass. The cry of a hawk brought his father's attention toward him. The boy held up four fingers and patted them on his thigh, indicating he had spotted a four-legged animal. He pointed to the east.

From below, his father, Two Rivers, removed an arrow from his quiver and placed it in the bow, waiting in silence for the beast to enter his sights. He kept a keen ear for the second hawk cry that signaled him to aim. Mouth-watering visions of a venison feast sent pangs to his belly.

A searing snap pierced the air as the branch under the boy's moccasins gave way. "A-a-ah!" he yelled as he fell.

Two Rivers turned at the sound of a scream. In a panic, he dropped his bow and ran with outstretched arms, intending to catch his son.

"Cedar Claw!" Two Rivers bellowed.

The boy landed on the rocky area below, only inches away.

In a chaotic moment, the bottom of Two Rivers's buckskin pant leg tangled in the branches, and he dropped to the ground like a fallen tree.

Aster approached the two still bodies. She gasped. "Cedar Claw? He could be me."

Blood oozed from a gash on Cedar Claw's forehead. At the sign of life, she placed her hand over the cut to stop the bleeding. Nothing happened. Aster had forgotten she was only an observer, not a participant. The teen's deep-set eyes were closed, and his wide jaw was slack. The father, who was just inches away, was not getting up to help. He looked like a bigger version of the boy.

Hovering over the body of Two Rivers was a cloudy-eyed old woman wearing black robes. She waited patiently. Aster had seen the death crone before. The way Two Rivers's face was embedded in the rock made it clear that his nose had been pushed into his skull. In a short time, his breathing stopped. The death crone greeted his spirit with a nod and led him off, out of sight.

Aster stared at Cedar Claw, searching for any ancestral resemblances to the Snowden family line, but there were none. Determined to find an answer, she used all her might to ask, "Are you the old me?" As soon as she asked, a sparkly gold cord emerged from the boy's chest and attached to her heart. Instantly she felt a kinship, and she knew Cedar Claw was a part of her.

Female laughter had Aster turn to see a tan horse led by a rope and pulling a travois. A group of young women encircled the horse to ensure the cargo made it back to the village. They had come down from the mountain with a load of firewood on the crude sled, which consisted of two poles strung together with a framework of laced buffalo sinew. The pole ends not attached to the horse dragged along the ground behind them. Each woman carried a basket; some rested the baskets on their shoulders, some tucked them in the crooks of their arms, and others held them dangling from their hands. All the baskets contained a variety of freshly foraged supplies to replenish their hogans.

A woman's voice said, "Moon Pebble, look! There's a fallen branch. More firewood for the hearth."

"I'll drag it back, if you take the rope and lead the horse back to the village," Moon Pebble said, offering the rope to her friend.

Moon Pebble, a new bride still wearing her wedding necklace, strode over to the fallen limb. Peering behind a large boulder, she screamed. With a scrunched-up face, she pointed at the two bodies.

Two Rivers's outstretched arms stuck out of the sleeveless buckskin. Moon Pebble checked, and his hands were already cooling. She shook her head, signaling to the others that he needed no tending. The sight of Two Rivers's body left the other women shocked. Several covered their mouths.

Cedar Claw lay on his side. His breathing was shallow. A red puddle had formed by his head. Moon Pebble set her basket of pine needles on the ground. She squatted, avoiding the blood, then placed a hand over Cedar Claw's forehead to slow the bleeding. With her free hand, she pointed toward the village, saying to the others, "Go deliver the wood. Bring the sled back. Fetch the healer too."

The women left quickly.

Moon Pebble shot a nervous glance at the dead body behind her. Gooseflesh ran down her spine. "A-a-agh!" she let out a dreadful groan, her shoulders shaking.

She turned toward Cedar Claw's placid face. "Y-you g-gave more blood to the earth than women do each moon. Be thankful that coyotes usually sleep at midday. One downwind whiff would bring the hungry ones running."

Keeping a watchful eye for any other creatures drawn to the scent of blood, Moon Pebble babbled until help arrived.

* *

Barely conscious, Cedar Claw felt hot sunshine on his face. Perhaps he was dreaming, for his eyelids turned translucent, with a surreal, glowing pink light shining through them. One thing seemed real: the sound of horse hooves clopping. Something jostled his body. A weak moan left his lips, and he slipped into darkness.

The medicine man walked along the travois, chanting a healing prayer. His brown, wrinkled face stayed somber as he opened his heart to the Spirit. Briefly, in his youth, his peers had called him Short Legs, One Who Walks Low to the Ground. He was always undersized. Eventually, the name changed to Turtle. The same genetics that cursed him as a runt also blessed him with an animal name. Each morning when he greeted the sun, he thanked the Creator for giving him a small, round chin, saggy eyelids, and a triangular nose, for all these features contoured to the shape of a turtle's head. Even his breastplate, constructed of tubular bone beads, was patterned to look like the underbelly of a tortoise shell.

Cedar Claw lay motionless in the sled. He had a broken ankle, and a cloth bandage was wrapped around his head. At the fall site, Turtle set the ankle bone as best he could. Excessive swelling concealed the extent of the injury. Turtle gave thanks to the Great Spirit, for the Spirit favored the boy by giving him passage into the dreamworld, sparing him the pain. The jagged cut on Cedar Claw's forehead now bulged in the shape of an egg. In a moment of reverence, Turtle nodded to himself at the speed with which his fresh yarrow leaves had stanched the bleeding. During the short trek back to the village, he took a mental inventory of the medicine supply. It was clear other plants needed to be gathered.

Turtle's nephew, Wild Arrow, stood impatiently at the healing bed with a clay jar in hand. His intense eyes were wide, much like a sheep's. The bottom half of his front tooth was broken from a fight, giving him a slight lisp. "Uncle, our s-supply of little mountain dais-sy is-s low. He'll need it with all that s-swelling. Whew."

"Arnica," Turtle instructed.

Wild Arrow puffed his chest like a proud warrior. He hated his scrawny shoulders and the fact that Cedar Claw stood taller than he did. Pretending to hold a cocked bow and arrow, he said, "On hors-seback I can reach the mountain flowers-s with the s-speed of an arrow." He took aim and fired the imaginary bow.

Turtle scrutinized his skinny nephew, who matched his height, eye to eye. "Huh, on my mare, Farwalker. She bites reckless riders," he lied. "A broken arrow if you come back empty-handed. Pick some nerve weed too."

"Ahi!" Wild Arrow let out a whoop and hopped a few dance steps.

"Ahem. Focus, young buck! Arnica and nerve weed," Turtle scolded, well aware of his nephew's enthusiasm for horses.

Wild Arrow looked confused. "White or yellow flower?"

"Nerve weed," he ordered, holding his hand as high as the plant grew. "Remember, it lives next to flat rock. The yellow flowers have many hairs standing in the center. Five thin petals. Tiny black dots line up along the edge of its petals. Gather some of its leaves too."

"My ears-s hear you, Uncle," said Arrow.

Turtle shook his head in disappointment. "Wild Arrow, your heart is not that of a healer."

Looking at the position of the sun, the medicine man said, "You'll probably miss the funeral rites."

He turned around and realized Wild Arrow was nowhere to be seen.

Wild Arrow mounted Farwalker, a gold-speckled horse, and rode to the fire pit in the center of the village. He stopped in front of a group of boys who were sharpening tomahawk blades on sandstone slabs.

The eldest of the boys shouted in disbelief, "What are you doing on the medicine man's horse?"

"Uncle gave me the tas-sk of a man. By mys-self, I will gather the herbs-s to s-save Cedar Claw's-s life," Wild Arrow boasted.

"You speak truth?" the boy said testily.

"The wound can fes-ster. I get to be the hero, ris-sking my life on top of this-s wild beas-st. Uncle hinted he might give me this hors-se if I ride like the wind." He gloated over the idea of owning a horse, for it was every boy's dream to have one.

Envy shone on each boy's face.

The eldest one replied, "Collecting herbs is women's work."

"Not on a hors-se," Wild Arrow said smugly. He circled around the fire pit and sped off at full gallop.

The sun shone high in the midday sky. The increased temperature made it too warm for Turquoise, Cedar Claw's mother, to shoulder her blanket. Instead, she hugged it as a comforter.

She arrived at the lean-to, her eyes puffy and her heart filled with grief. Standing before the medicine man, she grabbed the end of her waist-long braid, and used it to dry the tears on her prominent cheekbones.

Saggy eyelids blinked as Turtle nodded a hello.

Turquoise forced a smile. Her disheveled hair and wrinkled dress displayed an abnormally haggard appearance. She pointed toward the healing bed with trepidation. Out of respect, she did not wish to interrupt any spirits assisting in the process. At once, a wrinkly hand signaled her to proceed.

Turquoise's full lips quivered as she bent forward to examine her son. The simple act made her scream, "Ahh, Cedar Claw wears Two Rivers's face! My husband's spirit haunts me!"

Her eyelids fluttered as she swooned.

Turtle caught her by the shoulders, guiding her gently to the ground. "Talking Bird!" he yelled for his niece.

Turtle folded Turquoise's blanket and placed it under her head for a pillow.

The sound of tottering footsteps halted at the supine body. Talking Bird's long brown braids were pulled back behind her ears and tied together with a beaded hairpiece. Her slanted eyes froze in disbelief. In a trembling voice, she said, "Oh my! Not the mother too!"

"She merely fainted. Hold her feet and sing the Earth Song to invite her back into her body," instructed Turtle.

Turtle shook his gourd rattle over Cedar Claw to chase away evil. He then proceeded to chant while he applied the last remaining nerve weed, along with evening primrose buds and powdered deer antler, creating a poultice to lay directly over the ankle. In attempts to stabilize the joint, he constructed a brace of shrub-oak branches, willow, and leather. Foreseeing the lack of cooperation of his patient, he deliberately bound the knee to restrict any further motion. Asking Cedar Claw to be still was like asking the leaves not to be blown by the wind.

When Turquoise came to, her pretty face paled. She

whimpered, "Dear Mother, I cursed our family. I called the spirit of my husband to come back. I said his name. I actually said Two Rivers's aloud. No. Not again! I must leave ... to save my son." She kicked her legs free of Talking Bird's hold and sat up.

The medicine man and Talking Bird glanced at each other, both stunned at the taboo. Custom forbade speaking the name of the dead prior to burial. The sheer utterance of the name not only called the spirit back to the old life, it also disrupted the journey of the soul, cursing the family and possibly the entire tribe.

Silence prevailed for a few moments before Talking Bird spoke. "I'm sorry your heart aches for your husband. He was a good man."

"Shut up, little girl; I am dead to you. I leave now to be with my husband," Turquoise said stubbornly. She grabbed her blanket and stood up, full of defiance.

"I can help you cleanse," Turtle said. The base of his triangular nose broadened with a smile.

"No. I will lure the spirit of Two Rivers to follow me out of the village. I will call his name at sunup, midday, sundown, and in my sleep. I will wrestle with the Spirit if I have to. Anything to spare Cedar Claw from being haunted or cursed," Turquoise declared.

Clutching the blanket, she shuffled through the maze of hogans, with downcast eyes. Taking no notice of the conical mud homes that surrounded her like earthen beehives, she passed her own dwelling. Turquoise headed north out of the village in the direction a spirit leaves the earth.

Cedar Claw opened his deep-set eyes and realized he was lying in a lean-to. Strips of leather fastened brush and tree branches into a cozy shelter from the sun. Above his head fresh bundles of herbs hung to dry. Various feathers and bones dangled over his feet. His curious fingers felt the edges of a fur-lined sheep hide sticking out from under layers of blankets. He had not been in this healing bed since last spring when Turtle had sewn a gash in his arm. Every muscle in his body hurt. A dull ache in his head gradually grew stronger. He emitted a loud groan that summoned Talking Bird to his bedside.

"The tree climber is awake. You slept most of the day," Talking Bird said, touching his shoulder. "You are the first injured person under my care as learner. How do you feel?"

He looked up at her, still drowsy, and thought, *She looks pretty wearing that worry face. Never noticed that before.*

Cedar Claw tried to sit up. Intense agony rippled through his foot, and he had no time to mask the embarrassing cry that escaped him.

"Sorry! You are not supposed to move," Talking Bird said, looking troubled.

Cedar Claw tried hard to get his breathing back to normal, to prove he could handle the pain.

"Here, let me fix the blanket. Good. Can I get you anything?" She fidgeted, as she was unsure what else to do.

Ignoring the intense pain in his head, Cedar Claw smacked his lips and whispered, "Thirsty."

"I have something here for you. Now hold still," she said with a smile, holding a horn to his lips and spilling a few drops into his mouth. "This is one of Uncle's healing teas. Swish it in your mouth and wet your tongue before you swallow."

Afraid to move again, he surrendered, acting like a downy fledgling with its mouth gaping open for more nourishment. He managed a tiny chirp. At first, he wanted to guzzle the entire horn, but in his haziness, patience came more easily. To Cedar Claw's surprise, Talking Bird seemed more than a girl in the village; for some unexplainable reason, he actually liked her caring touch.

Talking Bird giggled. "Feeling better?"

Cedar Claw talked slower than normal. "Like earth under horse hooves."

"I see. Does your head hurt much?"

He blew air through his lips, imitating a horse. "No big cloud of smoke."

"So, if I touch the bandage on your forehead, you feel nothing?" Talking Bird lightly caressed the bulge under the bandage.

"Ahh, what did you do that for?" he complained.

"To find truth. I will keep touching you until you say how you feel. Uncle Turtle wants me to find out as much about you as I can." She feigned an attempt to touch him.

"Stop. My head throbs." He winced in pain.

"How bad?" She held her hand inches away from contact.

"Like wearing a headband so tight that the eyes blur," he confessed.

"And when I touch the side of your head?" Talking Bird pushed lightly near the temple.

"Yow! That is a tiny tomahawk chopping my head in two. No more poking," he complained, pushing her hand away.

"Sorry I made your pain worse. You men always hide your feelings. I had no choice but to force it out of you."

For a moment, Cedar Claw forgot his pain. He reveled in the fact that Talking Bird called him a man, not a boy.

Wild Arrow approached the healing lean-to, a leather sack full of fresh herbs slung over his shoulder. He scowled, witnessing the camaraderie between his older sister and competitive friend. "Look what I got! Medicine to s-save Fumble Foot's-s ankle," he said smugly. "I ris-sked my life getting thes-se. Farwalker got s-spooked by s-something. Probably a rattler. Yeah, that's-s what it was-s. We flew to the lake. I s-stayed on his-s back like a warrior." He expanded his chest and pounded it with his fist.

"Set the herbs down on that mat," Talking Bird said, uninterested in her brother's story.

"You know what els-se?" Wild Arrow said enthusiastically.

"A red-tailed hawk s-swooped in front of us-s and sh-showed us-s the way to the medicine plants-s. He dropped a feather for me. I gave thanks-s by throwing up a berry at his-s beak. The hawk caught it in his-s mouth and flew away."

Talking Bird exchanged looks of doubt with Cedar Claw. She blew out her cheeks, indicating that Wild Arrow's mouth was full of scat. They snickered over the private joke.

Wild Arrow strutted over to Cedar Claw's side. He said, "What are you two women laughing at? Is the Claw blowing wind out of his ass-s again?"

Cedar Claw raised his fist, saying, "Come here and say that."

"Ignore him. I'm going to clean the dried blood out of your hair," Talking Bird said, placing a wet cloth above Cedar Claw's forehead.

"Look, s-see who is pretending to be an all-knowing medicine woman. When playtime is over, you'll s-see how important my tas-sk was-s. Where is-s Uncle? I want to sh-show him the herbs-s," Wild Arrow demanded.

She gave Wild Arrow the silent treatment.

"S-sister, I as-sked you a ques-stion," Wild Arrow scoffed.

Talking Bird drew a hand across her throat, hinting for him to shut up. Her urgent plea fell on blind eyes.

Wild Arrow snapped at her, "Why does-s your tongue s-sleep in your mouth? Ans-swer me!"

Talking Bird worried that the tragic news about Two Rivers might encourage Cedar Claw to try to stand or crawl away on all fours to the funeral. His stubborn eyes would want to see the grave, and his own ears would want to hear Uncle Turtle chant the burial rites. She said abruptly, "Come, I'll take you to the medicine man."

Talking Bird headed toward the center of the village.

"Ts-sk," Wild Arrow grumbled impatiently, following her.

With each step, contempt filled Talking Bird's thoughts. Once out of earshot, she fumed at her brother, "How can you be as thick as river mud? Do you not know Cedar Claw's father lies in the earth? Our uncle chants at this moment to send the spirit north."

"I did not know the father died," Wild Arrow said, puzzled.

"Because all you care about is yourself," she said sternly. Her voiced calmed as she told Wild Arrow the remaining details of how Two Rivers had died, adding that Turquoise had fled, cursed.

Later that evening, Cedar Claw awoke from a deep slumber. The stars shone brilliantly in the sky. The air was cool. The smell of mutton cooking in the fire pit sent hunger pangs to his gut. He attempted to roll onto his side and then grumbled in pain like an ornery bear. He was vaguely aware that Turtle had rubbed something slick on his leg. Feeling confused because the sun no longer lit the sky, the voice of the medicine man filled his ears.

"We need to keep Cedar Claw as still as possible while he heals. That means you, young buck, do not get the last word in and rile him up," Turtle said, a direct order to Wild Arrow.

The sound of crackling flames had Cedar Claw crane his neck toward the hearth. Turtle, Wild Arrow, and Talking Bird sat around the glowing orange fire, eating from clay bowls.

"Yes-s, Wis-se Elder. It will be a difficult tas-sk. Cedar Claw threatened to hit me this-s day," Wild Arrow whined.

"You called me a woman!" Cedar Claw yelled, defending his honor.

"Sh-shut up, Cedar Claw," snapped Wild Arrow.

With the back of his hand, Turtle cuffed Wild Arrow in the mouth, reprimanding, "Tomorrow, the scarf for you, young one. Will wisdom ever enter your heart?"

Weary of the constant bickering between the boys, Turtle shook his head in disgust.

"The scarf of shame you shall wear will tell the entire village you are still a boy, not a man," Talking Bird added.

Wild Arrow made a sour face.

Turtle pulled out a long, flaming torch from the fire pit and placed the handle in a tall clay urn, casting light onto the healing bed. A smile lit up his leathery face as he addressed Cedar Claw. "You are awake, young buck. You need rest to get strong again."

Turtle moved closer to the bed. He removed the head bandage with great care and examined the cut for signs of infection.

"Does it fester?" Cedar Claw asked.

"No. The healing powers of the Spirits have blessed you."

"Ouch," Cedar Claw complained as the medicine man applied a disinfecting salve made of honey, echinacea, and chaparral on the open wound.

Turtle scooped up a spoonful of it and handed it to Cedar Claw.

"What is it?" Cedar Claw said, leery of the medicine man's concoctions.

"Prevents festering. Take this and lick it off the spoon," instructed Turtle.

"Mm, honey!" said Cedar Claw, relishing the sweetness melting in his mouth. Crinkling his nose, he asked, "What's the bitter stuff?"

"Good medicine," Turtle answered in that firm tone Cedar Claw knew not to challenge.

Humming softly, Talking Bird tidied up after Turtle. She picked up the discarded honey spoon. With those beautiful slanting eyes, she looked down at Cedar Claw.

"Are you hungry?" she asked.

Not realizing he was staring at her, he said, "I could eat an entire flock of sheep and chase away any drooling wolves intent on stealing my meal."

"I'll go fetch some flock-of-sheep stew," she quipped back at him, trailing off to the hearth.

Turtle observed the interaction between his patient and his student. He said softly to Cedar Claw, "At least my niece is a promising apprentice."

He had offered to teach Talking Bird and Wild Arrow healing skills while their parents spent the summer with Pueblo Indians in Taos, planning a rebellion against the controlling Spanish priests.

"Which speaks louder, your head or ankle?" Turtle asked.

"Foot area. Ankle, I guess."

"It's broken. I braced it. Take a look."

Cedar Claw tried to sit up to look at the medicine man's handiwork. Dizzy, he swayed and fell back into the bed.

Turtle inched the torch closer for better light, removed the blanket, and supported Cedar Claw's torso while he inspected the brace.

"You made a cradle board for my leg. How am I supposed to move?" Cedar Claw demanded.

From the waist down he was naked. Modesty had him cover his privates, as Talking Bird would be returning with food.

"You are not," Turtle said in response to Cedar Claw's question, flashing warning eyes.

"What if I have to pass water?"

"A piss pot."

"Great," Cedar Claw sulked.

Talking Bird returned, carrying a bowl of stew. "Let's see if this fills you up," she said cheerfully.

"He cannot sit up yet. You will have to hold him while he eats. I must thank the Spirits for their help," said Turtle as he returned to his mat and sat by the warmth of the fire.

"Can you move your arms?" Talking Bird asked.

Cedar Claw winced as he lifted his right arm. "My other one works better," he said in a disappointed tone, now realizing he had more injuries than he thought.

The spicy stew tasted delicious. The way Talking Bird embraced his body felt nurturing. Surprisingly, he felt desire in his loins. His back rested against her breasts, and the sensation made his penis rise. Because he wore no breeches, the blanket bulged. Cedar Claw glanced down and blushed.

"You stopped eating. Are you dizzy? Do you not like the stew? Or did you spill? I cannot see the bowl; you are blocking my sight," Talking Bird said.

"No, no, stay where you are. I'm savoring the taste is all." He spooned in another mouthful, feeling grateful she saw nothing. Desperately, he turned his attention to the sky and searched for shooting stars.

Talking Bird chatted away endlessly. By the time Cedar Claw finished the stew, all his body functions had returned to normal.

Moving carefully, Talking Bird stood up and helped Cedar Claw recline in the bed. "Look, another shooting star. Seeing this many streak in the sky brings luck," she commented.

Wild Arrow, who hid behind a hogan watching, sneaked closer to listen to what Talking Bird had to say. In the evening darkness, he slinked among the shadows.

"Cedar Claw, what do you remember last?" she asked.

"Hmm. Hunting with father. Climbing a tree and looking for deer. ... Ah ... and then, waking up in this bed."

"You fell and clunked your head. Uncle said you might feel like your head had rocks inside," she said, teasing.

Talking Bird's nose was almost as narrow as the Spanish who had migrated from the south and from across the great ocean. He thought, *Curious that I never noticed that before.*

"Rocks? Maybe turquoise rocks," he joked. "Seriously, I do not recall falling."

"The tree branch you stood on broke," Talking Bird said, pushing a strand of hair out of her eyes. She had the lightest color hair in the village, a medium shade of brown, not the usual black.

He smiled at her, daydreaming. *She is so beautiful, I want to kiss her. I think her birth father is from a different part of the world.* He imagined her real father was not Horned Bull, the man who had raised her. People said Talking Bird's mother lay with the Spaniard for a knife trade, a wedding present for her soon-to-be husband.

Parents? Cedar Claw's thoughts changed suddenly, and he craned his neck, looking around. "Where are my parents? Why are they not here?"

Worry clouded Talking Bird's face. How could she explain without causing Cedar Claw more pain? Ever since infancy, her mouth chattered like a bird. Unusual, as it might be, she said nothing now, just cleared her throat.

"Have you seen them?" Cedar Claw asked.

"I-I think your mother is away at another village. Your father, well, um ... I believe he is resting," she said nervously.

"For eternity," Wild Arrow blurted, coming out of hiding. The scarf of shame hung around his neck, no longer covering his face. He inched closer, full of malicious intent. "Your father died. Bled from his ears-s."

He then abruptly shut up.

Turtle, who hurried over to Wild Arrow, lunged and cuffed his outspoken nephew on the backside.

"You speak too harshly. No respect. Three more days wearing the scarf," the old man scolded.

Wild Arrow flashed an I-got-you-last smirk as his uncle dragged him into the hogan by the ear.

"Is this true? My father!" Cedar Claw's voice trailed off. He looked horror-struck.

"I'm sorry to bring you sadness. Yes, it is true," Talking Bird said, biting her bottom lip.

"How can this be?" he pleaded. "We were hunting."

"Like his son, he hit his head. He must have tripped and fallen fast," she said.

Cedar Claw's face contorted in unbearable pain. "Where?" he asked through trembling lips.

"Right next to you," she said, sniffling.

"It's my fault he died. I begged him to take me hunting. I stepped on the branch that broke. Did I land on Father and kill him?" Cedar Claw moaned.

"No," she replied, trying to lessen his burden. She had no idea if he did or not.

Talking Bird kept Cedar Claw still by holding him while they both cried.

❋ ❋

The sun hid behind a small patch of clouds. A light breeze kept Cedar Claw cool as he lounged in the shaded confinement. Feeling like a prisoner of the lean-to, memories of his father came and went, rekindling the ache in his heart. Out of habit, he expected to see his mother braiding his father's hair, but as he brushed the sleep from his eyes, he was all too aware of their absence. He had wept a good portion of the night. By morning, emptiness enveloped him until he remembered having two dreams.

The first dream was of his mother. Turquoise's cheeks were thin. She sat in a crevice of a rock outcropping, her shoulders nearly touching the steep sides. She reclined on her back, nestled in the fissure, and fell asleep. Short as the dream was, Cedar Claw found joy in her smile. He wanted to hear her voice, but, somehow, he knew she would never come back.

The second dream he had was of bedding Talking Bird. Kissing her felt like magic, as though they became their own ancestors, from the beginning of time, generation after generation as husband and wife. The glorious recall of their naked bodies rising together until ecstasy made him shudder. Over and over again, he replayed the scene, trying his best to cast aside the abandoned feeling of an orphan.

The medicine man's necklace jangled softly against his beaded breastplate as he walked to the bedside. A strand of teeth intertwined with seeds and bones protected against bewitching foes and alerted man and critters alike of his approach. At a glance, he saw a bored teenaged face. "How is your day going, young one?" he asked.

"Life is hard sitting here like a rock. I'm useless. I should be the one who died," Cedar Claw complained.

Turtle studied his patient. The lanky teen before him was no longer a boy and not yet a man. He said, "You speak with grief in your heart. You are very much alive."

Unable to contradict the truth, Cedar Claw sighed. "True. Turtle, I wish to speak of something else. I had a dream last night. I want to know what the Dream Spirit is showing me. Can I tell you?"

"Yes."

Cedar Claw chose to keep the dream about Talking Bird private and proceeded to share the dream about his mother.

Turtle exhaled a long breath. "The Spirit sent you a vision. Before I tell you, young buck, much has changed while you slept. Like the first snow turning brown leaves white."

"I know this," Cedar Claw said bitterly, motioning toward his foot.

"Let me explain," Turtle said. He squatted, picked up a stone, and with it drew the four phases of the moon in the dirt. Pointing at the half circle, he said, "Your father joined the spirit world during the wane of the moon. When Sister Moon shrinks, so does her power. Women ebb and flow with this power. It is this time, the wane of the moon, when emotions make women do foolish things, things they may regret."

"Are you telling me that Mother did something stupid?" blurted Cedar Claw.

Turtle pounded his fist against his heart twice, commanding respect as an elder.

Silence fell.

The old man's pause seemed to be deliberate, intended to keep Cedar Claw waiting. Cedar Claw wished for the riddle to end. He stared at the elder until his eyes went out of focus.

Finally, Turtle cleared his throat and said, "Your mother was unwise. Before your father rested in the earth, she spoke his name."

"No!" Cedar Claw gasped.

"The truth is hard on the ears. I am sorry."

Cedar Claw's heart went numb. He said, "Please tell me everything. I cannot understand until you do."

Word for word, Turtle recounted his interaction with Turquoise.

With piercing insight, Cedar Claw asked, "In the dream, when Mother smiled, do you think she greeted Father's spirit?"

"It is possible. I believe it was her plan to protect you, to lure your father's spirit away. A good woman like her swallows mouthfuls of shame each day for cursing her family. Her death would mean the curse is lifted. For your sake, she hungered to live in the spirit world instead of the earth," Turtle said.

"I think living without Father added another stone on her heart."

"True. You speak like an old man," Turtle said, taking note that no hot embers shot out of Cedar's lips, nor did grief show in his eyes. The poor boy was too shocked to feel.

Ignoring the compliment, Cedar Claw swallowed hard, trying to making sense of it all. Matter-of-factly, he said, "It is true; winter has fallen upon me. Turtle, I have no family. I may never walk or hunt again. I am the weakest one in the herd. Maybe the dream tells me I am to follow my parents into the spirit world. I am brave enough to go there."

"No, that is not your path. The Spirit has spoken in my ear. You are gifted with clever hands. I will teach you the medicine way," Turtle said, unwilling to witness the dark cloud end another life and destroy an entire family.

"You already teach Wild Arrow and Talking Bird."

"Wild Arrow has the heart of a warrior. He would rather fight."

"That means Talking Bird and I will learn together?" Cedar Claw asked.

While considering all these life changes, his heart clung to the idea of working side by side with the girl who had nursed him so tenderly.

"Yes. She and I will be your family."

Tears filled Cedar Claw's eyes.

❋ ❋

The following day, Talking Bird maintained her vigil, sitting beside Cedar Claw and twirling wool into yarn. Her slender body was planted straight, like a young pine sitting on top of a woven mat. Her fingers moved skillfully, keeping the yarn at an even thickness.

Cedar stole a look at Talking Bird. Her movements and doe eyes captivated his attention. Engulfed in fantasy, he wanted more than dreams.

Turtle came clanking up to the lean-to with a leather sack full of sage.

"We are making smudge sticks, yes?" Talking Bird asked.

"Yes," answered Turtle.

She glanced in the sack and said merrily, "I believe there's plenty of sage to make extra for gifts or trade."

"Now there's a thought. We will use the thread Talking Bird made to tie the bundles," said Turtle.

"I'm ready to make smudge sticks," Cedar Claw said. No longer dizzy, he looked enthused, eyeing the parcel. His fingers moved greedily, like a hungry spider climbing to retrieve the fly caught in its web.

Turtle gave a little chuckle. He placed a mat on Cedar Claws lap and said, "Now watch. Take a hand-sized bundle of sage, place it on the edge of the mat, and use the mat to roll the sage tight, like this. See how firm it gets? Then, remove the bundle from the mat, using a strong grip. While you hold it, Talking Bird will wrap and tie it with string. See? Just like this." Turtle gave the finished piece to Cedar Claw.

"It looks easy," Cedar Claw said, inspecting the smudge stick.

A shadow moved over Cedar Claw's body, causing everyone to look up into the sky. A large bird with expansive wings glided overhead, presumably looking for a morning meal.

"A golden eagle," Talking Bird said in awe.

"Ahh-eee-waak," Cedar Claw cried out to the enormous bird.

There was no reply. The sacred bird dived out of sight, obscured by the terrain as it swept up its prey. The eagle rose up with a limp rabbit clutched in its talons. Three powerful strokes of the wings swiftly propelled the bird to a lofty altitude.

Awestruck at the elegant maneuvers of the great hunter, Turtle said, "This is a good sign. The eagle soars at great heights above the earth, close to the Spirit, experiencing a farsighted wisdom that all tribal members dream to have."

"Why a good sign?" Talking Bird asked.

"The eagle cast his shadow onto Cedar Claw. There is a special message for him," Turtle said.

"What kind of message? I could use a good omen," Cedar Claw whined.

With a slight curl of his lip, Turtle said, "The eagle has shown you the cycle of life; for out of death comes new beginnings. He has shown you the power to rise above and go forward into your next journey. You are very lucky."

"Me. Lucky?" Cedar Claw said, screwing up his face.

"Yes, you are. Learning to be a medicine man is an honor," Talking Bird said, appearing to catch on to Turtle's cheering-up comment.

Cedar Claw gazed at Talking Bird. Her small breasts poked from her dress in a pleasant way, and her lovely slanted eyes hypnotized him into replying, "My hands wish to heal. I want to be useful. I have no desire to be a burden."

"Good choice," Talking Bird replied.

Turtle gave a nod of satisfaction and left his students alone to finish their lesson.

Content to be near Talking Bird, Cedar Claw said, "With all this sitting, I want to do things with my hands. When we finish making the sticks, I can help prepare for the rebellion. I can help fasten arrowheads, sand arrow shafts, or sharpen tomahawks—anything to keep my claws moving."

"Speaking of the rebellion," Talking Bird said, "I heard a funny thing at the rebellion meeting yesterday. Do you know why the robes of the Catholic priests are black? Because they use the cloth to wipe the poop from their behinds."

Cedar Claw snickered, saying, "I agree the priests are not wise. They call us heathens, when in truth, they speak of themselves."

Talking Bird said incredulously, "The dishonor angers me. The priests pretended to be our friends. They called a gathering of our holy men, and forked tongues promised horses to all that came. The lie became clear when the medicine men were led into the church at gunpoint, and then given the choice to repent for devil worship or die."

"Demanding savation was an evil act!" Cedar Claw exclaimed.

"Salvation," she corrected.

Cedar Claw rolled his eyes and said, "What do the priests know about the way of the Spirit? They jailed five of our shamans who refused salvation and then hung four of the five the next day."

Still wearing the scarf, Wild Arrow had stopped at the water urn for drink. Upon pulling the scarf from his mouth, he downed a full mug, and then cut into the conversation, "The fifth sh-shaman was-s like me, a cactus-s jumper. He was-s the cleveres-st becaus-se he hung hims-self in jail, preventing the priests-s the pleas-sure of killing a s-savage."

"You are always picking thorns out of your butt, aren't you?" Cedar Claw, said not in the mood for the unwanted intrusion.

Wild Arrow's wide set eyes glowed like fire, and he said, "I was firs-st pick for the food, mend, and tend clan. I am joining the tribes-s that are banding together for revenge. Together, we will be big in numbers-s and s-spill blood of their holy men."

“More like force them back from where they came,” Cedar Claw said.

Wild Arrow retorted scornfully, “Look at little know-it-all. Cannot move, can you?”

“Shut up. You were first pick because you are no good at medicine,” Cedar Claw shot back.

In a cocky tone Wild Arrow said, “S-so? I will be helping the warriors-s while you lay around doing woman’s-s work with my s-sister. S-sorry I cannot s-stay; firs-st picks-s lead the war dance. Enjoy your mis-sery.”

Chapter 3

The Ride Home

Aster rolled over on the yoga mat and frantically jotted down key points about her journey into the Navajo past life. In huge letters across the bottom page, she wrote, "REBELLION OUTCOME?"

When Aster sat up, Galen's puffy eyes were staring in her direction. Aster asked, "How'd your journey go?"

Galen yawned and said, "Not so good. I fell asleep. Had a weird-ass dream about selling peanut butter-and-jelly tacos and jewelry in St. Louis. And then—poof!—I was mining crystals in Arkansas, using a laser gun."

"Any clue as to what it means?" asked Aster, smiling at the oddity.

"No, it's way too wonky. How about you? Where did you go?" Galen seemed overly eager.

"New Mexico area. I visited a Navajo life," Aster answered briefly. She felt hesitant to rub in her "success."

"Was it like a movie, or a bunch of snapshots?"

"Hmm. It seemed like a virtual-reality show."

"Cool. I'd love to hear the story over a cup. Are you free now?" Galen suggested.

"Too late for coffee. I'll never sleep," Aster said shyly.

"Tea?" pressed Galen.

"Not now; I have to make a phone call real soon. Perhaps another day." Aster came off as aloof.

"I know. Let's do a yoga class together, like old times. Here's my business card. You got one to give me?" Galen said, determined to be Aster's friend.

Aster read the italic lettering on the card: "Galen Barlow, Jeweler and Craniosacral Therapist. Best Hands in the Business."

Friendships were something Aster usually botched up. Not expecting any follow-through, Aster exchanged cards.

"Great! There's a yoga class on Sunday, at nine in the morning. I'll swing by and pick you up."

"Okay. Sunday it is," Aster replied, taken aback by how quickly the arrangement happened.

"Nice. This will be fun," Galen said, tucking Aster's card into her purse.

Galen seemed nice but pushy. Aster's discomfort triggered anxiety. Aster struggled to stuff it down.

She looked at the wall clock and said, "Oh my gosh, look at the time. I gotta run. J. J. is expecting my call. See you Sunday."

Aster waved a thank-you at Jack and left.

Engaged in conversation with another student, Jack glanced up at Aster's abrupt departure.

What Aster did not see was the disappointment on his face.

Aster began to talk herself down. "Okay, there's truth to the phone call. J. J. and I talk every Monday. Thank you, cousin, for an excuse to escape. I get so awkward around strangers. But Galen is no stranger; I can do yoga with her. I've toyed with the idea of taking classes again."

It was eleven o'clock. Aster walked out of the air-conditioned Discovery Center, with glazed eyes. The assault of sweltering heat felt far worse than any hot flash. She set off on her bike, slicing through the wind and riding under as much shade as possible. Recapping the last hour, she thought, *That Navajo life was incredible. It kept unfolding like a chapter in a book!*

At the corner of Twentieth and Pearl, the blast of a horn

snapped her out of her reverie. She had failed to stop at the light. Mistaking the angry driver for a greeting client, she waved merrily at the car. The relationship between Cedar Claw and Talking Bird drew Aster back into oblivion as she pedaled home.

Her red-brick ranch had a breezeway that attached the house to the garage. A tall blue spruce practically blocked the sidewalk that led to the door. A few of its branches had been cut away, forming an arched passage that made Aster feel charmed every time she walked through it.

In her haste, Aster ignored the full mailbox in the breezeway. She grabbed her phone and dialed up her cousin, Jeraldine Jansen (more commonly known as J. J.), on FaceTime.

J. J. and Aster had become best friends during junior high, and until they graduated high school. J. J., the more gregarious of the two, had big boobs, which were an automatic ticket to popularity. Aster had always been a shy loner. Cruel as the rite of passage was, her training bra kept her social status at the bottom of the totem pole. J. J. once punched Steven Plato in the mouth for comparing Aster to an ironing board. Word spread fast not to tease Aster the Late-Blooming-Flower. No longer mocked for her looks or her loco conejo abilities, Aster started to feel normal. From that point forward, the two girls spent much of their time at Aunt Gertie's house, Aster's home, and J. J. seemed to never want to go home.

While waiting for her cousin to answer the phone, Aster remembered a scene from childhood.

Her preschool-age self-stood in the bathroom, watching her mother dab brownish liquid on her finger, and asked, "Mom, what's that stuff you're gonna put on?"

"War paint," Mom replied as she began applying streaks to her cheeks and forehead, similar to Indian face paint in western movies.

Young Aster giggled as her mother made the marks disappear by blending the streaks into her skin.

Aster reflected that her daily routine was exactly like her

mother's, except Aster's war paint was moisturizing cream instead of makeup.

"Hiya, Aster, what's new?" J. J. asked in a Southern drawl. Her chubby round face appeared on the screen. A blond tuft of bangs hung on her brow. The rest of her hair was cut a half-inch from the scalp, making her head look like a furry volleyball.

"Oh my God, J. J., you cut off your gorgeous blond curls. I barely recognized you!" Aster said, unable to compliment the unflattering look.

"Yeah! I got a butch. It's much cooler in all this heat. Atlanta's been a hundred degrees all week."

"I met a guy today," Aster announced.

"Did you actually have a conversation, or did you run like a scared rabbit?"

Aster said with a hint of pride, "We connected. Felt like I knew him forever. He's a loco conejo, not a dreamer like me; he takes people on past-life journeys. He said we've shared many lives together."

"Are you sure he's not a wacko street person?" J. J. cautioned.

"Jack is for real. He invited me to a class at the Discovery Center. So I went. I was safe. There was a classroom full of people. He guided everyone to a past life. I visited a Navajo life I lived in. Jack was supposed to be in that life too, but I had no idea who he was in that lifetime."

"My shy cousin came out of her shell. Did you chat with Jack after class?"

"No, I bolted. I had a little anxiety," Aster said, wincing.

"Aster, did you at least thank the man?"

"I sorta waved."

J. J. shook her finger, saying, "Girl, where'd you get your manners, at the five-and-dime? The man was nice enough to give you a free class, maybe he wanted to ask you out. No more playing the widow card. You're ready to date. I know, 'cuz you watched the last Super Bowl game. You said ya missed havin' a man in the house, so ya invited tons of testosterone into your livin' room. For you, that's one hell of a U-turn, since ya always thought football was too violent to watch."

Aster shrugged, saying, "At least the extreme measure worked. It helped me through a lonely patch. Might I remind you, you're no stranger to abrupt life changes. J. J. the Minnesota farm girl moves to Georgia, and in no time speaks with a drawl and discovers she's gay."

"I'm the queen of U-turns. Change keeps me tickin'." J. J. chuckled, snorted a bit, and chuckled some more.

The familiar laugh warmed Aster. She smiled wide and said, "What a goony pair we are."

"All right, then. Y'all gonna tell me 'bout that Navajo life?"

That night, Aster dreamed about lounging on a purple velour cushion. Lying on their sides, she and Grannyme faced each other, talking about the Navajo life.

"What's your impression of Cedar Claw?" Grannyme asked in her raspy voice.

"A handsome lad. Weird how he was a stranger, and yet at another level I knew him. The whole vision left me feeling sorry for Cedar Claw."

"Because?" Grannyme's green eyes searched for the truth.

"He lost his parents, and he felt responsible for his father's death. The whole ordeal made me tear up."

"Think he was?"

"Responsible? No. That was grief talking," Aster said.

"I see. And what about losing his parents?" Grannyme pried deeper.

"Part of life, isn't it?" Aster rolled on her back, hoping to change the subject. She resented the way Grannyme poked her like a specimen under a microscope.

"You expect me to believe that line of baloney?" Grannyme scrunched her face, deepening the wrinkles tenfold.

"I'm overly empathic is all. I always am. You know how I weep when someone else is crying," Aster said in her own defense.

Grannyme's voice cut through the fog. "I find an interesting parallel between you and Cedar Claw. He suffered abandonment by his parents, and so did you."

"Not the same. I left my parents. They did not die until I was an adult," Aster refuted. Her pulse quickened at the thought of unveiling unwanted memories.

"You were both fosterlings. Take heed of repeats; lessons, dear one."

"Whatever," Aster said.

"You both suffered from abandonment issues. In fact, it's all here in this folder, the agenda for this year." Grannyme shook the file with vigor. A light-blue sheet of paper fell out onto the cushion.

Aster snatched it up and frantically scanned the short message. "Thank Jack for the free session. Hint: he loves food."

"This has absolutely nothing to do with my parents. Wait a minute! You are in one of those conniving modes. Are you trying to tell me to ask a guy out?" Aster's face colored a bright pink.

Grannyme nodded.

"Really? You have a funny way of showing it, jumping from life lessons to the dating game. There's no end to you nudging me out of my comfort zone. Is there?" Aster snorted.

"Have I ever led you astray?"

Chapter 4

The Farmers' Market

The cloudless sky forecast another sweltering day. To enjoy her bike ride, Aster woke up early to pedal around in the cooler part of the day. Leery of getting too much sun, she put on a sun hat, tossed a reusable shopping bag in her bicycle basket, and rode to the Boulder Farmers' Market.

The farmers' market stretched along the east side of City Park. Local vendors keeping cool under the shade of white canopies sold a variety of wares, such as organic veggies, goat cheese, flowers, jams, coffee, baked goods, meats, and honey.

Aster bought the usual, an iced watermelon juice. Parched from the ride, she guzzled it. As she headed toward the recycling bin, a high-pitched voice assaulted the air.

"Hello, Aster. I knew that was you hiding under the hat and sunglasses," said the voice.

Aster cringed at the sight of Lydia Driftwood, one of her bloodsucking, needy clients. She tossed her empty glass into the bin.

Lydia's curly black hair hung to her shoulders. She wore a polka-dot summer dress and an excessive amount of makeup. Aster thought Lydia looked like an aged hooker, and she knew the woman was a classic nymphomaniac.

"The sleeping remedy you recommended didn't work. I took

them with a glass of red wine. I was out like a light. Then, two hours later, I woke up. I got up to pee. I couldn't go back to sleep. I even used my vibrator. It wore me out, and then, finally I conked out," exclaimed Lydia.

"Lydia, we are not in session right now. Remember, sharing your sex life is for you and your therapist, not me," Aster said. She glanced around, hoping no one had heard the conversation.

"Oh, you prude," Lydia retorted playfully. She ran a hand over her curls and pouted. "You always tell me to give up the wine. I'm not going to. It gets me in the mood."

Desperate to flee, Aster said, "I've got things to do. Bye."

Aster turned to leave.

"Wait!" cried Lydia, scraping her front teeth over her bottom lip. "See this malachite necklace? I paid three hundred dollars for it at a fund-raiser. And the auctioneer got an erection when I hugged him."

"No! I don't wanna hear about it. Good-bye," Aster said in a hushed tone and gave a quick wave.

Lydia gasped. "How rude! Proceeds were for starving children, African children."

Feeling many eyes upon her, Aster broke into fast strides, escaping into the crowd. Shaking off the creepiness, she headed for the vegetable stands, looking for soup vegetables. Choices this early in the season were mostly greens and root veggies left in the ground all winter. Aster bought spinach, carrots, and onions, and planned to add them to the leftover roast in her refrigerator. As she approached a booth that sold European foods, she came upon a man in a straw fedora, Hawaiian shirt, and flip-flops. A double take left her staring at Jack McFadden.

Their eyes met.

Dazzled by his perfect teeth and attractive hazel eyes she froze, thinking of Grannyme's and J. J.'s advice. There was no way she could slink away now. Holding her breath, she said, "Hi, Jack."

His face lit up. "Well, hello, Aster. I didn't get a chance to speak with you after class. How did the journey go?" Jack said.

Despite the intriguing sensation, the way she'd felt when they met by the creek, she had no courage to ask him over for a meal. Instead, she said briefly, "It was great. Thanks for the class."

"My pleasure. Did you journey to the Navajo life?"

"I did. I got the impression I was Cedar Claw. There were others too: Turtle, Turquoise, Two Rivers, Wild Arrow, and Talking Bird," she said.

"Talking Bird! That was me," Jack said excitedly.

"Oh. I had no idea."

"How about if you tell me your story over a cup," Jack suggested.

"Sorry, I can't. I have to make Irene some soup for lunch."

"Darn. Sick friend?" he asked.

"No. An old friend. She's retired on a fixed income. I give her a meal once a week, change her light bulbs, and help her with little tasks," Aster said, describing in more detail than she had intended.

"So, you're standing me up to be a philanthropist?" He checked his watch. "It's only eight thirty. How about a cup to go?" Jack grinned.

His alluring smile seemed to cast a spell. Before any logic formed an excuse to leave, Aster faltered, saying, "Well, um, I am on my bike, and I do need to stay hydrated. An iced coffee it is." Not knowing what else to say, she nodded toward his purchase and asked, "Whatcha get, baklava?"

"No. I bought spanakopita. Viola makes the best in town." He gave Viola a wink as she watched them from behind the counter.

Viola looked German. She appeared to be seventy-plus years old, with silvery hair in a tight bun. Her portly figure was clothed in a shirtwaist dress ironed to a crisp. She stood tall, like a marble statue. In a surprisingly soft voice, she said, "Zack, you flirt. Zee tzatziki sauce make it veal good. You spread on. Varm in zee oven wiz tomato on zee top, and you vill love it."

"Sounds delicious. I love spinach pie," Aster said, admiring Viola's broken English.

"Ever try Viola's? Here, have one." Jack retrieved a plastic-wrapped spanakopita from a paper bag and offered it to her.

Aster refused, saying, "I couldn't. You are way too generous."

"I insist. I bought four." Jack dropped the spanakopita and a side of sauce in Aster's bag.

"Thanks." Aster reached for her pocketbook.

"No worries. Put that away, and come with me," he said. "They sell hydroponic tomatoes down a few stalls. You can buy your own tomato. You'll be glad you did."

Her feet followed Jack before her brain could resist. They wove between people until they stopped at baskets of succulent, beefsteak tomatoes. She pushed her sunglasses atop her head to pick the best ones.

"These are gorgeous, aren't they?" Jack said. Beneath the straw hat, his piercing gaze made her feel naked.

Relieved to break eye contact, she bought a bagful instead of the planned two. Putting her sunglasses back on, she gave a tomato to Jack. "There. Now I won't feel so indebted to you." *Or overexposed*, she thought.

"Coffee?" Jack raised curious brows.

"It's on me," Aster insisted, once again swept away by his enthusiasm.

For a short moment, Jack placed his hand on Aster's mid-back and guided her in the direction of the coffee stand. Brief as the touch was, a warm tingly sensation enveloped her. She flashed back to Cedar Claw lying in the lean-to while Talking Bird helped him sit up. As Jack led them to the java stand, Aster noticed he smelled of sandalwood.

As they stood in line waiting to order drinks, Aster asked, "What kind of coffee do you want?"

"Ethiopian, with lots of cream."

❋ ❋

The swamp cooler kept Aster's house briskly chilled. She turned it off. The roar from the fan made too much noise to hear the voice message on the landline answering machine. Every day, she listened to her late husband, Keith, greet callers. His baritone voice, a treasured comfort, filled the empty spaces in her heart: "You've reached Aster and Keith's phone. Leave a message after the beep."

Aster set the bag of vegetables on the kitchen counter and began talking to the answering machine, as if Keith lived inside. "Darling, I just got back from the farmers' market. Gonna make soup for Irene. It's so cold in here. Think I'll whip up some bread too. Love ya always."

While the soup cooked on the stove, and a pan of corn bread baked in the oven, Aster wrote an entry in her journal:

> Saturday: I bumped into Jack at the farmers' market. He smelled great—sandalwood. He looked great too, but I think I'll leave it at that. ... I'll enjoy him as eye candy.
>
> I will admit he is easy to talk to ... engaging as heck ... a nice acquaintance.

Bzzzzz!

The timer on the stove startled Aster out of deep thought. A wonderful fresh aroma wafted her way when she opened the oven door. As soon as the bread cooled, she packed it in a cardboard box, along with a quart of soup, and drove to Irene's.

Aster pulled into the Mapleton Mobile Home Park and

stopped at a barn-red, sixteen-foot-wide trailer. Admiring the new paint job she had done with her own hands, she knocked at the front door.

A bespectacled woman with blue hair coiffed in short waves stood in the doorway. Irene's polyester outfit, a floral top and matching pink slacks, reminded Aster of her grandmother.

"Hello. Knew it was you. Come in, come in. Set that down on the counter so I can give you a hug," Irene said. She hung her walking cane on the back of a kitchen chair.

They embraced. Irene smelled of lilac perfume.

"There's corn bread and veggie-beef soup, warm and ready to eat," Aster announced flatly.

"There you go again, trying to fatten me up. It won't work. I eat like a horse, and these old bones refuse to budge out of size five," Irene said merrily.

"Lucky you. I got a two-fisted burrito living under my shirt. Are ya hungry?" Aster asked.

"You bet. I'm starving. How about if you set the table? I'll put the kettle on."

The women settled around the kitchen table. Only one bowl sat on the checkered place mat.

"You're not eating soup," Irene protested.

"I had a bowl before I came. The bread will do." Aster frowned as she slathered butter on a piece.

The teakettle whistled.

"I'll get it," Aster said, hurrying over to the stove.

Irene scooped freeze-dried decaf coffee into the cups and added water. "I like this organic brand you gave me. It tastes better than the old stuff."

Aster held her tongue, preferring fresh ground. "It's okay. I'll get the cream."

"Aster, what's bugging you?"

"Nothing."

"Girl, if your face got any longer, I'd have to wrap it in my support hose, lest your jaw reach the floor," Irene chided.

Aster rolled her eyes and then complained, "I went to the farmers' market this morning. I ran into Jack. He gave me a free class at the Discovery Center on Monday. Then, today, he tossed a spanakopita in my bag. Why does he do that? Now I feel obligated to outdo his gifting."

Irene's grunt was followed by a full-on reprimand. "He wants to get in your pants. Men are scoundrels, always leading with their doohickeys. My ex left me for Suzy Perky Boobs, who gave him sex five days a week. The tramp was young enough to be his daughter. My advice is you're better without a man in your life."

"But he's nice."

"They always are in the beginning. Why so bent on the payback?" Irene asked. Her knobby arthritic fingers struggled to grip the spoon, so she switched hands.

"I don't know. Maybe after getting burned in the divorce settlement, I crave fair play."

Irene gave an incredulous snort. "That was twenty years ago. To what's his name. Oh yes, Bill the Pill."

"Hearing his name still makes me cringe."

"That's because he's a jerk who gave thirty thousand dollars to his brother and claimed he paid back a car debt—a lie to avoid splitting the money with you, knowing full well he'd get the money back from his brother after the divorce. You never challenged him," Irene protested.

"Yep, that money was from selling Aunt Gertie's house," Aster said, accepting defeat.

"A mean, gotcha-last type, if you ask me. Remember he burned up your childhood photo albums in the fireplace? And you gave him the house!"

"Yes and yes. I hurt him. My lust, my affair with Keith, made me a fallen woman—the family destroyer. My shame had me believe I deserved less. Plus, I did not want to fight him. I wanted to get the mess behind me," Aster confessed.

"You put up with a lot of crap from him. You said he was an emotionally abusive ass."

"For the longest time, I overlooked his shortcomings. Bill wasn't as abusive as my own father, so I put up with it," Aster said. To ensure a peaceful marriage, Aster had kept her predictive dreams a secret. Being a plain old intuitive woman had felt safer.

"Until you fell out of love. Good thing you left him. You mothered him too much. The scoundrel needed to grow up," Irene assured her.

"Yuck! I know. And I don't want to fall into that trap anymore. My therapist told me that if I ever feel out of balance with a man, I should stop everything, back off, and say no if I need to. That's what I'm doing with Jack. I'm not going to even try to go there," Aster said.

With Keith, life had improved. At that time, it had felt safe to disclose the predictive dreams to him, as well as Iris, her daughter. Nevertheless, Grannyme still remained a secret.

"Good reason to be gun-shy," Irene stated firmly.

"Ya think?" Aster muttered.

"Well, getting divorced by the first hubby and widowed by the second makes you cautious. Jack, the spinach-pie guy, strikes up interest, and you are smart enough to back away."

"I guess so. How's the soup?" Aster said, wanting to change the subject.

"Soup is delicious. You haven't touched the bread."

"I wasn't hungry after all," Aster said.

Despite the company of Irene, Aster felt lonely. The conversation added a doleful weight, lowering her mood to somewhere below the knees. She made an excuse to leave.

❋ ❋

That night, Aster lay in bed unable to sleep. Her mind vacillated as to what she should do. *I don't want to fall asleep. Grannyme will hound me about Jack. He did give me a free class. What is it going to take to even the score? It feels rude to snub him.*

Why do I care so much? If I did call him, the Navajo journey would give us something to talk about. He seemed genuine. But it's much safer to be alone.

Occasionally she checked the nightstand clock, and the hours slipped by, one ... two ... three in the morning. Eventually Aster drifted into a dream.

She sat in front of a laptop computer. Her toes squished luxuriously into a purple fabric. Blurry words appeared on the screen. Not sure if Grannyme would show up or not, she pressed the space bar, bringing the letters into focus:

Solution to pay back Jack.

1. Relax.

2. Invite Jack over for dinner.

3. Talk about Navajo life.

(He's a good guy.)

The chimes of the doorbell woke Aster from a deep slumber. Clumsy hands found the armholes of her bathrobe and struggled to locate the belt as she shuffled to the door.

"Hello, come on in," Aster said, absently scratching her scalp.

Dressed in leggings and a sporty sleeveless shirt, Galen inspected the puffy eyes before her. "Morning. Obviously, you overslept," she said in a practical tone.

"Yeah. Couldn't sleep." Aster rubbed her eyes.

"Yoga starts in ten minutes."

"Oh dear. I'm not gonna make it. You can go without me," Aster said.

"No, we can take the next class in two hours. How about a cup of beans while we wait?"

"Good plan."

The women retreated to the kitchen.

While Aster filled the electric teapot with water, Galen asked, "What kept you up? Did you solve the world's problems last night or your own?"

"My own. I met Jack at the farmers' market," Aster remarked.

"McFadden?"

"Uh-huh," Aster muttered. Deeming it safe to share, and desperate to get another opinion, she proceeded to explain the details to Galen, stopping only to pour boiling water into the french press. She set a fresh cup in front of her guest.

"No big whoop. Invite Jack over for a thank-you dinner. That would even the score between you two," Galen said, stirring cream into her coffee.

Challenged by the words *thank-you dinner,* Aster flat out refused. "No dating! It's been decades since I've gone there. Platonic, maybe."

"Isn't it a bit lonely playing the widow card?" Galen had a way of being overly honest.

"Absolutely. I feel awkward calling a guy. I like him, but it's way easier to blow him off. Platonic or not, relationships make my life too complicated." Aster grimaced.

"Loneliness is no fun either. I had a feeling you two would hit it off. I have his number." Galen picked her phone up off the table and pressed Jack's name on the screen.

"Hang that up," Aster said urgently.

"I need to ask him about class. It got moved. I don't want to miss it." Galen's petite face resembled a pixie up to no good.

Aster hung on her every word.

"Hello, Jack. This is Galen. Say, I was wondering what time class starts on Monday. ... All right, in the room down the hall. ... Great, thanks. ... One more thing. I'm over at Aster's. She couldn't find your phone number, so I told her I'd dial for you. She wants to ask you something. Hold on."

Through gritted teeth, Aster whispered, "No! I'm not ready."

Galen pressed the Mute button, saying, "Want me to ask for you?" Releasing the button, she shoved the phone at Aster.

"Hello. Hi, this is Aster. Yeah, I guess you already know that," Aster said, frantically twirling her hair.

"Aster, hello. So nice you called. Are you ready to compare notes on our Navajo lives?" Jack said.

In one breath, Aster replied, "Yeah, I am. I want to pay you back for the free class. How about dinner at my house?"

"Splendid. I'm free tomorrow night," Jack suggested.

"Sounds good. I'll text you my phone and address. Um, err, ahh, on Galen's cell," Aster said nervously.

"I'm looking forward to it."

"Until then. Bye-bye." Aster hung up and shot Galen a look.

"That wasn't so bad now, was it?" Galen chided.

"You little rascal." Aster shook a finger. The twinkling of bells ringing in her hand interrupted the rant. She gave the phone to Galen.

Galen answered, "Hello. Oh, hi, Jack. ... Okay, I'll ask. Aster what time is dinner?"

"Seven o'clock," Aster replied.

Chapter 5

The Dinner

Aster spent the afternoon tidying up the covered patio. She planned to barbecue salmon pesto on the grill and serve it with a salad. Having no idea if Jack had any allergies, it seemed a satisfactory gluten-free meal for a guest.

Just before Jack arrived, she fixed her hair in a french braid. Out of sheer habit, she checked for phone messages to hear Keith speak.

As if leaving a message, Aster said, "Hey, sweetie cakes, a male friend is coming over for a BBQ. You would like Jack. He's a gentle soul. Gotta get ready. Love ya. Later. Bye."

Jack arrived, carrying a liter of Chilean cabernet. "Hello. Hope this goes with dinner. It's ten years old. Thought tonight would be as good a time as any to part with it," he said, showing her the label.

Nervous, she said, "No wonder it's so dusty. I mean, it's probably a good vintage. Hey, let's pop the cork. How was your day?"

He pulled a corkscrew from his pocket and said, "Just in case you didn't have one." He proceeded to open the bottle.

"Thanks. I'll get the glasses," Aster said.

A bead of sweat rolled down her side. Desperate to stay cool, she turned the swamp cooler knob to high. She took a quick, nonchalant moment to smell her armpit as she reached above her head for wineglasses. Relieved there was no odor, she set the glasses on the counter.

"To answer your question, my schedule was full. All day long, the thought of a home-cooked meal smoothed all the rough spots. I'm not great in the kitchen. My mother was. The little boy in me misses coming home to wonderful smells and fantastic food."

"Been cooking since I could hold a knife. Let's hope I pass inspection," Aster replied.

"Don't see why not." Jack poured the wine and handed her a glass.

"Thank you. Nice color," she said, peering into the burgundy sheen.

"To your health," he toasted.

Aster took a large gulp, wondering how long it would take the alcohol to calm her down.

"Mm, it's good. I usually add water or ice cubes to dilute the bitter taste. Don't need to. This is real smooth," she remarked.

"It's a great vintage. The grapes come from Maipo Valley, near Santiago," he said, taking pleasure in a sip.

Uncomfortable as ever, she blurted out, "It's not fair! You're as calm as can be, and I'm a wreck. I'm afraid my nerves will ruin the dinner."

"Bad day?"

"I'm a little off," she said in an edgy voice. "You're the first man I've cooked for since my husband, Keith, died three years ago."

"No worries. I'm a little keyed up too. This wine is taking me down a few notches."

"Good. It's not just me. That said, ya hungry?"

"Starved," Jack said, rubbing his ample belly.

Aster let out a big sigh. "Okay, then. The grill is fired up. I'm gonna put the fish on." As she opened the fridge she asked, "Can you take the plates outside? They're in that the hutch across from the table."

"Sure," said Jack. He walked across the kitchen and let out a gasp. "Whoa!"

Aster turned, worried. "Is everything all right?"

Jack opened the glass door and removed a blue-and-white plate. Astounded, he said, "Can't believe it. These must be antiques by now. Currier and Ives dinnerware. I ate from these as a kid. What a flash from the past!"

"Really? I inherited them from my mother. Every week, Mom got a free piece at the supermarket. Friends and family helped her collect the whole set," Aster said.

Impressed, Jack said, "Interesting synchronicity. We shared an Indian life together, now dinnerware."

During the second glass of wine, they were so engrossed in conversation about the Navajo life that their laughter moved freely across the table.

Jack reflected, "The characteristic I repeated from the Navajo life and into this life is the gift of gab. Whereas you continued with healing arts."

"So, you're saying fragments of past lives repeat into other lives?"

"Absolutely. When you began studying herbs, was it sort of like remembering a forgotten language?" Jack questioned.

"Now that you mention it, learning about herbs was the easiest thing I ever did. My classmates swore I had a photographic memory. I never studied, while they spent hours poring over books. It stirred up a little resentment," Aster said sheepishly.

"That's because you tapped into your Akashic records. You downloaded past-life memories. In fact, to become that proficient, I'd be willing to make a wager you've had multiple lives as a healer." Jack gave a flirt-filled wink.

"It'd be interesting to find out, wouldn't it?" Aster said, flashing him a smile in return. Suddenly she changed the subject. "How's the food?"

Realizing her voice carried through the screen door, she flinched. It seemed indecent to flirt within earshot of the answering machine, the very place where Keith's endearing voice lived. Then, it hit her: *Keith is gone, you idiot. Get over it.*

"Hmm, this is tasty," he said, with a mouth full of fish.

"Goes well with the wine, doesn't it?" Aster said.

"Yes indeed." He swallowed. "You keep staring at my chin. Am I wearing my meal?"

"Pesto. Right there." She pointed. "How rude of me."

"No, not at all. You had a cute little worry face. Knew something was up." The oily blob quickly disappeared onto the cloth napkin.

"I'm sorry. Didn't mean to embarrass you," she apologized.

"Let's make a deal. Any time there's food on my face, let me know sooner. If the dribble were on there any longer, I'm afraid it'd sink in; then, surely, I'd turn green," he said, grinning.

She laughed, enjoying his easygoing attitude.

Jack offered to refill her glass, but she declined. He filled his own glass, saying, "I'm so glad we met in the park. Destiny drew us together. Let's toast to old-soul recognition."

"Destiny or not, I'm shy. Usually takes me a long time to open up. Jack, you're so easy to talk with. You seem like family; perhaps a brother," Aster said, feeling a bit tipsy.

Jack said nonchalantly, "Think about it. We, Talking Bird and Cedar Claw, worked side by side as Turtle's apprentices. We had a close kinship. True, that was only one life. But in my book, you and I are part of the same soul family that recycles life after life. At some point, we might be quicker to say, 'Oh, it's you again.'"

Aster lifted curious brows. "You're saying our heritage comes with perks. Like a built-in icebreaker to attract each other into our current lives?"

"Absolutely." Jack touched her forearm and eyed her appreciatively.

His touch sent a warm glow all the way down to her toes. Aster wanted to say *Slow down, buster,* but she could not.

Unsure of what to do next, she faked a cough. "Gonna be right back. I'm dry; need water. I'll get us both some."

She fled indoors to the kitchen. Dazzled by the sensation, she marveled at how inviting, how familiar, it felt. Caught in the moment, she fancied Jack a possible mate. She would never grow tired of looking at his handsome face. He was funny, full of surprises, smart, and employed. Just as Aster thought about what it would be like to kiss Jack, she shot a furtive look at the answering machine and threw a dishtowel over it. Temptation gnawed at her. Suddenly the line of a Beatles song popped into her head: "Gotta be good looking, because he's too hard to see." *Okay, got it. I'll move forward with caution. He's got an alluring cover. I wonder how smooth the pages turn and how the story unfolds.*

After dinner, they toured the herb garden. Burdock bloomed, displaying an unusual flower shaped like a martini olive with thorny spikes. An unfinished penciled sketch of its large leaves hung on a portable drawing table set up nearby.

Aster raced across the grass. "Oh, I forgot. I should put this on the patio. It might rain tonight," she said, wheeling the table toward the house.

"Not so fast. Did you draw that? Let's see!" he said.

"It's nothing, just one of my hobbies. Usually I don't let people see my work until it's done."

"Please. I appreciate art."

"Call me superstitious, but I'm gonna say no." She turned the backside of the table toward him and pulled it into the far patio corner. "I'll show you some finished ones. I study herbs. I watch them grow and draw them," Aster said rapidly. She entered the house and gestured for Jack to follow.

"Do you make calendars or note cards with your art?" he pried.

"Let me show you." Aster led him down the hallway. She pointed at two portraits on the wall. She said, "These are my children, Sam and Iris. Sam lives in Denver; he's an accountant. Iris is teaching third grade in Fort Collins.

"Nice-looking kids. Can tell they are yours," Jack commented.

Appreciating but pretending she did not hear the compliment, Aster continued, "I adore them completely."

Jack followed her into a room lined with bookcases. A six-drawer desk stood in the middle. Neatly piled on top were padded mailing envelopes, labels, and bubble wrap.

He took inventory. "You have a mail-order business?"

Aster handed him two books, saying, "This was my thesis at herb school. I self-published and sell them on line."

Jack read aloud, "*The Herbal Workbook,* volumes 1 and 2, by Aster Snowden. Wow, you're an industrious woman!"

"This is where my sketches end up. Flip through it. Every herb has a drawing."

Jack thumbed through pages and stopped at the illustration of astragalus. He said, "I'm impressed. Labor of love, or what?"

"Yes, it is. Actually, my favorite part is exploring the history of each herb. I acquired several old books in my research. There's one book in particular I want to show you." Aster pulled a thick hardcover from a shelf. The book was big enough for a child to use as a stool. "Let me set this down. It's heavy," she said as she gingerly placed it on the desk.

Except for the spine, which read, "*The Herbal or General History of Plants,* by John Gerard, revised edition, 1633," the rest of the cover was a plain olive green.

"That edition is a toe breaker!" exclaimed Jack.

"It's a reprint of the original copy." Aster ran a finger under the author's name. "Gerard writes in old-fashioned English. Every time I open this book, I get overwhelmed, as if somehow it's a part of me. Can't figure it out. What do you think?"

"Sparks a little intrigue, doesn't it? There's definitely a life inside awaiting discovery. Got the feeling in my bones," Jack replied.

"Ever since the journey into my Navajo life—" she began.

"*Our* Navajo *lives,*" Jack interjected mirthfully.

She forced a smile. "Right. Our lives. Do you think I wrote this book? Printed it? Or simply knew the author?"

Jack grabbed a sweater that hung on the back of a chair and wrapped it around his head like a Swami. Comically, he took on an accent from New Delhi and incanted, "I am the meek who will find what you seek." He sat down cross-legged on the floor and closed his eyes.

Aster twirled the end of her braid, waiting. The sweater had fallen. Automatically, she hung it on the back of the chair.

"You lived in England. No, you did not write the book; however, you were involved in the process," Jack said.

"Tell me more. Who was I?" Aster inquired.

"Let's see. Ah, somehow you knew the author."

"Who was I?" Aster wanted to know.

"Not sure. I couldn't focus the blob into view."

"Were you in the life?"

He gave a yawn and said, "Sorry, I don't know. I just got a glimpse. The wine clouded my journey. That was a potent bottle of grapes. We'll have to continue another time."

"Are you gonna leave me hanging?" she admonished.

"Great excuse for us to meet up again."

Chapter 6

The Apology

On Wednesday morning, Aster received a text message from Galen: "You like Beatles music and seventies rock?"

"Yes. It's the music I grew up with," Aster texted back.

"Tonight, Retro Monkeys are playing at Band on the Bricks. Wanna go?"

"Free music! Yeah," Aster answered.

"Meet ya there at seven by the taco kiosk."

"Okay."

That evening, Aster entered the Pearl Street Pedestrian Mall, the main street in downtown Boulder, paved in red brick. "Sergeant Pepper's Lonely Hearts Club Band" boomed from the temporary stage set up in front of the courthouse.

How ironic! A song dedicated to me, she thought, approaching a throng of baby boomers milling about food and drink kiosks, stomping their feet on the dance floor, and sitting on folding chairs.

Galen stood by the taco stand, swaying and mouthing the words of the song.

"Hi! I made it." Aster tapped Galen's shoulder.

"Aster. Yay! You're here. Don't they sound great?" Galen flicked her hand toward the stage.

"Just like the record." Aster glanced at the band. A quintet of graying men played merrily on their instruments. The bass, lead, and rhythm guitarists stood in a line in front of the keyboards and the drums.

Galen eyed Aster with a curious look. She suggested, "Let's get a beer so we can loosen up and go dance."

"Beer? Nah, too filling," Aster replied.

"They got margaritas."

"I'm not much of a tequila drinker. One is my limit," Aster said, hesitating.

"It'll be fun. Come on, there's no line, and I'm buying." Galen coaxed her forward.

Galen and Aster sipped their salt-rimmed drinks and chatted.

"How did dinner go with Jack?" Galen asked.

"I was a little nervous, but he brought wine ... nice icebreaker."

"I like laid-back Jack; at least he talks."

"I know. He wants to take me on another journey," Aster shared.

"To the Navajo again?" Galen asked. She raised her brow in an approving way.

"No, this time to England."

"Great idea," Galen said as the song "China Grove" blasted from the amplifiers. She said excitedly, "The Doobie Brothers! I love them! This is their best dance song. Come on." She urged Aster onto the dance floor.

Galen bounced around enthusiastically while Aster moved with reserve. The soulful sound that came from the keyboards began to loosen up Aster, and before the song ended, she had worked up a sweat. The friends danced to two more songs until the band took a break.

"I told you this would be fun." Galen chuckled lightly.

"Yeah, makes me feel young again," Aster said.

"Nice to see you enjoy yourself," said a man's voice.

Aster turned and said in surprise, "Jack! Hi. Did you just get here?"

"No. I was here at the very start," he answered.

"Jack, those ivory keys were smoking," Galen complimented him.

"Thanks," he said, feigning embarrassment.

"Am I missing something?" Aster said, confused.

"Jack is the keyboard player," Galen explained.

"Really? I didn't see you. The guitar players blocked my view. And Galen failed to mention it," Aster said. Suddenly feeling hoodwinked by a friend playing cupid, she shot a look at Galen.

"Sorry. Brain fart," Galen apologized with a goofy smirk.

"Jack, how long have you been in the band? Sounds like you've been playing forever," Aster said, making a quick recovery.

"I started playing when I was six. I played in garage bands in high school and college. This summer, I'm filling in for Michael. He's got a family emergency back east," Jack explained.

"He's a lucky man who gets to follow his heart. You know, past lives and music," Galen chimed in.

Jack glanced at his watch. He said, "Well, duty calls. You girls want to grab a bite to eat afterward? We only have one more set."

"Sorry, no. I work tomorrow. I have to wake up early," Aster said.

"Maybe another time," Galen interjected.

"Absolutely," Jack said.

"Break a leg," Aster offered.

"Thanks." He broke into an award-winning grin and headed for the stage.

"Jack's a bit easy on the eyes, don't you think?" Galen sighed.

Aster glared at Galen and in a flat tone said, "I'm going home."

"But we're having fun," Galen protested.

"It's not fun being a pawn in a matchmaking game. It's embarrassing," Aster whined.

"Aster, I was trying to help things along. You're so shy."

"It's easier to trust an honest friend than a conniving one. Bye-bye." Aster left.

Stewing over the fact that Galen had gone too far, Aster could not deny that Jack was talented as well as handsome. At home, she flicked on the answering machine, ready to unload her frustration on her late husband, but heard nothing. She pressed the button again, and there was silence. Desperate to hear Keith's voice, she unplugged the cord and plugged it back in, removed the cassette, replaced it, and tried again. No matter how many times she pressed Play, Keith had disappeared.

"No! Don't leave me," she cried.

Feeling like a metal spike was piercing her heart, she sobbed in earnest, "No, not again. I don't want to feel this. I'm tired of mourning."

Desperate to numb out, she strode over to the liquor cabinet, uncorked a bottle of rum, and downed two shots.

"Ugh!" She gagged on the strong liquor. The next two drinks she mixed with water.

The following morning, the alarm woke Aster at six. With a headache the size of a house, she drank electrolytes, took B vitamins, and moseyed off to work. Twenty-three years ago, she had vowed to never drink that much again. It was during her divorce with her first husband, Bill, when she craved an escape from the stress and consequently suffered a magnificent hangover. Regretting her lapse in judgment, Aster unlocked her office door. The ten-by-ten square room had the illusion of being bigger because of the east wall of windows and a solid mirrored wall on the southern end. Her first client was a no-call no-show. Wishing there was room to lie down, she did the next best thing, resting her head on the desk until there was a knock at the door. The next two clients were difficult, resistant to dietary change and questioning every nutritional suggestion. When the fourth and last client walked in, Aster winced involuntarily, as if an annoying fly had entered the room.

Lydia Driftwood's beady eyes and bright-red lips worked

together, forming a pathetic pout. In a nasal voice, she whined, "I need an apology from you. You had the audacity to snub me over the simple act of making love."

"I deal with health issues, not sexual oversharing," Aster stated firmly.

"A good sex life keeps you healthy. An orgasm a day keeps the doctor away. And let me tell you, the one last night nearly blew the roof off. We laughed hysterically over the positions in the *Erotic Sex Book,* how the numbers eight and twelve guarantee success every time. We added a move; you've got to try it. First, we—"

"Stop!" Aster interrupted, demanding, "I don't want to hear about it."

"But it's adorable."

"No! Let me tell you about boundaries. In the privacy of this room, we discuss health issues. Not at the farmers' market. In this room, I do not ask about your sex life, because I don't want to hear about it," Aster raised her voice.

"Sex is part of life. What is your problem?"

"It creeps me out that you have no filter," responded Aster.

"There you go again, being uptight and rude. Maybe I should find a new health coach," Lydia retorted.

"You're going to have to, because I'm not booking you into my schedule anymore. A better fit for you is a mental-health therapist."

"Well, I never," Lydia huffed. With an indignant swipe of her hand, she flipped the black poodle curls off her shoulder.

"Good day, Lydia."

Lydia stormed out the door.

At the sound of heavy heels clicking down the hall, Aster clapped her palms over her eyes thankful the conversation had ended. The headache that had been vexing her all morning turned up a notch.

Aster's cell phone let out a ping.

A text from Galen Barlow said, "Sorry I upset you. The

matchmaking wasn't as helpful as I expected. Let me make it up to you. Come over for lunch tomorrow, and I'll treat you to a craniosacral session."

Through watery eyes, Aster texted back, "Thanks. I'm having a bad day. I could use a little TLC."

❋ ❋

The next day, intent on cheering up, Aster drove to Galen's house. Galen lived in Louisville, nine miles east of Boulder. Instead of ruminating over Keith, Jack, or clients, Aster sang along to the songs on the radio. The familiar sight of a farmer driving a tractor in a field reminded her of Minnesota, where she grew up. Things were looking up. In no time at all, she parked in front of Galen's yellow bungalow surrounded by a large fenced yard.

When Aster knocked on the front door, her petite friend was setting up the massage table on the screened-in porch.

The two women greeted each other with a hug.

"Glad you could make it," Galen said sincerely.

"Me too. It was sweet of you to invite me over."

"Last thing I want to do is alienate you. You feel like the sister I never had. I want us to be friends."

"I could use a friend, believe me." Aster opened her eyes wide.

"Come on in. I bet you're thirsty; it's a hot one today. I made lemonade," Galen said, entering the house.

A wooden sign carved with the words "Please remove your shoes" hung on the inner door. Aster obliged.

"Nice place," Aster said, walking through the living room and dining room decorated in a country motif. The narrow kitchen served as a hallway to the back door, as well as a room where every square inch burgeoned with cookware, spices, and appliances.

Galen nipped off a sprig of mint from a potherb on the windowsill, mottled the leaves in each glass, and stirred in the lemonade. "Here, this is my grandma's recipe," she said, giving a glass to Aster.

"Mm, good," Aster said as the citrus soothed her throat, which was dry from too much singing in the car.

"The food's all ready. Before we start eating, I want to show you a shipment of turtles that came in today. They're very rare."

Galen led the way to a bedroom off the small living room. Strings of beads in all shapes and colors filled a wall. Shelves filled with all sorts of semiprecious stones carved into figurines, balls, pyramids, and faceted crystals lined the remaining walls.

"This is a miniature gem-and-rock show in here!" Aster exclaimed, amazed on the selection.

"I sell this stuff online and at festivals. Take a look at these," Galen said, pulling a turquoise turtle too big to fit in one hand out of a bubble-wrap bag. The detailed carving made it look real.

"That's beautiful," Aster said.

Galen took out a second turtle. She said, "These are a pair. They're old Navajo pieces. Hard to find. You'll never guess who they're for."

"Apparently not you."

Galen said, "They're for Jack. He journeyed into the Navajo life you shared."

"He mentioned that," Aster said, flashing on Turtle, Turquoise, Talking Bird, and Cedar Claw.

"Jack is a nostalgic history buff. He collects artifacts, but only things with personal meaning."

"He's got expensive taste. He's either broke or a spendthrift. My late husband was a spendthrift. It was the only thing we ever argued about," Aster said, masking her intrigue.

"Okay, then Enough show-and-tell. You hungry?" Galen changed the subject.

"Yes, I am."

As the two women dug into Cobb salads, Aster said, "Gotta tell ya. My answering machine died Wednesday. Destroyed the only recording I had of Keith's voice. The loss devastated me."

"Your late husband's voice erased? That sounds awful." Galen pushed gray strands of hair behind her ears. Her elfin body, almost childlike, did not match the age in her deeply lined face.

With a dull look, Aster said, "It felt like he left me one more time."

"Why didn't you call me?" Galen said in mild disapproval. "You can tell me anything."

"You were still at the Band on the Bricks. Besides, I grieve in private. Easier to cry that way," Aster said, reassuring her.

"How about now, are you still sad?" Galen studied her face.

Green eyes stared back. "I was yesterday. Had a good cry. Then, I got extremely impatient, feeling grief once again invade my life. When will it end?" Aster complained.

"Never!" Galen exclaimed. "Grief cycles like that. After my mom died, I cried at the smell of coffee, at random, unexpected moments. Life's little treasures."

Aster clutched her heart. She said, "Losing Keith's voice was intense. I wanted to numb out and needed a change. I found an old bottle of Jamaican rum and did something I never do. I took shots. Wow, it lit my throat on fire. I put music on and danced like crazy until I staggered into the bathroom and hugged the toilet bowl. Don't know which was worse: the alcohol going down or coming back up."

Galen said compassionately, "You poor thing. One more blow of the hammer. Ouch. Aster, I can hardly imagine you drunk. You're such a health nut."

Aster turned her palms up, exposing them to the ceiling and saying, "Yeah, I know. Well, I got what I asked for—a distraction."

"Yes, you did." Galen took a sip of lemonade.

They sat across from each other. The tasteful way the cloth napkins, the floral-print tablecloth, and the white dinnerware blended had Aster say, "Galen, I like how artful your table looks. I grew up with my aunt, and nothing ever matched."

"Was your aunt a colorful character?" Galen asked.

"Gertie Olsen was a bighearted person with no style," Aster

said fondly. "She took me in, rescued me from having to live with an abusive alcoholic father."

"Bless old Aunt Gertie. Did her lack of fashion make you want to match everything: your house, your clothing, and probably your license plate to your car?" Galen teased while mopping up salad dressing with a piece of cheese.

Aster wiped her mouth with a napkin and confessed, "I am a bit type A. I crave harmony. My therapist said matching and neatness provide a way for me to process the chaos from my childhood."

"Yeah," Galen said with a smirk. "But you're a lovable neurotic."

"Gee, thanks. Now I'll have to put you on my Christmas list," Aster said, laughing.

"Fair enough. I'm dying to hear about that Navajo life that you and Jack share." Galen's blue eyes cast softness, creating a safe atmosphere to open up and speak.

"That's right; I never told you. Well, it was in New Mexico. The first person I saw was my old self, Cedar Claw, falling from a tree," Aster began and then proceeded to tell the entire story.

"What great recall! That's interesting how you and Jack met up again. He taught us in class that it's common to reincarnate in groups. I wonder if I'm in that group too," Galen said hopefully.

"Probably so." Aster shrugged.

"I wonder if Cedar Claw ever got his kiss."

"No idea."

"Jack told me you inspired him to buy those turtles. I bet McFadden's lips are pining for a kiss. You know, for old times' sake," Galen joked.

"Galen! Not again," Aster remarked.

"I'm sorry. Cancel, cancel, cancel; I take it back. I'm a hopeless romantic. All the women in Jack's class have a crush on him. We all agree he's like a pair of wind chimes sending tingles to the bones. It's hard not to let fantasy carry me away," Galen apologized.

Despite Galen's comments, Aster wanted to explain. "Jack and I are platonic friends. There's a brotherly type of bond we share. It made me feel safe enough to invite him over to my house. A first since I've been widowed."

"So, you haven't dated yet." Galen appeared very interested in this news.

"Nope. I haven't been willing to let anyone in."

"It's been a while for me too. I don't think I remember how to be with a man. Whew! Menopause puts such a damper on my libido; it's a guaranteed relationship killer. We're a regular pair of man magnets, aren't we?" Galen chortled.

"Downright pathetic."

Galen nodded and said tenderly, "Are you ready for some bodywork? Craniosacral really helps you let go of unwanted feelings."

"More than ready," said Aster, getting up from the table.

Aster lay faceup on the therapy table. The patched plaster on the ceiling showed a blemished repair shaped in an elongated oval. She pointed a pinched nose at it and said, "Galen, most people put a nature poster above their table, but you have a whale on your ceiling."

"Yeah, that's Oscar. He came with the house. I never had the heart to get rid of him. He's good mojo," Galen said while wrapping her long gray hair into a bun and using a chopstick to hold it in place.

A fan lodged in the screened window blew in a welcoming breeze. Galen's adept hands-on touch smoothed muscles in Aster's face. She said dreamily, "I'd love to have luxury like this every day."

Toward the end of the treatment, Galen held the back of Aster's head. Covert fear dislodged from its hiding spot and floated away from Aster's skull.

"Whoa. Can you feel that release? A lot is coming out," said Galen.

"Let 'er rip. I wonder where all that tension comes from."

As soon as she asked the question, Aster had a vision.

An idyllic rural scene of a two-story farmhouse with a vegetable garden and a backdrop field of corn came into view. The farm belonged to her parents during her childhood. Subtle sounds of cows, horses, and chickens chorused with the noise of her giggling. The sensation of swinging from the drooping branches of a willow tree tickled her belly. She shouted, "I'm Tarzan, King of the Jungle."

Dirty-blond pigtails blew in the breeze. Hands callused from farm work suited the tomboy activity of dangling through the air until her arms got tired. Landing like a cat, she scraped her legs on raspberry brambles and left broken willow branches in her wake. A trickle of blood ran down her shin. A scattering of ripe raspberries fell to the ground. Aster picked up the berries, holding them in her palms. They began to mush, and berry juice soon ran down her arm. The only logical thing to do was to pop the berries into her mouth and run for the garden hose to clean off.

Regina Snowden, her mother, stepped out of the house in a tizzy. A scarf tied over curlers framed a face in full makeup, a dead-on look-alike of actress Katharine Hepburn. A full-length starched apron fastened tight over a shirtwaist dress accentuated a slim figure. Her failed attempt to make food for the church potluck pushed her past irritability.

Fuming, Regina said in a single breath, "Aster, I can't believe it. The angel cake fell, and the potatoes are too mushy to make salad! Go see if there are any eggs in the coop."

Aster knew the fiasco in the kitchen had happened because of her mother's obsession with applying makeup. The daily beautifying ritual kept Regina's depression at bay. For a mother, she measured sparse in the nurturing department, often depending on Aster to take up the slack.

Looking at her daughter, Regina gasped in disbelief. Blood dripped down Aster's sock and splotched onto her shoes. Raspberry stains smeared her hands, face, and dress.

"Good heavens! Those berries were supposed to be for dinner tonight. Your dress! It's ruined. Damn it to hell!" Regina's pious lips rarely spoke vulgar syllables, but when she uttered such words, one could easily imagine steam billowing out her ears.

"A-a-ah!" Regina screamed. Enraged, she knocked Aster down onto the grass, grabbed a fallen willow branch from the ground, lifted the stained dress, and whipped Aster's behind. "You little devil! I'll teach you to behave," she yelled, repeating blow after blow.

Aster struggled to crawl away. The last whack caught the back of Aster's head before she bolted into the cornfield. She ran until a stitch in her side prevented her young legs from going any further. Holding a cornstalk in each hand, she dropped to her knees, disappearing into the foliage. The pain from the lashings did not hurt as badly as the daggers piercing her heart. Aster was used to Dad's brutal fists, but not Mom's. Regina had never hit Aster before. Horror-struck that Mom had become an evil turncoat, a downright betrayer of love, Aster wished she was never born. Sad green eyes released silent tears.

As the scene disappeared, Aster felt Galen's hands shift position.

"Good release. Here's a tissue to dab your eyes," Galen said softly.

"Wow! I flashed on a memory from childhood—a spat with my mom. All the anger I felt at that moment was stored in the spot you were holding. Thanks for helping me free it from my body. Felt cathartic as hell!"

Over a cup of chamomile tea, Aster filled Galen in on the farmyard scene.

Chapter 7

London, 1589

Aster rode her bike to the Acorn Market health-food store to buy yogurt for breakfast. The aisles teemed with shoppers. She wove around people gawking at shelves of food. As she closed the dairy-case door, she overheard a man with a Bronx accent.

"My good friend, the Dalai Lama, suggested I go to a higher level and teach meditation as well as yoga. You know, embrace body, mind, and spirit to become one with the divine law of a Buddhist master."

"That's nice, Fred. Excuse me, I need to get into the door behind you," said a familiar male voice.

Aster turned to see Jack McFadden open a glass door and remove a pint of half-and-half.

Fred had a severe comb-over and the pear-shaped body of someone who sat a lot. Disturbed by Jack's blasé response, he brandished his cell phone. "Look, I've got Princess Fergie's phone number here. My wife is her cousin."

Jack wore an expression of doubt. He looked to his left and spotted Aster.

"Hello, Jack," Aster said, as she joined the men.

"Aster, there you are. So, we're on for tonight? We'll be late if we don't hurry along. Later, Fred," Jack said in full grin. He put an arm around Aster's shoulders and strode away quickly, moving her along with him.

Aster found the little ruse delightful. A magnificent rush coursed through her, almost as if Jack's energy could match Keith's magic touch.

"Oy vey! No manners," Fred complained. His voice soon faded away.

As soon as they got out of earshot, Jack said, "Thanks for the save! Fred is one 110 percent full of himself. He teaches at the Discovery Center too."

"I get it. I've got a former client, Lydia, who's as self-absorbed as he is," Aster replied.

"I'm serious about getting together tonight. Let's explore that English lifetime. I bet it'll be a great adventure," Jack suggested enthusiastically.

"I can't. I'm hanging out with Irene tonight. It's her birthday."

"How about tomorrow?"

"Sorry. I'm processing a lot of garbage from my past, and I don't want to examine another life right now," Aster said, masking her true feelings about how fun it sounded to take an adventure and be with him.

"Oh darn. I was looking forward to hanging out with you," Jack said, crestfallen.

"Maybe some other time. I gotta go. See ya," Aster said quickly.

She walked away, flattered that he'd asked, intrigued by his touch, and scared to move forward.

❋ ❋

Early that evening, Aster picked up Irene to take her to the Shakespeare Festival. For the special occasion, Irene wore a red dress, had lipstick to match, and carried a black walking cane studded with rhinestones.

"My, don't you look like a dapper birthday girl. My sundress is rather plain next to you," Aster said, holding the car door open.

"Thanks. Flattery will get you everywhere. Here hang this on your review mirror. Parking on campus is impossible without it," Irene said, handing Aster a handicapped-parking pass. Moving painfully, she plunked into the seat and tucked her legs in.

"You sure this ain't illegal?" Aster said, hanging up the pass.

"Not with me in the car. With eighty-year-old hips like mine, I'm not hobbling a quarter of a mile to see *A Midsummer Night's Dream,* even though it is my favorite play in the world."

Aster found close parking. Only a few feet away, they approached a banner that hung between two trees: "Welcome to the Shakespeare Festival." A teenaged boy dressed in clothes from the 1600s tore their tickets in half. The wooden benches of the outdoor theater gradually descended to the stage. Aster offered Irene an arm, and the two women descended the wide stairway. They took seats about midway down.

Aster said, "Would you like something to drink? There's a kiosk over there."

"A wine spritzer."

"Okay. These benches aren't very soft. I'll go get the blanket out of my car, for padding, and then I'll get our drinks," Aster said.

Since wine spritzers had been popular several decades ago, Aster came back with concoction made of half rosé, half carbonated water, and a splash of white soda. As soon as the women settled on the blanket, Aster took a lemon muffin out of her purse, inserted a candle, and lit it.

"Oh, look at you fussing around, making my birthday special." Irene flushed.

Aster glanced at the people sitting behind them and said, "This is Irene's eightieth birthday. Can you help me sing?"

A chorus of voices joined in singing happy birthday to Irene. They clapped when she blew out the candle.

While Irene and Aster nibbled on the muffin, a trumpet blew, and the crowd hushed.

A narrator welcomed everybody and announced act 1 of *A Midsummer's Night Dream.*

Only a few lines into the play, Aster heard the sound of a drink spilling onto the ground, followed by "damn it" from someone in the audience. A few rows away, a white-haired man stood up abruptly and dashed over to the kiosk. Aster's jaw dropped as she recognized Jack when he grabbed a napkin and started mopping his pants. He returned to his seat with both wet and dry napkins, and cleaned up his mess.

What the heck is Jack doing here? she wondered. Thankful to be hidden from view, she craned her neck to see whom he was with. A woman with long black hair and a red dot painted between her brows encouraged Jack to scoot down the bench a bit. She kept leaning into Jack and whispering into his ear. Jack put an arm around the woman and motioned for her to be quiet. For a bit, the woman rested her head on Jack's shoulder.

Aster went numb. She struggled to sort it out. *I thought he was interested in me. He wasted no time in finding another woman to date. No big loss. I have no claim on him. Hell, I never got past intrigue or even kissed him. The way he's snuggling up to that woman, it's clear we are just friends. I'm embarrassed I thought otherwise.*

No matter how many rationales flooded her mind, Aster could not pay attention to the play. She literally watched Jack interact with the woman the whole time. They appeared to be comfortable in each other's presence, as though they had a history together.

Damn. So, Jack is not single. I wonder if his girlfriend knows how flirty he is. The little scoundrel, Aster mused.

Irene clapped vigorously at the end of the play. "What a great performance. Don't you think?"

"Oh yes, it was marvelous," Aster lied. "Great costumes too."

"Thanks for making my birthday special. Tasty as the

spritzer was, it went right through me. Let's go. I need to use the ladies' room," Irene said. She grabbed a hold of Aster arm and laboriously worked her way to the top of the stairs.

"Aster," called out Jack.

Aster pretended not to hear the call and kept trudging along to Irene's slow pace. She wished Irene could move faster.

"Hey, Aster," Jack tapped her on the shoulder.

"Oh, Jack, hello. This is Irene. We're here celebrating her birthday," Aster said, noticing the woman he was with dressed and looked as though she was from India. The woman was a bit curvy and somewhat attractive.

"Are you Spanakopita Jack?" Irene asked, looking him up and down.

Jack looked puzzled.

"Yes, he is. He gave me a spanakopita at the farmers' market. Jack, please introduce me to your friend," Aster said, curious as to how Jack would respond.

"I'm Amanda," the woman said, hiccupping. "Sorry. I drank one too many cocktails. My husband is out of town, so Jack is my chaperone tonight."

Shocked that Jack would date the wife of a man who was probably a friend, Aster stole a look at Jack, only to find him as calm as could be. Aster maintained her composure. Wanting to show distance, she said, "I'm Aster. Jack took me on a soul journey a few days ago."

"Sorry, folks, I gotta break this up. My eighty-year-old bladder waits for nobody. C'mon, let's go." Irene pulled Aster's arm.

"Nice meeting you," Amanda slurred.

"Happy birthday, Irene," Jack called to their backs.

"Thanks," Irene said, tottering away.

Aster turned and said, "Bye." She felt thankful for the quick getaway. The whole scene with Jack seemed too weird.

They found a portable toilet near the entrance. On the drive home, Aster commented, "I was surprised to run into Jack. He wanted to hang out with me tonight. Then, presto change-o, he's with a married woman tonight. Fast mover, or what?"

Irene replied, "Amanda called him a chaperone. He could be a professional male escort, for all we know. Guys like that are charming as sailors—regular salty dogs with girls in every port. I'd watch my step if were you."

"Jack and I are nothing more than friends," Aster said in defense. Saying the words aloud stung a bit. To think she'd actually toyed with the idea of Jack as a potential candidate for the dating pool. Succumbing to her own ruefulness, she crossed him off the ballot. Once again, fate pushed the UA button: unlovable and alone.

The minute Aster got home, she called her cousin in Georgia.

J. J. answered, "Aster, hello. It's late. I'm in my pajamas already. What's up?"

"Sorry it's a bit late, but I gotta tell you about Jack."

"Did you two hook up?"

"No. I ran into him at the health-food store, and he wanted to explore that English life. But I said no because I had plans with Irene," Aster started and then explained every detail of the evening, including Irene's comment about the male escort.

"That's sort of a slap in the face, isn't it?" J. J. said.

"A bit. It made me feel unlovable. It shouldn't. I have no claim on Jack. He made it clear that he's a free, roaming bachelor. The thing that trips me up is that he flirts as if he's interested in me." Aster rolled her eyes.

"I'm sorry, but how many times have I said you are lovable? Tell me, was Jack awkward confronting you tonight?"

"Not at all. He made a point of greeting me. He treated me like an old friend. That's what we are, friends, because all we've ever done is talk and hug."

"Nothing wrong with a good buddy." J. J. yawned.

"Between you, me, and my answering machine, I admit I let Jack in, he stirred up fantasy in me. As fate has it, he's on a different page," Aster confessed.

J. J. chuckled. "I'm delighted he stirred you up. You need a little action in your life."

"What's the use? I'm a lousy player. I don't have any game," Aster whined.

"It really bugged you that Jack was with a married woman. Ain't that right? In that case, I'm gonna play devil's advocate here. You have no idea what the situation was with Jack and Amanda. You're assumin' the worst. What if you're wrong? Because you are the shyest person on the planet, you'll never find out the truth of the matter. You could simply ask him," J. J. said.

"Thanks for the slap in the face. It's very sobering." Aster sighed.

"Anytime, dear cousin. Sleep on it, and let's talk Monday. I'm getting tired. I'll catch ya later," J. J. drawled.

"Okay. Good night."

Aster lay in bed, trying to figure out why Jack had come into her life. As much as she had resisted, he stirred interest; and yet, it ended up a disappointment. She thought, *What was the purpose of it? I learned about a past life. Big deal! I was a healer with a lame foot. Now I know I have a soul family—oh joy. It feels like my lot in life is for men to rake me over the coals. Did I do something horrid in a past life to deserve bad karma? Why do I need a man to love me?* Drowning in self-loathing, she drifted off to sleep.

Aster had a dream. Grannyme was dressed in a black and white–striped referee outfit. She stood at the shore of a waterway similar to a moat. On the far shore, a double door expanded the entire background. Nailed to the wooden center was a copper chalice nearly the height of a horse.

"My dear bumpkin, I'm here to help you on your quest. Now

you need to get to that door," Grannyme said, pointing across the water.

Eager to find the answer, Aster said, "There's no drawbridge, is there?" She gauged the distance too long for one. The length seemed about the size of two Olympic pools end to end.

"A bridge would be too easy," Grannyme said, snapping her finger. Her hair changed from hanging loose to a ponytail, and so did Aster's.

At the shift, Aster looked down to notice she was wearing a wet suit. She said, "I get it. I'm supposed to swim to the other side. No problem. If you remember, I used to swim across Crystal Lake as a kid all the time."

"Think again, my dear," Grannyme said, waving her hand in a carefree manner.

Out of the water, a balance beam emerged. Three stuffed duffel bags dangling from ropes hung across the path. Beyond the beam, a one-person raft moored alongside a small dock.

"Whoa! An obstacle course," Aster said, thinking that getting wet was the worst that could happen.

"Yes, and this key unlocks that door," Grannyme cocked her head toward the door while she held up a gold-chain necklace attached to a gold skeleton key. "The challenge is to keep it dry. For the key won't work if it's wet."

"Pshaw, a granny-twist. Do I have to wear it around my neck?"

"Whatever works."

Aster put the necklace on and walked to the balance beam. The minute her foot touched the wood, the first duffel bag began to spin like helicopter blades, forcing her to crouch into a crawling position. Praying to stay dry, she inched along the narrow beam, like a snail. Memories of walking on eggshells to avoid angering her father lingered until she was able to stand again. Glad to let that task fall behind her, Aster inhaled a cleansing breath and kept her balance. The next duffel bag swung like a pendulum across the beam. Getting safely past involved timing.

For some odd reason, the rhythm reminded her of jumping rope. She had never mastered the feel of when to enter the moving rope because her peers refused to play with a loco conejo. She paused, watching the path of the duffel bag.

"I'm not good enough to do this one, am I?" Aster fretted.

"Just put one foot in front of the other," Grannyme encouraged.

"I can't move slow on this one."

"No worries. That suit will keep you warm if you get wet."

Extending her arms out for additional support, Aster waited for the bag to clear the beam. She took several steps to safety.

"That's my girl!" Grannyme cheered.

Impressed that taking action kept her dry, Aster began to sway.

"Breathe!" shouted Grannyme.

Not realizing she was holding her breath, Aster took in air and found center.

The quest had seemed easy until she faced the last duffel bag. It hung at the end of the beam, blocking passage. Unsure if pushing the bag aside would work, Aster touched the surface. It felt as soft as a down pillow. Without warning, the bag suddenly split in half, creating an opening to go through, as if pulling a curtain open. Then, the two halves quickly slammed back together, closing the passageway. After watching the opening several more times, she discovered there was no rhythm or logical pattern to determine safe passage. At each closing, as the two sides met, a disturbing whack knotted her stomach.

The erratic sounds reminded Aster of her father's punches. In an attempt to stuff the feeling down, she whined, "At least the blow won't be as hard as Dad's iron fists. Oh dear! How on earth am I supposed to navigate something I can't predict?"

"Take a gamble," Grannyme cajoled like an excited spectator.

"Great odds," Aster moaned.

Less than enthused at the blind insight yet determined to reach the grail, she stayed balanced and stepped forward. In a swish, the duffel bag closed up and held fast onto her calf. Seconds later, the bag reopened. Thrown off balance by the sudden impact, Aster fell. "A-a-agh!" she screamed in defeat and landed with a thud. Of all things, she crashed on the dock. Aster got up, inspecting her body for injuries.

"Don't worry. The only bruise you will find is your ego!" Grannyme cackled.

"Stop goading me!" Aster cried.

"You better catch the raft; it's floating away." Granny snickered.

Sure enough, the raft was adrift. Too annoyed to fear any danger, Aster dived toward the craft. Partially missing the mark, the lower part of her body had submersed in the moat. As luck would have it, her elbows hooked over the sides. By sheer determination, she pulled herself into the raft. Delighted to find the key still dry, she paddled toward the far shore. Halfway there, raindrops plunked on the water's surface. This seemed weird, for the sky was clear. As if by magic, a rain cloud hovered directly in her path. Thinking fast, Aster tucked the key under the wet suit. The metal felt warm against her heart. She slouched forward, using her back as a shield, as the rain pelted down. Crouched in the awkward position, her visibility poor, she paddled with all her might until the cloud disappeared. Thankful the raft had stayed on course, she beached it on the shore.

Grannyme raised her arms, declaring a touchdown, while Aster clambered out of the raft.

Breathing hard from the exertion, Aster removed the key from around her neck. It sparkled in the sunlight. She broke into a grin, saying, "It's dry."

"You did it." Grannyme clapped. "Now go unlock that door."

Aster strode over to the gigantic doors. Up this close, they looked like sliding barn doors that stretched on without end. The copper chalice was actually in two pieces: half was on the left door, and half was on the right. Nervous, she dropped the skeleton key, plucked it from the sand, and inserted it into the lock. When the doors slid apart, it felt symbolic, signifying cracking open a mystery. Aster's face fell upon seeing an old fashion gramophone with a hand crank, topped with a speaker that looked like an oversize morning glory. She laughed hesitantly. "What kind of joke is this? That's no grail."

"It's a clue. Play it." Grannyme giggled. "Isn't this fun?"

Rolling her eyes, Aster turned the crank and set the needle on the record. Crackly orchestra music played a few bars and then stopped.

Then, out of the speaker, Grannyme's raspy voice boomed, "Congratulations, Aster! You made it. You have officially begun your quest. In honor of your triumph, I will advise you on the next step in finding the grail."

A trumpet played, as if introducing a member from the royal court.

Grannyme cleared her throat, saying, "The next step involves giving Jack a chance to explain himself."

The record slowed down to a stop.

Aster cast an expectant glare at Grannyme and said, "What? This is getting more absurd by the minute. Jack? C'mon, can't you circumvent the uncomfortable and be more specific?"

"My darling bumpkin, I cannot tell you. Feeding your mind is pointless; you need to feel the answer, truly anchor it into your cells," replied Grannyme.

"What does Jack have to do with my quest?" Aster scrunched up her face.

"He's helping me out, getting you to the finish line."

"You mean he's a pawn in your game."

"More or less. I love playing games," Grannyme said, giggling once again.

The next day, Aster went to the Boulder library. Curious and eager to get more clues about the quest, she checked out a book entitled *King Arthur and Holy Grail.* She stood in the lobby, reading the prologue, when the smell of sandalwood had her look up. Jack McFadden stopped in front of her, with a large book tucked in his arm. Stunned to see him, she said, "My word, you're everywhere I turn."

"Believe me, I'm not stalking you. I came here to pay a fine on this overdue book. Glad to see you, though." Jack broke into a grin.

Heeding advice from Grannyme, Aster stayed patient to engage. She held up her book for him to read the cover and said, "I picked up an old classic."

"One of my favorites. I love historical pieces. Which reminds me, how did you like the play last night?" he asked.

"It was good. I adored the costumes."

"I wasn't able to enjoy it much. Amanda was plastered. She spilled her drink on me and kept apologizing repeatedly in my ear," Jack explained.

"She a heavy drinker?" Aster asked coolly.

"Hardly. Earlier, we were both at the same wake. She overdid it grieving over Kate, her best friend, who died. I offered to drive her home, but Amanda insisted on going to *A Midsummer's Night Dream* first.

"Did she want a distraction? I get that," Aster said.

"It was more about honoring the dead. Amanda and Kate had season tickets to the Shakespeare Festival and went to every play. Being a sucker for a hard-luck case, I agreed to escort Amanda. She's an old friend," Jack said sincerely.

"Oh, I see. You were consoling a tipsy friend," Aster said, delighted to hear the circumstances.

"Well, yeah. I'd much rather hang out with you and check out that English life. How about it? You game for tonight?"

Deeply touched by his words, she wondered if this was part of the quest to follow. Unclear how to decipher the moment clearly, she said boldly, "Sure. Seven sound good? I'm curious too. How about my place?"

"Great. See you then." He walked away with a slight bounce in his step.

A red flag waved inside Aster's mind. *Damn it, what did I get myself into? I've got to stay neutral and not get attached. Galen warned me: he's a spender.*

Jack arrived exactly at seven o'clock, bringing a long-necked, liter-sized green bottle. His khaki shorts and purple golf shirt appeared brand-new.

"Hi. Come in." Aster led him into the house. She had dressed up in a floral skirt, loose tank top, and a little eyeliner. Makeup was a sparse frivolity worn only for special occasions.

"Good to see you. Been ages since we last met." He laughed lightly. "Here, I brought this."

"Is that wine?" Aster asked, wary of Jack losing his ability to journey. She peered skeptically at the label.

"No. It's carbonated mineral water. My parents engrained in me to bring a beverage whenever I'm a houseguest. It's an old family tradition," Jack replied, kicking off his flip-flops.

"Oh, bubbly water! That's very thoughtful. I've got a lime in the fridge. If you add it to the water, it makes a good thirst quencher."

"Sounds great."

While Aster fixed the drinks, Jack said, "I journey into the past for a living. I love it, but after a bit, it becomes an ordinary phenomenon. It's weird, though; today, as I drove over, the mere thought of journeying with you felt exciting, like a kid setting off to go trick-or-treating. Makes me wonder if you and I are twin flames. It's what I've been searching for my whole life."

"And twin flames are?"

Jack replied, "They share a deep connection, bound to each other forever. Sort of like the yin and yang of a soul when it's created. Some lives they are best friends, and other times not.

All depends on what karmic agreements the souls made before each incarnation."

His eyes penetrated into hers, and she felt the inkling of seduction. The longer he stared, the more she felt exposed.

"That's a lot of depth," Aster said, wishing he would withdraw his gaze.

"I'm sorry. I thought you'd share the excitement with me, but there's reluctance written all over your face."

"I'm uncomfortable. The way you looked at me shocked me. I'm not sure how to read it."

"What do you mean, the way I looked at you?" Jack said, taken aback.

"As though I'm transparent. Like you reached in and saw all my secrets," Aster said, wondering if he knew why she only wanted to be friends.

"Believe me. I don't have those types of omnipotent powers. Sorry. I didn't mean to offend. The other day, at the store, when I touched your back, a jolt of energy shot up my arm. It dazzled me. It made me wonder if that was what a twin flame would feel like. Just now, the little boy in me was looking for a light flickering in your eyes, something—anything—to confirm my hunch. Granted, you and I are old souls revisiting each other, and I simply want to know to what extent. Stuff like this excites me. Will you forgive me for being too intense?" Jack apologized in earnest.

Aster's shoulders began to lower. Sensing honesty, she said, "No problem. I got it. That was you being excited."

Jack asked, "Aster, did you feel anything when I touched your back?"

"Oh, just a bit," she said shyly.

"I knew it," Jack said enthusiastically. "I love historical stuff. My spider sense knows we go back to the beginning of time, and I bet we are twin flames too. I'm gonna check it out."

Aster raised her brows, impressed by how candid Jack was about being a loco conejo.

"Aster, do my time-travel abilities weird you out?" he said, concerned.

"Your excitement amuses me. You know, I'm a little woo-woo too. I often have predictive dreams, but I'll be the first to admit, I'm not used to your la-la land. The one time I visited, it was fun. I'm looking forward to doing it again."

"Great! We could take a woo-la, woo-la journey right now. You game?" Jack said.

She warmed to his play on words. "Sure. We'll be more comfortable in the living room. Come on." Aster led the way.

They settled into two matching tan recliners across from a maroon sofa.

Jack guided them into a deep breathing exercise. Once they grounded into a meditative state, he set the intention to visit the life with John Gerard, author of *The Herbal or General History of Plants*.

Aster floated into timelessness. In her mind's eye, blue and pink morning glories clung to a gray stone archway. Led by curiosity, she walked through, a bit more confident than she had been during her previous journey to New Mexico.

Within a matter of seconds, Jack and Aster soared across the Atlantic Ocean and descended in England. The scene stopped in a still frame similar to a map. The legend in the corner read, "London, 1589." The metropolitan area was smaller than in the twenty-first century. Just west of the city, on the Strand Road to Richmond, they touched ground. Humidity tinged with a hint of coal smoke filled their lungs. A smattering of gardens bordered the cobbled thoroughfare.

The sound of clopping hooves drew Aster's attention toward two people approaching on horseback. A teenage girl wearing a rust-colored dress with a brown laced-up bodice straddled a pony. Her chestnut braids formed a scalloped ring from forehead to nape, much like a laurel wreath in ancient Greece. A bonnet rested in the center of the braided coronet. The male beside her, slightly older than she, sat at ease, as if his tall black steed were a lower appendage. He wore a knee-length tunic over leggings that defined a lean body. His broad shoulders rose and fell in rhythm with the horse's gait.

In the next moment, Aster drifted over the girl and hovered above the saddle, and then, like a ghost, entered the younger body of the girl. Her awareness shifted, as if looking through the girl's eyes. The point of view was different from the Navajo life, where she had observed from outside the body.

Aster thought, *Wow! I know how to flow naturally with the gait of a horse.*

"Ah!" the girl let out a startled cry as gooseflesh shot up her back.

"Margaret, what's wrong with you this time? Bug bite you?" her riding companion asked, growing impatient with her moodiness.

"Got the willies, Emery. Like I stepped over a grave," she said, shaking her head.

The late afternoon sun shone warm on Margaret's weary face. The journey from Kent to west London had eaten up half the day. Her gentle pony, a Welsh cob that had been her constant companion since early childhood, let out a tired snort.

"Daisy, easy mate. Almost there. At least we have each other." Margaret stroked down the taupe neck until her fingers touched something flimsy. A renegade leaf from the mugwort girdle stuck out from under the saddle. It reminded her to give thanks to the Nature Spirits for the gift of endurance the herb bestowed on the pony.

"You and me are castaways. Rather be home doing chores." Her hoofed friend listened to everything in confidence and habitually bobbed her head, as if agreeing to Margaret's opinions on life.

Sitting taller on his stallion, Blacky, Emery shot her an impatient glance. "Be done with it. You've been in a foul state all morning."

"Could it be any worse? I'll have no family; not a soul who knows me." Her pouting amber eyes stared ahead, lost in misery.

"Worse? Yes, it could. Papa could have arranged for you to wed Dr. John Gerard," Emery parried.

"Oh, how dare you! That old codger." She soured.

"If it wasn't for your complaining, this would be a bonny trip. It's sunny, and the roads are dry. At the very least, you could have told stories instead of storing a teacup on that enormous bottom lip of yours." Emery got the last word, for Margaret was too annoyed to retort.

Papa had entrusted Emery to escort Margaret and deliver a pull horse named Ginger to Dr. Gerard. The mare, a two-year-old Suffolk bay, was an impressive thank-you gift for the doctor providing the shelter and safety of his daughter. A horse breeder by trade, Papa could afford such a present.

Attached to Ginger's back were the remnants of Margaret's former life, which included satchels of clothes, sundries, a roll of fresh bedstraw, and a potted plant.

A tabby kitten chasing after a mouse darted out into the road. Ginger reared from the sudden movement, dislodging the halter. The plant, a last-minute cargo add-on, fell off the bay. The sound of breaking pottery spooked the horse into a bolt.

The rapid jerk of the lead rope sent Blacky bucking his hind legs. Intense, loud neighs filled the air. Emery struggled to stay on. As soon as his horse settled, he reeled in the rope and sprinted into a gallop.

Daisy let out the whinny of a seasoned matron. Her mature nature stayed calm, and she moved out of the way of the excited younglings.

Margaret watched her brother race off, knowing the speed of his horse would soon catch up with her belongings. During the last quarter of the trip, she'd felt a dull ache in her legs. She gladly dismounted to inspect the fallen plant. Hidden behind the broken pot, the kitten lay still, its tail trapped under the weight.

"Are you dead, little one?" Margaret asked. The stillness rekindled a raw sensation in her heart. Grief oozed in as memories of Mum wove their way into her thoughts. Only a fortnight ago, her mother was hung at the gallows, wrongly accused of being a witch.

How lonely it was without Mum, Catherine Colton, the best midwife in all of Kent. *We were so close. I could tell her anything.*

Margaret freed the cat. The tail bent like a broken reed. Tears fell onto the black and gray–striped fur. Dread overcame her as she tried to find a heartbeat. As a last resort, she raised the limp body to her ear. At the sound of a faint pulse, she instinctively cradled the injured feline, praying for vitality to enliven the poor thing.

Emery returned with packhorse in tow. The young man's amber eyes glowed with excitement. "What a great chase! Blacky took off like lightning. Best part of the trip."

"Oh joy," Margaret replied.

Wet cheeks met his stare, dampening his glory. He grumbled, "You're a pathetic weeping willow. Crying over a broken pot?"

"No," she snapped. "This kitten's near death. Got hurt when the horse spooked."

He knew from experience not to challenge her stubborn nursing nature. To hurry things along, he suggested, "Let's bring it to the doc; maybe he can fix it. Hop on. Let's go."

"The plant," she pleaded.

"Leave it. How you gonna carry that? It's in pieces," he said, certain his logic was the best answer.

"It's the kind of gift Mum would give. I have an old sun bonnet I can wrap it in," she said, walking toward the packhorse.

Keeping the kitten in the crook of her arm, she held the reins while her brother bundled the roots and soil into the headpiece. Emery hoisted the package onto Ginger's back, and off they rode.

The sound of hooves droned on as she jostled to the smooth

gait of Daisy's stout legs. Coming closer to her new destiny of living with a dreadful barber surgeon, she wondered what type of monster he was. Mum, a French-trained midwife, rarely trusted that type of healing, for more often than not, surgeons would bleed people to death. She decided right then that her new foster father and employer would never touch a scalpel to her skin. *He'll never know I'm sick. I know what herbs to take. He will not prescribe my death.*

Emery broke the silence that fell between them. "Hey, we're almost there. Look, there's Cecil House!"

The three-story brick manor, crowned with corner turrets, boasted of wealth.

"Aye," Margaret replied in a dry tone, not looking.

"Don't be such a dolt. Place looks nice. Cheer up, or you'll be sent to a nunnery in France," he said, attempting to tease her.

Margaret winced.

Not wishing to deliver a crying sixteen-year-old girl, Emery said, "Don't worry; they're going to like you. Besides, this filly is right smart dowry for fostering." He looked Margaret in the eye and winked.

"Lucky me. Payment to live with an old quack," she said sardonically. "And dowries are for marriages, you silly git."

"Look up ahead; that must be Gerard's cottage," he interrupted.

A two-story stone cottage sat recessed twenty feet from the road. An orange-breasted robin flew to a nest secure under the overhang of the thatched roof. Coal smoke rose from the chimney.

Before going to the door, Emery asked, "Do I look presentable?"

His eighteen-year-old face produced a sparse goatee. The leather on his knee-high boots and his cap matched, obviously cut from the same hide. He looked exactly like who he was: a horse breeder's son dressed for riding, not in his Sunday best.

"You look like a billy goat who forgot to shave. Whoever

answers the door might offer you hay clippings and tea," Margaret remarked.

Emery lifted the brass-ring knocker and struck rapid taps.

A curtain moved in the front window. The Colton siblings stood staring at the weathered door of nine square wooden panels, waiting for it to open. Emery hoped to say the right words—the kind of words that were spoken by a man, not a boy. Margaret wished she were back in Kent with her family.

An older woman wearing an apron past her knees answered the door. Her somber gray dress clung snug around a plump midsection. As she stood in the threshold with the stance of a centurion, her squinting blue eyes scanned new faces. A plain, white, close-fitting cap covered her ears and the top of her forehead, hiding all of her hair. It was an old-fashioned style commonly worn by the elderly. The base of her rectangular face produced not droopy but soft jowls of a once extremely square chin. Margaret marveled that except for the clothes, this person could masquerade as either man or woman.

Emery cleared his throat. "Ahem! Hello, ma'am. I am Emery Colton, and this is my sister, Margaret. Pleased to make your acquaintance."

Margaret gave a short curtsy. She held her tongue, surprised to hear Emery be so formal. His nervous fingers were busy clicking nails.

"Greetings. I'm the housekeeper, Mrs. Wakefield. Yes, we are expecting you. Humph! Rather frail for a gardener," she replied curtly.

Margaret froze.

The housekeeper paused to finish scrutinizing the new arrivals. Of late, fashion statements were measured by collar height and frivolity. Margaret's simple low-lying ruffle collar showed no status, yet its beige color offered a rich accent to the rust dress. Emery had no collar whatsoever. His jerkin fit rather handsomely, offering no fashionable correctness, only a rugged appearance.

"Two skinny descendants of a merchant," Mrs. Wakefield scoffed.

Margaret bowed her head politely, not happy with the reception.

Mrs. Wakefield shook her head, as if remembering good manners. "Oh, right! I see the family resemblance—same chestnut hair and pinched nose as your father's."

She noted Margaret's hat, which sat further back than her own. "Those new caps are scandalous, exposing hair like that. In my day, we wouldn't think of flaunting our ears in public. Did that skimpy thing stay on your head riding all the way from Kent?" she asked tartly.

"Yes, it did. I pinned it to my braids, to be sure." Margaret felt unclear as to how to read the lack of warmth, so she offered no more than what was asked.

Leaning on the side of caution, she thought, *The housekeeper is a regular gatekeeper dog. Barks a bit. Need to stay calm and move slow, so she doesn't bite.*

"Wouldn't want that." Mrs. Wakefield spat instructions like a drill sergeant. "It's nearly teatime. Stable the horses out back. No cats in the house. Wretched things make me sneeze. Wipe your feet before entering. There'll be no filth in my kitchen."

Emery and Margaret entered the cottage, carrying the satchels. The messier bedstraw bundle and plant remained on the porch. Everything in the room was larger scale than at home—the cook stove, the washtub, the table. An array of pots and pans hung from the rafters; cupboards and shelves lined the walls. A large pantry off to the side proved the occupants enjoyed a richer life than any common folk.

"Smells good in here." Emery sounded hungry, inhaling the aroma of onions sautéed in a frying pan. He presented Mrs. Wakefield with a bottle of mead. "It's Mother's finest brew."

"How kind. Thank you," the housekeeper replied in a bored manner.

"It was voted best in the village at the spring fair," Margaret interjected.

With an air of superiority, Mrs. Wakefield said, "My mead is favored by Lord Burghley. When he entertains the queen at his home, Her Majesty claims the mead is the finest in the entire kingdom."

"Must be tasty then," Margaret said, feeling thwarted that the gift did not impress the receiver as a thoughtful gesture.

"So I hear," Mrs. Wakefield said, looking down her long nose. She then announced, "I'll serve this with our meal today; use it up."

After a bit, she muttered sharply, "Don't want to mix it with the good stuff."

Two minutes later, John Gerard entered the kitchen from outside. The thin-framed doctor set the black leather bag carefully on a small table. He had just returned home from making a sick call, and his energized movements belied the exhaustion evident in his sleep-deprived face.

Margaret's first thought was that Dr. John Gerard looked like a well-groomed old fox. His long, skinny legs maneuvered gracefully with each step. A red handlebar mustache angled up like a chevron, and his beard came to a point. Beneath puffy eyelids, a pair of green squinting orbs focused keenly.

He reached out his hand politely to Emery, saying, "Hello, then. John Gerard, at your service."

"Emery Colton," he replied, shaking hands.

Following the advice of his father, Emery inspected Gerard's hands. The index finger and thumb bore smudgy ink stains—the sign of a writer. Papa had mentioned that Gerard was writing a book about herbs. Emery felt cautious, not wanting to insult the doctor, so he refrained from drawing attention to the soiled fingers.

"Yes. Roy Colton's son," Gerard opined, memorizing his budding adult features. "Been expecting you. Your father and I met years ago on a ship crossing the English Channel. He was bringing a horse back home to breed. I was the ship's surgeon."

"And you've been friends ever since," Emery added.

"Right," Gerard said, nodding.

"The ginger-colored bay in the stable is a gift to you from Father." Emery stroked his chin while wearing a prideful smile. "Raised and trained her myself."

"I saw her." Gerard gave a short whistle. "Splendid husbandry. Yes, indeed, a smart-looking mare. Make sure to thank your father for such a fine gift."

Emery gave a derisive snort, saying, "Margaret named her Ginger. Despite the plant name, I can guarantee the horse is a good puller. Do you ride carriage often?"

"Yes, when it rains." Gerard turned to face Margaret, who was staring at the worn doctor's bag as if the tools inside were possessed by the devil. "And you, Miss Margaret, must be our new house guest. Welcome to our home. It's a bit humble looking next to Lord Burghley's estate, there across the garden. By the way, Ginger is a splendid name. I am very fond of plants." He picked up her hand and kissed it briefly, as if she were a princess.

Margaret's lips moved before she could speak. She could hardly believe a surgeon would speak in such a casual and kind manner. While curtsying awkwardly, she muttered, "Yes, I am … ah, sir."

The doctor eyed her inquisitively. "You look so much like your father; I feel I should know you already."

"Thank you, sir. Papa sends his regards," she said politely.

Gerard opened the back door and focused to his left. "Healthy wood betony specimen you brought here. Never seen a bonnet used that way before."

"The pot broke." Margaret raised her shoulders.

They both stepped onto the porch.

"Mum called it 'bishopswort' because it's planted in every churchyard in the kingdom." Reciting memorized words, she added, "It drives away evil that gives you headaches; good for colds, sweating sickness, and lung ailments."

He wet his fingers on his tongue and twisted the ends of his mustache, saying, "Interesting you brought this particular plant. I was just at Richmond Palace, administering a betony concoction to the queen," he explained.

"Queen Elizabeth?" Margaret's brows rose in astonishment.

"I'm filling in for her personal physician, as he suffers the same illness as Her Majesty. The queen is bedridden with a high fever. Too early to tell if it's a serious ague." He looked worried.

"Sir, Mum was a midwife. Pardon me, but would it be too forward if I told you what she would do?" Margaret risked asking.

Gerard yawned from fatigue. "And what would that be, elder syrup to reduce the fever?"

"Not exactly." Using a finger from each hand, she drew a rectangle in midair as she explained, "Apply a poultice of garlic to the soles of both feet. Then, feed her bone broth for strength."

"Hmm. I'll consider it," the doctor said, impressed.

Barking interrupted the conversation. The dog, Chester, came running over to greet his master.

"There you are, old boy," Gerard said, as he stroked the beagle's head. "Be good, and sit."

Dutifully the dog obeyed.

"Chester, come meet Margaret. Give her your paw."

Margaret smiled at the reception; it was the least-threatening one of the day. Chester went to work smelling the new scents from Kent.

"You're so handsome," she said, scratching behind his ears.

"Enough sniffing already." Abruptly, Gerard ordered, "Rabbit, go fetch."

For a short moment, Chester raised his nose in the air, then tore off into the garden, disappearing behind the shrubbery.

"Now that you've met my most loyal friend, allow me to show you around. Come over here," the doctor said, motioning with his hand as he walked toward the winding fence. A perimeter of stone, roughly four feet tall, protected the flora from grazing fauna. With a sweep of his arm, Gerard explained, "This acreage is called Emerald Gardens."

"Oh dear! Look at all those plants," she said incredulously. "How many?"

"Roughly a thousand. I daresay, the herbal manuscript I'm drafting has grown quite large, for I have documented the virtues of them all. In the course of my endeavors, I've grown very fond of each and every one. Consider them my children, since I have none." He glanced at her in adoration.

"Weeding alone will keep me quite busy," she said. At the same time, she thought, *Oh God! Is he implying I am to bear his pups? Never!*

"I daresay it will." He tilted his head. "Over there, on the far side, is Cecil House."

Half-listening, Margaret turned. Her mouth dropped at the size of the three-story brick manor and the paved tennis court that she hadn't paid attention to when they arrived.

"Pardon me. What did you say about children?" Margaret said, utterly confused.

"I treat these plants like children, because I have not had the pleasure to sire my own," he responded quickly, seeing the dismay on her face.

"I thought you had married," she said.

"I was married, for the shortest two years of my life. My Emily suffered ill health. She died childless. With all my knowledge, I could not save her."

"I'm sorry for your loss. I misunderstood what you said. For a moment, you looked at me rather strangely as you spoke," she apologized.

Gerard slapped a hand to his cheek, saying, "Wonderful start we're having. Forgive me for staring. Something about you reminds me of my sister who died twenty years ago. As such, your presence makes me overly comfortable. My mind plays tricks, for I'm talking as candidly to you as if we'd grown up together. How rare of me to do so. Please excuse my illusion of a closeness not yet earned. Surely you think me full of pretense."

She thought, *My initial judgment of him was wrong, for he is a sensitive soul.* An awkward silence made Margaret nervous. It seemed as though there was an invisible hand held over her mouth, preventing her from speaking. Eventually, she cleared her throat. "Not at all. I prefer to speak openly, sir. Mother and I were very candid. Father is very witty, and my brothers are extremely frank. If any household matter needed discussion, the concerns were addressed in the bluntest fashion imaginable. Believe me, I prefer casual."

"I have no family left alive. Yours live far away. Perhaps we could extend our friendship into a kinship as it suits." He rubbed at tired eyes. "Now, where were we? Ah yes, the tour." He pointed toward the manor, explaining, "The orchard is over to the left. William Cecil owns all of it."

Dazzled at the wealth, she asked, "Is Mr. Cecil a lord, then?"

"Yes. His proper title is Lord Burghley."

"He's part of the royal court?" she asked.

"Queen Elizabeth appointed Sir William Cecil as Principal Secretary. Soon afterward, Her Majesty granted him the title Lord Burghley, Leading Councilor," Gerard explained.

Margaret took it all in, wanting desperately to become familiar with her new surroundings, so different from her former ones. She felt like a newly transplanted flower needing to secure its roots.

"Sir," Margaret said inquisitively, "Of all the plants in the garden, are there any you cannot grow?"

"Ginger. Tried everything. The frost kills it," Gerard said in regret.

"It's an expensive root. We had some once. It's spicy," Margaret said, remembering the taste.

"The queen had hoped we could corner the market. Ginger's high trade value would bring in sizable revenue. She has Sir Drake and Sir Raleigh looking for a tropical island on which to cultivate it. Oops! Actually, that last bit is confidential. Daresay, please do not tell Mrs. Wakefield, or all of London will know before sundown. I am hopeless. Again, I confide in you."

Margaret gestured, as if buttoning her lips. The fear of him being a monster slowly subsided. She found the nerve to say, "Sir, there's a kitten with a broken tail in the stable. Would you take a look at it?"

"The matter is attended to already. After leaving my horse with the groom, I heard a little voice mewing for help. I had to snip the tail off at the bend so it wouldn't fester. The rascal gave me this, thanking me for my service." A thin scratch marred the back of his hand.

"So, we didn't kill it," she said, relieved. Margaret told the doctor everything about the spooked horse incident.

"Stripes will be fine. By the time I left, Russ, the stable man, fetched a cup of milk. Never saw a tongue lap that fast. Poor thing was hungry," Gerard said, letting out a chuckle.

"Stripes? You named her already? Shall we keep her, then?" Hope filled her eyes and swept across her face.

"We shall see. If she is a good mouser, she may dwell in the stables. Must earn her keep," he stated casually.

They walked back to the porch. The betony plant slumped in the shade. Loose dirt scattered onto the floorboards.

"Sir, the roots are drying. Not enough soil in the bonnet to keep it happy. It needs to find a home. Where should it go?" she asked.

Gerard motioned with his head. "Over next to the elder tree, by the others. What do you call it, bishopswort?" He handed her a spade that leaned against the cottage. Before taking leave, Gerard held up his ink-stained index finger. "I must inquire. Can you read or write?"

"No, sir."

"I have a remedy to cure that."

"Pardon?" Margaret had not caught his meaning.

"I shall teach you the alphabet. You are more useful literate than not." Dr. Gerard gave a friendly smile and turned to enter the house.

The thought of learning to read and write astounded Margaret. Her brothers had the skill, but Papa deemed it unnecessary to educate a girl. The promise of literacy along with the sight of the magnificent elder tree increased Margaret's hope for the future, for every successful herb garden grew next to a sacred elder.

❋ ❋

The next day, after a breakfast of crumpets, plum sauce, and sausage, Emery bid farewell to Dr. Gerard and Mrs. Wakefield. Emery then went to the stable, with his sister in tow. Margaret watched Emery fasten the saddle onto Blacky, a Yorkshire Dale stud Papa favored in breeding. Slowly her fingers stroked the ebony muzzle, wondering if she would ever see her eldest sibling again.

As Emery guided the stallion out of the stable, Margaret blurted, "I could hop on Daisy and ride with you to the bridge."

Emery frowned, shaking his head. He barked a stern order, "You shall walk me to the road. On horseback you would be too tempted to follow me home."

Margaret swallowed hard. "I promise to be good."

Together, they walked, elbows hooked, a rare intimacy she thoroughly enjoyed. She breathed in the scent of his musky hair, mixed with leather and hay, locking the smells into memory. Secretly, she adored her brother. He was three years older, aloof as ever, and barely willing to tolerate his "bratty little sister." Throughout her entire life, very few words were ever exchanged between them, beyond jabs and teasing. Temporarily, life seemed dreamy while she clung to his arm.

The glory ended too fast. They stopped at the road.

Emery gave her a brief hug, saying, "Behave yourself, ya little gnat."

He swiftly mounted Blacky and rode away.

She stood there stunned and mute, watching until he disappeared. Tears blurred her vision. Feeling abandoned by her family was not as painful as enduring Mum's death; but, alas, it still hurt.

From summer to fall, Margaret practiced writing with a slate board and chalk every night after dinner. Once she learned the entire alphabet, the doctor had her sounding out three-letter words. Toward the middle of September, she took delight in forming simple sentences.

The fall equinox proved to be a dreary day. The sky turned the darkest gray. Foreboding low-lying clouds reached for the treetops. By midmorning, torrential rains drenched London, turning the soil into notorious mud that could suck the shoe off any unfortunate soul. Margaret was working indoors in the pantry on this soggy day. She removed the lid from a ceramic crock, and the pungent vapors that rose up made her eyes water. The aroma confirmed the batch was ripe, for the apple scraps inside had decomposed nicely into vinegar. She stuck a funnel lined with cheesecloth into a gallon jug, and by the cupful, strained the apple cider vinegar until it filled the container. Hoisting the heavy gallon onto her hip, she carried it into the apothecary.

Hanging brass oil lamps cast flickered light onto the ceiling. In addition, candles burned throughout the shelf-filled room, keeping it well lit. A glowing fire in the hearth removed the dampness, creating a cozy atmosphere. Dr. Gerard sat bent over the table, printing onto labels that read "Garlick Vinegar." Since Margaret had not yet graduated to the level of using quill and ink, Gerard demonstrated the proper way to form precise lettering. If one drop or smudge of ink soiled the paper, a crinkled wad flew into the kindling basket. Using paper to start fires was an odd extravagance Margaret had noted but never mentioned aloud. It seemed safer not to remind adults of their mistakes.

A tray of two-ounce medicine bottles half-filled with a potent infusion of garlic, boneset, and oregano waited to be topped off with vinegar. As Margaret measured and poured, she said, "Dr. Gerard, Mum used to make medicine similar to this. She called it 'plaguewort.'"

"Did she now? How clever; the name explains exactly what the remedy is for."

He scratched more letters onto the label. As the ink dried, he showed his student another use of grammar. In parentheses, underneath "Garlick Vinegar," he showed her that it read, "Plaguewort."

After the doctor explained the use of the punctuation mark, Margaret repeated the word *parentheses* until the four syllables flowed smoothly from her mouth. Pleased to learn something new, and deeply touched, she gave a polite curtsy and said, "Sir, how kind of you to honor my mum."

Mrs. Wakefield, who had come from upstairs, became extremely miffed to once again witness Dr. Gerard's doting fondness for the gardener. She angrily squeezed the decorative box in her hands. As an idea struck, she pulled a nail loose from the hinge and barged into the room, saying, "When I was dusting, I noticed a nail sticking out. A few taps of a hammer ought to set it right. I shall fix it straight away. Sir, I know you cherish it so."

"Yes, of course. It is a lovely stationery box that belonged to my late sister," Gerard explained to Margaret.

Mrs. Wakefield said in an overly sweet voice, "Margaret, have you ever seen such fine carving? Crafted from Asian cedar, the most fragrant cedar in the world. Go ahead, open up and smell it."

Margaret adored the smell of cedar. Eager to take in the aroma, she held the box up to her nose, flipped open the lid, and let out a horrible scream. With a sudden slam, the lid closed, and she glared at the housekeeper.

Gerard looked inside to see what stirred such a commotion. "How ghastly! Get rid of it," he said in disgust, pushing the cedar box toward the housekeeper.

Mrs. Wakefield snatched up the box and exclaimed, "Oh my, I forgot. I caught the cockroach yesterday. Thought the smell would kill it. It worked. Look, the legs are not moving. How clever of me!" A forced laugh escaped her lips as she tossed the roach into the fire.

Too stunned for words, Margaret stewed. She wished the hammer would smash the old bat's thumb when she fixed the box. A rumble of thunder reverberated overhead, causing her to flinch.

"Sorry, Miss Margaret. Please excuse us. Mrs. Wakefield, I want a word," the doctor said sternly, marching off to the kitchen.

Gerard shook an angry finger and spat, "Mrs. Wakefield, I will not tolerate a ruse such as that under this roof again."

"It was only a joke." Her voice started to tremble.

"In the twelve years you have been in my employ, humor has not proved to be one of your daily practices," Gerard retorted.

Eyes welling with tears, the housekeeper said, "It is awfully lonely watching you two carry on. When you two get together, I don't exist. Your eyes no longer see me because they are always on her."

"Oh, nonsense. I'd be lost without you. Margaret is a bright girl. Her work is valuable to me. Do not forget, the three of us in this household are servants to the Cecil family. If we fail to get along, perhaps bring shame to the estate, our homeless shoes will tread heavily on the cobblestone. Now go and apologize at once," he ordered.

Tucked away in the far end of the apothecary was Margaret's bedchamber. A squared-off room with a curtained door gave her a modicum of privacy. She'd expected, at best, a wobbly cot. Instead, she had a wooden box bed with thick leather straps woven into a lattice that held the bedstraw in place. The bed ate up a large portion of the floor space. A trunk and wall hooks housed her clothes, and a crate turned on its side served as a nightstand.

Margaret lay in bed, praying for the braid of garlic bulbs that hung above the door would do its job and protect her from evil. She considered tucking a bulb into her dress pocket to ward off further mischief from the housekeeper.

Her thoughts drifted to her two brothers, Sheldon and Emery, and how they would pull pranks on each sibling's birthday. *Today is the day after the fall equinox; it's my birthday, she suddenly realized. I'm seventeen.*

Her mouth watered, craving a birthday apple pie. As she imagined the wonderful taste of cinnamon in each bite, a movement in her peripheral vision had her sit up. Something moved along the wooden beam overhead. She clambered upright and stood on the bed to get a better look. A crawling spider scurried away from her. Margaret said to the fleeing creature, "I know not to kill you, or else it will rain today."

She stepped out of bed, plaited her chestnut hair, and dressed before anyone else in the household awoke. Plenty of light shone through the kitchen window as she tore a huge chunk of rye bread from a loaf, buttered one end, and went outside to find Chester, the watchdog, curled up in a small cubby next to the coal bin nestled under the roofed porch. Voiceless, the pooch awoke to the coddling of gentle strokes on his head. Immediately, slumber returned while he kept one ear listening for the opening of the stable door. To free her hands, she held the bread in her teeth. Onto Daisy's back she strapped a double saddlebag with large pouches, grabbed a two-pronged hoe, and set off for the orchard.

"Daisy, we are after apples today. What a perfect day for pie! It's my birthday." Out of habit, Daisy nodded her head at the chatter of Margaret's words.

By now, all the puddles had dried up, presenting favorable conditions for a ride. The sun hung low in the east, casting soft hues of gold onto everything in reach. Patches of blue sky served as a backdrop for the clouds that shape-shifted with her imagination. A serving platter formed in the direction she was headed. *What a good sign! This means bountiful food at mealtime today.* She beamed a toothy smile as she reined Daisy forward, heading south. To extend the short trip to the orchard, she rode over to the Thames River.

Much to her delight, the ducks that were milling around swam toward her. Margaret ate the buttered end of the bread. The remainder she broke off, a small piece at a time, and threw toward the ducks. They fought greedily over the treat, even though each bird received several helpings.

A large mallard swooped down onto the river, slapping webbed feet on the surface of the water to break his speed before gliding to a graceful landing. He paddled toward his companions and interrupted their feeding with aggressive jabs of his beak, a hostile attempt to dominate and secure the food source. The other ducks were quick enough to move out of his way, avoiding injury.

"A splendid entrance, Prince Mallard," said Margaret, bowing her head to the drake. "Sorry you missed breakfast, Your Highness. I'm off to Lord Burghley's orchard for the apple festival. Ta-ta!" Pursing her lips, mocking as much regal stiffness as she could muster, she gently kicked her heels in Daisy's sides and set off.

At the orchard, she tethered Daisy to a garden post. Margaret used the two-prong hoe to reach the apples high in the branches and dislodge them one at a time. After filling both saddlebags and closing them securely, she gave Daisy an apple and ate one herself. "Fresh picked are the tastiest," she slurred while swallowing the last bite.

Instead of a nod, Daisy's ears suddenly shot back in alarm. She jibbed to the side and let out a startled neigh. Margaret stopped to listen as well, perceiving the cackle of a woman's laughter nearby. She turned toward the noise and sensed an object plummeting out of the sky. The sound through the leaves was of something moving faster than an apple. Reaching down, she pulled an arrow out of the ground. Feeling the razor-sharp tip, she thought, *This is too serious to be a birthday prank. Who on earth would shoot an arrow at me? Oh my God! Beatrice Taylor. That evil woman had Mum killed. She wants revenge because I was at the birth too. I've got that sinking feeling in my chest that means I'm next.*

Crunching steps in the fallen tree leaves sent a wave of nausea through Margaret's gut. Dropping the hoe, she mounted Daisy and set off in full gallop toward home. Tears blew off her cheeks as she envisioned her own freshly dug grave next to her mother's.

Back at the stable, her hands shook as she slung the saddlebags over one shoulder, hoping the thick leather would act as a shield from additional arrows flying her way. In a purely visceral state, she allowed only one eye to peek out the doorway. She found no predator in pursuit. As if captured in a surreal dream, her rubbery knees would not move fast enough.

Chester lazily raised his head, yipped twice, and returned to dreamland.

It took an eternity to sprint up to the house. Margaret quickly entered, breathing fast, to find Gerard and Mrs. Wakefield sitting at the kitchen table, drinking tea. She held up the arrow in front of Gerard's face, dropped the saddlebags to the floor, and rapidly recounted the chain of events.

"Where are your manners? That's not very lady like, bruising apples," the housekeeper growled.

Gerard's forehead creased as he scrutinized the arrow. "High-quality feathers and a straight, smooth shaft," he muttered under his breath. "Undoubtedly, this was the property of a wealthy owner." He tugged at his beard repeatedly, as if the hairs could engage his very brain and capture an idea floating just above his head. "I'll go over to Cecil House and inquire within."

Before leaving, he turned to Mrs. Wakefield. "Make her some of that nerve tea."

"Yes, sir. Tut-gotten she is. In a regular state of panic, that one," Mrs. Wakefield said, as if Margaret were not in the room.

Gerard went outside and headed toward the orchard. His long thin legs moved gracefully, his steps scarcely making a sound.

More than anything, Margaret wanted a hug and assurance she was safe. Only thing warm she ever got from Mrs. Wakefield was a cooked meal. Her first instinct was to go and hide under the covers of her bed, yet she feared being alone. *The old buffoon will have to do. It's gossip she's interested in, not me.*

Mrs. Wakefield poured hot water over a blend of chamomile and catnip. "Idle hands are the devil's workshop. Move it! Give me those apples. I'll cut and core. You make the dough."

Shaky hands placed the saddlebag in front of the portly cook.

Mrs. Wakefield narrowed her blue eyes and scolded, "Tsk-tsk. Toughen up. You're such a little pansy."

The words stung, for they were an echo of a nasty remark Emery had made in the past. Margaret turned away to hang her shawl on a peg near the door. She held onto the back of the chair to steady her hands. "Right," she said, wishing the old tart would shut up.

"Can't trust you with a knife; you'll curse my kitchen in blood. That would give the good doctor another reason to dote over you like you're something special," Mrs. Wakefield scowled.

Shocked at the harshness, Margaret hated the old bat more than ever. A bowl filled with flour and butter slammed on the table in front of her.

"Hold on," said Margaret.

She dashed to the window and pressed her nose against the glass. No foes approached. Chester sniffed peacefully at the garden gate. Along with chasing rabbits, his enjoyment in life was to announce the arrival of visitors.

"You sinful dodderer, mix the pie dough," the housekeeper barked.

Through gritted teeth Margaret said, "Let's make pie."

Accustomed to busy work, Margaret squeezed the butter, watching it ooze through her fingers. Besides eating it, this was her favorite part of pie: mixing the butter into the flour.

All Margaret could think of was the last conversation with her mother. While in jail before the trial, Catherine had explained, through a barred window, that the death of the newborn was the fault of ridiculous fashion, not witchcraft. Beatrice Taylor, the woman in labor, had been bound in tight corsets ever since she grew out of swaddling clothes. Obviously, the crushed torso gave no room to carry a baby to full term.

Just as Margaret was about to add the water, Mrs. Wakefield yelled, "Stop! Add a dash of whiskey to the dough."

"You're joking!" Margaret said, wary of trusting the old hag.

"It makes for a flakier crust, and the dough rolls out better. A French baker told me his secret. Let me pour a little in. Here's your tea."

"Do what you must," Margaret said, not caring.

She glanced into the tea, checking for bugs floating within. In silence, her mind ticked away. She formed the dough into a ball and then cut it in half. The dough obeyed the pressure of the rolling pin. It even molded into the pie pan with ease. At last, a good omen.

Unable to hold her thoughts back any longer, Margaret blurted out, "Beatrice is a wicked woman! She killed Mum and now wants to kill me!"

This was the first mention of the scandal since Margaret's arrival.

Seemingly intrigued by the juicy news, Mrs. Wakefield smiled. The muscles in her face, generally unaccustomed to this expression, made her look like a hungry hound dog. She said,

"No need to snivel about old news. What your little head might not understand is that your mother was French."

"So?"

"Beatrice Taylor loathes anything French because French designers relentlessly steal all her fashion ideas. She hates the entire country. I know this because she stays at the queen's castle when she is in London. I chat with the castle servants at the market every Saturday." Mrs. Wakefield spoke with an air of superiority.

Margaret hissed, "What a stupid reason! Mum delivered Beatrice's stillborn. Beatrice accused Mum of being a witch and had her hung."

"Too bad your mother was not sentenced to the clucking stool instead of the noose. Life would be different." Mrs. Wakefield popped an apple slice into her mouth.

"What are you talking about? What is a clucking stool?" Margaret asked.

"For heaven's sake! You're not very worldly, are you?" Mrs. Wakefield commented while chewing.

"We didn't have one in our village," Margaret retorted.

"It's a chair you get bound to. The crowd scolds you, and then you get dunked into the river. The device looks like a see-saw. One end of the log is a chair, and the other end has a rope attached. A huge man controls the rope and thus the fate of the chair. If he lets go of the rope, the chair and the person get soaking wet," explained Mrs. Wakefield.

"I see. It's a punishment. One doesn't drown?" Margaret asked.

"No drowning. It's a public humiliation. And to make matters worse, they also remove your hat and shoes before the seating. Ew-w-w! Utterly disgraceful!" Mrs. Wakefield's chubby cheeks shuddered.

"Humiliation would have been juster than the unfair trial. Beatrice bribed the judge. She made two gowns for the judge's wife and only charged her for one," Margaret said bitterly.

Mrs. Wakefield raised her brows, hearing the new tidbits. She commented, "Beatrice can afford to pay hefty bribes. She made a small fortune creating the high ruff collar. Her wares are sold to the ladies in the queen's court. Rumor has it that Beatrice cannot sew fast enough to keep up with demands. And to think, those pleated neckpieces are extremely uncomfortable—one can hardly move the head—yet, unfortunately, for the rich, fashion is as important as ever." Mrs. Wakefield stopped slicing apples to sip her tea.

"Minus the cussing, Papa calls her 'the high-ruff devil'!" Margaret crinkled her nose in distaste at the mention.

Mrs. Wakefield dug for more information. "Were any church bells rung to announce your mother's death?"

Margaret let out a long sigh. "Yes, the passing-bells chimed. They are very large and heard for miles."

Waving her knife dramatically in the air, the housekeeper punctuated her words. "How fortunate for her soul! Evils spirits detest church bells the most. The louder the bell, the further the evil spirits need to travel to clear the sound. It buys the soul time for an unmolested passage to heaven."

Clenching her jaw, Margaret replied, "I know." Saddened by the memory of the gonging church bell, the horrid sound that shouted to the world that Catherine Colton was dead, tears ran down Margaret's cheeks.

Moments later, Chester announced the arrival of his master. A few short yips, followed by a muffled "down boy," confirmed it.

Gerard entered the kitchen, shaking his head in disbelief. "Our landlord's grandson-to-be, Sir William Hutton, was teaching archery to his fiancée. That young miss, who happens to be Elizabeth Cecil, attempted to hit the target center. From a flirtatious poke, she lost her grip, making the arrow go awry. The arrow landing at your feet was no more than a courting couple's folly."

"Thank God," Margaret said with a sigh.

"Woe to the dangers of romance! Archery should be left for men," Mrs. Wakefield opined. "Did he offer an apology?"

Gerard explained, "Sorry. Sir Cecil said, 'No injury, no harm done.' For Sir Hutton to reach below his social status and apologize to the gardener warrants drawing blood."

Dr. Gerard turned to examine Margaret's tearstained cheeks. He placed a hand on her shoulder and asked, "Are you all right?"

Of late, he had come to yearn for her company.

"I am now," Margaret said, appreciating some kindness.

Mrs. Wakefield gave a fake cough, with tight fists dug into her hips. Her glowering blue eyes disapproved of the open display of tenderness. She spewed, "Sir, you have a patient that should be arriving any minute."

In his shyness, he confessed, "So true."

Pink-faced, he darted into the apothecary.

❋ ❋

At noon Dr. Gerard, Mrs. Wakefield, and Margaret sat at the kitchen table, eating rabbit stew.

"The white chunks in the stew are the potato, are they not?" Margaret asked.

"Indeed. They are the tubers you dug up yesterday," Gerard answered.

Margaret marveled at how the potato easily squished on the roof of the mouth. It had a subtle sweetness just like bread. "I like how these potatoes taste. Where did they come from?" asked Margaret.

"South America," Gerard answered.

"Sir Walter Raleigh presented them to Queen Elizabeth. His chambermaid keeps me up on the latest news between those two," Mrs. Wakefield offered.

"Ahem," Gerard interrupted. Directing the conversation away from gossip, he said, "My housekeeper, lady of invention, prepares potatoes in a variety of ways: baked, fried, boiled, pied, ground, and stewed. Believe me, Margaret, you will enjoy feasting on her concoctions."

Mrs. Wakefield bowed her head slightly, soaking up the adulation. Her tongue was rather loose after emptying her glass of mead. She slurred, "Wait until you taste my pie. With every first bite, I make a toast to King Henry VIII for planting apple orchards all over England. Margaret, did you know, because of good ol' King Henry, your homeland, Kent, is riddled with pippin apples?"

Margaret drifted. The image of pink apple blossoms infusing the spring air made her homesick. Placing chin in hand, she looked how she felt.

"Elbows off the table, girl," Mrs. Wakefield bellowed.

"Ahem. If you please, Mrs. Wakefield, I believe our gardener is having a moment." The doctor pointed his eyes at Margaret.

Feigning sympathy, Mrs. Wakefield said, "You poor girl. Betcha miss the beautiful gardens back home. Family too, I suppose. And to think, your mum rests in her grave without you tending the weeds above."

It took little effort for grief to invade Margaret's thoughts. Her eyes filled with tears. Speaking past the lump in her throat, she managed, "Sir, if you'll excuse me."

"Do call me John," he said, uncertain how to offer comfort.

Margaret gave a slight bow before fleeing outside.

"John? How forward. I don't even call you that," the housekeeper scoffed.

"She's upset," Gerard said.

"Let her cry; it'll do her some good. She's a simple girl," Mrs. Wakefield assured.

"With a tongue as harsh as yours, I remain Dr. Gerard to you," he said as he strode away.

Margaret escaped to the comfort of the stable. The aroma of leather, hay, and manure smelled the same as Papa's stables in Kent. The moment she sat on the three-legged stool, Stripes jumped into her lap. The tabby's shortened tail had mended, sticking up like a sawed-off mast. Gentle fingers petted the gray stripes of fur.

"Thank God you're a good mouser, you cuddly thing. You are nothing like Mrs. Wakefield. She is vile! She deserves a turn on that dunking stool. How dare she salt my wounds. I miss Mum, Papa, and my brothers. But it's my lot in life to be here with you," Margaret whimpered.

A rough tongue licked Margaret's hand. Touched by the affection, she stroked the kitten's cheeks until loud purring seemed to dry up her tears.

Daisy poked her head out of the stall at the sound of Margaret's voice. A soft neigh greeted her old friend and master.

Setting the cat down on a bed of hay, Margaret walked over and rubbed Daisy's muzzle. A familiar equine snort of pleasure echoed against the walls. Margaret twisted her mouth into a playful scowl, and said, "Looks as though Mab, the queen of fairies, was a bit spiteful. She went and turned your forelocks into elflocks." She began untangling the bangs between the horse's ears with her bare fingers.

"Daisy, do you think anyone will ever love me as much as Mum did? The pastor said I should be thankful for what I have—and what I had. Plenty of children grow up without a mother. Yet my heart still feels sore. I wish I were the one who died, instead of her. Together, we should have fled to across the sea to Virginia, but we had no warning they were coming to arrest her." Margaret batted a fly away from Daisy's eye, and continued grooming.

"I had a bit of a scare today with the arrow ... a cockroach too," Margaret continued.

"Did, did, did, you now, lass?" stammered Russ Culpepper, the groom, who had been eavesdropping.

With his broad shoulders, fitted waistcoat, and curly brown hair, cut short, he looked like a soldier. Margaret usually enjoyed viewing his physique, but not today.

"Good day, Russ. You have your greeting jacket on. Has a

patient arrived for the doc?" Margaret asked. Wishing for a friend, she willed herself to be strong and not sound overly emotional.

"Nay, lass; not, not a patient," Russ stuttered. "I escorted a haughty woman to, to Cecil House. A blimey dark heart she w-was. I steadied the horses while she cl-climbed from the c-carriage. The hag h-hit me with a glove ... called me a br-brainless harelip. She hit her hip on the d-door; she blamed me ... said the c-carriage moved. I beg to differ. The carriage did not b-budge a knuckle." Russ had a look of disgust.

A scar above his mouth gave the impression that he was a harelip. Men at the local pub called him Lippy, implying he had one. Mocked for his shortcomings, rarely did Russ go out in public. He preferred the company of animals.

"H-heard y-you crying. You h-hurt?" He scrunched up a worried face, which pulled the scarred lip higher than normal, exposing part of a front tooth. He appeared to be scowling.

"Mrs. Wakefield is mean. Acts up whenever the doc gives me attention," Margaret said, grabbing hold of his forearm.

A bit stiff, uncertain how to react, he said awkwardly, "She f-f-fancies the doc." He pulled his arm away.

"Sorry if I offended you," Margaret said, looking surprised.

"I only t-touch animals, n-not people," Russ stuttered. Leery of a repeat, he kept a distance, as though she were poison ivy.

Pity, not rejection, surged through Margaret's heart. A simple scarred lip kept him from human contact. His fate made her own seem less severe. Collecting enough wits to calm down, she said, "It is safe to say we both had mishaps today with wretched old hags. A pathetic lot we are."

"W-we deserve b-better," Russ said.

Margaret nodded.

Daisy pressed her muzzle against Margaret's shoulder. Gaining no response from her master, the pony let out a snort. Margaret absently stroked the mare's neck, just under the mane.

Its silky texture felt soothing to her fingers, and Daisy responded with a contented whinny.

A crooked smile shone on the groom's face.

Immediately, Margaret understood that she had entered Russ's world. She could tell he approved of the affection between her and Daisy.

Russ said, "M-mighty fine pony you g-got there."

The stable door flew open. John Gerard stepped into the room, clutching his black medicine bag in one hand.

"Sir, sh-shall I saddle up your h-horse?" Russ asked.

"No need. A guest at Cecil House has collapsed. Margaret, if you will assist me?" he motioned her to follow.

"Yes, sir. I shall dig up valerian root if the guest is in great pain." Margaret quickened her step to catch up with Gerard's long strides.

"Please call me John," the doctor insisted.

"Not in front of the old battle-ax. She would flatten me with her broom."

"She owes you an apology. I daresay the woman has the propensity to be overly possessive toward me."

"A polite way of saying jealous," Margaret said testily.

"Perhaps."

"Then I shall find neutral ground and call you Doc."

"Doc it is."

At a brisk pace, they strode through the culinary section of the garden, where combined aromas from rosemary, sage, and mint stimulated their sinuses. At the kitchen door of the manor, Gerard pulled a braided cord that rang the delivery bell.

A petite blond woman opened the door. With an Irish lilt she said, "Dr. Gerard, Maggie, come in. Do excuse me messy state. I'm makin' bread." She absently dusted flour off her apron, which nearly reached the floor.

"Good day, Mrs. Moore. I understand a guest has fainted," Dr. Gerard said informally.

"Yes, indeed. Poor thing hollered like a birth gone wrong and fell onto the sofa, but she is nay with child. 'Tis coming around, though; I heard moaning a bit ago," Mrs. Moore said, leading them into the parlor.

A woman in an expensive dress, with auburn hair pulled taut into a bun, was doubled over, with a hand over one kidney. She let out a horrifying scream. The high ruff collar immobilized her neck, giving the impression of a stiff doll flopped over.

Gerard knelt at the sofa and said, "Hello, ma'am, I'm Dr. Gerard, at your service. Is the pain moving down or staying in one location?" He dared not move her, leaned in best he could and peered into the terrified profile of a woman who appeared to be about thirty years old.

Gasping, she replied, "Moving down."

Gerard turned to Margaret and ordered, "Do go dig up valerian straight away."

Margaret nodded. She took leave immediately, for it was difficult to watch another human suffer.

"Mrs. Moore, if you could be so kind to boil water. I suspect the passing of stones. A malady as such requires a strong concoction," the doctor instructed.

Mrs. Moore darted into the kitchen, calling out, "Maggie, wait, I be fetchin' you a basket."

Margaret hated the name Maggie, which she thought befitted a horse or a cow. Nevertheless, she thanked Mrs. Moore politely and hooked the basket handle into the fold of her arm.

"A-a-ah!" another scream came from the parlor.

"Best get on my way," Margaret said as she flew out the door, eager to escape the suffering. The shriek brought memories of that difficult birth—and the delivery of a dead baby—all leading to the accusation of Mum being a witch. Feeling haunted, she retrieved a spade from the shed and strode over to the wilted valerian plant. Full of determination, she unearthed the roots with a kind a fury, until sweat cooled the fire within.

Margaret rinsed the roots off in the miniature pond. A group of water nymph statues posed leisurely around the bench at water's edge. Reminded again of the Cecil family wealth, she stowed the valerian in the basket and scurried off to the manor. Through the kitchen window, she saw Mrs. Moore shaping the bread into loaves, and Russ seated at the table, sipping tea. Before entering, she prayed, "Dear God, please help the ailing woman. Please stop the suffering."

"I am back. Here are the roots," Margaret said at the door.

Mrs. Moore's blue-gray eyes showed duress. She said, "Thank heavens. I swear, my bread shan't rise if she keeps carrying on like a banshee. Gonna need the cleaver and a strong arm to chop those up. Russ, no more lollygagging, we need your strength."

"A-a-agh!" another agonizing scream came from the parlor.

Margaret flinched and noticed that Russ seemed almost pleased. She met his eyes and asked, "The wailing does not bother you?"

"Perhaps this is penance for her evil ways. The coach never moved, mind you," Russ said.

He made that toothy sneer again and snatched the cleaver from the rack of knives on the wall.

As he chopped the fresh roots into smaller pieces, Margaret used mortar and pestle to crush them flat. She hummed a church tune to help drown out the sounds from the parlor.

When Margaret finished, she stood up to relieve a crick in her back from sitting too long. The sound of a "psst" drew attention to the doc. He waved her over.

"What is the progress on the concoction?" Dr. Gerard asked.

"We are ready to steep the roots," Margaret reported.

"I see," Gerard said, twisting his mustache, obviously calculating his next move.

"Doc, if you don't mind me asking, what have you done so far?"

"Garlic poultice on her feet, mallow to soothe the innards, and vinegar water to soften the stones. Poor woman clutches me so, I barely have time to think. What remedy cures one wrought heavily with fear?" he wondered.

"Borage makes one glad," Margaret suggested.

"Splendid. There should be an elixir in my bag," Gerard said, slapping his forehead.

"I shall bring a cup of valerian as soon as it is ready," Margaret said, trying to be helpful.

Once the liquid inside the china teapot darkened to the correct brown hue, she carried a saucer and cup to the parlor door, and hesitated. She urged Mrs. Moore to come along for an update, and to introduce her properly to the lady who was in pain.

Mrs. Moore feigned disinterest, but the desire to know the goings-on and collect potential gossip had her scramble to put a jar of honey and serving spoon on a tray.

Margaret made her way around a fine love seat. Worried about spilling on the tapestry carpet, she moved carefully. She set the saucer down on a carved end table next to the ruffed collar Gerard had removed from the patient. By the time she straightened up, Mrs. Moore stood next to her.

Mrs. Moore took the liberty to say, "Mrs. Taylor, I apologize fer not properly introducing you to Dr. Gerard or his assistant, Maggie. Mrs. Taylor is here to sew Lizzie Cecil's wedding dress. Her reputation for bein' the best seamstress in the land 'tis the reason Mrs. Wakefield recommended her highly."

Margaret cast darting eyes on the withered body sprawled on the love seat. A linen sheet underneath the body made the garment stand out. An exquisite dress with matching corded hem, cuff, and embroidery boasted great wealth. Through darkened eyes, pride shown on a face Margaret recognized. Upon close inspection, the yellowed protruding canines and tight lips were surely those that had bellowed obscenities and told the lie that accused Mum of witchcraft. It had to be. It was! Beatrice, the hag who ruined her life!

Hatred boiled up inside. *To think I prayed for her,* Margaret thought.

Unable to contain herself, Margaret shouted with contempt,

"Lord, have mercy! Beatrice, the high-ruff devil. You killed my mum! The only witch I've ever known is you."

"Oh dear," Dr. Gerard moaned.

Mrs. Moore's mouth gaped open in shock.

"Catherine Colton's daughter! Evil runs in the family. The trash that spewed from your mouth was a spell trying to defame me. You should have hung too, because you are a witch just like your mum," Beatrice snarled.

"Liar! Too-tight corsets killed your baby. You are trying to bewitch everyone in this room. We are all too clever for your hex to work on us. Today, God is punishing you for lying," Margaret volleyed back.

"How dare you speak to me so!" Beatrice shouted.

"Go to hell. And take those ugly collars with you," Margaret spat.

In a flash, Mrs. Taylor's hourglass figure sprang up. With demonic eyes, she wrapped her venomous fingers around Margaret's neck.

The doctor tripped over his black bag before he could reach the women and pull them apart. He hit his head on the corner of the end table and slumped against the sofa, seeing stars. All sorts of medicine bottles scurried about across the carpet.

Mrs. Moore screamed, "Stop it, stop it, stop it!"

Try as she might, Margaret could not pry the strangling hands away. "Dear God, release me from Satan's grasp, for I have not sinned," she wanted to say, but her vocal cords were not working. Unable to breathe, her body jerked, and she fell backward. Beatrice fell on top of her and held on tightly, intending to kill.

A dull thud added to the din. Beatrice's head whipped forward, as if hit by behind. The old bat collapsed over Margaret's torso and finally let go.

Russ dropped the frying pan, unaware of the blood on the bottom, unaware that he had cracked open a skull. Hastening to free Margaret, he lifted Beatrice with ease and dumped her aside.

The room became silent.

Dr. Gerard's vision cleared. Horror-struck at the stillness of both women, he crawled over and blew air into Margaret's mouth several times. Frustrated that he had failed to protect the woman he adored, he pumped her heart. Spotting camphor among the bottles strewn on the floor, he snatched it, quick as a fox, and ran it under her nose.

Margaret gasped as the air returned to her lungs.

"Stay with me, Margaret." The doctor placed a gentle hand on her diaphragm, willing it to work properly.

It took several inhales before Margaret's breathing returned to normal. She remained on the floor, exhausted.

"Maggie lives; thank the Lord," Mrs. Moore sighed.

Dr. Gerard caressed Margaret's cheeks, saying, "Welcome back, dear one. You stay put while I depart for a bit." He did not dare mention the name of the person he was to examine next.

"C-can I help with something, Doc?" Russ asked anxiously.

"Throw a blanket on Margaret," he answered.

Russ placed the sheet from the sofa over Margaret. He stuttered to her softy, "T-there you go, missy. You're just like a d-downed filly. D-don't you fret now. W-we be takin' good care of you."

Gerard approached Beatrice, who lay crumpled on her side, and examined her.

"Is she? Is she gone?" Mrs. Moore inquired.

"May God be my witness, yes," Dr. Gerard said soberly.

Chapter 8

A Trip to the Hospital

Jack whispered, "Let's go back."

The heat of the summer day had waned after sundown. Aster's house was quiet except for the hum of the swamp cooler blowing cold air from the hallway ceiling. Arms and legs full of goose bumps stirred Jack and Aster out of the dreamlike past and into the present.

"Wow, we're back at my house. What a trip!" Aster said, rubbing her upper arms.

"Interesting history, wasn't it?" Jack said, delighted.

"I went inside Margaret and merged with her body. I was actually her. In the Navajo life, it was like watching a movie. Is one way better than the other?"

"Nah. The different viewpoints are more like getting what you need for clarity. You know, aha moments," Jack explained.

"Oh, like self-learning."

"Precisely. It's part of my mojo. People keep coming back for more."

"There's a ton of people in Boulder eager to clean their slates. Bet you have a waiting list," Aster said, prying because she wondered how successful he was.

"I do. Usually a month out," Jack said matter-of-factly.

Aster took note, then asked, "Jack, who were you at Cecil House? I couldn't tell. Being Margaret was all I could handle."

"Dr. Gerard."

"Really? You were a healer back then. Do you think there's a correlation between being a doctor in that life and being a past-life traveler in this life?"

Jack stared, thinking, and then answered, "Hmm. I'd say the jobs are different ways of helping people get better."

"That's insightful. Comparing my lives is a simple overlap: herb lore. Anyway, Mrs. Wakefield was a piece of work, wasn't she?" Aster commented.

"Nasty old turncoat. She instigated the meeting of Beatrice and Margaret. Makes me wonder if her ass got fired for that," Jack said.

"Whew, the strangling was intense! I felt the whole thing. My neck feels sore as we speak," Aster commented. She got up and turned off the swamp cooler. "That's better. Dang thing only has two settings: high or low. That was on low."

"Soul travel is more intimate than going to the movies, isn't it? I'm curious what's going to happen next. You want to do this again tomorrow?" asked Jack.

The word *intimate* reminded her of sex, and heading in that direction felt too big. "What I really need is to write all this down before I forget the details. I want time to process it too. You teach your students how important it is to do both. By the way, tomorrow I'm busy helping Iris with a teaching project all week," Aster lied.

"Too bad," he groaned.

"Thanks for everything. I'm hoping the journey will give me profound insights. There's always room for growth," Aster walked to the door and grabbed the handle.

Appearing crestfallen, Jack stepped into his flip-flops and said, "It's all about the process. I tell my clients that every day."

She opened the door, "We'll journey some other time then."

"I'd best get going. Before I do, any objections to a hug?"

Aster glanced at the answering machine, half expecting Keith's ghost to float out of the speaker and make a scene. As common sense clicked in, she changed her mind and took pity on Jack. They embraced.

Once again, Aster noticed a lovely energy surge, similar to what she had felt in the grocery store. She pulled away fast. "Sorry. My imagination got the best of me. I envisioned Keith watching me. Felt weird, like I wanted his approval."

Rather confused, Jack asked, "Keith?"

"My late husband. This may sound creepy, but I get the feeling he watches me sometimes."

Jack wore a goofy smirk as he said, "Right. Oh, in that case, if Keith can hear me, I'd like to tell him hello. I'm a great guy. A little chubby around the middle, but once you get to know me, Keith, you'll like me."

"Jack. You're making fun of me. Get going before you embarrass me further. If you were my brother, I'd be socking you in the arm," Aster said with a laugh.

Jack paused at the door, gave a little wave, and said, "Bye. See ya later."

"Good-bye," Aster replied.

Still feeling a warm glow from the hug, she retreated down the hall to her office. Mustering all her strength into stubborn mode, she thought, *We're just friends. Enough of this emotional stop and go. I want to focus on the sensation of riding Daisy down the Strand Road.*

Seated at her desk, pen in hand, she wrote, "London, England, 1589."

The doorbell rang, interrupting her writing. She ignored it. It rang again, impatiently, like a needy child. Curiosity guided her feet to the window. Like a sleuth, she peeked through the curtain to see who it was. She opened the door to Jack.

His hazel eyes looked unhappy.

"What's up, Jack?" Aster inquired. "Did you lock your keys inside the car?"

Holding his breath, Jack grimaced. He then moaned, "Not that lucky. Hospital."

"Are you hurt?" Aster's concern grew.

Jack lifted his arm. "Yeow! My hand," he said.

"What did you do?"

"Tripped off the curb," he said, trying to suppress the pain.

"Oh dear! Sounds serious." She could not see anything abnormal. It was a dark, moonless night, and the porch light shone poorly on the injury. She sped to the refrigerator and removed an ice pack from the freezer. "Let me grab my purse and keys, and let's go."

En route to the hospital, the pain in Jack's hand made it hard for him to speak. He struggled to explain what had happened. "Journey spaced me out ... you wanted to write ... I left hastily."

"Are you grounded now?" Aster asked, not knowing what to say to comfort him.

"Painfully so."

"So, the English life distracted you?"

Jack whimpered, "Yep. ... Then, whammo! I was lying ... in the gutter."

"Not the first time for ya," she said, in an effort to make him laugh.

"Nope." The ice bag fell on his foot, which caused his four limbs to jerk. He gasped in pain.

Aster saw the misery on Jack's face and sped up the car. Trying to engage his interests, she said, "I bet being a history buff was the catalyst that gotcha into soul journeying."

He struggled to say even a single word. "Bingo," he pronounced, then winced.

Aster sat in the waiting room while the doctors set the broken bone in Jack's wrist. She'd forgotten to bring her journal. Desperate to record the English life before losing the details, she checked the trash can for something to write on. A lone wad of gum stuck to the inside of a plastic bag liner. The printer at reception spat out carbon triplicates on a continual feed of paper, the kind with perforations at both ends of the page. Hospital policy did not allow disrupting the flow of documents. The receptionist, Georgia, muttered something about a broken paper trail.

"What about that paper bag? I could write on that," Aster said.

Indignant, Georgia said, "That's my lunch." Her blue eyes appeared lopsided. The penciled right brow arched up like an over expressive clown's, and the left one was too low, compressing the lid.

"I'll pay you five dollars for the bag," Aster offered.

The oppressed look of Georgia's left eye took Aster back to her body-psychology class. She remembered that the left eye expressed a person's feminine view of the world. Aster could not help but wonder if Georgia was experiencing mother issues. For it would take a few simple strokes to even up that botch job by drawing in Elizabeth Taylor's brows.

The lunch emptied onto the desk. As soon as the money was in Georgia's hand, she said, "I would have taken one dollar if you offered."

Ignoring the comment, Aster had pen in hand and sat down to write. A *People* magazine served as a lap pad. Small letters quickly flowed across the top of the brown bag, to economize the writing space. When both outer sides had filled up with words, she carefully tore it open along the seam. A smattering of crumbs rudely dotted the faces on the magazine cover. Aster cringed and dumped the litter into the trash can. Trying to keep up with her thoughts, she smoothed the paper and wrote madly.

Aster looked up at the wall clock behind the desk to relieve the crick in her neck. The time was ten fifteen. Without trying, she overheard a distressed Georgia talking on the phone. "I want to have a small wedding in Taos. ... My mother wants it in Denver, so she can help plan it. ... Yuck! You know what that means. She'll invite all her relatives and friends."

Aster smirked. *Bingo on the brow lady! Bingo? Oh my, that's Jack word.*

A nurse wheeled Jack into the waiting room. Puffy fingers poked out of the end of a cast that rested peacefully inside the fold of a blue sling. His sleepy face gave evidence that the pain pills had kicked in. He sat there helpless. Aster folded the bag into a perfect square and slid it into her purse. Her heart felt slave to two masters: the writer and the caretaker. If only she could clone herself and become both. Out of pity, she drove Jack home.

Inside Jack's townhome, Aster noticed the coffee table cluttered with half-full coffee mugs, popcorn kernels, books, and mail. The kitchen was no better. Blended together in an untidy collage, dirty dishes covered every surface.

"Jack, you need to lie down. Let's get you to bed."

Aster felt too uncomfortable to sit anywhere, surrounded in someone else's mess. One spot seemed easy on the eyes, the bed. The smooth blankets and neat corners were pristine enough to pass military inspection.

Jack shuffled along, a bit wobbly. He said, "I'm woozy."

"Great job on making your bed. Sit down before you tip over." Aster held on to his upper arm, guiding him to a safe landing.

"I love smooth sheets. Gives order to my chaos." Jack sounded medicated.

"I can imagine," said Aster, peering inside the walk-in closet, searching for pajamas. On the floor lay a sea of dirty earth-toned clothes. The pile was more than a foot high and not free of odor. Aster shuddered at the sight and backed away from the smell.

"Jack, you remind me of my brother. How can you look so neat and live like a slob?" Aster said, bypassing politeness.

"Rosita left me to myself. She's staying at Mom's while the baby is still a newborn," he slurred.

"Rosita?" Aster's brows lifted. She removed Jack's sling and hung it over the bedpost.

"Yep," said Jack.

He'd never mentioned anything about a wife or girlfriend. Trying to sound casual, being careful not to reveal how bothered she felt, Aster asked, "Did Rosita have a boy or girl?"

"A boy. Cute as a bug's ear." He laughed affectionately and in baby talk he said, "A little cutie pie."

"What's his name?" Aster asked, wanting the full name. She helped him out of his shirt.

"Rocky. The little man doesn't look like a Rocky. Should've named him after me, but Rosita thought Jack was too common a name."

"Is Rocky your son?" Aster blurted impatiently.

"No."

"Then, Rosita is not your wife?" Aster asked.

"Rosita is my maid."

"I see," Aster said, letting out a sigh. Not breathing through her nose, she tossed his shirt into the closet.

With his good hand, Jack played the air piano and began to sing the lines of a Neil Young song, "A maid. A man needs a maid. When will I see you again?"

"Okay, rock star. Don't quit your day job." Aster giggled. "Where do you stash your pajamas?" Suddenly she felt much lighter, and happy.

"Too warm for pj's. I sleep in my boxers." Jack yawned.

"Fair enough," said Aster, relieved there was no need to return to the closet.

Jack slouched on the bed. "Damn, handicapped here. Gonna need your help to take off my trousers," he slurred.

"Oh my! Trousers! Well, yeah ... um, sure. Not easy being a one-handed Jack. Is it?" Feeling a bit awkward, she removed the flip-flops.

Jack fell backward onto the mattress and proceeded to curl up in fetal position. "I'm sleepy," he mumbled.

"Okay, you lummox, before you drift off to never-never land, lift your butt so I can get in your pants. I mean, take off your pants." Aster blushed, hoping he was too out of it to recall what she'd just said.

A faint smile revealed he was still of this world. In slow motion, Jack uncurled and lifted. As soon as his body returned to the mattress, his jaw slacked, and he was out.

Aster studied his nearly naked body. With every breath, a rounded belly rose and fell. He looked soft enough to cuddle, like a contented teddy bear. There was very little chest hair. It was blond, not white like his beard. A scar, undoubtedly from a surgery, interrupted the lines of wide masculine shoulders. He looked so adorable, she fought the urge to kiss him.

On the way home, Aster could not stop thinking of Jack. *He rings up a lot of pluses on my criteria list. But ... a slob is not a good sign for a potential mate. He's got a maid, though. How weird is that? Good thing I didn't kiss him—it'd probably lure me in to wanting more.*

That evening, Aster had an assortment of run-on dreams that made no sense until a rhythmic thud drew her attention. Through the thinning mist, shimmering golden robes rose and fell in erratic patterns. As the image came into focus, it became obvious that the person dressed in the robes was none other than Grannyme. Soaring with the agility of a gymnast, she bounced on the purple cushion as if it were a trampoline, performing flips in the air.

"Aster, come join me. This is fun," her raspy voiced urged.

Aster clambered on top of the cushion. She stood dumbfounded, watching the old crone tuck and spin one, two, three rotations. An infectious cackle made Aster smile. Defying gravity, Grannyme floated in slow motion, making a soft landing.

"How do you do that at your age?" Aster noticed Grannyme's disheveled french-braided hair.

Aster automatically set off to fix her own. Deft fingers

repositioned a hair clip to control a loose tuft. Suddenly, as if by magic, both women displayed neat, smooth coifs.

"Just believe you can do it, and it'll happen," Grannyme said with a shrug.

"You're awfully happy."

"Progress, my dear. Your progress."

"Mine?" Aster said confused.

"Darling, you completed a vow." Grannyme snapped her fingers, summoning a folder. Huge letters across the front read, "Jack." She opened it, allowing Aster to read the page.

Eager eyes scanned to find a lone sentence: "Dazzle Jack with home cooking on blue-and-white dinnerware."

"That's a vow?! Is that part of my quest?" Aster said incredulously.

"Most certainly. You solidified a friendship bond. All it took was triggering warm and fuzzy memories from Jack's childhood. Because you opened his heart in this manner, you'll be his friend forever."

Still confused about the quest, Aster admitted, "*Forever* is an attractive word. I crave having a good buddy. The thing is, though, Jack's currently a wounded puppy. I fear I'll slip into the caretaker role with him instead of being a whole person. I already have two kids. I gave so much to their dad, it hurt. I'm not going there again."

"And because of that wound, you isolated yourself to the point of loneliness. Aster, Jack is the type of guy who will give back," Grannyme encouraged.

Aster's eyes filled with tears. "Hitting core here."

"My little bumpkin, be Jack's friend. He's suffering a broken wrist, and he won't ask for help. You can at least bring him soup."

"As long as it stays platonic, I'll do it. The guy is a slob. It's a big barrier for me." Aster raised her palms away from her chest, indicating a wall.

"Fair enough." With a swipe of her wrinkly finger, Grannyme made a red check mark above the written vow.

The file disappeared instantaneously, and with a wink of her eye, so did Grannyme.

❋ ❋

Late the next morning, as the heat of the day began to invade the temperate air, Aster arrived at Jack's place, a purple backpack slung over one shoulder. The front door was wide open, exposing a spotless living room.

Wondering if she was at the right place, Aster double-checked the address on the door. Number twenty-two was definitely Jack's house. An electric piano sat in front of an entire wall of CDs. Four woodblock paintings hung over the leather sofa. Each picture evoked a southwestern landscape. Last night, she had not noticed the beautiful artwork.

"Hello, Jack. Are you there? Brought you some soup," she called out.

"Come in. Be right there," yelled Jack.

He came out, wearing an orange Broncos T-shirt and dark-blue gym shorts. His wet hair was slicked straight back, away from his forehead.

"You a football fan?" Aster asked.

"Not really. Christmas present. Only thing clean."

"How's the hand?"

"Throbbing."

"Perhaps you should elevate it," suggested Aster.

Raising the cast next to his head, Jack said in a whimsical tone, "How! Me Chief Big Hand, formerly Chief Talking Bird."

They smiled at the cheeky connection.

She said, "I think you watched one western too many. Did ya sleep?"

"Pain meds knocked me out and wore off early in the morning," said Jack, rubbing puffy eyes.

"Your fingers are very swollen. Did you gimp around one-handed and clean up?"

"No, too groggy. Rosita came over for a couple of hours. She had to stop cleaning. She sprang a leak." Jack touched his nipples. "Her shirt got wet in the front. She had to go home to breast-feed Rocky. Have a seat." He motioned to the sofa.

"Okay." Aster took a few steps forward.

He watched Aster's firm butt move in knee-length spandex shorts.

The entire room boasted a southwestern decor. A display of arrowheads, a bow, some arrows, a tomahawk, a coup stick, and a dream catcher loaded with feathers all hung on the walls.

Instead of sitting, she studied the artifacts. A quick glance at Jack made her forget what she was going to say. "What are you smiling about? Do I have a leaf in my hair or something?" she worried.

"Glad to see ya, ah, enjoy my collection."

Above the dining room table hung a worn rug. She pointed to it, asking, "Is that Navajo?"

"Yup. Sure is," Jack said with a hint of pride.

"Looks old. You have a museum here. Wow! Those turtles on the mantel are striking next to the pottery vase. Wait a minute. They're the ones Galen showed me, aren't they?"

"Yep, the very ones. I really dig the fact they symbolize my Navajo mentor. Actually, *our* mentor," Jack said, breaking into a large grin.

"That's right. Turtle did mentor Talking Bird and Cedar Claw," she said, adding, "Jack, you certainly have a strong affinity for the Navajo."

"Absolutely. Don't get me started. My tongue will start moving like a tumbleweed in a windstorm." Jack motioned to the purple bag. "You brought soup? I'm starving!"

"Chicken noodle, and a salad." Aster took steps toward the kitchen, clutching the backpack. "Show me where you keep the bowls. Let's eat."

They brushed shoulders in the small kitchen as Jack reached for spoons. His touch warmed her. She grabbed a potholder hanging on a hook and fanned her face. "Little hot flash here. Whew!"

They sat on bar stools at the counter, slurping soup.

"This is very thoughtful, bringing me food," Jack said, licking his lips.

"You aren't supposed to drive on that medication. Tomorrow, Galen is bringing you food. Some of your other students will feed you as well. Galen is setting it up."

"Sweet," Jack said, rubbing his ample belly.

After washing the dishes, Aster pulled a yellow vial out from the backpack. She said, "I brought a potion for you."

Jack watched her confident hands place the bottle gracefully on the table. "I see you have modified your medicine bag to have shoulder straps. Much more practical than the drawstring bag Cedar Claw used," he observed.

With an eyedropper, she squeezed several drops of clear liquid into a glass and filled the rest with water. "It took me a few centuries to streamline the design. Here, Chief Big Hand, drink this," she said, playing along.

"What is it?"

"A flower essence. After what you went through, you need it. You keep smiling at me," she observed.

He raised his cast, saying, "Being in gimp mode, it's more fun focusing on you. You're mighty easy on the eyes."

"I'm blushing. Bottoms up," she said. As she flirted with him, she felt another wave of heat course through her body.

Jack gulped it down. "That was painless. Tastes just like water. Not nasty like an herb tincture." He let out a big sigh, followed by another.

"See? You're releasing. Flower essences are good for emotional upheavals. This particular one is for trauma," she explained.

"Trauma that a lummox might experience?"

"Sorry. You did hear me last night. That's an old word! My grandma used to call my grandpa a lummox when she wanted to motivate him out of laziness. Sort of like a fond little jab." She gave a slight laugh.

"Oh, I'm honored. You're treating me like family," he mocked.

❋ ❋

As soon as Aster pulled into her driveway, her daughter pulled up behind her. Iris lived over an hour away, in Fort Collins. Iris's high cheekbones showed the same angles and curves as Aster's. What set Iris apart was her long, curly brown hair and rounded nose.

Surprised by the unexpected visit, Aster said, "Hi, sweetie. What brings you here? You missing your mama?"

The two embraced.

"Mom, where have you been? I left you messages," Iris whined impatiently. She looked very thin in her sundress. Her unruly curls stuck out of a ponytail, as if she'd woken up that way and never fixed it.

"I was with a friend. What's wrong? You seem upset."

"Bad news," Iris said, her voice trembling.

"Come inside, out of the sun and we'll talk. Are you okay?" Aster asked, unlocking the kitchen door.

Iris plunked down at the kitchen table wearing a long face. She removed her sunglasses and gray-blue eyes stared aimlessly at the floor. She said, "It's not me. It's Dad."

"He didn't poison the neighbor's dog? He's been threatening to get rid of that yapper for years," Aster said, pouring a glass of water and setting it in front of Iris.

"He had a heart attack," Iris said in squeaky voice.

"Oh, I'm sorry. Is he all right?"

Iris shook her head. She worked her mouth but nothing came out. Watching her daughter struggle, Aster guessed, "Did Bill die?"

Iris nodded.

Aster pulled Iris into a stand and hugged her. Nestled into

the safe haven, Iris began to wail and out of empathy, Aster joined in.

An ironic thought crossed Aster's mind, *"It's so fitting Bill died of a weak heart. He was a classic narcissist who loved only himself. His biggest wound took him out."*

Iris calmed down and with a blotchy face she said, "Mom, I'm the executor of Dad's estate, and I don't know what to do. Sam refuses to help. He's drowning his sorrow in a bottle of scotch."

"Don't worry. I'll help you with everything. I know the hoops you gotta jump through. I did all this three years ago with Keith," Aster assured her.

It did not surprise Aster that Sam was dodging an unpleasant task. Like his father, Sam focused on the good times and ignored the bad.

"Thanks, Mom. You're the best," Iris said, drying her eyes.

Aster handed Iris a tissue and said, "There's no rush for a funeral since Bill is being cremated. Easiest thing to do is have a potluck memorial at your dad's in three weeks. That will give the out-of-state people a chance for better flight options, and it will also give you more time to adjust."

"Good idea," said Iris.

The next day, Aster made phone calls, wrote emails, and put an obituary in the *Daily Camera* newspaper, announcing the death of her ex-husband.

When she called her cousin J. J. with the news, Aster said, "I'm helping Iris with all the arrangements, but I'm not going to Bill's memorial. I don't have it in me to honor him."

"I don't blame you. He played a nasty game of I-got-you-last during the divorce. He hid money from you, burned your photo albums, claimed you were an unfit mother because you had an affair, and then claimed he wanted full custody of the kids. He rarely lifted a finger raising Sam and Iris. You did it all."

Aster let out a "tsk" and then said, "Yep. That's a bunch of old garbage I don't wanna think about. Wanna hear something weird? This morning when I packed up Bill's clothes I found my wedding dress hanging in the back of a closet."

"That white skirt and tunic top? You graduated high school in that," J. J. said.

Aster replied, "Yep. Got my money's worth out of it at least. Surprised Bill didn't burn the garment along with the photographs. Anyway, it felt very strange being back in that big house. Old memories of being Mrs. Felman haunted me. I spent twelve years caretaking Bill's needs in lieu of my own."

"And you endured his know-it-all rants while he enjoyed a life of leisure with his friends," J. J. added.

"Yeah, my role as wife literally meant being a single mom. You'll be happy to know I had a payback moment when I carried his stuff down the hallway. Just in case he was hanging around listening, I ranted at him, 'You selfish bastard! I'm still cleaning up after you. Thank God, this is the grand finale.'"

"Nice job clearing the air. I never liked Bill. Hopefully, in his next life he won't be so arrogant," J. J. said.

"Amen," Aster said with a snicker.

Chapter 9

The Hike

One week had passed, and Jack phoned Aster. The call went to voice mail. Moments later, he received a long text that ended with "Call me back in an hour." He did.

"Hello, Aster. I got your text. What an intense change of plans. It must be one hell of a chore cleaning out your ex's home," he said.

"I'm doing it for Iris. Poor thing spends a lot of time sobbing."

"Give her my condolences. Is it a big house?" he asked.

"It's one of those huge homes on Oak Street. There's a ton of storage, and he's lived here for more than thirty-five years. We're donating and recycling everything we can."

"I'm going stir-crazy with this cast and thinking you need a break too. You want to go for a walk? It's a great day to get outside," he said enthusiastically.

"I put in some long days. Fresh air sounds tempting. Sure. How about Chautauqua Park?" Aster replied.

"Great. I'll pick you up in an hour. Are you at home?"

"I will be soon. I just cleaned the stove, and I need a shower. See ya in a bit. Bye." Aster hung up the phone and thought, *Holy crap! I gotta think before I do. Wait a minute! Grannyme said he and I would be friends for life. I can have a male friend.*

There's nothing wrong with that. Somehow, Jack is part of the quest.

At home, after Aster showered, she packed a small backpack with water, first-aid supplies, sunscreen, a whistle, and a flashlight. It gave her comfort to be prepared, for according to Murphy's Law, anything could happen.

Jack arrived exactly one hour later. Aster sat waiting on the front stoop, filing her nails with an emery board. She slung the backpack onto one shoulder and hopped into his red Subaru Sport Outback.

"How's that wrist healing?" she asked.

Jack beamed a gorgeous smile. He said, "Hello, kiddo." He showed her his hand.

"Looks as though the swelling has gone down in your fingers," Aster said, stashing the emery board in the pack.

Jack said, "Damn cast itches. I shouldn't complain. I'm able to grab the steering wheel. It's great to be mobile again."

While he spoke, she watched his lips, those same lips that allured her nightly. She snapped out of her dream state and put on a serious tone. "Bet you're looking forward to getting the cast off."

"Absolutely. Five more weeks, and counting."

The two chatted freely as they headed toward the west end of Boulder.

Baseline Road climbed uphill to Chautauqua Park. As they pulled into the parking lot, the Flatirons, a unique geological landmark, towered in the sky. The famous view consisted of a series of craggy slabs of rock shaped like the bottom of a clothes iron and tilted into the fascia of the foothills. Whether true or not, there was a rumor that the scenic attraction was larger and photographed more frequently than the four faces carved at Mount Rushmore.

Jack parked his car in front of the dining hall. As he turned off the ignition, he said, "Maybe we can grab a bite here after our hike."

"Brunch? Yeah, I'm game," replied Aster.

"Cool."

Aster pulled sunscreen out of her backpack, dabbed some on her nose, and said, "Mr. McFadden, your Irish nose could use some protection."

Jack chuckled, removing his sunglasses. "Thanks. I burn easily." He used the visor mirror and slathered his entire face.

Ready to go, Aster stepped out of the car and slung the backpack on her shoulders. She looked smart dressed in matching baby-blue sun visor and tank top.

They walked down the road until they reached the trailhead. Gazing, up she said, "I never tire of looking at the Flatirons. I love how frost, snow, and fog change their appearance. The whole array is simply gorgeous."

"You know about Chief Niwot's curse on the Flatirons?" Jack asked.

"Once white man cast his eyes upon such beauty, he is cursed to always return. Many will gather at the splendor until the land overcrowds and the air turns foul," she quoted.

"'Course you'd know. The prophetic chief was Arapaho?" Jack queried.

"Yep."

The trail climbed up the foothills, through an open grassy meadow sparsely dotted with yarrow and lupine. They set off at a slow pace, and soon their lungs worked harder to carry on a normal conversation. A group of spandex-clad runners passed them by like agile hares leaving the turtles behind. In a comical way, Jack shook his thumb at the athletes, indicating they were show-offs. Aster rolled her eyes in agreement.

About a mile up, they came to a stand of ponderosa pine trees emitting a distinct scented blend of butterscotch, vanilla, and pine tar. The familiar smell, mixed with Colorado dry air, made Aster feel at home. They stopped in the coolness of the shade. At that elevation, the panoramic overlook of Boulder Valley spread below.

Instead of enjoying the view, Jack paled and slumped forward.

Aster rushed over and gave him a drink from her water bottle. "This has electrolytes in it. You need to hydrate," Aster said with concern.

"My heart." He caught his breath. "It's pounding."

He paused and took another breath. "Like a tom-tom," he said, holding his chest.

"Sit down and rest. Park yourself on that boulder over there. You'll be okay." Aster made her voice sound composed and hoped what she said would be true.

After Jack's breathing calmed, she wished to relax, but the hair on her neck stood up. She asked herself fiercely, *What am I sensing? Is Jack gonna have a heart attack?*

Jack poked a small twig under the cast to satisfy an itch.

"Jack, how do you feel?"

"Little dizzy. My heart is happier."

"Does your arm ache?" She reached over to hold his wrist and found his pulse almost normal.

"No. I'm okay." Jack patted his round belly. "Just out of shape. Perhaps I should start working out at the gym, so the mountain won't beat me up."

"Foothills, dear chap," Aster corrected in a playful British accent. She took her amethyst necklace off, using the pendant as a pendulum to ask if Jack was okay. The purple stone spun a clockwise circle, a yes. *Then, what am I feeling?* Unable to clasp the necklace back on without a mirror, she stuffed it in her pocket.

A raven squawking in a nearby tree distracted her. Aster answered the raven, matching the inflection and the deep guttural tone.

Jack stared in amazement. "That was incredible! You speak raven."

"I grew up talking to birds. Kept me out of the house, away from my parents' reach." Aster rummaged in the backpack and pulled out binoculars. “That sounds like Grampa Gus. He’s the biggest raven I’ve ever seen. His body is about the size of a chicken. His left foot has a blue band on it; tagged by a bird watcher.”

The raven was not visible to the naked eye. She adjusted the focus on the binoculars and scanned the trees.

“Gus? You have a favorite raven?” he said incredulously. “Those birds are dumpster-diving scavengers.”

“We banter back and forth. He’s quite verbal. Come on, Gus, show yourself. Come and meet Jack.”

“Besides ravens, you imitate ducks and farm animals too?” he joked.

“Yeah,” she admitted. “I think ravens are adorable janitors of nature. They’re suave. They dine at the road-kill grill, all decked out in dapper black. Sort of reminds me of James Bond, dressed in a suit for all occasions.”

“Since you put it that way, I get it,” Jack said, flirting.

Almost directly overhead, she spotted something tan. A tail dangled from a branch, attached to a sleek fur coat. A mountain lion lounged on a tree branch. Fear ran down her limbs like a lightning bolt. “Oh God. Jack, we need to go.” She threw everything into the backpack and shouldered it before Jack stood. She grabbed Jack by the arm and pulled him up.

“What’s the hurry?”

“Bathroom. I’ll want toilet paper.” Her mind raced for safety tips when confronting mountain lions. Worried about Jack’s heart, she thought it best not to shock him.

“Go off in the trees,” Jack suggested. “You have one of everything in that backpack. Surely you have tissues. I’ll just sit and enjoy the view.” He parked his butt back down on the rock.

In a swift lunge, Aster picked up two long branches at the base of the tree. Intensity rose in her throat. “Get up. You can use this as a walking stick.”

“You need to chill out. Just go. Nobody will see ya,” he insisted.

Teeth clenched, she uttered, "There's a mountain lion in that tree."

Jack looked up and froze. "Not for long," he gasped.

Powerful claws sank into the pine bark as the cat descended the trunk.

Thrusting the stick at Jack, Aster commanded, "Come on, stand tall and look big. Don't run or stare it in the eye." Her knees shook.

He obeyed. In one graceful leap, the large cat landed on the ground and paused, undoubtedly smelling the fear. Aster stood on the rock Jack had previously sat on and raised her arms, trying to appear big. A thunderous roar assaulted the air.

The intimidating sound soared through Aster's torso, tightening her gut. She knew terror. The little girl inside had felt the same tension hearing her father's booming shouts. Back then, she was too small to fight. Now, the adult Aster had the strength to holler, "Get out of here."

A menacing growl challenged her.

Disappointed that her voice lacked a mean thrust, Aster tried another shout. Her body trembled. Her vocal cords strained as she spewed out the nastiest locker-room smut she could muster, mimicking her father's worst abuse.

Stunned by the situation, Jack shook his stick and added to the screaming. Bark flew into the air as the top quarter of the weathered branch broke off. He continued to flail desperately.

The mountain lion bared its teeth and hissed. It eyed them both, one at a time. As if bored, it snarled, backed up a few steps, and then proudly retreated into the wilds of the foothills.

Aster said rapidly, "Whoa! That was scary."

On impulse, she flung her arms around Jack.

"No kidding," Jack agreed, returning the embrace.

"Are you okay?" she asked, pulling away to study his face.

"Bit rattled. Much better now," Jack said, smiling down at her.

Aster kept watch for the return of the mountain lion. Staring toward the west, she said, "Thought we were goners."

"Let's go down to safety," Jack muttered.

As they descended, Aster reflected in an excited tone, "Can you believe what just happened? Holy crap! We were potential kitty snacks!"

Jack shook his head. "What a harrowing experience! We could be dead right now. Never again am I going up that trail."

Aster rambled on anxiously, "Mountain lions usually don't come down this low. They prefer remote areas near their food source. They don't like to be around humans."

Jack interrupted, "Vice versa."

Aster paused to retrieve the water bottle. She commented, "My throat's a bit raw. I cussed up a storm." She took a drink of water. Inspecting the empty trail behind them, she sighed.

"You're a regular potty mouth, Old Spitfire Snowden."

"Here," she said, handing him the water.

"Felt like I channeled my dad's anger. He had a litany of swear words that would win the Olympics. Never thought his raving would keep me safe," Aster said, amazed by the irony.

They relived the encounter all the way back to the car.

Aster dropped the backpack in the front seat. As she shut the door, she said, "I panicked. I thought of your heart giving out. You, lying on the ground, presented as a special-delivery meal for a feline. It was awful." Her eyes filled with tears.

Jack leaned over and kissed her cheek. "Being the heroine is a bit nerve-racking," He pointed to the dining hall. "Let's get a drink. You and I could both stand to take it down a notch."

Aster blushed.

They walked to the dining-hall entrance. The reception podium was outside, at the top of the stairs.

The blond host asked the rattled pair, "Would you like to sit on the porch or indoors?"

"Inside," they said together.

Sheltered within the enclosed walls, Jack made the first toast. He lifted his cabernet and said, “To safety.”

“Hear, hear,” agreed Aster.

Because of the stress, they ordered only appetizers. On their second glass of wine, Aster calmed and took interest in bolstering the spirits of her companion by bringing up a favored topic. “Hey, Jack. My Indian past life ended at the dispute of Navajos and Spaniards. Do you know the date?”

Jack flicked a lazy hand. “The date didn’t pop up during the journey, so I Googled it last week. The site did not have much information. The Pueblo Revolt happened in 1680. The Spanish, in search of gold, settled in Santa Fe. They made peace with the local Indians, giving gifts of metal knives, tools, and pots and pans that did not chip or break like pottery or rock. Less often, they gave horses—obviously, a hot commodity. Hunting on horseback improved food supply tenfold. When the priests arrived, all hell broke loose, because they wanted to convert the Indians to Catholicism.”

“A nasty move, to say the least. Hmm, come think of it, that lifetime would come after my English life,” Aster commented thoughtfully.

“Our lives, Ms. Margaret-Cedar Claw-Snowden.”

“Right. Mr. Psychic Jack the Maniac,” Aster quipped.

They laughed at their silliness.

Aster squinted, asking, “Whatcha find out about the fighting during the revolt?”

Jack took a sip a wine and said, “Okay, here’s the short version. The rebelling Indians, who gathered in Taos, outnumbered the Spanish soldiers in Santa Fe. Most of the Spanish soldiers were away fighting the Apache. The clever natives cut off the water supply of the enemy and then eventually barricaded the governor in his palace. The Indians won.”

“Amazing how things work out. Did the Spaniards stay away long?” she asked.

"No idea. But I would like to make a toast to the Pueblos." Jack raised his glass. "Cheers," Aster said.

The two clinked glasses.

Finishing his wine, Jack leaned over and kissed Aster on the lips. "I've wanted to do that for some time now. Whew! Courage in a bottle is probably better than none at all." He looked delighted.

"You pack quite a punch there. Wind chimes tingled and spread all the way down to my feet. Now I know," said Aster.

"Know what?"

"If you're a good kisser or not. Hmm! Show me how you did that," Aster said, not feeling shy at all.

He picked up her hand and kissed it as though she were a queen. "Let's go over to my place, and I'll show ya right properly," said Jack. His hazel eyes sparkled.

Jack paid the bill, and Aster left a tip. They held hands all the way to the car. Sitting inside the car, their lips joined madly, as if starving.

"It's hard to stop. We're like magnets pulled together," Aster said, her whole being in a radiant glow.

"I'm not complaining. Feels like a reunion. We've done this before, many, many times." In a soft voice, Jack sang, "I could drink a case of you."

"Thank you, Joni Mitchell," Aster said, beaming.

She ran a finger down his short nose and palmed his cheek, like a sculptor memorizing a work of art. After a long kiss, she said, "Let's go before the magic spell wears off."

The wine seemed to have dissolved any resistance. She hungered for all of him.

❋ ❋

Jack took Aster by the hand and led her into his bedroom. One passionate kiss after another, and then in a frenzy, clothes flew to the floor. They lay side by side on the bed. The moment their naked bodies pressed together, a magic force bonded them, as it had thousands of times throughout history.

"We haven't even had sex. It feels incredible to be in each other's field. Every cell in my body is firing off joy," Jack said. He planted little kisses on her neck.

"I know. It's so familiar, safe, yummy. ... I'm overwhelmed," Aster said, opening to his touch.

"Intoxicating, isn't it?" He moved to her nipple and ran his tongue along the surface.

"Yeah. My heart is in celebration mode like never before. Oh my God! I'm building already. I want you inside me now," Aster said, amazed at the dormant feelings coming to life.

After three years without a partner, it took very little to reach desire. Without hesitation, she lubed his penis with coconut oil and mounted an eager mate. The second Jack entered her, the welcoming sensation built with every thrust. Pleasure groans filled the room. As she convulsed into climax, Jack rode the same wave.

Chapter 10

The Birth

The next morning, Aster and Jack lingered in bed, naked. They could not move. He was blissfully spent. She felt a bit sore, even with the use of coconut oil as a lubricant. All her performance fears vanished. Save for the first round, Jack approached sex like a savory meal, slowly enjoying every bite. Sated, in an ethereal afterglow, she melted into the mattress. From the window, rays of sunshine cast rectangles on Aster's pouchy belly. Not wanting to spotlight her least favorite feature, she draped the sheet over the unsightly mound.

After their lovemaking, Aster had a dream that added an interesting twist to hooking up with Jack. Grannyme had a starring role. She sat behind a desk with a pair of reading glasses halfway down her nose. Instead of robes, she wore a shimmering gold business suit. The purple dais looked more like carpeting than a cushion.

"My darling bumpkin, congratulations! You completed another vow," Grannyme said as she made a large red check mark across the paper in front of her.

"You mean using my father's anger to confront the mountain lion?"

The crone smiled. "Challenging as it was, no; not that. You

needed a little help, so I nudged you toward the goal. I told Snuggles to get out of the tree and greet you."

"The mountain lion's name is Snuggles?" Aster said, utterly flabbergasted.

"Why, yes. Isn't he a gorgeous cat?"

"You told a mountain lion to terrify us so that we could overcome our fear?" Aster raised her voice.

"No, silly, so that you and Jack would hug, bond over surviving a threat, and consummate your relationship."

"Aside from all your shenanigans, you're saying the bonding was the vow?" Aster spoke through clenched teeth.

Grannyme smacked her lips and said, "To be more precise, an eternal lover's vow. In every life you and Jack share, the goal is to rekindle the flame. In some lives, you've missed your mark. In this life, however, the potential has just begun."

"Wait a minute. First, you said Jack and I are friends for life. Now we have a lover's vow? Can we have both?" Aster asked in disbelief.

"Yes. You two made the vow."

"Okay, so Jack and I have an incredible history as lovers. Why is the goal so important?" Aster said, calming down.

"The goal brings the chalice into closer proximity. On a soul level, completing a vow is sort of like graduating to a higher place. It's part of your destiny. You and Jack, basically, team up and enhance each other's lives. The eternal lovers' vow has more to it than you might think. I'm talking about the magic you feel when you embrace. That sensation is angelic love, and it's bigger than you are. Think of your union as magnetic north meeting south, emitting a radiant energy that travels beyond the walls of your bedroom, orbits around the earth, and spreads joy to all inhabitants."

"Come on. You're sounding a tad grandiose, here." Aster snorted, still nowhere nearer to understanding the quest.

"Never underestimate the power of love. It's good medicine to spread around. Aster, you of all people needed a double dose to heal your lonely heart. You can thank Snuggles and me for helping you loosen your grip on that criteria list."

"Right, good ol' lovable Snuggles," Aster said sardonically.

Grannyme shot a look over her reading glasses and said, "Dear bumpkin, the fright was a small price to pay for such a profound residual effect."

Then, with a click her fingers she disappeared.

Aster glanced at the naked body next to her. Casting aside the criteria list took merely a nanosecond. The intimacy with Jack felt right. She said, "Jack, I'm enjoying the cuddling more than you know. It's sort of like basking in an enchanted haven."

"Yummy, isn't it?" agreed Jack. "There's nothing like eternal lovers reconnecting once again."

Aster rolled on her side, with a hand supporting her head. "Eternal lovers? That's what I dreamed about last night. Grannyme, an old wise woman who's the conductor of my predictive dreams, said that you and I made a vow to be intimate in every lifetime we share. Apparently, every now and again, we fall short of reaching that goal. Jack, do you think our old selves in that Navajo life, Talking Bird and Cedar Claw, reached our goal?" she asked, staring at his profile.

"Probably," Jack said lazily. "I like your conductor, Grannyme; she confirms my theory. We are twin flames."

"That probably explains how last night and this morning we knew how to please each other so effortlessly. Like we—" Aster sneezed, interrupting herself. Dust in Jack's bedroom caused a tickling sensation in her nose.

"Had lifetimes of practice," Jack said, finishing the sentence for her.

She nodded, thinking about how satisfying the orgasms were. It also astonished her that, without thinking, she had freely shared her deepest secret: Grannyme.

"We were amazing—nothing short of spiritual ... downright sacred. Makes me wonder how many lifetimes it took our souls to tune in to that level of intimacy," Jack said, choosing his words carefully. He avoided saying the word *love*. It was too early in the relationship to admit the truth.

"I'd say we reached somewhere around master's—no, more like PhD—level. It felt like we read each other's minds. Doesn't it make you want to revisit New Mexico so we can find out if we completed our vow? You know, check out our status."

"As long as I don't have to move, I'm game," said Jack.

Side by side, they lay on their backs. Together, they grounded, found neutral, and listened to Jack's slow-paced voice. "In your mind's eye, see the beckoning light."

Aster floated into timelessness. In her mind's eye, golden rays of sunshine lit an archway of stone burgeoning with blue and pink morning glory blossoms. She recognized the portal and entered. Semiarid air permeated her nostrils. New Mexico terrain and a brilliant blue sky came into view. Long shadows of a scrub oak darkened the dry soil. Aster had the sense it was late in the afternoon.

At this point in the year, the tribe migrated to a mesa. On the edge of the flat shelf, a creek flowed. A tall butte ran west, along the water, supplying shade from the afternoon sun.

Cedar Claw set up their hogan in the trees, providing as much comfort as he could for his pregnant wife. He had become the medicine man. He wore eagle feathers attached to both braids, and a smooth chunk of turquoise hung around his neck. The adornments were only a small portion of his status, for he owned four horses.

Many from other clans walked for miles to receive the shaman's legendary healing forte: the ability to relieve pain. All clients bestowed gifts. The majority brought food, for hunting was nearly impossible with a lame foot.

Cedar Claw's forehead and the skin around his eyes showed creases from constant sun exposure. He stood, balancing on his walking stick, watching his three sons—Blue Star, Thunder, and Wee Cub—approach the outdoor hearth.

The youngest, Wee Cub, a dimple-fingered three-year-old, held up a feather. He said, "Father, look! A baby-eagle feather." Wee Cub resembled Cedar Claw the most.

The creases around Cedar Claw's eyes deepened as he smiled. In a deep voice he explained, "That's a grouse feather, Wee Cub. See the marking here?"

"Told ya! It's not an eagle feather," Thunder bellowed. His fists rested on both hips as he looked disapprovingly at his little brother. Snorting a nasal grunt, he added, "When you're six autumns old, like me, you'll be smarter too."

Cedar Claw shot a disciplinary glance at Thunder. "That mouth of yours is always brewing up a storm. You remind me of your uncle."

What Cedar Claw did not say aloud was how haunting it felt that his own son, Thunder, looked like his late uncle, Wild Arrow. Thunder had his uncle's wide beady eyes, but his redeeming feature was the smile he had inherited from his mother.

Wee Cub jumped up and down in excitement, saying, "Put the feather in my hair, Father, just like yours."

"Hold still." Cedar Claw's deft hands unwound the leather hair tie and effortlessly rewrapped it with the feather in place. "There ya go. Just like mine." He patted the little one on the butt, encouraging him along. He said, "Go see if Mother has finished her nap."

"Baby's comin' soon, isn't it?" said Wee Cub in his expectant, young voice.

"Yep. See if she needs any help," Cedar Claw instructed.

"I want a little sister." Wee Cub skipped away. "I won't be the youngest anymore."

Blue Star was nine years old. He was the pretty one, with the slanted eyes and narrow nose of his mother. Influenced greatly by his great-uncle, Turtle, Blue Star was a philosopher. He and his great-uncle, the wise elder, had often spent many nights under the stars telling stories, gazing at comets, and tracking heat lightning.

During Blue Star's fifth summer, Turtle had died of old age. Most memories of his great-uncle had faded, but one stuck out in his mind. This memory set Blue Star apart from his brothers. It was the moment Turtle had said, "You, Blue Star, were born an old man, wise beyond your years. Not until you become an elder will you act more childlike."

Now Cedar Claw whispered in Blue Star's ear, "Help me with this." Cedar Claw sat on a tall tree stump. He picked up Thunder by the ankles, hanging him upside down. "We're gonna let laughter chase away the storm." Struggling to keep the six-year-old in the air, he commanded, "Blue Star, come tickle his belly."

"But, Father, Thunder ate juniper berries. He might spit them up."

Cedar Claw beckoned with his head. "Just for a bit, son."

Thunder's hearty laughter was contagious. Soon all three chorused their laughter in unison. Thunder's ponytail swung madly as he tried to twist free. He managed to squeal out, "Puke." Within seconds, he found himself upright and sprinted out of arm's reach. In an excited voice, he said, "Just kidding."

"You little squirrel," said Cedar Claw. A quick lunge caught the youngster. Hoisted in midair, Thunder somersaulted and landed in a sitting position on his father's shoulders.

"Look at me. I'm a big chief up here. Voice of all nations," Thunder declared.

"Chief Big Mouth is more like it," Blue Star snapped.

"Come, Blue Star, pluck your brother off my shoulders. Let's gather firewood from the great pile."

With his two elder sons in tow, Cedar Claw limped to the community fire pit using the Y-shaped walking stick as a crutch.

"That's women's work," complained Thunder, holding Cedar Claw's free hand.

"Mother's too heavy with child," reasoned Blue Star.

"Our little sister," said Thunder.

"Brother," insisted Blue Star.

A while later, Cedar Claw, Blue Star, and Thunder dropped several tree branches at their hearth. Cedar Claw hobbled to the lean-to and took out the saw hidden under the blankets. Few of the Spanish man's tools were integrated into the Navajo way of life. All seemed to turn a blind eye, pitying the crippled medicine man's inability to do it the old way, balancing on one leg while whacking powerful blows with a hatchet.

Talking Bird waddled over toward the sound of the saw, her swollen belly in the lead. Massaging her lower back, she watched and waited until her husband finished the cut. She said, "Cedar Claw, it's time."

Cedar Claw wiped the sweat from his brow. He said, "For what?"

"To sing the birthing chant," said Talking Bird, stroking the sides of her belly. "Number four will probably be quicker than the last."

Cedar Claw rubbed his nose with the back of his palm. Particles of sawdust tickled his nostrils, making him sneeze. His whole body jerked in response. "Yeow!" Cedar Claw yelled as the saw grazed his leg. A warm trickle of blood ran down to the scar on his ankle.

"Are you so sensitive that you are feeling the birth already?" said Talking Bird.

"No. I nicked my leg with this thing," Cedar Claw replied with a look of distaste as he brandished the saw.

"Put it away before it causes more injuries," insisted Talking Bird, noticing the small hole in his pants.

After Cedar Claw shoved the saw under layers of blankets, he sat down and rolled up his pant leg. The three-inch gash was not fatal, but deep enough to make a wide red streak down his shin.

Blue Star pulled Thunder by the arm to look at the wound.

"See, boys, how dangerous that saw is?" Cedar Claw said, looking at his sons. He scanned the area, asking, "Where is Wee Cub? He should see this."

Thunder, squeamish at the sight of blood, quickly volunteered to check the hogan. He ran inside. Moments later, he shouted from the door, “Wee Cub’s not in there. I’ll go check the village.” He took off at a run.

“I told Wee Cub the baby will be born today. He probably went looking for you,” said Talking Bird.

“How do you feel?” Cedar Claw asked.

“I feel pressure on my hips. The Great Mother is making room for the birth. I believe that I will be nursing our baby before sunset. What is that moving by the bushes? Maybe it’s Wee Cub.” She waddled a few steps toward the bushes, only to find a pair of fluttering moths.

Cedar Claw rose. From behind, he reached around and held her abdomen until he felt a contraction. He hobbled around her until they stood face-to-face and then asked, “How long has the womb been quickening?”

No matter how many times Cedar Claw looked at his wife, he continued to find joy in the beauty of her slanted eyes.

“This morning, the quickening was mild. I thought nothing of it. Not until the sun moved toward the west did the intensity increase. My womb prepares for birth. We need more water and the midwife,” said Talking Bird.

Cedar Claw raised a brow as he turned toward Blue Star. “Son, the water jug is over there. Before you fill it, tell Rabbit Tail we need her skills.”

Blue Star loved responsibility, for it made him feel grown up. Off on his errand, he walked tall. He could hardly wait to boast to his brothers about this task, the most recent privilege of being the eldest.

“Cedar, do you think Wee Cub is safe?” Talking Bird gave an adorable frown.

Cedar Claw faced north and asked for all-seeing wisdom. An internal voice said, *Caution to the wind.* “Wee Cub will be fine,” he lied to his wife.

A short while later, Rabbit Tail approached. Her

salt-and-pepper hair, tied in a braid with a beaded leather thong, hung at the back of her head. Jostling freely with each step was an assortment of rabbit tails that hung from a belt fastened to her narrow waist. The wrinkles above her lip disappeared when she smiled a hello to the expecting parents. She handed a pottery jar containing raspberry leaves to Cedar Claw.

"The usual," Rabbit Tail said.

Cedar Claw smelled the leaves. "Delivery tea."

Rabbit Tail held up four fingers. "This isn't your first delivery and probably not your last." She snickered at their fertility, having delivered all three of their sons.

The medicine man bowed to the midwife, giving her silent permission to take charge. He knew she spoke polite words to keep the spirits happy and the mother-to-be calm. What Rabbit Tail did not express was the fact that a lame father fails to provide for yet another child without taxing the wife, the older sons, and the entire village.

Reminded of his limitation, he groaned, thinking, *My lame foot curses me. I cannot hunt. Other men teach my sons how to track. I am a burden. If it not for my medicine knowledge, I'd have been thrown to the wolves. From now on, Talking Bird must drink the no-baby tea.*

While Rabbit Tail attended to Talking Bird, Cedar Claw made a fire. As soon as the embers glowed orange, he placed a water-filled iron pot, a relic from the Spanish visitors, on the coals.

Blue Star came back, hoisting the water jug on one hip and struggling with the weight.

Thunder loped in alone, shaking his head. He said, "Wee Cub must be hiding. I cannot find him."

Cedar Claw checked the position of the sun. Dusk began to dim the sky. He set the prayer gourd rattles next to the fire, freeing his hands to remove the boiling pot. Into the clay jar, he poured the scalding water over the raspberry leaves. In the distance, a coyote howled. Hairs on his arm stood on end. To nobody in particular, he said, "While the tea is steeping, I'm gonna wash the blood off my leg." Before anyone could respond, he limped off, worried about Wee Cub.

Cedar Claw checked points of interest—the horse corral and the grazing sheep—but there was no trace of his youngest son.

Female laughter caught his attention. A group of young girls grinding corn stopped what they were doing at the halting footsteps of the medicine man. They had not seen Wee Cub, but they promised to send him home if they did.

A coyote howl came from the creek. Alarmed, Cedar Claw walked toward the sound as fast as his lame ankle allowed. The maligned bone mend prevented him from running. Panic tensed the muscles in his chest. His mind raced, far faster than his feet, warning, *Coyotes hunt at dusk.*

On a flat rock that jutted out into the water, he saw a small body lying facedown. A mangy lone coyote stood leering, as if waiting for his pack to join in a feast. The carnivore had not grown to full size, probably on its first hunt.

Breathing hard, Cedar picked up a branch and a stone. He let out a menacing shout: "Get away from my son!"

The canine bared its teeth, let out a growl, and took ferocious bites at the air, threatening the enemy with its flesh-ripping jaws.

Cedar Claw spun the branch over his head and advanced. The coyote backed up. A stone flew into its hindquarters. The coyote let out a yelp. Out of sheer determination, the beast stood defiant, intent on overcoming the cripple. Focusing on the smell of blood, the coyote advanced, mouth open, ready to clamp its jaws down on Cedar Claw's leg. Just inches before the sharp fangs met their mark, the tree branch knocked the furry head aside. Another blow hit the rump. A painful yelp sounded, and the creature ran off.

Wee Cub had witnessed his father scaring off the coyote. He said, "Father, you smacked him good! Just like a powerful warrior!"

In a sharp tone, Cedar Claw said, "Come on, let's go." He scooped up Wee Cub with his free arm.

Loud screams bellowed in Cedar Claw's ears. Ignoring the fuss, he walked on. Slow, burdensome strides brought them to the center of the village, where Cedar Claw set Wee Cub down on the ground.

"Whew!" He breathed hard, groaning at the pain in his ankle. Turning to his son, he said, "Why are you crying so hard? You are safe with me."

Wee Cub's lower lip quivered. He pointed to his back. "Sunburn," he moaned between sobs. Tiny blisters speckled the little back.

Of the three brothers, Wee Cub had the lightest skin; he was prone to sunburn. His coloring was the only trait to show up from his mother's side, as his grandfather, a white man from across the great waters, had sired Talking Bird during a knife trade.

Offering a hand to his son, Cedar Claw said, "Come. Let's go home. We'll fix it."

Cedar Claw leaned heavily on the walking stick. Halfway there, he calmed down to the point where he felt the effects of his actions. Wee Cub's extra weight had torqued his ankle, causing the joint to freeze up. The pain was too intense for him to even be able to drag his foot. In all humility, he got on all fours and crawled the rest of the way.

Thunder saw Cedar Claw and Wee Cub enter camp. He ran to meet them. "Father, you're hurt."

"Get me a mat, raw wool from Mother's basket, and my salve," Cedar Claw said, wincing.

Wee Cub had watery eyes. Thunder smiled, thinking his little brother must have gotten a good walloping for running off. He yelled, "Where you been?"

"Creek," Wee Cub said, pouting.

"Mother's giving birth," said Thunder, pointing at the lean-to.

At a glance, the two women across the way seemed to be carrying on fine without him.

"Son, fetch me the salve. Now!" ordered Cedar Claw.

Thunder sped to the hogan. He returned, placing the mat and basket of wool on the ground and handing the clay pot to his father. He cast a smug look at Wee Cub and said, "I get to do the important stuff. I'll be one up on Blue Star, serving the medicine man."

Cedar Claw rolled his eyes at the competition between his sons. At the same time, he felt thankful the rivalry manifested in helping, not hitting.

Pain shot up his calf, so intense that Cedar Claw could hardly think. He touched Thunder's shoulder, saying, "Son, now get me a clean wet cloth."

Thunder obeyed.

"Good job, Thunder," Cedar Claw said as he cleaned the dried blood from the cut. He scooped out a generous dollop from the salve jar and gingerly applied it to both ankle and cut. He knew cold soaks from the creek, along with warm poultices, would offer added relief, but there was no time for such comforts.

"Father, my back hurts," Wee Cub said with a long face.

Cedar Claw flooded with affection. "Cub, you look like your grandfather right now."

Wee Cub smiled. "Mother told me that you, he, and I look alike. He died when you fell from the tree."

"True." Cedar Claw recalled his father's name, Two Rivers, but did not say it aloud.

"My back stings when I move," complained Wee Cub.

"We'll fix it. Thunder, grab the pitcher," Cedar Claw instructed through gritted teeth, feeling the pain again.

Thunder stood, peering into the empty vessel. "What am I supposed to do with this?"

"Pee in it," Cedar Claw said, letting out a sigh.

"I don't have to go." Thunder looked disappointed.

"Drink water," Cedar Claw ordered.

"Not thirsty." Thunder raised his shoulders, confused.

Nostrils flaring, Cedar Claw barked, "Drink." He cupped his hands around his mouth and yelled, "Blue Star, come."

Blue Star's face fell as he turned to see his father motioning him over with hand movements. Blue Star had been watching his mom squatting and enduring waves of pain. He tore himself away reluctantly and went to answer his father.

Thunder chugged down a mug of water. He wiped off his mouth and belched. Then, he walked over to a nearby tree to hide behind it while passing water into the jug.

Blue Star arrived, curious as to what was so important. He gave an expectant glance at his father. "What?" he asked impatiently.

"Remove the feather from Wee Cub's hair," Cedar ordered.

"Not my feather!" moaned Wee Cub.

Blue Star smirked as he untied the leather, delighted to join in on his little brother's punishment.

Thunder returned. "Here's my pee. What should I do with it?" he asked.

"Today, that is sunburn medicine. Wee Cub, lie down on the mat," said Cedar Claw.

Wee Cub hesitated. "You speak true words Father?" he questioned. On several occasions, his elder brothers had duped the three-year-old.

Cedar Claw's deep-set eyes darted toward the mat. Without saying a word, he commanded action.

Wee Cub obeyed.

"Blue Star, you place the wool along Wee Cub's sides. Thunder, pour a small amount of pee over the burned area. Use the feather to spread it," Cedar Claw instructed his sons.

Blue Star and Thunder exchanged glances. They dared not laugh. Of all the chores they had been given, this one topped them all.

Some of the liquid rolled off and wet the absorbent wool.

Wee Cub moaned, "That stings!"

In a measured tone, Blue Star said, "This will teach you to run off all by yourself. Father, why is Wee Cub so badly burned?"

Cedar Claw shook his head at the three-year-old. "He fell asleep on the flat rock downstream where we bathe."

"Why did you do that? I searched the entire village for you," said Thunder. His eyes squinted in disbelief.

Wee Cub's small voice said, "I was hunting for a shiny stone in the water. A gift for Mother's new baby. Got all wet when I reached for it."

"You fell in," Blue Star corrected.

Embarrassed, Wee Cub nodded. "I was cold. I lay on the warm rock to dry my belly. Rolled over to dry my back. Then, I heard screaming."

"That was me," Cedar Claw said. "I scared a young coyote away. The young beast licked its big teeth hungry for a Wee Cub snack." Cedar Claw bared his teeth and gave a fearsome growl. His actions instilled fear and also made it clear that Wee Cub had been in mortal danger.

"Whoa! And I thought father was teaching me how to be brave," the child murmured. He twirled his ponytail nervously until a finger caught in a tangle. Tears wet his round eyes. "I'm stuck."

Blue Star reached for the small knife at his belt and cut Wee Cub's finger free. He handed the cut strands to Wee Cub. "Here, put these in your totem bag." Blue Star grinned as he tickled Wee Cub under the chin.

Wee Cub let out a giggly snort.

Blue Star quipped, "Little brother, now we can call you Coyote Snack."

"More like Smelly Pee," Thunder snickered.

All but Wee Cub laughed.

Cedar Claw crawled over to his wife. The lean-to opened to the north; the other three walls that held up the roof blocked out the intensity of the sun. Constructed with strips of leather fastened to brush and tree branches, the healing bed served the entire clan. Herbs, feathers, and bones hung above Talking Bird's slouched body. She no longer squatted. Her face strained as she bore down.

Forgetting his own pain, Cedar Claw stroked the top of Talking Bird's head. His loving touch rekindled her strength to push. The baby's head had emerged into the world. The puffy newborn face looked blue.

In a state of panic, Rabbit Tail commanded, "Stop pushing!"

The umbilical cord was wrapped tight around the baby's neck. Rabbit Tail struggled, trying to pry a finger under the cord, intending to slide it over the baby's head. Just as her finger slid into place, a contraction expelled the baby. The cord tightened, pinning her finger to the neck. As she worked one-handed, trying to maneuver a slippery newborn, Cedar Claw slid over on his butt to help. He lifted the baby while Rabbit Tail unwound the cord.

For a brief moment, Talking Bird closed her eyes, relieved that the intensity was over.

Curious to know the baby's gender, she lifted her head and said, "Boy or girl?" Watching the midwife and her husband, she gasped, asking, "What are you doing?"

Rabbit Tail grabbed the limp form out of Cedar Claw's hands. Using a hollow raven bone, she suctioned fluids from the baby's airway. She blew air into the tiny mouth, but there was no response. As a last resort, she tenderly rubbed the diaphragm, hoping to encourage life.

No matter what efforts ensued, the baby did not stir.

Talking Bird moaned, "Is it a girl? Alive?" She reached her arms out to hold it.

Rabbit Tail shook her head no. She presented the baby in plain view for the mother to witness the still body.

"Send your blessings, Talking Bird and Cedar Claw," Rabbit Tail instructed. She forbade the mother from touching the baby girl. No bonding allowed the spirit an easier journey to the afterlife.

Overwrought with emotion, Talking Bird cried, "Give her to me!" Enraged, she struggled, trying to get up.

Cedar Claw hugged Talking Bird, holding down her arms.

Talking Bird twisted fiercely as she shrieked, "My baby girl!"

"Shh, shh," Cedar Claw soothed. He held his wife in a tight grip until exhaustion rendered her still.

"I prayed for a girl every day," Talking Bird sobbed.

Cedar Claw spoke softly. "Let go, and set the spirit free." His insides churned with guilt for not singing the birthing chant. "I did not honor the new soul coming in. It's my fault our daughter is dead."

"Oh, my baby!" Talking Bird cried, burying her wet-cheeked face in Cedar Claw's shoulder.

"Let it all go, my darling birdie," Cedar Claw said.

He kissed the side of his wife's head. The very act overwhelmed his senses. He cried too. Everything had happened so fast. He recalled how one event had unfolded after another that day. *The Spirit has not favored me today—the saw, the coyote, the birth, the death, my distraught wife. The Spirit punishes me so.* He grimaced at the intense pain in his ankle. Once again unable to walk, he wept over his disability and the loss of his daughter. In fact, every loss in his life seemed to line up to take a turn at crushing his heart.

Blue Star kept an ear on alert, listening to the dismay coming from the lean-to. He realized that the wails of childbirth had turned to sobs of grief.

Thunder was preoccupied, telling a bear story to Wee Cub. The two younger ones had no clue as to what had just happened.

Curiosity led Blue Star to find out what Rabbit Tail was doing with the baby. Still holding the grouse feather, he strode away so abruptly that the two younger brothers stopped what they were doing and followed.

The boys approached Rabbit Tail. She held a wrapped bundle in her arms.

"Hope it's a girl," Wee Cub said excitedly.

Rabbit Tail put up a palm for the brothers to stop. "Sorry, boys. The baby did not survive."

"Can we see her?" Blue Star asked.

"Does she look like me?" Wee Cub wondered.

"Is there any blood?" Thunder clenched his teeth.

Rabbit Tail pushed the salt-and-pepper braid to her back. "You are family. With your own eyes, you can see that the Spirit has left your sister." She removed the coverings from the baby and held the tiny naked form before her for all three boys to see.

A full head of black hair, matted down wet from birthing fluid, contrasted with the stark pale face. In her smallness, she resembled Talking Bird, notably the narrow nose and full lips.

"She has dimpled hands just like Cub," Thunder said. Relieved, he added, "There's no blood."

"I'm way too big to ever be this tiny. Looks like she's taking a nap," Wee Cub said in awe.

"Pleasant journey, little one," Blue Star said solemnly. He extended his palms, as if making an offering to the Spirit. The grouse feather fell, unnoticed, to the ground.

The other two, unsure of what to do, copied their big brother's hand movements.

Wee Cub reached to touch the lifeless little body, but Rabbit Tail shook her head no and pushed his pudgy hand away.

"Young bucks, head over to the lean-to. Your parents need you." Rabbit Tail shooed them away, knowing newborns had an infectious way of burrowing into the hearts of onlookers.

The three brothers stood in front of their swollen-faced parents. Overcome by a wave of sadness, the boys joined in a family embrace, and they all had a good cry.

Rabbit Tail had already collected the placenta and wrapped it in another blanket. She carried it away now, letting the family mourn. If the baby had lived, she would have cooked the afterbirth and fed it to the mother to help her regain her strength.

As night fell, the first evening star accompanied the waning crescent moon. An aura of light shone in the western sky.

"Father, everything is ready for the burial rights," said Blue Star.

Cedar Claw heard nothing. In the deepening darkness, he sat with his arm still slung around Talking Bird, who had dozed off. His stony face stared off into the trees, as he inwardly apologized to the Great Spirit for his inadequacy.

"Father, come on. They're ready for you to lead the ceremony," Blue Star persisted.

Cedar Claw hesitated, afraid to put weight on his ankle. For, surely, the Spirit might not forgive him and leave him even further crippled than before. He let go of his wife and reached for his walking stick. Unable to breathe, he became light-headed.

"Father, lean on my shoulder; I will help you. Grief has stunned you," Blue Star said.

Cedar Claw stood up, but the second he put weight on his foot, he collapsed in pain. "Son, find two braves to carry me. Be quick. Soon the sky will blacken." His voice cracked as he stuffed down the fear of the Spirit's curse.

While Cedar Claw sat waiting for able lifters, he realized how dizzy he felt. His last meal had been at sunup. The possibility of food staying in his knotted stomach had him grab the only thing in reach: the pot of leftover raspberry-leaf tea. He drank all of it.

After the burial, his family had gone to sleep, but Cedar Claw lay on a mat, staring up at the stars. He drank valerian tea to dull the pain; and yet, rest did not come. Pondering what kind of lesson the Spirit had planned by leaving him too crippled to walk, the young medicine man reviewed the events of the day. Everything pointed to lack of duty.

Riddled with remorse, he fretted. *I did not honor the soul of my own daughter's entrance to earth. I could have waited to treat Wee Cub's sunburn until after the birth. Then, perhaps the Spirit would have been satisfied, and my wife would have a daughter. I hate being a cripple. If I could trade a horse to walk like a man, I would. Why is it that when I attempt to be a man, I get struck down? First, when I fell from a tree as boy to prove myself a hunter, and again today when I rescued my son. Turtle, I wish you were here to give me advice.*

As soon as he thought of Turtle, the medicine man's wisdom came to mind. *The old man warned me that my ankle wound was not a spiritual punishment. He demanded that I think again ... that I ask for wisdom. For a wise man knows to wait moons, even seasons, until the lesson becomes clear. I had little patience for answers to fall from the sky. I cringed when Turtle said I was not a normal man, because too many stones blocked that path. However, it did soothe my ears to hear that my pain and suffering would give me the skills to be a great healer. Is such knowledge worth the cost?*

"Father."

Cedar Claw heard a boy's voice as one of his sons shook his shoulder. He came out of his thoughts to listen.

Thunder leaned toward Cedar Claw's ear, saying softly, "Father, I can't sleep."

"All right then," he said with a sigh. "What's bothering you?"

"I had a dream about an old man, an elder. He wanted me to give you a message," Thunder said.

"Dreams can be tricky messages. Lie down and tell me about it." Cedar Claw scooted over to make room on the mat.

Thunder snuggled up, placing his head against Cedar Claw's shoulder.

"Father, look, a shooting star! Look over there," Thunder said, pointing.

"That means your dream must be important."

Thunder smiled at that. He said in awe, "The dream was so real. The elder's face had many wrinkles, and he was not much taller than I am. His voice had an echo, as if it came from the sky."

"What did the old man say?"

Thunder mimicked the airy voice, stating, "Tell Cedar Claw to listen to his own words."

"In your own voice, tell which words, Thunder," said Cedar Claw.

"He said many things while he fed his horse, Farwalker. He said the Spirit gave you a priceless gift. You heal pain. Tribesmen travel far to see you. They trade and give you food and hides so that you can provide for your family. You live a unique path, as only a medicine man can. The Spirit takes care of you because you take care of your people."

"Is that so?" Cedar Claw said, intrigued that Turtle spoke through Thunder. The old teacher had slipped in another lesson.

"Yes. And you know what else? He said that I remind him of my uncle, Mother's brother. The only difference is that my spirit is much kinder."

Mindful not to say the name Wild Arrow aloud, Cedar Claw replied, "The old man in your dream was the medicine man who taught me. His tongue speaks the truth: you are kinder."

Thunder nodded appreciatively. Then, he asked in a serious tone, "Father, how did Uncle die? The one I look like."

Cedar Claw tucked his hands under his head. Blurring out the myriad stars in the sky, he said, "Hmm. Let's see. Your uncle was a wild spirit. He was part of the group at the revolt; his job was to provide food, aid, and supplies. One day, instead of staying at camp, he sneaked along with the braves as they overtook the governor's manor. Your uncle saw one of the Spanish soldiers cast his gun aside before raising his hands in surrender. The gun landed in a bush, somewhat hidden. Your uncle went to retrieve the gun. It tangled in the bush. He gave a hearty yank, and the gun fired into his chest."

"Killed himself, didn't he?" Thunder said in awe.

"Yes, because he did not pause to think."

❋ ❋

Within seconds, the father and son under the starry sky vanished, and Aster and Jack lay in Jack's bed, staring up at the drywall ceiling.

Aster's cell phone rang. She scanned the room, still in a daze from the time travel. Her phone was somewhere amid the disarray of clothes strewn on the floor.

"Ugh. The switch to modern technology seems too abrupt at the moment," she said.

"Let it go to voice mail," Jack suggested.

"Good plan."

Jack said, "I got the sense we entered that Navajo life about twelve years later than the first time we journeyed."

"Yeah, and we did hook up," Aster said, recalling the eternal lovers' vow.

"I knew we'd end up husband and wife. Added proof to my theory that we're twin flames." He laced his fingers behind his head, full of confidence.

Aster rose up on her elbows to look him in the eye. She said, "And to think we had four kids. They were so cute. It was sad to see the baby girl die."

"It was." He reached over and gave her a consoling stroke along her arm.

Chapter 11

A Shared Memory

On Labor Day weekend, the temperature had cooled to light-jacket weather. Aster pulled a chaise lounge out from the shaded patio and into the sunlight of the backyard. Reclining in comfort, she basked in the sunrays, imagining her face was a solar panel recharging her battery.

A car door slammed in the driveway. Jack came walking into the backyard, saying in a happy tone, "Look, my cast is off. At last, freedom to move." He pulled up his long-sleeved shirt to show a scaly, dry wrist.

"I've got lotion to put on that," Aster offered.

"Sure enough, dear lassie. Do ya fancy dining with the likes of an Irish lad?" he asked in an overdone Irish brogue.

Aster's lilt sounded more authentic. "Well, Mr. McFadden, if it's green eggs and ham, I reckon so." She got up to kiss Jack.

"You English vixen! Ya hungry?"

Jack smelled of sandalwood aftershave. Aster inhaled the delightful scent and said, "I'm starving."

"Can't go until you wear these." Jack held out a little green box.

"For me?" she said, surprised, and opened the box. A pair of hoop earrings rested above a label that read, "14 karat."

"What luck! You found a pot of gold." He beamed.

"Oh my! They're lovely." She gasped. A lump formed in her throat.

"What's the matter?" he said to her scrunched-up face.

Aster patted the spot over her heart. "Hoo-hoo." A tear left a wet streak as it rolled down her cheek.

They hugged.

She finally found her voice. "Thank you. No man has ever been so randomly kind to me in my entire life."

Jack winked as he lilted, "Lassie, didn't ya know? A spot of gold at harvesttime melts two hearts into one."

"Love that about you, Jack. You're such a hopeless romantic."

"Hopeless? Let's go eat before you call me more names."

❋ ❋

After their breakfast, Jack and Aster agreed to walk off some of the calories. They drove to Scott Carpenter Park. From the parking lot, they crossed a small grassy hill and headed toward the bike trail along the creek. The smell of a wet lawn reminded Aster of being a kid. From out of nowhere, a dreadful memory sent her heart pounding as the younger version of herself ran out of the house to escape her father and the terror he wrought.

"Hey, Jack. Walking on this grass gave me a childhood flashback."

"You mean your tomboy era?" he asked.

"Yeah. Flashed on my dysfunctional family," Aster said blandly.

"Sounds like ya got a story. You rarely speak of your parents. I've told you about my helicopter mom and dad. It's your turn to spill the beans. How abnormal can it be?" Jack pleaded.

They reached the bike path and walked along the creek. The water current sounded hypnotic and seemed to flow with her thoughts. "I'll let you in on a family secret. My dad, Henry the Horrible, was a raging alcoholic. He was mean too. Ya'd walk around on eggshells, not wanting to piss him off. His anger made me feel guilty for being alive."

"Wow, what a rough childhood. And you seem to have survived quite well," Jack said in his soothing voice.

"I've mellowed from years of therapy." She had a glazed look on her face, thinking back on her youth.

Jack had witnessed this expression before. When she came back to the present, she had a clever way of changing the subject.

He stopped walking. He lifted her chin, making sure their eyes met. He asked, "Will you share your memory with me? I feel left out."

Touched by his caring nature, she said, "Okay. Here goes. I was nine years old. Dad and I had finished watching a program on TV. I got up to leave and tripped on an empty beer can left on the floor. As I was catching my balance, he hauled off and slugged me in the arm. Like an ornery boot-camp sergeant, he yelled, 'Get the hell out of here, you clumsy shit.' His flattop haircut and massive forearms gave the impression he'd never left the army. Not wanting more, I hightailed it out of there and escaped to my room. I was so brokenhearted at his meanness, the swelling and bruise on arm did not hurt. Nothing new—I grew up as Dad's punching bag. I hated him. My biggest wish was for a change, perhaps a loving embrace, so at least I'd have one single moment to cherish forever."

Jack commented, "What a piece of work. Where was your mom?"

"Regina was in the basement, doing laundry. I went down there to show her my injury," Aster explained.

"Bet that rattled her feathers. My mom would have been in a tizzy," Jack said.

"Hardly. She was lost in her world, singing 'Moon River.' Mom was a carbon copy of Katharine Hepburn. She identified so strongly with the actress, she never left the house without hair, nails, and lips all lacquered perfectly."

Jack interjected, "My parents loved Hepburn. You'll have to show me a picture of her. What did your mom do?"

Aster continued, "Regina's hair was rolled up in curlers, and she was ironing one of Dad's shirts. The laundry room was her private space, and I hated to invade it. Nevertheless, I asked her to check out my arm. Reluctantly, without looking, Regina huffed, 'Can ya move it? Ain't broken if ya can.'"

Jack interrupted, "I broke my thumb playing baseball. I whined how it hurt, and my coach told me to suck it up. Ate me up inside; it was like he felt my pain didn't matter."

Aster replied, "Oh, I know what you mean. I had to beg Mom to look at my arm. Mom stayed planted next to the wooden ironing board. Mechanically, she adjusted the sleeves of a plaid shirt to lay flat, grabbed the iron, and smoothed out the wrinkles, as if crisp linen made life a better place. Finally, Mom glanced at the bruise, with an insipid look on her face, and said, 'Ice it up and take aspirin.'"

"You're kidding. She didn't offer to help you? My mom would have acted like a caffeinated nurse emptying out the medicine cabinet," Jack offered.

"Like an ostrich with its head in the sand, Mom advised me to ignore Dad. She said if I did, everything would get better. 'Don't push his buttons,' she'd always say."

"Great problem solver," Jack said sarcastically.

Aster replied, "Mom's version of not rocking the boat sucked. On my own once again, I went upstairs and sat at the kitchen table, icing my arm. Dad came in to get a beer. His eyes got puffy underneath when he was drunk. Right then, I knew I should have gone to my bedroom, instead of hanging out in the kitchen. It was too late. Dad offered to put a cold beer can on my arm. I cringed and drew away."

"What a drunken asshole, scaring you that way!" Jack shook his head in disbelief.

Aster nodded. She then continued, "In a fit of anger, Henry roared, 'Won't let me help ya, huh?' He smashed the beer can on the table. His aim was true, for it caught my pinkie, breaking it. The pain was so intense, I yelped. Desperate to flee, I stood up. This set off Dad. He bellowed, 'I'll give ya something to cry about.' He punched my gut. Got the wind knocked out of me. I curled forward in a panic."

Jack gasped, "What? What type of man would do that to a nine-year-old kid?"

"The asshole wasn't done yet. He uppercut me to the face." Aster made a fist and imitated the blow. "I fell to the floor. Stars twinkled in front of my eyes. My old man stood there gloating at my submissive position."

Jack's eyes filled with tears. "I can't imagine what you've gone through. To have a parent literally beat the crap out of you. That's sick. And to think, back then, battering kids wasn't considered child abuse. It wasn't a crime."

"It was terrorizing," Aster said, twisting her hair with fervor. "I wanted the blows to stop, but I did not dare say anything; begging for mercy only coaxed Dad's fury. Thank God, child beating is thirsty work. He took time out to open the flip-top beer can and take a swig. Before he could bat at me again, I crawled to the back door, knocked over a coatrack by the entrance, and escaped outside. I heard Dad yelling as he struggled, clearing the coatrack from his path. By the time he stepped into the yard, I was on my bike and, one-handed, pedaled away. I feared for my life."

Jack picked up both of Aster's hands and kissed each one. "I don't know which one got broke, but a little TLC goes a long way. Worked for me as a kid."

"You're sweet," she said, taken aback at his gesture.

Aster and Jack approached a small pond. Noisy geese flew overhead. Their dapper bodies looked stylish, especially the long, narrow, black necks. The three-toned feather motif was not as formal as a tuxedo, but it was sleek, like a nicely tailored suit. The birds stayed in formation as they circled clockwise down to the water.

"Aren't they beautiful!" she said with a sigh.

"Wait a minute. You never told me how far you got on your bike," he said, curious.

"Right," Aster said. She blew a breath of air from billowed cheeks, returning to her memory. "In a blur, I rode my bike to Aunt Gertie's. She lived a mile down the road. I pulled into her yard and found her in the garden. Her wide-brimmed polka-dot sunhat clashed horribly with her rose floral dress. The mere sight of Gertie's mismatch attire set my knees shaking. 'I got hurt' was all that came out."

"You must have been pumped with adrenaline to ride that far. Gives me the willies thinking about the angels that helped you pedal to safety," Jack said.

Aster nodded and continued, "Auntie G. sputtered her famous saying: 'Good God.' She hobbled over on an arthritic hip. Her mouth dropped at the sight of me."

Aster took a breath and then recalled, "The tank top I wore exposed my bruised arm and bent finger. One eye had already started to swell shut, and blood dripped over my lips.

"Gertie said, 'Land's sakes, Aster! Whatcha do?' Her wobbly soft arms reached out to steady me. 'You need to see the doctor. I'll bring you home so your parents can take you.'

"'No. Can't do that,' I said.

"'My brother is drunk again, isn't he?' she said in disgust. 'He did this to you?'

"Reluctantly I nodded my head.

"'That monster!' Gertie stormed.

"Next thing I knew, I was lying in a hospital bed," Aster finished.

Jack said in a serious tone, "Your father could have killed you."

Aster grimaced, "I know. I spent a week in the hospital, with a broken pinkie, a bone-bruised arm, and a black eye. The internal bleeding in my liver seemed to take forever to heal. Every time I saw the rectangular bruise on my belly, in the shape of Dad's fist, it gave me terrible flashbacks."

"How traumatic! Did your dad ever hit ya again after that?" Jack said, concerned.

"What is this, twenty questions?" she asked.

"Yes. Play with me."

Aster crossed her arms and groaned, "Okay."

"Well, did he?" pressed Jack.

"No. I lived with Gertie until I graduated high school. By then, Gertie was a widow. Uncle Charlie had died of lung cancer. Auntie G. lived off his life insurance policy and a meager social security check. Her no-frill lifestyle had her shopping at thrift stores and garage sales. Humble as it was, we had all the comforts of life."

"Did she have children?" Jack asked.

Aster said, "No. Fostering me was the closest thing to it. My aunt doted on me. Her go-to solution for many problems was making ice cream on Saturdays. We had a cow that supplied the cream. Anyway, life got mellower. The only discord in the house was the decor—nothing matched. It was like living in a Pippy Longstocking world. You know, a mishmash of florals, plaids, polka dots, and stripes. Eventually, I trained my eye not to focus on the funky decor. For the most part, I felt safe at Auntie's house, but not 100 percent. Horror lived only a mile down the road."

Jack wrapped his arm around Aster's shoulder. He said with a chuckle, "Now I know why you match everything, down to your panties. It's the glue that holds ya together."

Aster gave a slight pout. "Either you're making fun of me, or you really get me."

"Quit being so adorable." He pointed a thumb to his chest. "Psychic Jack the Maniac has known you for eons. Seriously, though, I've got another question. For the remainder of your childhood, did you see your parents much?"

Aster complained, "Very few people know all this stuff about me. Last question."

"I promise," said Jack.

"Every other Sunday afternoon, I visited Mom and my brother. Dad was never there. Gertie filed a restraining order. She arranged for him to fix things at church on those Sundays, to spare me the trauma of being near him. Auntie got a lawyer and drew up adoption papers. Dad was given the ultimatum to stay sober and attend AA for a year, and then I would move back home; or, if he chose to continue drinking, he'd lose custody. Dad dropped out of AA after a week."

"What about your brother, Leroy?"

"He was the favored son who could do no wrong. I envied the hell out of him," Aster recalled. "My therapist insisted the reason Dad beat me was not only because I looked like Grandma Snowden, my dad's mother, but because I had predictive dreams like she did. Her foreknowledge of the future freaked Dad out. After growing up with a witchlike mother, it did not sit well with Dad to raise a witchlike daughter. In a haphazard manner, Dad tried to beat the intuitive blood out of me. His plan backfired."

"Not very fair, was it?" Jack sounded a little flippant. Perhaps realizing it, he frowned, showing great concern, and said, "To suffer the sins of your father had to have been brutal."

Aster replied, "I'll say. Mr. McFadden, you have a way of burrowing into me and unlocking all my secrets like no other."

"Isn't it obvious?" he said.

"Yes, that you're a sucker for a sad case," she quipped.

"Think again, Miss Snowden. I love you. Actually, it was love at first sight—for me," he said and flashed a winning smile.

Aster pressed her lips tight and laughed through her nose. "God, really? I've been smitten by you all summer but afraid to say anything, in case I would jinx it."

"I don't buy earrings for just anybody." He feigned being hurt.

Her heart flipped in delight. She squealed, "So glad we finally said it."

"And mean it," Jack added.

Chapter 12

The Spat

On Tuesday morning, heavy rain pelted Aster's roof. The dip in air pressure from the storm encouraged Jack to sleep in. His light, rhythmic snoring, not loud enough to scare away spiders, sang contentment.

Aster had risen early and left for work, leaving behind a peaceful Jack who was dreaming that someday Aster would be his wife.

The furniture in the bedroom gave the impression that Aster had bought an entire bedroom showroom of cherry-stained Mission furniture, complete with matching bedspread, curtains, and plush accent rugs.

At nine o'clock, the phone rang, sounding like an obnoxious alarm. With one eye cracked open, Jack snatched his cell phone from the nightstand. A client, Tasha Wingstrom, demanded that he add an extra half an hour to her appointment that day. He agreed they needed extra time to talk about an upcoming seminar, so he cut half an hour off his lunch to accommodate her. Immediately regretting his decision, he groped for something to write on, finding a pink spiral notebook. He opened the notebook to a random page and scribbled down the data.

After a quick shower, Jack returned to the notebook to enter the appointment in his cell phone. Below his messy handwriting was a passage in very neat print. "Oh shit. I didn't use a blank page. Is this important?" he said. He glanced at the first few sentences.

Before he knew it, he had read the entire page:

> Last dream of morning involved Herman Palfrey, my massage therapist, and me. We were having outrageous sex. The intense build and prolonged climax had me sing out, "Simply the best, better than all the rest,"–that line from Tina Turner's song.
>
> I woke up confused, like the dream was real. I felt as though I'd just had an orgasm. Reminded me of crying in my dream and waking up sobbing.
>
> I went to the store to buy groceries, deliciously enveloped in a post-coital glow. As fate would have it, the first person I saw was Herman. He sauntered up the produce aisle and gave me a warm hello.
>
> He must have thought it was rude of me to have sex with him and then leave abruptly after. At the very least, I could have thanked him for making me feel so good.
>
> He looked unabashed. In fact, normal as hell.
>
> I, on the other hand, felt embarrassed. Unable to address the issue, I made

up an excuse that I was running late for an appointment.

I fled to the other end of the store, and then it hit me. Herman had no clue as to the bedlam in my mind, because that was a fantasy dream! Not the usual prophetic kind ... my supposed gift.

In hindsight, I can see how my reality filters went berserk. Why do I experience such a muddled segue between the sleep world and the awake world?

Curious point: I've admired how passionate Herman gets when he massages. I had joked with Galen, "If Herman has as much zeal in bed as he does at work, his girlfriend must be a happy woman.

Jack stopped to cover his eyes. The idea of Aster enjoying outrageous sex with Herman had Jack spew, "Holy crap! Apparently, I'm not good enough for her. She's fantasizing about another man. Her dreams forecast the future. She wants Herman." Gruffly, he tossed the blankets to the floor, leaving the bed unmade.

On the drive home, Jack smashed his fist on the dashboard, muttering, "Wish that was Herman's face. Damn him."

Jack's cell phone rang and he glanced at it to see a call from Aster. He turned the phone off in a fit of pique.

Later that day, Jack tidied up his office. A verdant curtain of plants huddled around the window. He picked up a dead philodendron leaf from the floor and threw it on top of the potted soil. The sound of voices in the reception room prompted him to open the door to greet his next client.

Tasha Wingstrom, with bleached-blond hair puffed in short bob, stood in spike heels. In a pretentious, sultry voice, she said, "Jack, so good of you not to make me wait. I'm a busy woman. First hour will be the session. Then, I need to update you on the seminar you are giving. Some last-minute changes."

"For you, Tasha, I'll do my best," Jack replied. With a sweep of his hand, he invited her into the office.

Tasha walked in, poised as if she owned the place, leaving behind a pungent trail of baby-powder perfume. Her smooth china doll complexion made it obvious she was no stranger to face work.

"Delightful day, isn't it?" she said, offering a cheek for Jack to kiss.

"Yes," he responded dutifully with a little peck.

"I'm ready for one of our exciting adventures into my past. We need to record this so that my ghostwriter can turn my lives into a book," she said smugly.

"Ms. Wingstrom, you'll always be ageless," said Jack. He became aware suddenly of how natural Aster appeared, compared to Tasha.

"Oh Jack, you're such a charmer," Tasha smiled. Her upper lip appeared stiff from injections, and only the bottom edges of her front teeth showed.

Tasha's assistant, Darla, arrived at the door. Darla was a stocky young woman who appeared to be college aged. Her red hair hung in sassy tufts akin to unmown crabgrass. She set two iced lattes on the table next to the recliners.

Tasha said impatiently, "There you are. Here set this up." From her handbag, she presented a recording device to Darla, who was preoccupied listening to her phone headset.

Disgusted by the lack of response, Tasha knocked on Darla's forehead and scolded, "You pudgy thing, I'm speaking to you. Turn this thing on for me."

Darla's freckled face fell. She replied, "Yes, ma'am. It's a digital recorder."

"Of course it is," Tasha said, as if talking to an idiot. "That will be all." She waved a hand of dismissal.

Appalled at the behavior of his most frequent client, Jack waited for the mop-topped aide to leave the room. From the beginning, Tasha had literally built his practice through word of mouth. Her current interest in furthering his success pushed every tolerance button within reach.

"Shall we get started?" he said, pointing to the recliners.

"I brought you some iced kona. My favorite," Tasha said, smoothing a crease in her royal-blue dress as she sat down.

"Thank you. Just how I like it: lots a cream," said Jack.

The soul-journey part of the session took the usual hour. During the additional half hour, Tasha updated Jack about his upcoming seminar in Sedona, Arizona. She took out the brochure and pointed a manicured finger to the title above Jack's picture. She read aloud, "Explore Past Lives with Jack McFadden."

Jack nearly blushed.

Tasha held the photo, saying, "An unplugged retreat. No phones or internet access. Since I'm the sponsor, my picture is on the back."

"Tasha, you've outdone yourself," he said, embarrassed.

"Jack. Don't be so modest. I'll share you with the world. Just think," she encouraged, "You'll make a ton of money at the retreat. All seats are sold out. Afterward, you could fly your girlfriend to Europe. First class. The only way to go."

"Now there's a thought," he said, stroking his chin.

Tasha rambled on with more details. The next words Jack actually heard were "We leave tomorrow. So you can meet with the ghostwriter. We'll fly in my private jet."

As she was speaking, Jack eyed her critically. Her low-cut dress exposed ample cleavage from breasts too big for a woman so thin. It took little imagination to wonder if the pair of perky jugs would pop out of the dress if Tasha lifted her arms.

"Impressive a package as it is, how can I say no?" said Jack.

"You can't. I thought of everything." She gave Jack a hug. Her chunky amethyst necklace dug into his chest.

"Ouch. Your half-ton necklace is dangerous." Jack rubbed his chest.

"Poor baby." She took hold of his face and kissed each cheek, as if she were French and greeting family. Tawny-colored lip prints marked his cheeks. She tousled his hair. "You're so irresistible. Like a little teddy."

Repulsed by her forwardness, he reached for the door to show her out.

"The spa awaits me. Lars is focusing on my abs today. He's so brutal. I'm forced to reward myself with a facial and massage afterward. Such is life! Ta-ta!" She blew him a kiss.

Aster sat in the waiting room, observing. Seeing the lip prints and the disheveled hair, she wondered what had happened behind closed doors. She stood up, blocking Tasha's way, and said curtly, "Hello. I'm Aster, Jack's girlfriend."

Shocked to see Aster, the Herman-loving vixen, Jack said, "What are you doing here?"

Tasha cleared her throat, shooting a pointed look at Jack.

With forced calm, Jack said, "Aster, this is Tasha Wingstrom, the promoter of my Sedona retreat."

Uninterested, Tasha said, "Hello, Astro." She turned to Jack and winked. "Jack, that was fun. Oh, my Gucci. I forgot it. Darling, will you get it for me?"

"What?" he asked.

"My handbag. Could you?" Tasha batted her eyes.

"Oh. Yeah, sure." Jack darted into the office.

Tasha seized the moment. Lowering her voice, she said, "You should get some laser work on those wrinkles. Then, maybe your man won't have such a wandering eye."

The brashness combined with the sickeningly sweet perfume

made Aster wince. Within seconds, distrust turned to loathing. Nostrils flaring, she struggled for words. Before she had time to reply, Jack stood in the doorway.

"Here it is," Jack said, handing the enormous bag to Tasha.

"Darla, come. We're off." She left, waving her fingers, and said, "Ta-ta."

Aster pushed Jack into the office and closed the door. "You stood me up," Aster said, her lips taut. "We were supposed to have brunch."

Jack slapped his forehead. "Sorry. Forgot. Updates on the seminar."

She stiffened, smelling baby-powder perfume on him.

"What's the matter? You seem pissed off." He stepped back.

Aster snapped, "Looks like you enjoyed her more than me." She scowled at the lipstick on Jack's face.

"Look who's talking!" Jack spat back.

"What?" Aster said, incredulous.

"Herman. Apparently, you enjoy him more than me. Or will in the future." His voice rose.

"You ... you read my journal?" she said, outraged.

"You admit it then."

Aster planted her fists firmly on her hips. She huffed, "Can't believe ya did that. To top it off, you stood me up to have a roll in the hay with that bitch."

"How can you say that? I'd never."

Aster interrupted, "There's lipstick all over your face, your hair's a fright, and you reek of baby powder."

Worry spread across his face. "Liar! You won't admit it, but you don't want me. You lust after Herman."

His words struck like a blow to the chest. Aster trembled. "I ... I can't do this." She turned and stormed out of his office.

❋ ❋

Once home, Aster hurried to the bathroom to vomit. The nausea, shortness of breath, and chest pain made her worry that she was having a heart attack. Just in case she was, she took some magnesium to relax her muscles. Right now, dying felt like a viable option. To be hurt by Jack, a man who loved her, felt ten times worse than being hurt by a father who hated her.

Betrayal and despair fought like dragons in her mind. Her eyes filled with tears. *How could he do that to me? Every time I get close to someone, I get hurt.*

She flopped into bed, hugged a pillow, and cried herself to sleep.

Jack called the landline because Aster had apparently turned off her cell.

On the first ring, Aster sat up in bed. The old answering machine still worked. She had replaced the worn-out tape of Keith with a new one. She rushed into the kitchen to listen to herself say, "Hello, this is Aster. Please leave a message." Too emotional to deal with anyone, she did not answer the phone, but listened to the caller leaving a message.

In a peaceful voice, Jack said, "We need to talk. I'm leaving early tomorrow. I'll call ya when I get back." He hung up without saying good-bye.

Caught in an inner whirlwind, a wave of loneliness struck Aster heavily. She already missed Jack. Not sure which emotion would rise up next, she hesitated. Deep down, what she really wanted was to talk to him, smell him, feel secure in his arms. Conflicted about whether to call him or not, she paced up and down the hallway. Feeling hopeless, she thought, *What am I, a huge bottle of relationship repellent?*

Trying to cope, she hopped on her bike and rode around for hours, pedaling on Boulder's bike trails. If her mind wandered to Jack, she reverted to her childhood church-choir days and started singing "Hallelujah." Sounding like a choir alto on skip, she found fragments of solace, riding among colonies of prairie dogs sunning their backsides.

The torturous three days Jack was gone, Aster tried to find order in life by cleaning. No matter how vigorously she scrubbed the bottoms of pots and pans, he haunted her thoughts. *I trusted him. Never again. I'm done with relationships.*

Her sleep-deprived eyes fixed upon Jack's prescription bottle on the windowsill over the sink. *This is a Jack-free zone. I'm throwing these away right now,* she thought. Rattling the bottle, she removed the lid to find two pain pills left over from his broken wrist. Fed up from lying in bed at night and obsessing about the situation, and feeling like a zombie suffering from jet lag, she dumped the pills in her mouth, desperate for sleep.

It was midafternoon, and her neighbor was mowing his lawn. Neither the drone of the mower nor a thought of Jack was going to get in the way of her sleep. Aster turned off the phone, pulled down the window shade, inserted earplugs, placed a sleep mask over her eyes, and slid into bed.

❋ ❋

The first rays of sunshine brightened the backyard. A robin at the bird feeder chirped merrily. Thirsty and in a drowsy haze, Aster filled a glass with water and shuffled to the patio. Squinting, she said to the bird, "Tone it down, would ya?" Wrapped in a pink velour floor-length bathrobe, she curled up in the chaise lounge.

Hearing footsteps, Aster yelled, "Hello!" She pushed a wisp of hair behind her ear.

Standing at the screen door, with his head hung low, he said, "It's Jack. How about a truce?"

Aster wanted to lunge into his arms, but she was too groggy. Unsure whether to raise her defense shields or not, she settled for the path of least resistance. Feigning apathy, she said, "Pull up a chair."

Jack noticed her haggard appearance. "Looks as though toothpicks would collapse under those eyelids. I'll go make coffee."

"Okay," she said, feeling itchy from the medication.

Jack waited in the kitchen for the coffee to brew before returning to the patio. He found his empty prescription bottle next to the sink. That was curious. Aster was too tidy to leave anything on the counter. Determined to get answers, he clenched his jaw and entered the patio, carrying two creamed cups of coffee.

"Thanks," Aster said, taking a large mouthful.

He sat there watching her, not sure where to begin.

"What?" She met his worried eyes.

Jack removed the empty prescription bottle from his pocket and waved it in the air. He managed to ask calmly, "Did you toss these or eat them?"

Aster confessed, "Couldn't sleep since ya left. I downed the last two like candy." Her puffy eyes had a hint of defiance.

Jack wrinkled his nose, and his voice escalated to a scold. "They're strong pills. One knocked me on my butt. Not exactly an overdose, but it's so unlike you to be that reckless."

"I wasn't myself. I lost it. Reality seemed too cruel. Right now, I'm paying for it. I got brain fog from ear to ear. Forgot how debilitating pain pills are," Aster said, rubbing a hand over her forehead.

"How long did you sleep?" he asked.

Getting annoyed at his attitude, she raised her voice. "Don't know. Twelve, maybe fifteen, hours. Grand total for the past three days! I checked out. Unplugged the phone and got some rest."

More agitated, Jack no longer held back. "I don't know where I stand between you and Herman. I called you all day, from both airports, at home, and in the car. You never picked up. My worst fear was that you were hooking up with him, and I got the boot."

"Herman? My massage therapist?" she said incredulously.

"You get naked for him every week."

She snorted, "I'm under sheets."

"You enjoy his hands on you so much, he turns you on," Jack blurted out.

"Oh yes. Cheap shot, the fact that you read my journal."

"An accident! I was half-awake and needed to write down a phone message. When I realized there was writing on the page, I felt bad I had ruined it. I glanced down and saw the passage about you and Herman having outrageous sex. I read only one page."

Aster remained curt. "Don't know whether to call you a voyeur or intruder. Actually, the dream weirded me out too. As you know, my dreams typically foretell the future. Carl Jung, the dream guru, would have called it an unconscious fantasy. His advice would be to 'live the dream.'"

"You mean have an affair?" he said worriedly.

"Not literally. Experience the dream to the fullest. Then, symbolically analyze how I feel about it."

"And the answer to that is?" Jack inquired.

"Purely whimsical. Logically, the dream stretched reality to an absurd level."

Jack whined, "Not much of an interpretation."

"Herman makes me feel good every week. I love how his hands help me relax. He's an obsessive-compulsive, meticulous about relaxing muscles. That is all he is to me in my real life. Befriending his neurosis on a personal basis would drive me up a tree. I like him for what he does. And I pay for that service. Period."

"You sure?" Jack questioned.

"Duh," Aster rolled her eyes. "Absolutely. Because the person I love is you, Mr. McFadden."

"But Herman aroused your sensuality," Jack pouted.

Aster exhaled heavily. "Historically, I have intense, vivid dreams. My brother used to call me a crazy rabbit, shaming me for being a fortuneteller. It's part of who I am. If it threatens you, I don't want to cater to your fear, because it will mean you don't understand who I am. That's an old wound I refuse to open."

"Still hurts. Thought I was enough for you," Jack said ruefully.

"You are. Just don't expect me to control my unconscious mind. Sometimes I struggle knowing if my dreams are true or not. That's why I dream journal, to help me sort it out. If I were interested in Herman, I would have never gotten involved with you."

"So, you choose me, huh?" His mood lightened.

"I hope it's a good choice," she confessed.

"Why wouldn't it be? We're old mates drawn together by destiny." Jack lifted his empty mug. "Refill?" He disappeared into the kitchen and came out with the coffeepot and a carton of half-and-half. He prepared the coffee.

Resting chin on fist, Aster said, "I'm too exhausted to volley with you. Just tell me straight out. Are you and Tasha hooking up?" She stared into his handsome hazel eyes, wondering if this would be her last savory look.

"What?" His tanned face soured.

Aster frowned at the memory of Tasha's lip prints on his cheeks.

Struck with shock, Jack's eyes enlarged. "God, no! Tasha is not my type. I can barely tolerate her."

"Truthfully?" demanded Aster.

"I swear. Believe me," Jack said as he held his heart. "You are jealous over Tasha! That woman is total pretense. She is not genuine like you. Everything about her is overdone. The person I'm attracted to is you, Aster Snowden."

"Tell me what happened in your office that day."

Jack explained Tasha's every move. As he stated every fact, Aster muscle tested his statement with her fingers. So far, Aster sensed Jack was telling the truth. Troubled by one more question, she asked, "Then why did you do the seminar in the first place?"

"For one, a career boost. Then, it occurred to me to use the money to take you on a trip. Thought it would be an adventure to visit places in our past lives. Stir up feelings and old memories."

"Really?" She looked surprised. Her inner eye saw the word TRUTH in large capital letters. A quick muscle test confirmed it. She said, "Whoa! You mean that. Don't you?"

He broke into a huge smile. "Absolutely! Sorry I missed brunch. Also, reading your journal—my bad."

"Trusting people is my biggest issue in life. Gonna take me a while to let the dust settle," said Aster, finishing her coffee.

Jack held his hands over his shoulders as if calling a truce. "You made your point. I'll never open your journal again. I hate arguing. This is our first spat. I'm a Libra. I love harmony. How about a hug?"

Chapter 13

Soaking Wet

Aster lay sprawled on the couch, reading travel brochures that offered alluring getaways to Europe, Africa, and Australia. For the past two days, she had no choice but to be indoors. A raging monsoon from the Gulf of Mexico had overtaken Boulder, violently rinsing off September's dust. A sudden whack of thunder lifted her right off the upholstered cushions.

After a moment, she drew breath again. "That's close," she said, and counted, "One, two." With that, another boom vibrated the dinnerware in the hutch. She sat up and listened intently. The next crack sounded five seconds later. As she counted to seven, the electrical potency dissipated, thankfully drifting that many miles away. Keeping an attentive ear to the sky, the sound of a waterfall had her rush to the window. A swipe of her hand erased the mist on the pane. Unable to see the source of pouring water, Aster slipped on a burgundy raincoat and an old pair of tennis shoes, went to the front door, and stepped outside.

The street had transformed into a flowing stream. The gardens turned to mud. Aster walked through the ankle-deep water of the recessed sidewalk. On the south side of the house, she shielded her eyes from the downpour and looked up at the problem. Rainwater gushed over the edge of the gutter and flowed into the basement window well. Only a trickle came out of the downspout.

Aster thought, *Damn! Must be clogged. I'd better fix it before the well fills and the window blows.* She began to fret as sirens screeched out flash-flood warnings. *It's only gonna get worse. Last thing I want is a flooded basement; that could lead to mold.*

Trying not to panic, she fetched an aluminum extension ladder from the garage and set it up against the eaves. Armed with a bucket and long barbecue tongs, she climbed toward the roof. Halfway up, her left foot slid along the rung until it met the ladder's side. She stopped and nervously said, "Yikes! It's slippery. I can do this. I'll go slower." Reaching for the next rung, she grasped it with a white-knuckled grip. Wedging her foot against the side of the ladder, she rose another rung and proceeded with the other foot, using the same precaution, doing a bull-legged climb up the ladder to the eave. Even though every muscle in her body tensed, she willed her mind to remain calm. The oncoming volume of rain made it impossible to look up. To see properly, she climbed until her head rose above the eave, positioning her face to look down upon the clog. Thankful to stop and lean into the ladder to secure her position, she let out a sigh.

Wasting no time, Aster removed the twigs and pine needles with the tongs, depositing the debris into the bucket.

Then, somehow, the whole situation seemed absurd to the point of her feeling giddy. She thought flippantly, *I used to climb like a monkey as a kid. Once I figured out the footing, no problem scaling the ladder. No big whoop with this rain either. Heck, if I had soap, I could strip down and take a shower.*

Once the clog was cleared, Aster exclaimed, "It worked! No more waterfalls! I didn't need a man to fix it."

Aster dropped the tongs onto the grass and hung the bucket in the crook of her arm. As she clambered down the ladder, she marveled inwardly, *This wasn't half as scary as dealing with my father's rage. I'm not a helpless kid. I'm a tough old bird, taking care of myself.*

Before she knew it, she lost focus on her technique, and the tread-bare shoe slid across the rung. Both feet swung off the ladder and arced up like a swinging pendulum. The momentum tipped the ladder, causing her to lose her grip.

"A-a-agh!" her own terrified scream resounded.

Inches before touching ground, the ladder pushed Aster headfirst into the egress window. Her splayed arms folded on impact inside the narrow cavity. Her head plummeted deep into the muddy water, leaving her feet, still in the tennis shoes, in the open air, kicking madly. Tangled in the raincoat, trying to jockey out of the position, she could not budge. Submerged in a good four feet of water, she struggled fiercely, thinking, *Damn! Can't breathe! Need air! Help! Someone—anyone—find me!*

Then, she stilled. A vague sensation of her shirt wicking up moisture was her last corporeal memory. As she floated backward, she saw a tiny golden dot growing larger. An archway made of clouds appeared. Keith stood at the gate beckoning her forward. Her late husband looked vibrant. Just as she reached for his hand, everything went blank.

Jack pulled into the driveway and thought it curious to see a bucket tipped over next to the house. Before he got out of the car, a yellow raincoat zipped past him. By the size, the person appeared to be a man who ran to the house and began pulling on something. Jack got out quickly, checking out what the man was doing.

"Hey buddy, what's up?" Jack asked, shielding his eyes from the rain.

"Grab a leg and help pull her out," the stranger shouted. His yellow rain gear glistened. A constant stream of droplets fell from the bushy brows and pug nose that stuck out of the oval opening of the hood.

"Oh my God, Aster!" Jack panicked, recognizing her shoes.

The two men squatted on the sodden ground and hoisted Aster up from the window well.

"Let's get her onto the breezeway. It's too wet out here. Come on," ordered the man.

The rain pelted them relentlessly. By the time they carried her inside, Jack was soaking wet from head to toe. He paid no heed, for Aster lay on the floor, nonresponsive.

The stranger initiated CPR and managed to get water out of Aster's lungs.

Jack knelt beside her. He prayed with all his might, "Come on, Aster, take in air. ... Breathe! Please breathe!" Tears coursed down his cheeks.

More CPR by the stranger, and more water seeped out. ... And then, finally, Aster retched.

"That's good; get it all out," said the unfamiliar voice of the helpful stranger.

"Thank God! Babe, you're alive!" Jack cried.

Aster coughed, her ashen cheeks streaked with mud.

"I'm Felix Carelli," the man said, taking off his raincoat. He had a balding crown and the broad shoulders of a football player.

"Who?" Aster mumbled before suffering another coughing fit.

"I'm your neighbor from across the street," Felix answered.

"Oh," she said dumbfounded. Her vision shifted in and out of focus.

"We need to get you out of these wet clothes. I want to move you into the house where it's warmer. First, I want to check for more injuries. Aster, can you move your ankles?" Felix asked.

Mechanically obeying orders, Aster flexed her ankles. In fact, all her joints worked fine. Aster did not say a word until the exam was over.

She looked at Felix, perplexed, and asked, "Keith's gone? I'm not dead?"

"You're very much alive. Aster, you're home in your own breezeway. I'm here," Jack said tenderly, rubbing her cold hand.

The sound of his voice coaxed Aster out of the fog. She said faintly, "Jack McFadden. Wh-what happened?"

"Felix and I pulled you out of the window well. You nearly drowned. Felix gave you CPR," Jack explained, forcing his voice to stay calm.

"I fixed the clog ... floated up to the clouds ... met Keith," Aster rasped. The talking made her cough again.

Felix interjected, "I looked out the window, and I noticed you on the ladder, clearing the gutter. I went to get my rain gear on, figuring you might need help. It's very dangerous to be clearing the gutter in this type of weather. As I crossed the street, I saw the ladder and bucket strewn in disarray, but it took me a minute to see your feet sticking out of the window well. Jack arrived just in time; he helped me pull you out."

Aster's lips quivered, and she shivered. Flashes of being upside down and unable to breath began to unnerve her. Through chattering teeth, she managed to say, "Th-thanks."

"You're chilled," Jack said worriedly.

"Can you stand? You need dry clothes." Felix offered a hand.

Aster rose unsteadily. She swooned on wobbly legs.

Felix caught her. His bulky arms scooped her up effortlessly and carried her to the living room.

"Put her on the sofa," Jack said leading the way. He removed her raincoat and began untying the soggy laces of her tennis shoes.

"I'll get towels. Bathroom must be down the hall. Right?" Felix said.

"On the right," Jack answered.

Felix came back, holding Aster's bathrobe. He said, "This was hanging on the back of the bathroom door. Here's a towel to dry her off."

Aster stared off into space, reliving the terror over and over—falling, almost drowning, and having a near-death experience—while Jack undressed her, dried her with the towel, and wrapped her in a bathrobe. Her blue lips shivered frantically as he placed a blanket over her.

Jack lost his composure. "Aster needs another blanket, maybe a doctor. How do we deal with this?"

"She's in shock," Felix reassured him. "We could take her to the hospital, but the roads are flooding. Probably not safe to drive. Let's get a weather report on the news."

Agitated, Jack grabbed the remote and turned on the TV.

Observant of the charged atmosphere, Felix took control. "Fix her some warm tea. Perhaps something stronger for you and me."

"Okay." Jack paused, frantic, unsure what to do first.

Felix held out a palm for the remote. "Give me that. I'll find an update."

"Good. I'll dig around in the cupboards," Jack said.

As the newscaster announced the weather update, a ticker tape ran across the bottom of the screen for the hearing impaired: "Flash-Flood Warning for Boulder County."

Moments later, the voice of a newscaster projected through the living room: "A hundred-year flood has swelled Boulder Creek past its banks. The bike trail is under water. The creek is now reaching the underside of the Broadway Bridge. City officials demand that everyone stay off the streets. All canyon roads are closed. Residents along the mountainsides, evacuate to higher ground."

Jack brought a mug of ginger-chamomile tea for Aster and set it on an end table. He dashed back into the kitchen and brought out two white-colored mixed drinks for Felix and himself.

"This is a horchata with rum," he told Felix

"Horchata?" Felix asked.

"It's a spiced Mexican drink made of rice. Cheers," said Jack.

Felix took a sip. He said, "Not bad. Did ya hear the news?"

"Yep. Time to build an ark," Jack said, taking a large gulp.

"Intense hundred-year flood. If you ask me, Aster should see a doctor. By the way her eyes failed to track my finger when

I checked her, I can tell that she has a concussion. If she starts vomiting, I can drive you two to the hospital. My pickup truck has high clearance, and I've got oversize tires on that puppy," Felix offered.

"Thanks. I'll take you up on that if need be. I'm so relieved you got Aster breathing. Man, I don't know what I would have done without you. You were this yellow blur that came out of nowhere. I hadn't a clue Aster was stuck in the window well. I couldn't have pulled her out by myself. I owe you big time," Jack said.

Felix gave an acknowledging nod. He added, "The way she was wedged in made her dead weight even heavier. We did some great teamwork getting her out that fast."

The tea helped Aster calm down. She let out a sigh and said, "Whew! That whole thing was so intense."

"Aster, how are you feeling?" Jack said. He knelt by the sofa and peered into her tired green eyes.

"Like I just came back from the dead," Aster said in disbelief.

"You did, thank God. I prayed so hard and loud, I think the archangels had to cover their ears," Jack said, caressing her cheek.

Aster smiled at Jack. A dose of love was exactly what she needed. Her spirits lifted sufficiently, and she turned to the pug-nosed guy. She raised heavy eyelids, asking, "And you are ... my neighbor?"

"The blue house." He pointed in the direction of the street. "I'm Felix."

"The whistler," she blurted without thinking. The annoying, tuneless neighbor whose mouth she had wished to cork with a carrot.

"He saved your life. Our hero of the day," Jack said proudly.

"It's nothing. I'm a retired firefighter. Makes me feel like I'm back on the job. Miss it a bit," Felix confided.

"You're too young to be retired," Jack remarked.

"Disability. Lung cancer in remission," Felix explained.

They all shared their stories over tea and rum. After they toasted to their health, Felix announced that he had things to do.

"We ought to have you over for a BBQ. Aster's a great cook," Jack said.

"Sure. Sounds good." Felix nodded his approval.

"If it ever dries up. Thanks again, Felix," Aster said slowly. She looked worn out.

"My pleasure. Glad to see you pull through. You seem better. Jack gave me a business card. I'll call you later on and see how you're doing." Felix headed toward the door.

"Thanks again, buddy." Jack gave him a bear hug.

Felix patted Jack on the back. "Good teamwork there. Catch ya later. Bye." He left.

Once they were alone, Jack said, "I was so worried. Don't ever do something like that again. Can't bear it. You could have died." He sat next to Aster on the couch and embraced her fervently. Into her ear he uttered, "You mean everything to me."

"Same here," she said, sounding spacey.

The possibility that Aster suffered from an unseen brain injury had Jack suggest, "My sweet vixen, you need to see a doctor. Get some scans to make sure you're okay."

"We're supposed to stay off the roads. It's unsafe. There's too much flooding."

"But this is an emergency. What if you go into a coma?" Jack said.

Aster insisted, "Little cold and sore is all. A hot bath with Epsom salts would be nice."

"I'm staying in there to keep an eye on you in that water. In case you pass out."

"Relax. I know the drill. If I start puking, you can take me to the ER."

He shot her an admonishing glance. "You sound like a tough chick that grew up in boot camp. I'm tempted to take you to the hospital for X-rays now."

Aster said, "No need. A hot soak ought to do the trick. I've got goose bumps piggybacking on one another."

While the tub filled, Jack went to the basement to check how badly the water had seeped in through the window. A steady stream went down the wall, forming a small puddle on the floor; a few inches away, the water drained into the sump pump. The muted light that came from the window suddenly turned dark. Wondering if a tree had blown over, he rushed upstairs and ran out to the porch to find Felix placing a large rock onto the plywood that newly covered the opening.

Jack yelled over the roaring rain, "Felix, what you up to?"

Felix walked closer. He said, "Preventing more rain from coming in."

"You didn't have to do that. Thanks again. The sump pump is right below the window. There won't be much damage," Jack told him.

In a matter of fact way, Felix said, "I'm all about prevention. As much trauma as I've seen on the job, it's always more intense when it's close to home. This whole ordeal got me all worked up. I love fixing things. Had to do something constructive so I'd sleep tonight."

"Can't thank you enough for being such a guardian angel."

"Right place, right time. Things happen. Glad I could help you. Got a Crock-Pot of chili calling to me. See ya." Felix waved.

"Bye," Jack called after him.

Jack went back inside and called out to Aster. "Hey, sweetie, there's only a small puddle in the basement. No biggie. Can't believe it: Felix covered the hole with plywood. That guy is something else."

Aster had not moved. "Good," she said, sounding fatigued.

Jack bolted into the bathroom to turn the water off in the tub. He returned to find Aster still shivering.

"Ready for a hot soak?" he asked.

She nodded.

Jack helped her to the bathroom. "Whew, tipsy," she said, holding onto him.

He gave a short chuckle. "It's okay if you want to call me Talking Bird. Nurturing you is nothing new."

Aster smiled at the Jack-ish nostalgia.

The minute she removed her bathrobe, Jack said worriedly, "Look at those big bruises on your arm! They're new."

Aster looked in the mirror. "Yep. Get me the arnica cream on the back of the toilet. I'm starting to feel stiff too."

"Here, I'll dab some on your finger. Let it work its way in before you get into the tub," Jack said squeezing the tube.

"A-a-ah," Aster said, sighing as she sank into the slanted-back tub.

Jack knelt beside the tub, staring at her in a contemplative manner. He said, "Never seen your hair in such a messy, disheveled state. You look like one sassy mama. Sort of turns me on. Makes me want to marry you. But first things first; I'm washing the mud out of your hair."

"Aren't you the romantic type! There's a plastic rinsing cup under the sink," Aster slurred, as if in a stupor.

Chapter 14

A Family Affair

The next morning, nausea gripped Aster's stomach. Hoping oatmeal might settle her gut, she braved several spoonfuls, but as soon as they landed, the food came back up, soiling her lap.

"Yuck. Reminds me of morning sickness," she groaned miserably.

"That's it! You're going to the hospital," Jack said, holding his nose. He slid the kitchen trash bucket beside her feet.

"Gross. I can't deal," she said, removing her pajamas and tossing them into the trash.

Breathing through his mouth, Jack grimaced, sealing the trash bag. He said nasally, "Babe, let's get you dressed, and then I'll call Felix. Okay?"

"Yeah. Can you get my yoga outfit? I just wanna lie down on the couch," she said, clutching her stomach.

Jack helped her dress. He set her purse and phone on the end table.

"Thanks. I'm tired," Aster said. She dozed off on the sofa while Jack talked to Felix.

"Felix, I think you ought to drive your truck into Aster's garage," Jack said. "I just need to move her car to make room," Jack suggested.

"Good plan; best to keep her dry. I'll be right over. Bye," replied Felix.

Jack hung up the phone. He called to Aster, "Babe, wake up. It's still raining like crazy. Felix is giving us a lift."

She did not answer.

"Aster, did you hear me?" Jack spoke louder. He tensed up as he neared the sofa, for she lay too still to be in a deep sleep. Unsure if Aster had suffered a fatal brain bleed, or if she were in a coma, Jack panicked. He placed an ear over her chest; he heard nothing. Then, realizing he was too far over on the wrong side, he moved to the left, listening intently for signs of life. "Thank God!" he cried, hearing the faint rhythm.

A car horn blasted from the driveway.

"Felix is here. C'mon, Aster, wake up," Jack coaxed. He rubbed the back of her hand, to no avail.

Jack grabbed Aster's car keys and hurried to open the garage door. He got into Aster's car and drove it outside. The heavy rain on the windshield came down in such clear sheets, he did not need to use the wipers. Reluctant he had not at least grabbed a garbage bag for protection, Jack sprinted back inside, getting completely drenched.

Felix wasted no time backing his four-door red pickup truck into the garage. Wearing his rain gear, he promptly climbed out of the cab.

Felix hadn't been kidding about the oversize tires. Looking at them, Jack said, "What the heck you got on that puppy, one-and-a-half-foot clearance?"

"Just about," Felix replied matter-of-factly. He looked Jack up and down and said, "Nasty out there."

Jack nodded. He motioned for Felix to enter the house and then said anxiously, "Aster vomited earlier. Now she's conked out, and I can't wake her."

"Okay, Jack. You and I need to stay calm. Go get a towel and a bucket, just in case she vomits again. And I'm going to my truck. Meet you back here," instructed Felix.

Jack sped down the hallway.

Felix returned, carrying a plywood plank and bungee cords. He said to Jack, "Sorry I made a mess dismantling a shelf in the garage. We need to use this as a board to transport Aster into the truck. Does she have a yoga mat to soften it up?"

"Yeah. I'll go get it."

When Jack returned with the mat, Felix had put three bungee cords parallel on the floor and placed the plank over the cords.

"Here's the mat," Jack said.

"Hold onto it for a second. We're going to make a taco out of the blanket and wrap Aster in it," Felix said. He removed the blanket that covered Aster and placed it alongside the plank.

"So, you want the mat on the inside of the taco or the outside?"

"Inside."

Jack placed the mat.

"Okay, good. Now help me lift her onto the mat and then cover her up," Felix said, scooping Aster up by the shoulders while Jack lifted her legs.

With a few grunts, they set Aster in place. At her shoulders, waist, and feet, Felix used the bungee cords to fasten her to the cushioned plank.

"Nice custom stretcher. Shall we?" Jack said, eager to get going.

The two men hoisted Aster into the pickup truck bed. They used cushions from the sofa as wedges to prevent her from rolling around at turns. With Aster's purse slung over his shoulder and the bucket in hand, Jack clambered into the back as well, to keep an eye on her.

Aster awoke on a gurney rolling down the hospital corridor. She had been unaware of Jack talking into her ear the whole way to the hospital; unaware of the truck weaving a zigzag route through Boulder, avoiding flooded streets; unaware of the emergency-room doctor prying her eyelids open. Each ceiling light she passed under shone overly bright.

"Dim the lights," Aster uttered.

The gurney came to a halt. A black man with bristly short hair, wearing green scrubs, leaned in for a close look. He said, "Ms. Snowden, you're awake. I'm Nurse Cory. We are in the hospital, on our way to an MRI."

"I'm not dreaming, am I?" Aster said, noticing the intense constriction in her head. A constant stream of tears ran down the sides of her temples.

The MRI felt claustrophobic. Aster imagined the experience was similar to being in a sarcophagus. That seemed too dreary, so she changed the mental image to a time machine. Undoubtedly, Jack would appreciate the choice. More than anything, she wanted to sleep, but the deafening noise of the machine kept her on the edge of dreamworld. A vague thought that her brain was swelling gave a possible reason for the extreme headache.

When the scans were complete, Cory wheeled Aster back to the emergency room.

No longer in his wet clothes, Jack wore Denver Rockies sweatshirt and matching sweatpants that he'd purchased at the hospital gift shop. He lit up at the sight of Aster. Stroking her cheek ever so gently, he said, "Welcome back, love. You nodded off for a while. How ya doing?"

"Been better," she said with a sigh.

"The doctor said they want you to spend the night for observation. I'm staying too. They have a cot for me. I've texted Sam and Iris to let them know you are here."

"Thanks. Glad you're staying," Aster said, fatigued. She closed her eyes to shut out the flickering aura surrounding Jack.

Iris called after lunch the next day. She offered to drive down from Fort Collins, but because of the bad weather, Aster insisted that she stay put.

Sam, however, did not call. Ever since the divorce, Sam had lost respect for his mother. He sided with his father, blaming Aster as the selfish cheater. How dare his mother have the audacity to fall in love with Keith, another man. Sam was the center of his mother heart. He relied on her heavily because dad was either busy at work or out with friends.

For more than twenty years, Aster had prayed for forgiveness. She'd always wished for a stronger connection with Sam. She only saw him on birthdays and holidays, and even those occasions did not guarantee visits. She wanted to tell her son that she was spending the night in the hospital. She wanted to share the MRI results that her brain had been bruised. She wanted to report the advice the doctor had given, such as having bed rest, taking naps, moving her head slowly, not bending forward or lifting anything, and, most important of all, returning to the hospital if vomiting reoccurred or the blurred vision increased. However, in her current state, it felt like too much work to do all that explaining. Above all, she knew Sam would have no interest in the details.

Appreciating the one male in her life who cared, she adored Jack for sitting at her bedside in his new sports outfit, especially since she knew he was no baseball fan at all.

Aster said, "I wish Sam would call."

"Why don't you call him? Here's your phone," Jack said, giving it to her.

"Eh. I can't get my eyes to focus on the buttons," she complained. Secretly she felt relieved to have a valid excuse to put off making the call.

"I'll do it. He's probably eager for an update," Jack said, glad for something to do.

"No, stop. Sam and I are a bit estranged."

"I can't imagine anybody not liking you, especially your son," Jack said.

Aster cringed. "I'm embarrassed to say that Sam blames me for wrecking the family. You know, my affair with Keith. Never thought I'd be that woman, but I was a lost soul catering to everyone else but me. I was starving for love. I put my family in second place and chose Keith's affection. As a result, I suffered from guilt—and the loss of my son. So, as far as Sam is concerned, the ball is in his court. Last thing I want is to alienate him even further with too many messages. He'd think I was a whining old nag."

"I see. You endured dysfunctional love in both your family of origin and your first marriage," Jack said matter-of-factly.

Aster rolled her eyes. "Tsk. Shoot me point-blank. Yes. You recap quickly. It took my therapist years to convince me that I'm worthy of being loved."

"I agree 100 percent with your therapist." Jack gave a meaningful wink.

Jack touched Aster's core. Her eyes filled with tears.

"All right then, Aster, how about a compromise? I'll use my phone to give Sam an update," said Jack.

Aster looked hopeful. "Okay. Send a text. Make it short and sweet."

Jack pressed Sam's number and said, "Okay, ready. What should I say?"

Aster replied, "Tell him, 'Your mom spent the night in the hospital. She has a slight concussion. Doctor said all is okay.'"

❋ ❋

At dawn the next day, the rain finally stopped. The doctor, a round-faced man with Japanese features, entered Aster's room. He examined her pupil response and had her squeeze his fingers. Aster smelled a strong waft of coffee breath when he explained, "Remember, you need to rest your brain. That means very little jostling of the head. No bending forward. No fast head movements."

"Does that mean no bike riding?" Aster frowned.

"Absolutely. Your balance will be off," replied the physician.

"Yeah, I am a bit dizzy."

The doctor started listing other symptoms, counting them off on his fingers. "You may also experience some hypersensitivity to light, sound, smell, and/or high-activity situations."

"What type of activity?" she asked.

"From people. An intense person might overstimulate you, and so might a whole crowd," the doctor said.

Unenthusiastic about the limitations, Aster said, "If I promise to behave, can I go home now?"

The doctor looked at Jack and asked, "Are you family?"

"Boyfriend," Jack replied.

"If you can tend to her needs during recovery, for at least two weeks of nursing, I'll sign the release forms. If not, I want her here for a few more days," the doctor stated firmly.

Aster held her breath, craving the comforts of home. Jack took a quick glance at Aster, reading an imploring face similar to a begging dog at the dinner table. He said, "Of course I can; no problem."

Even though Aster wore sunglasses on the way home, she pulled the windshield visor down in the car. Getting little relief, she closed her eyes, but the motion of the car increased the nausea. When she cupped a hand over her brow, she found greater comfort.

Aster said, "Jack, my eyes are freaking out at the brightness. It feels a lot like getting my pupils dilated at the eye doctor's office."

"Bummer. Hang in there; we'll be home soon. Close your eyes."

The minute they arrived home, the drapes were drawn, and Aster retreated into bed.

Iris dropped in after lunch. Her tall and lean body entered Aster's bedroom, loaded down with a laptop bag slung over one shoulder, a purse over the other, a coffee mug in one hand, and bouquet of flowers in the other.

"Hi, Mom. It's weird to see you lying down in the middle of the day. How ya doing?" Iris set the purse and coffee on the dresser and the computer on the chair.

"Hi, sweetie," Aster said feebly.

Iris said enthusiastically, "Here, I brought you these. Look, baby's breath and daises. Aren't they cheery? The vase is blue and white; it'll match your kitchen." Her fishhook mouth broke into a smile as she placed the vase on the nightstand.

"They're beautiful," Aster returned in flat tone.

"Missed ya; just gotta kiss ya," Iris said, giving Aster a peck on the cheek.

The scarf around her neck had fallen to the pillow when she leaned over. Iris made her presence known. As usual, a mess ensued in her wake within a matter of seconds.

"Ditto," Aster said, returning a kiss.

"Got a headache?" Iris said, pushing her curly brown hair over her shoulder.

"Yeah, a whopper," Aster said, unconcerned by the clutter. It lifted her spirits to be in her daughter's company.

"Best cure for that is staying away from window wells. I can't believe you got up on a ladder in the middle of a storm," Iris said incredulously.

"Got in one of my fix-it modes. It was incredibly gratifying unclogging the gutter without a man's help. Getting caught up in the egress pit wasn't as much fun." Aster shrugged.

"That Wonder Woman move nearly killed you. It really rattled my cage. The possibility of losing both parents in the same year freaked me out," Iris scolded, reaching for her coffee.

"Looking back, it's all one big blur. Got some sense knocked into me, though. I'm paying for it now, bedridden with my head in a vise grip."

"Jack said you were in a zone. You couldn't remember your zip code or phone number," Iris said, changing her tone to a light reprimand.

"I'm better. The numbers came back today," Aster said in self-defense, then ran both numbers in her mind to check if she was telling the truth. She was.

"Good. Where is Jack? Is he working?" Iris asked.

"No, he's picking up some food."

Iris removed the phone from her purse, took a picture of Aster lying in bed, and then snuggled next to her mom and took another.

"Put that damned thing away. I'm a mess."

"Look. Here's proof you're slacking in bed in the middle of the day," Iris joked, showing her the pictures.

"Ugh. Delete them. My eyes are half closed in one, and I look hungover in the other," Aster said, disgusted.

"No. I'm sending them to Sam. He has deadlines at work. He won't be able to see you," Iris said, making excuses.

"Really? Why don't you just say it? Sam won't come because he doesn't want to."

Unable to deny the obvious, Iris changed course. "Sam is stubborn; runs in the family. We talked, and he asked questions about you."

"Yeah, like what? Am I dead yet?" Aster sounded agitated.

"Sam cares. He just has a funny way of showing it. His thick head is slowly getting the fact you were dying inside being married to Dad. Between Sam, Dad, and me, you came last. More often than not, you weren't even in the race. At some level, he gets it, because he doesn't want kids. He's a lot like Dad, not willing to give up his throne."

Aster rolled her eyes and said, "You really think he understands that I'm a person with needs too? My therapist said Sam and Bill were so codependent on me, they suffered great loss when I left. Plus, Sam's better off; the divorce forced him to be responsible. Iris, you were Little Miss Independence. You caught on really quick. Thank God, you understand."

Iris gave her a look like this was old news. "Yeah, I know," she said. "Mom, don't give up on Sam. He's coming around. We just lost Dad, and you're the only parent we have left."

Iris opened her laptop, typed a message, and sent it.

Iris did not stay long. She had a parent-teacher conference concerning a troublesome student later in the day.

* *

After two weeks of bed rest, Aster grew tired of staring at the four walls. She got up to go shower. The hot water felt soothing on her stiff muscles. She figured out that anchoring her elbow on the tiled wall would steady her balance, enabling her to close her eyes when washing her hair.

There was a knock on the bathroom door. Jack stuck his head inside and asked, "You okay in there?"

"Yeah." She turned off the water and grabbed a towel. As she dried off, she said, "Guess what, Jack? I feel hungry."

"That's a good sign. You need a change from miso soup, green drink, and cottage cheese. Hey, there's chicken soup I got at the deli in the fridge. I was gonna whip up my specialty: grilled cheese sandwich. You game?" he said.

"Sounds wonderful. I'm tired of wearing pajamas. I'm gonna put on my favorite jeans. After we eat, let's take a walk. I need some fresh air."

Jack set off for the kitchen.

Aster wrapped her wet hair in a bun. She put on her new pink cable-knit sweater and the jeans. The pants felt too loose to be her favorite pair. She went to the mirror to make sure she had the right ones. "Damn it," she said and then marched into the kitchen.

Jack stood at the stove, flipping over the grilled cheese.

"My favorite pants don't fit me anymore," she complained.

"What's wrong with them?" he asked.

She turned around. "Look. I've got diaper butt." She grabbed a handful of sagging denim.

"Oh, you mean your pants don't hug your ass like they normally do. I like your butt."

Not finding any humor in the situation, Aster changed into a pair of leggings. Determined get her butt back, she ate the entire lunch.

Afterward, she and Jack stepped outside for a walk up the street.

Garbed in dark sunglasses and visor, Aster said, "Sorry to put a wrench in our plans. We have to cancel our fantasy trip until my brain heals. Tomorrow, I'm clearing my health-coach calendar until after the New Year."

"No worries. Things happen for a reason."

While they strolled along Glenwood Drive, she said, "Look at all the debris from the flooding." An assortment of soggy drywall, mattresses, books, and carpeting were heaped at the curbsides.

Jack replied, "The storm left its mark. Lots of my coworkers are fighting mold and need to remodel. Interesting how some homes were hit harder than others. I'm glad my townhome didn't flood. I have no basement. Lucky your house sits up higher than the road, so most of the water drained into the sump pump. Felix told me all the hardware stores sold out of sump pumps. Hoyt Perkins, who lives in that tan brick house, drove to Denver to buy one." Jack adjusted his fedora for better eyeshade.

"I feel fortunate all we had to do was minimal mopping," Aster said, thinking about the time and money her neighbors had spent cleaning up their homes.

The walk around the block left Aster exhausted. They passed the egress window that nearly took her life, and neither had the wherewithal to acknowledge it. She said, yawning, "I really needed to get out of the house. But, right now, I need to lie down."

Jack held open the screen door of the breezeway. "After you, my dear."

Aster kicked off her shoes and shuffled through the kitchen. Too tired to obsess over the dirty dishes on the counter, she plucked a sunflower seed from the bottom of her foot and tossed it into the trash. She said, "Enough cleaning for today. This place is a sty."

"Looks fine to me." Jack avoided the hint.

Aster gave him a stern look. "I know."

"My mess tolerance is way different from yours. Got an idea," Jack said, grabbing his cell phone. "I'll see if Rosita can clean for you."

"Hire a maid? Too embarrassing. She'll think I'm a slob." Aster's languid tone hid her anxiety about frivolous spending.

"You're joking," he said incredulously.

"Don't want a stranger rifling through my things," she protested.

"Rosita's trustworthy. She's been working for me for ages." Jack placed the phone call and made all the arrangements for the following day. "I'm here half the week, messing things up. Rosita is my treat."

"No. I can pay," Aster countered.

"I insist. You're not working." He looked at his watch. "Come on. I'll drive you to your massage. It's in fifteen minutes."

On the drive to the appointment, Jack brought up the subject of money once again. He said, "I'm concerned about your welfare. Along with your head injury, your neck is sprained, and you have compressed vertebrae. Going every other day for a massage is expensive. You're paying out of pocket. It adds up quickly."

"Oh, I'm fine. Inherited some money when I sold Aunt Gertie's house," she said, telling a half-truth. Thirty thousand of it her ex had stolen during the divorce. She held her tongue about the millions she'd won playing the lottery, thinking, *Jack would be impressed to know the numbers came to me in a dream.*

An hour later, Jack picked up Aster. Looking rather content, she said, "I'm so glad I found this injury specialist, Tom. He says the massage is keeping my muscle tissue soft and opening up the compression in my spine faster than normal."

"Nice. Yeah, I can tell you are moving around better. I picked up a snack from the Greek Goddess," Jack said, setting the bag on her lap.

Aster opened the bag. "Ah, smells good. I'd starve if it weren't for you," she said.

"Don't want to jump a bag of bones, now, do I?" Jack joked.

"You goofball. I think it's romantic you feed me every day."

He smiled. "Restaurants and deli to-go food are my specialties." He pulled into Aster's driveway, offered her a hand out of the car, and held on until they got inside.

"Thanks for being so accommodating," Aster said. She kissed him and then pulled away at the sound of a stomach growling. "Was that me or you?"

"Me. Food's getting cold. Let's eat," Jack said. He strode over to the table and pulled out a chair. "For you, my lady. Have a seat, and I'll serve the food."

"Oh dear. It's sort of fun being queen for the day."

At each setting, Jack placed a small tray of gyros, hummus, and garbanzo balls, along with plastic forks and cups filled with pink lemonade. In a sanguine tone he said, "I even remembered napkins this time." He dropped one next to each of the forks.

"Jack, you're spoiling me," Aster said. She had hoped for lighter food, perhaps a salad, but did not have the heart to refuse.

"Look at this," Jack said.

Aster looked at the piece of paper that leaned against her pink lemonade. Obviously, the scrap had come from the bag of food. It read, "Goddess."

"How adorable," she said, cracking her first smile of the day.

Handsome hazel eyes glowed as he stuffed the half-eaten garbanzo ball into his mouth.

"You're in a cheerful mood. I thought only sex left you this happy. What's up?" she asked, wishing the brain fog would lift.

"Thought we could talk about it after our meal." He bit into the gyro. "Hmm."

Aster watched his jaw work. She grew impatient. "Not fair to leave me hanging. Come on, out with it."

"Since we did it before, I was wondering if you wanted to do it again." He took another bite mischievously.

"What? Can you be any more cryptic?" She played along with him.

He lifted a finger, indicating he had a mouthful of food. His slow, savory eating style left no room for speed.

Finally, after a swig of lemonade, he took hold of Aster's hand. "I'm asking if you'll marry me."

"You're serious." Aster flushed, studying his face.

Her first marriage, to Bill, had transpired too fast and ended in divorce. Keith and she lived together for a year before tying the knot, and the marriage had lasted until he died, twenty years later. Thinking the latter a wiser choice, she said, "Perhaps we should dwell under the same roof through the four seasons to see if we are compatible."

"I kinda asked you when you were taking a bath ... on the day you nearly drowned."

"Sorry. Aside from nightmares of falling and dying, the aftermath is one big blur," she said.

"Fair enough. You were out of it. Timing wasn't right because I didn't have one of these." He opened a black velvet box and presented a stunning diamond ring. A border of smaller stones surrounded the larger oval center stone.

"Jack, you maniac!" Aster gasped. Her eyes enlarged, first from surprise, and then at the thought of protecting her secret fortune. She balked inwardly; *I've got a perfect nest egg lined up for retirement. Marriage divides assets in half.*

Not expecting the hesitation, he frowned.

"Sweetie cakes, I love you dearly. You just caught me by surprise; that's all," she faltered.

"No pressure. I had the desire to ask you the night we consummated our relationship," Jack confessed.

"The day we encountered the mountain lion? At the beginning?"

"Yes, ma'am. Afterward, I dug through my old trunk to find this ring. Envisioned it on your finger," he said dreamily.

"Really? Ya never told me."

"I worried you'd think it was premature."

"Got that right," Aster admitted.

"Actually, that's not 100 percent accurate. At the park, when I first saw you, I felt a big gong vibrate in my chest. I wanted you as my wife right then. The fear of sounding desperate made me wait until now to pop the question. I believe it's the right time to ask if you'll marry me." He looked as if the cost of his words risked the very foundation of his being.

"You romantic, tortured soul." She faked a cough and drained her lemonade.

The words *prenuptial agreement* flashed in her mind. Unexpectedly, a wave washed over Aster, as if she were caught in a dream. A fleeting image of Grannyme snapping her fingers appeared, then vanished. Like magic, all Aster's worries disappeared. Somehow, the idea of being Jack's wife felt right. Not sure why such a goofy response followed, she found herself saying, "If you hang the toilet paper roll the right way, and don't pee on the seat, yes, I'll marry you."

Jack's face relaxed as he leaned forward for a kiss. He stopped inches away from her lips. "There's a correct way to hang toilet paper?" He sounded perplexed.

"Oh yeah, the open end goes over the roll, not under. That way, there's no struggle to find the end." Aster said, smiling at the offhand humor.

"I get it. It's the little things that make a relationship. I have a coworker who teaches a weekend course that's actually called The Little Things in Relationships," Jack quipped and then kissed her lightly. "Hmm, a citrus kiss."

Impressed that Jack even knew about the little things, Aster gazed into his hazel eyes and said, "You know it's uncanny how our destiny unfolded. We met, fell in love, and now plan to marry. The marriage will be a major bonus to our eternal lovers' vow."

Overcome by such wonderment, content to retain the state of bliss, Aster pushed away the vexing quest, the haunting riddle she could not figure out. Considering postponing or perhaps dropping the task completely, she reasoned, *why should I need to find the glorious grail? My cup is full right now. Does life get any better than this?*

"Yes," Grannyme echoed in her ear.

Aster tuned out Grannyme and focused on her future husband.

Jack lifted his brows up and down, "Yep. See if this fits; it used to be my nanna's." He passed her the heirloom ring.

"It's beautiful. This style is a floret," Aster said, awestruck.

"A flower for my flower." He beamed.

Aster slipped the band onto her ring finger and found the size too big. "Nanna must have been a big woman. The only finger the ring fits is my middle one."

"Rotund describes Nanna best. We can fix that; make it your own." Jack stood and aimed his cell phone at Aster. "Now hold your chin." He snapped several pictures.

Chapter 15

The Thrifters

By October, Aster's head cleared. Residual symptoms such as sensitivity to light, sound, and crowds remained. The constant bed rest inspired her to get out of the house. She perused the *Daily Camera* newspaper for local events. Spotting an estate sale, she phoned Galen.

"Galen, I'm going to an estate sale today. You wanna join me?"

"Yes, I do. I love thrifting. Actually, I'm at the used-books store in Boulder," Galen said.

Aster sounded excited. "Great! Pop on over to my house. The sale starts in an hour. I want to be there when the doors open. That way, we can brush wings with the early birds and get first dibs on the good stuff."

Half an hour later, the two women climbed into Aster's white Subaru Outback and headed west. Dressed in tattered jean shorts and an old cap-sleeved blouse, Aster opened all the windows. The inside of the car was much warmer than the balmy seventy-two degrees outside.

"You look like you're dressed to clean the garage," Galen commented. She wore a flat cap with blue and white engineering stripes. Beneath the brim, the wind blew wisps of gray hair back away from her face.

"I grew up thrifting with my aunt. Aunt Gertie used to dress in ratty old clothes, evoke pity in the sellers, and then haggle out of pure joy."

"Clever character. Bet she and I would have gotten along," Galen said.

Aster nodded and said, "Gertie was a hoot. We pretended to be sleuths rummaging through a stranger's home and picking up clues to figure out what type of person lived there. Then, on the ride home, we fabricated a bio on what the person did, looked like, and so on," Aster recalled fondly.

"Sleuthing part sounds like fun," Galen replied.

"Gertie made me laugh. She came up with odd voices and silly ticks that would have impressed Walt Disney," Aster reminisced.

"Goofy Gertie sounds so much better than Raging Regina," Galen said rather flippantly. She glanced at Aster.

Underneath her visor and sunglasses, it was obvious that Aster's face fell.

Galen had a way of painfully telling the truth. She said, "Sorry. Your mom was a drag; it must have been awful being ignored all the time."

"Forget Regina. Let's have some fun."

"Okay, but first things first; I haven't a clue where we're going."

"Fourth and Cedar," Aster said, holding up a folded newspaper clipping. Aster shrank the image of her mother to the size of a salt granule and stored the minuscule piece in a dusty memory compartment.

Galen snatched the ad and read it aloud: "'Estate Sale, Friday, Saturday, and Sunday, from 10:00 a.m. until 2:00 p.m. Something for everybody: furniture, kitchen utensils, books, jewelry, tools, and more.'"

"A mother-lode sale," Aster replied.

"We girls are gonna do some recycling," Galen sang out.

"Oh yeah. We're gonna wheel and deal," Aster sang back, happy to be in a different part of town.

After parking on Fourth Street, Aster said, "It's Jack's

birthday on the fourteenth. Maybe I can find him a present." She left the windows open, sensing that the neighborhood was safe.

The house appeared to be a ranch, but checking out the sloped terrain of the yard, it was obvious there was a walkout basement or lower level in the back. The decorative landscaping and elaborate etched glass door gave the impression the inhabitants were well off. A sign taped to the door read, "Please remove your shoes."

Aster and Galen walked barefoot on the oak floor and plush Navajo rug in the living room. The furniture and wall hangings remained in their original locations, whereas the smaller personal effects were arranged neatly on tables. Everything had price tags attached. By the quality of the window treatments, the marble around the fireplace, and the indirect lighting, Aster deduced that an interior decorator had spared no expense designing the room.

A professional estate vendor, a chubby, fiftyish, puffy-eyed woman wearing a red visor, greeted them. "Hello, I'm Vicky. Welcome. Feel free to shop around. Every room has something for sale. Downstairs and garage too."

Aster and Galen gave quick hellos and headed for the kitchen. Open cupboards, counters, and dining table displayed all imaginable housewares.

"Pay dirt," Aster said, finding a set of wooden spoons.

"Nice toaster oven. Mine's on the fritz," Galen said, picking it up from the counter. Since the toaster was bulky, she set it by the cashier's feet to purchase later.

As they left to check out the bedroom down the hall, Aster noticed a stack of blue-and-white sandwich plates with the Star of David in the center. She mouthed "Jewish." Aster had to step aside for a large man wielding a cane and coming out the hallway. The polite gesture caused her to bump into a coffee table and knock off a book. Embarrassed by the graceless move, she picked it up and took interest. The cover read, "*Hot Springs of the Rocky Mountains,*" by Curtis Stone. Judging by the dog-eared pages and slightly worn cover, Aster suspected the owner liked to soak in hot water.

The bedroom was spacious, almost as if two bedrooms had been converted into one. The room no longer had a bed or dresser; instead, in the middle an island of vending tables held assorted wares, exhibiting old western artifacts, both cowboy and Native American. Busy eyes scanned item after item. The "cowboy" paraphernalia consisted of gun cartridges, saddlebag, lariat, bridle, and a hand-crank butter churner. The "Native American" collectibles included things like beaded headbands, a turquoise necklace, a drum, wool blankets, arrowheads, and an animal skull. On the walls, old photos of Indian women, braves, chiefs, and Appaloosa horses hung among sandpaintings. In the walk-in closet fringed cowboy shirts hung from the rack. Leather riding boots and cowboy hats sat on the shelves. Aster got the impression a man had owned these clothes and ridden in parades, emulating Buffalo Bill.

The animal skull caught Aster's eye. It had the general shape of a booted moccasin and was decorated with semiprecious stones. She picked up the skull to read the tag: "Jeweled Coyote Skull, fifty dollars." Inspecting the stones, she identified them as green turquoise, red jasper, and blue lapis. Unsure what the black-and-gray speckled one was, she turned to Galen, "Do know what stone this is?"

"Snowflake obsidian. Helps get rid of anger and resentment," Galen said, drawing on her extensive knowledge of gem lore.

"Turquoise protects travelers, and lapis aids in communication. They're the only ones I know. What does the jasper do?" asked Aster.

"Assists in astral travel. The overall message of these gems grouped together is 'Speak peacefully while traveling in the spirit world.' Is that a dog skull?"

"A coyote. It's a perfect totem for Jack, the psychic maniac," Aster said affectionately. "He's getting this for his birthday. Just have to find a shoebox to wrap it in."

"Nice touch. When we're done with the lower level, let's go see what's in the garage. Bound to be treasures there," Galen suggested.

After finding nothing of interest on the lower level, they headed out the back door and descended on a flagstone path to the garage that sat adjacent to a paved alley. They did not want to bother going upstairs for their shoes, so they ventured forth barefoot.

The garage smelled of a lawn mower filled with gasoline; a fond reminder of the toolshed attached to the barn at Aunt Gertie's. Aster let out a contented sigh and scanned the tools, paint cans, and lawn furniture sprawled on the concrete floor. A cardboard box with dusty flaps caught her attention. She peered inside and smelled musty medical books that probably had not seen daylight in decades.

Galen snatched up the rake. "Nice new handle," she said, happy with her find.

Aster pointed at the box, saying, "The guy who lived here must have been a retired doctor."

"Who seriously played Cowboys and Indians," Galen chimed in as they returned to the house.

The house was now swarming with people scavenging for a deal. A line had formed at the checkout area. Galen and Aster stood in the queue, waiting for their turn to pay.

Galen whispered in Aster's ear, "That lady stuck a watch and cuff links in her purse. Check it out. The one with black poodle hair to her shoulders."

Aster turned to see Lydia Driftwood slipping a bronze statue of a horse into her handbag. "She was one of my clients. The worst energy vampire ever. Hide me."

It was too late. Lydia and Aster locked eyes.

Lydia's shrill voice assaulted the air. "Aster Snowden. My horoscope said I might run into a disappointment today. Stylish outfit." Disapproving eyes scanned Aster's tattered jean shorts.

"Lydia, you gonna pay for that horse you stuck in your purse?" Aster volleyed back.

"This is Dr. Schneider's house. He was an old friend. I lent him the horse. I'm simply taking it back," Lydia broadcast loudly, as if trying to impress all who were present with her connection to the late doctor.

"Taking without asking. Not an honest approach, now is it?" Galen said.

Lydia shook a finger. "Don't be absurd. You and your friend are too uptight." In a haughty manner, she turned and walked out the front door.

Vicky, the chubby estate vendor, heard the conversation. Aghast, she said, "She's a liar and a thief." With that, she took off after Lydia.

Galen acted quickly. She handed Aster the rake and fled outside.

Aster rushed to the door and watched Vicky stop Lydia from getting in her car. Galen slipped between the women and leaned against the driver's door blocking the entrance to the car. They were too far away for Aster to hear the heated conversation. Lydia angrily flung the purse into Vicky's arms. Galen moved aside, and Lydia got in her car and drove off.

Vicky and Galen came back into the house. Galen said, "I saw her take a watch and cuff links too."

"I hate liars. I gave Uncle Lenny that horse years ago. Can't believe she gave me the whole purse," Vicky said, peering inside the canvas bag.

"Bet her wallet ain't in there," Galen commented.

"One way to find out," Vicky said, dumping the contents onto the table. Every item that fell out had an estate-sale price tag: the horse, watch, cuff links, several pieces of turquoise jewelry, a bracelet, a ring, earrings, wooden napkin rings, salt and pepper shakers, and a postcard of an old Indian chief.

Galen said incredulously, "Look at that loot. There are no

personal belongings in the purse. She came here intending to steal."

"The nerve of that woman! I need to call the police. You said her name is Lydia?" Vicky said, steaming.

"Aster knows her last name," Galen volunteered.

"It's Driftwood. I'll write it on the back of my business card if you need to contact me."

"Her license plate said 'Boner' on it. Write that down too," Galen insisted.

Aster rolled her eyes. Once again, she was reminded that Lydia had no discretion when it came to sex. She handed the card to Vicky, saying, "Here you go."

"Thanks. Sorry about the ordeal, folks. My daughter, Rose, will be the cashier for a bit while I make some calls," Vicky said to the people in line.

A slender, young woman with bushy hair stood at the cash box.

Vicky stepped outside to call 911.

Aster and Galen, who were last in line, returned to their spot. Endless chatter about the theft rang in Aster's ears. She tuned it out, explaining to Galen, "Lydia can afford every piece she stole and still have money in her wallet. Why does she steal?"

"Probably a thrill," Galen answered.

"The way she overshares anything to do with sex, I thought orgasms were her big thrill in life." Aster sounded disgusted.

"At the car, Lydia got angry because Vicky wanted the stolen stuff back. She had this air of entitlement, as if she deserved the take. I think she's a psycho."

"No argument here. I refused her as my client. She's way too broken for me to fix," Aster said.

"No conscience and no boundaries are a bad combination that's gonna land her in jail. Thanks to you, me, and Vicky."

By the time it was Aster's turn in line, Vicky had returned to the cash box.

"Let me add this woman up," Vicky said to her daughter.

Aster said sympathetically, "I'm sorry you had to go through all that. I take it this is all your Uncle Lenny's stuff, and he passed away."

"Yes. We were very close," Vicky said. With a sad look, she took the coyote skull and wooden spoons from Aster to read the price tags.

"I had a favorite auntie who died. Selling her belongings was a tough job. And she'd probably turn over in her grave if I didn't haggle the price. I'll give you forty for the skull," Aster bartered.

"Favor for a favor. I'll sell it for thirty," Vicky offered.

"Deal," Aster said, more than pleased.

When Galen took her turn to pay, she wasted no time getting to the point, asking, "Are you going to take legal action against Lydia?"

"Oh yeah. Lenny's son, Bernie Schneider, is a lawyer," Vicky boasted.

"Not Bernie Schneider of Schneider and Schneider, Attorneys-at-Law?" Aster asked.

"The very same," Vicky said with a grin.

"He's my lawyer. He helped me with my divorce." Aster was careful to stop there and not mention her plan for Bernie to draw up a prenuptial; she knew to be wary of Galen's big mouth.

"Small world," Vicky said.

On the drive back, Galen reflected, "We were like a pair of detectives, solving a crime. I had no idea estate sales were this interesting. Despite all the Lydia shenanigans, you scored a nice birthday present for Jack."

"I'll say. He'll love your interpretation: 'To speak peacefully while traveling in the spirit world.' He'll probably stick it in his office," Aster said.

* *

The next day, Aster received a phone call from Bernie Schneider. She explained in detail what she and Galen had seen.

His gravelly voice sounded like that of a chain smoker. "I'm taking legal action against Mrs. Driftwood. I could use your help making a statement to the police. Sorry for the short notice, but can you and Galen meet me in front of the police station sometime this morning?"

"Sure. I could be there at eleven. I'll get in touch with Galen. I believe she is free to join us," Aster said, recalling that Galen intended to spend the day cleaning her house.

On October 14, Aster awoke early and slipped out of bed, careful not to disturb Jack's deep slumber. She planned to make a birthday breakfast for Jack. While the spinach-and-tomato quiche was baking, she fried up bacon and steamed some yams. Fresh-ground coffee measured precisely in the french press waited for a last-minute brew. As she set the table with the blue-and-white plates, the sound of water running in the shower cued Aster to boil water for the coffee.

Jack came walking down the hall, his wet hair combed back. He said, "The smell of frying bacon wakes me like an alarm clock."

"Happy birthday, Jack," Aster said enthusiastically.

They kissed.

Aster led him over to the table. She pulled out a chair and said, "A special seat for the birthday boy." On the plate before him rested a box gift wrapped in the Sunday comics.

"Is it food?" Jack said sleepily.

"Open it and see," Aster said patiently. She poured the coffee and set a pitcher of half-and-half on the table.

"Recycled paper. How green of you. Can I shake it and take a guess?" he said, adding cream and taking a large gulp of coffee.

"No. It's fragile—a one-of-a-kind item. You'll never guess," she said, getting him at his own game.

Jack tore the paper off with great zeal. He paused to examine an old boot box. "Antique shoes?" he joked.

"Don't know now, do ya?" Aster jived back. She buttered the yams and sprinkled on nutritional yeast.

Jack opened the box and stared in awe. "A jeweled skull. It's beautiful. I can tell by the golden coloring that it's old," he said, picking it up.

"It's a coyote skull. Got it at that estate sale. Apparently, it lived on Doc Schneider's mantel for more than forty years. It's full of meaning," Aster said excitedly. She explained what Galen said about the stones.

"Wow! How thoughtful. Thanks. I love it," Jack said. He leaned forward and kissed her across the table.

"You might want to decorate your office with it—tap into the coyote energy when you take people on soul journeys."

Becoming more alert from the caffeine, Jack said, "Absolutely. Come to think of it, in the Native American culture, Coyote is the trickster who forces folks to learn, even if they don't want to. The trickster is the role I play when I take my clients on journeys. Many clients come to me out of curiosity. Inevitably, it turns into 'aha moments' where they learn something about themselves," Jack said, shoveling a large forkful of yams into his mouth. "Hmm," he moaned agreeably.

"Like when you helped me figure out my affinity to John Gerard's herbal book; a dot connecter, if I ever saw one. You realize now that your clients are going to call you Coyote Jack."

"Oh. I like the sound of that. This is the best gift ever. Lots of depth in the choosing." He gave her an appreciative wink.

"Hold it up near your face, and I'll take your picture. Come on, show me those beautiful teeth." Aster grabbed her cell phone and snapped several shots.

"Hold on a sec. I'm gonna check something out," Jack said, embracing the skull. He closed his eyes and drew a breath.

Aster watched Jack prepare for a vision. His eyelids flickered as if searching, and then he stilled. She became tranquil as well and drifted into a daydream. In her mind's eye, pages of a photo album turned automatically, showing a husband and wife from various centuries in history. A progression of furs, togas, tunics, cloaks, hats, and gowns marked each era. Without a doubt, she knew every couple in the album was her and Jack. A shimmering gold aura radiated from her heart and encircled the couples. A spectacular sense of belonging confirmed the connection. She heard Jack call softly, "Aster, come back."

"Hello, sweetie," she said, reaching for his hand and squeezing it. The solid warmth assured her she had returned home.

"Hey, babe, where did you go?" asked Jack.

"A mini journey, I think. I paged through a huge book—a photo album of lifetimes. All these different faces appeared, and they were all you and me."

"Did the pages ever stop turning?"

"No," replied Aster.

Jack said enthusiastically, "The pages would have stopped if you had set the intention to enter one of the lives. You were at the index place. Since you didn't request where to go, the pages didn't stop."

"The index place. Interesting," Aster said, intrigued.

Jack had a twinkle in his eye. He said, "It's basically what I saw the first day we met. You felt familiar. I asked myself, 'At what level did we know each other?' I saw endless lives and felt an enormous burst of love, so divinely powerful my chest nearly ripped open."

"Seeing our old selves warmed my heart too. In fact, I'm sort of radiant at the moment," she said.

"Radiant beacons of love. That's what we are," he replied.

Aster ran a hand along is arm. She said, "What a romantic thing to say. You're so open with your feelings. I like it."

"It's effortless. You pull it out of me," Jack said.

"Jack, what did you feel when you held the skull?"

"An electric current radiated down my spine. My clue that I knew the last owner," Jack said.

Letting her hand linger on his, she said, "I can relate to the current down the spine. Right now, as I touch you, it's like hooking up to a battery. In a good way, though."

"I get it," he said, nodding.

"It's weird you got such a strong connection to Lenny Schneider. You never met him," she said.

"Not directly. I took a short journey and found out he's connected to our Navajo life."

"Really?" Aster said. She got up and gave Jack a peck on the cheek. "Hold on a minute. Lenny is gonna have to wait. I'll be right back." Aster headed for the bathroom. Moments later, she came out with nothing on except a bibbed chef's apron.

"Aster, I love your new look." He watched her go to the fridge, noticing how the bib failed to completely cover her breasts and how her butt cheeks peeked through the opening in the back.

She took out a blue canister, and said, "I planned on putting birthday candles on a chocolate croissant, but the baker was fresh out. So, I came up with another idea: whipped cream à la Aster." She flashed a provocative look, encouraged him to stand, and pressed into Jack's pelvis, inviting him to partake in the merriment.

By pure reflex, Jack kissed her. Their bodies lined up heart-to-heart, and a delicious energy bonded them together. They had not been intimate since before Aster's accident.

"Oh, you sexy vixen. Shall we carry on in the bedroom?" he suggested.

Aster smiled. "Only if you want dessert." She shook the whipped-cream container and sprayed a dollop on her neck.

"Happy birthday to me," he commented agreeably, kissing her shoulder and slowly working toward her neck.

He removed his shirt and without a care tossed it aside. She sprayed cream over the scar on his chest, saying playfully, "There's nothing like licking old wounds."

"Mm, good medicine," Jack said. He unbuttoned his pants and stepped out of them.

"I want to feel your skin next to mine. Come on, let's go get comfy," she said taking his hand, and placing the aerosol can in it.

Jack followed her down the hall, enjoying the view. From behind, she was virtually naked, except for apron edges draping the sides of her butt. "I'm gonna buy you an apron for every day of the week," he said, shaking the whipped-cream can vigorously.

From the bedroom, moans and heavy breathing ensued until Aster was unable to contain the oscillating pleasure. A surge rippled up and down her spine, making her gasp. "Sweet spot. A-a-ah!" she moaned.

Cued up and ready to go, Jack joined her.

"Whew, that was heavenly," he said, rolling onto his back.

"I'd say. I think we sent a lightning bolt to the core of the earth." Aster giggled.

After their breathing returned to normal, Jack said, "Hey, hot mama, you never let me finish my story about Lenny."

"Distractions, you know," she said with a smirk.

Jack ran his foot along hers, saying, "Hmm, I do. Before I forget, let me tell you, Lenny was our daughter-in-law, Warm Water, married to Wee Cub."

"Really?"

"Yes. For a wedding present, we gave them an Appaloosa horse. Wee Cub had a stallion of his own, so Warm Water now had a mare to ride."

Feeling completely content, Aster said, "Warm Water had to adore her horse big time, because, after many lifetimes, Lenny had pictures of Appaloosas on his walls."

"Isn't it mind-blowing I got Lenny's coyote skull?"

Chapter 16

A Disturbing Memory

The next day, Aster spent the morning raking leaves. Wearing sunglasses and a visor, she followed the doctor's orders and squatted instead of bending forward, to avoid dizzy spells. Determined to tidy the yard before her cousin J. J. arrived that afternoon, she packed the last of the leaves into the compost bin.

In the apple tree, two squirrels made a squeaky ruckus chasing one another among the branches. A lone apple in an upper bough, the instigator of the competition, hung passively as the rodents fought to claim it as a prize. As hard as the animals worked for their meal, the champion would leave a half-eaten core to rot on the lawn.

Aster spoke to the squirrels. "Finish the duel, and drop the apple already. I've got a lot to do before my cousin arrives."

J. J. had given Aster only one week's notice that she was coming for a visit. To make logistics easier, J. J. caught the airport shuttle. At one o'clock, she rolled a carry-on up the sidewalk of Aster's tidy yard. Her stocky body was dressed in jeans and a white oxford shirt with the sleeves rolled to the elbows.

Aster answered the door and received a hug that gripped her like a vise.

"Whatcha trying to do, crush my bones? Good to see ya." Aster winced, rubbing her ribs.

J. J.'s one-inch-long blond hair emphasized her fleshy cheeks, which once had been very chiseled and sleek. In a Southern drawl, she said, "Hey, cuz, how ya doin'?"

"I'm well. Too bad Jane couldn't come. It'd be fun with the three of us," Aster said.

"Jane's a big-shot real-estate agent. She's hosting an open house at a mansion. If she sells the place, I'm threatening to give her a new street name, Jane VanDyke, Best Gay Realtor in Atlanta," J. J. joked. Her slate-blue eyes appeared haggard despite the humor.

❋ ❋

That evening, the two cousins went to happy hour at Casa Verde, to drink the best mojitos in town and dine on empanadas. They sat at a secluded table nestled in an alcove walled off by a row of sculptured saguaro cacti.

"I have a favor to ask," Aster said, stirring her drink.

"What?"

"Will you be my maid of honor?"

"Again?" J. J. said hesitantly.

"Don't you want to?" Aster voiced concern.

"Yes, ma'am. Of course I will. Just weren't expectin' it is all. A toast to you and Jack—may y'all live happily ever after," J. J. drawled.

"Thanks." Aster smiled at the fairy-tale humor. During summers, J. J. stayed at Gertie's house too. "Happily, ever after" was what they called life at Gertie's.

J. J. put down her drink and commented, "These are good cocktails. They're sort of like glorified lemonade. I'd like to offer another a toast. To us—we who escaped our demented Minnesota families."

Aster crinkled her face, and asked, "What do you mean? You had it better than I did."

J. J. looked serious and said, "There's a dark secret you don't know 'bout. Neither does Jane."

"Really?" Aster said, taken aback. "Thought we shared everything during our teens."

"We did. I blanked this out until last month. Jane and I took a square dancin' class at a weekend getaway. The class was held in a barn on a peach plantation. A dog chasin' a cat came chargin' in, disruptin' the dance. Durin' the commotion, I lost my balance and fell onto a bale of hay. I was lyin' on my belly, and then—wham!—Jane fell on me, knockin' the wind out of me. All at once, the memories came back. Got so repulsed, I puked," J. J. said, shuddering. "Been sufferin' rage fits ever since. I beat a pillow so severely, it nearly broke open."

"Spit it out, J. J.," Aster coaxed.

"I'm an incest survivor," J. J. said slowly.

"No!" Aster gasped, as she placed a hand on her cousin's arm. In her mind's eye, Uncle Marvin appeared. "Your daddy?"

"Uhm," J. J. mumbled, nodding. "Lately, I've had payback visions of castratin' the old codger. Too late; he's dead now."

"When did it happen?"

"When I was 'bout twelve years old. I was up in the barn hayloft, readin' a Nancy Drew book. I heard a noise below. Reckoned I'd check it out, so I looked through the square hole in the floor. I saw daddy wankin' in the empty horse stall. He looked up and saw me peerin' down. That moment, I wished I were invisible."

Aster interrupted, saying, "I remember that. You said you hid like a mouse, quiet and unseen."

"Not quite. That's the amnesia version. There's more. He climbed up the ladder and forced me to sit on his lap. He slid me repeatedly across it. I got scared. When he let go of my arms, I ran. I smacked my head into a beam and passed out. Next thing I knew, Daddy was carryin' me into the house. He was cryin'.

My nose was bleedin.' My undies were stained with blood, and they smelled of fish."

"How awful! Uncle Marvin raped you while you were out cold," Aster said in disgust. "That monster! Did he do it again?"

J. J. brought her pudgy finger to her mouth and gnawed on her nail as she spoke. "Well, yeah. I tried hidin' under my bed. He'd find me, pull me out, and do the nasty. Remember the attic off my closet? He would find me there too."

Stunned at the revelation, Aster said, "You poor thing. I'm so sorry. He did it in the house?"

"Yes, ma'am," J. J. replied and spit out a piece of fingernail.

"Where was your mom?" Aster asked.

"Home. Maybe she was watchin' TV. Or out cold on sleepin' pills. Can't recall."

"How long did this go on?" Aster asked, feeling a tear in the corner of her eye.

"Until the end of high school," J. J. answered in a flat tone.

Aster shook her head, saying, "You endured abuse for that many years? And you never told me? Can't believe Aunt Paula remained clueless. She had to know."

"She never said anythin', and she acted as if nothin' was wrong. But, after my period started, she did send me off to spend summers with you, under the guise of Gertie needing help on the farm."

Sardonically Aster said, "So summers at Gertie's were her version of birth control. And I thought my mom was the best ostrich in the world. Our mothers were sisters from the same mold. And to think, I had no idea—not even a single dream of your abuse."

"I'm as shocked as you are to have recalled this buried trauma so late in life," said J. J. "Makes me feel dirty. I went on a fast. I wore white every day, to feel purified. Nothin' worked. Even considered drinkin' bleach."

"What about Peter? Big brother didn't come to the rescue?"

"Nah. He spied on Dad and me in the loft one time. He musta

got all worked up watchin'. I lay there, slung over a bale of hay, sobbin'. Next thing I knew, I heard him gaspin' and a bit later slinkin' down a ladder."

A tear rolled down Aster's cheek. Unable to take another bite of empanada, she set her fork on the square white plate and gasped, "You were just a girl! Violated by Dad while your brother watched in the shadows. Always thought Peter was a twerp. Yuck, the trauma you endured! It takes strength to withstand that."

"Insensitive assholes. I hate both of them. I'm angry at God too for not strikin' dead every rapist alive," J. J. admitted.

"You need to tell Jane. She can help you through all this," Aster advised.

"I'm afraid she'll think I'm too damaged to be in a relationship."

Aster shook her finger, as if scolding. "Jane has a big heart. She gets you. You have to tell her."

"I came here to tell you ... to practice voicin' my pain. Ya know, get the courage to confide in Jane. Shameful as it is, it helps tellin' you my darkest secret. You and I go way back. I can trust you. Jane grew up as a Southern Baptist. Findin' out about my past might shatter her moral foundations," J. J. explained.

"Releasing a secret taboo can be cathartic as hell," Aster said. "By the way, I seem to owe ya one. I poured my heart out to you plenty over my absentee parents."

When J. J. didn't respond, Aster added spontaneously, "Think we need a second round of mojitos to celebrate our sanity."

"I'll take another. One more thing I gotta tell ya." J. J.'s nostrils flared. "Bites me right in the craw to no end. Last week, I pieced this tidbit together. Durin' high school, Daddy used to call me a whore earnin' my keep."

Aster's mouth dropped open. "The audacity! What a twisted ass! He shoulda been locked up in jail."

❋ ❋

J. J. stayed with Aster for two nights. The next leg of her trip would take her to Minnesota to attend an Oktoberfest family reunion.

While driving J. J. to the airport, Aster asked a question that had been bugging her all through the night. “Do you plan on telling any family members about the incest?”

“Might. Maybe Jenny. She may not believe me.”

“Your niece is a smart one; she’ll hear it. J. J., please call me at any time if you need to talk. You’re my family. My oldest and dearest buddy. Nothing comes between us,” Aster said sincerely.

A tear fell onto J. J.’s cheek. She wiped it off and said, “Gertie and you were the best things in my life durin’ the dark years. I love you for it. Wish you were comin’ with me. We could kick up dust at Norma’s Bar. It’s awful that there’s bad blood between you and Leroy. Any chance you could forgive your weird brother?”

“I won’t set foot in Minnesota unless he apologizes for shooting the windows out of Gertie’s kitchen. If he can get pissed off because I inherited Gertie’s house and he got nothing, I can be pissed off that he’s a stupid jerk,” Aster spat.

“I know, I know; he got the nice side of your parents, while you got the bad. But when your mama died, Leroy sent you the blue-and-white dishes,” J. J. said.

“That was not an apology. It was in the will. I didn’t ask for them. In fact, I didn’t want any mementos from my crappy childhood,” Aster said, aware of how disconnected she felt from her family of origin.

“I can’t argue with the truth. I’m not gonna stir up the Leroy drama at the reunion. I’m tellin’ everyone y’all are too fragile to travel, ’cause of the head injury and all,” J. J. drawled.

“Say whatever floats your boat. I’ve got a wedding to plan,” Aster said, trying to lighten the situation.

At the airport, J. J. wiped away another tear. With false bravado she said, "Enough of this crap. I gotta catch a plane."

They hugged. J. J. got out and grabbed her suitcase from the backseat.

"Say hello to everyone for me. I'll miss ya," Aster said, teary eyed.

"Bye," J. J. uttered and choked back tears. She gave Aster a longing look, shut the car door, and walked into the airport.

The following night, Aster had a dream that J. J. could fly. Her cousin seemed happy, soaring like a free bird. She impishly showered Aster with daisies. "Tell Jane. I can't," J. J. said in the dream, and then she floated toward the stars.

The day after the dream, Aster received a phone call from Leroy. She had not talked to her estranged brother in more than twenty-five years.

Over the phone, he said, "This is Leroy Snowden."

"Leroy?" Aster said, leery of his intent. She wondered if he was trying to make amends or wanted money.

"I got something to tell you," he barked, as uncomfortable as ever.

"Make it quick," she said impatiently. His voice had the same tone and inflection as their father's.

"Bad news. J. J.'s dead," Leroy said.

"No! Not J. J.! I just saw her two days ago," Aster said, stunned. She regained enough of her wits to ask, "How?"

"Hung herself at the reunion, in her daddy's old barn."

"Who found her?" Aster's heart leapt, as she struggled to take in the information.

"Peter and I. Jenny told us J. J. had a present for us in the loft. We were instructed to be there exactly at one o'clock to find it. I don't know why she wanted me there. Probably to be witness to it all."

Aster could feel the tears prick. She asked, "Which Jenny? Peter's daughter or Aunt Jenny?"

"Peter's girl."

"Did J. J. leave a note?" Aster's voice quavered.

"Yep. Fastened to her shirt with a wooden clothespin," Leroy said in a repulsed tone. "Sort of a poem. I memorized it."

"Tell me." Aster placed a hand over her mouth to suppress any outburst as she listened.

Leroy cleared his throat and recited, "In this barn, rape killed my body. Incest killed my mind. Today, I freed my spirit. Returned to the Divine. My pa ought to rot in hell for violating me. And my brother ought to be whipped for watching."

Aster announced unnecessarily, "She killed herself to expose her secret in front of the entire family."

It all seemed unreal except for the pressing feeling in her chest, which Aster was unable to ignore.

"Yep. You can call her dyke girlfriend, 'cause I ain't got her number," Leroy replied gruffly.

"Her name is Jane! I'll call her. Good-bye." Aster hung up.

Along with disgust for her brother, she felt a pang of regret for not translating the flying dream correctly. There had been no purple cushion in the dream and no Grannyme. Berating thoughts vexed her: *This one of the few times my dreams ever failed me. If only I had a clue that J. J. was suicidal, I would have gone to Minnesota, despite the fact I didn't want to see Leroy. Because I couldn't get past my own crap, I wasn't there to support J. J.*

Blow by blow, the pieces of reality stung. No more Monday phone calls; no more best friend. Once again, Aster had been abandoned by a loved one. She slid to the floor and sobbed.

❋ ❋

Jack came over after work and heard Aster howling in misery. He raced down the hall and found her squatting on the bed, hugging a pillow. With her eyes puffed into slits, she looked like a pregnant owl surrounded by an array of used tissues.

"Hey, babe, what's wrong?" He sat beside her and drew her into an embrace. "You okay?"

Between sobs, she forced the words, "Leroy called."

"Leroy who?" Jack pulled away and looked her in the eye.

"My brother," Aster said nasally.

"Is he a drunk like your dad?"

"No. I can't stand him because he lost his temper with a gun, and I haven't spoken to him since," Aster said. She explained about the bullet holes in Gertie's windows.

"Aster, that's intense! Good thing you weren't in the house. I can't believe your family was so dysfunctional. Was Leroy a jerk growing up too?" Jack asked.

"Sort of. He rubbed it in that he deserved to be treated like a prince. I envied the hell out him. Life under Henry Snowden's roof was like living in a hurricane. Ya never knew when or where the storm would hit. I was the one who got pelted with debris, while Leroy relaxed in the mellow eye of the storm. He was the son who could do no wrong," Aster explained, grabbing another tissue.

"Is that why you are crying?" Jack asked, trying to understand.

"No. Leroy called because he had bad news." Aster's lips quivered.

"What happened to make you so upset?" he asked.

Aster choked on the words. "It's J. J."

"Your cousin. Is she okay?" Jack searched patiently.

Aster could not handle the finality of the word dead. Instead of saying it out loud, she drew a finger across her neck.

"Dead?" Jack guessed.

Barely finding her voice, Aster squeaked, "Ya." More tears followed.

"Sweetie, I'm so sorry," he said, caressing her hair. "I'm relieved you aren't injured. My heart about flipped at the intensity of your crying."

Jack encouraged Aster to lie down. He spooned her until the

wailing stopped. She rolled onto her back, stared at the ceiling without seeing it, and then shared the details of J. J.'s death.

"Sounds tragic," Jack replied.

"And the worst thing of all is that I feel responsible for J. J.'s unhappiness," Aster confessed.

"Why?" Jack questioned the absurdity of her statement.

"I feel inadequate. J. J. wanted me to come to the reunion. I refused to go. I ignored the dream. I could have called that morning and given her hope ... encouraged to live." Aster wiped a tear away.

"My dear, how on earth can you believe that? You had no idea she planned to commit suicide. You remind me of Cedar Claw, suffering remorse over his father's death; his newborn daughter's too."

"But I'm a dream weaver and an intuitive healer. I should've picked up on her sadness."

"Your predictive dreams are sneak previews of real life, not cryptic messages of death. Your dream was about J. J. flying and showering you with daisies. How can you translate that into a suicidal impulse?" he said.

Aster argued, "I've been plagued with recall my entire life. How come J. J. wasn't on my radar?"

"You need to separate J. J.'s karma from your own. For whatever reason, she had a miserable lot in life. Her reality was too intense to endure, so she chose to check out. It's free will," Jack emphasized firmly.

"That's cold. She could have held on and let me help her," Aster said, raising her voice.

Jack said serenely, "I see the death as merciful. Look at it empathetically. The other side of the veil is a much happier place for her than dealing with her haunted history."

"You can say that because you didn't love her." Aster's lips quivered.

"Precisely," Jack said in a practical way. "Why didn't you go to the family reunion?"

"Family feud with my brother. Plus, crowds are overstimulating! I'll stress out and get migraines. I had to postpone our vacation. Remember?"

Jack hid his disappointment over the delayed vacation. The peacekeeper in him piped up quickly, "Ya need to heal. There's always later. Now answer me this. If you had gone to the reunion, do you think you could've saved J. J.'s life?"

"Well, dunno." Aster twirled her hair, taking a minute to think. "If I'd known she was determined to kill herself, I'd have prevented the hanging at all costs."

"Apparently, J. J. understood she had to keep her trap shut around you for her plan to work."

"Yeah, but J. J. looked out for me plenty in life. I am past due to return the favor," she whined.

"Sweetie, you gave a tormented soul what she hungered for: love, trust, and a safe place to be. You invested your teen years doing so. J. J. probably felt indebted to you. So, lighten up; the score is in your favor." Jack watched Aster's brow furrow in deep thought.

"You always trump my emotions with rationale," she said and then let out a long sigh.

Chapter 17

Navajo Saga

Aster's heart ached. It felt like a train-track spike had lodged deep into her aorta. Lost in a surreal vortex, time slipped away from her. It was already dark outside, and she had not yet called Jane to tell her that J. J. was dead.

Aster picked up the phone with a shaky hand.

"Hi, Aster," Jane answered the phone cheerfully.

"Hello." Aster cringed at the thought of relaying such bad news.

"J. J. called this morning from Minnesota and told me the great news. She's gonna be in your wedding. J. J. is so happy for you. Congratulations!"

"Thanks, Jane. Jack is very excited; it's his first time getting married, and my third. Actually, that's not the reason I'm calling. I have something difficult to tell you," Aster said.

"Somethin' wrong?" Jane drawled slowly.

Aster's voice broke. "Yes. It's about J. J."

"What happened? She seemed a little distant. Is she breaking up with me?" asked Jane fearfully.

"No. Not that."

"She okay? Dear Lord, is she hurt? Tell me!" Jane began to panic.

Aster ground her teeth. She could not say the word *dead*

without violent sobs taking over. "J. J. passed away," she blurted as gentle tears cascaded down her cheeks.

"What?"

Aster sniffled. "She hung herself in her daddy's old barn."

"That can't be. I just talked to her this morning!" exclaimed Jane.

"I'm so sorry."

"My sweet Jeraldine ... gone?" Jane said in disbelief. "No!"

The dial tone rang in Aster's ear.

Ten minutes later, her phone rang. "Hello," she answered.

Jane strained to speak. "Why did she ...? How could she ...? Tell me."

"J. J. had recently recalled a buried memory. Apparently, she could not cope with the pain of it all."

"What happened?" Jane forced the words out.

"Incest."

"Dear Lord. Who?"

"Marvin." Aster shook her head in disgust at the family secret.

"Her dad! And she never told me. A-a-agh!" Jane shrieked and hung up, crying.

Wrought with sympathy for Jane and raw from her own feelings of loss, Aster used up an entire box of tissues.

An hour later, Aster texted Jane, saying, "I'll email you. I'm a sympathetic crier. It'll take forever to explain."

❋ ❋

The next morning, Aster was too upset over J. J.'s death to eat. In lieu of food, she and Jack went out for coffee. She ordered a chai with a shot of espresso. The smell of fresh-baked almond croissant was too much for Jack to resist, so he had one with his pumpkin latte.

"Hmm, these are good," commented Jack, scratching his thick torso. "Just got an idea. What if, right after you die, you are granted a choice of something to eat. What would be your choice of the last taste to enter your mouth?"

"Oh my, let me think. I know: raspberries or maybe coffee ice cream," she answered.

"Choose one."

"Depends on my mood. Today, it be would be the fruit," said Aster.

"Milk-chocolate pecan turtles would do me justice," Jack chimed. "What do you think J. J. would have eaten at the pearly gates?"

"Black licorice. We had to pick some up before we went to the airport."

"I forgot to tell you," he said with his mouth full, and then paused to wash it down with coffee. "My radar went off this morning thinking about J. J. Something was familiar about her. Did a quick meditation and found out she was in our Navajo life."

"No kidding. Who was she?"

"Guess."

"Come on. Give me a hint. A big one," Aster said.

"She was the first to find Cedar Claw when he fell from the tree," Jack revealed.

"Moon Pebble?"

"Uh-huh."

"She was nothing but a cameo. We know so little about her," Aster complained.

"We could take a little soul-journey trip and never leave the house," Jack suggested.

"Revisit our Navajo lives. Not sure if I'm up for that." She fidgeted with her coffee mug.

He shrugged. "Why not? It'll be interesting to see J. J. in a different light."

"All right then. Let's go to my place," Aster suggested.

Jack and Aster retreated to the most comfortable place in the house. They lay side by side on the queen bed, holding hands, intending to make a tandem journey. Together, they grounded, found neutral, and listened to Jack's slow-paced voice. "In your mind's eye, see the beckoning light."

Aster floated into timelessness. Golden rays of sunshine lit an archway of stone riddled with morning glory vines chock-full of blue and pink blossoms. She entered the familiar arid New Mexico climate, listening for signs of life. A bleating sheep among a scattered herd came upon a patch of prairie grass. Further to the left, a grouping of beehive-looking mud dwellings drew her interest like a moth to light.

She felt a tug on her arm.

Jack said, "Slow down. I'm right here."

She smiled a toothy grin. "Jack. It worked. Don't let go of my hand. I'm afraid I'd lose ya."

"Watch out! There's a pile of sheep droppings," he warned.

Too late. She stepped directly into the pile, making no footprint.

Aster inspected the clean soles of her shoes. "Gosh, almost forgot: we're spectators not participants."

"My bad. Distracted by a damsel in distress. I hear people. Let's go." He led them into the nearest hogan, at the edge of the village, and entered.

Their attention was drawn to the sound of rapid breathing, followed by an elongated groan. A woman with a round face and owlish eyes squatted over a birthing basin.

"It's Moon Pebble," Jack said.

Suddenly a grin widened on the face of the mother-to-be. Amniotic fluid trickled into the shallow pottery bowl, obviously soothing the muscles that were bringing the baby into the world.

"I can relate to that good feeling. It happened at my own births," Aster whispered into Jack's ear. She watched, fascinated.

"Shh. Listen," Jack warned her not to interfere.

An aged midwife, Rabbit Tail, with salt-and-pepper braids pinned to the top of her head, watched the container fill. The midwife turned to her young assistant. "This is a good sign. The color is clear, and it smells fresh. Go ahead, take a whiff."

"I pass." Talking Bird shot a wary glance toward the bowl. Unsure whether Rabbit Tail was in teacher mode or pulling a joke, she kept a safe distance away from the catch pot.

Rabbit Tail cleared her throat with impatience. "You and Cedar Claw are newlyweds eager at mating. Sooner than you think, this will be you. Such knowledge is a must."

Not wishing to annoy her elder, Talking Bird stuck her narrow nose into range. "Hmm, practically scent-free."

Night had fallen, bringing with it the crisp air of fall. Talking Bird placed the dwindling torch into the fire pit in the center of the hogan and lit the tinder. As she oiled the vaginal opening, Rabbit Tail sang a song that welcomed the new soul. The two women waited for the womb spasms to increase. Until now, Talking Bird had never paid much attention as to how hard the mother had to work to bring a child into the world.

The father-to-be, Big Bear, had stuck his head in the door more than once, asking, "Is it born yet?" His swarthy skin stretched taut over a large face, retaining the suppleness of a young man. His long nose bent at the bridge.

"No, Big Bear. Maybe I can hurry things along," Moon Pebble said in a soothing voice, between contractions.

Rabbit Tail grabbed his ear and pulled him outside. She scolded, "Listen here, young buck. Moon Pebble is working hard. Your impatience makes her nervous and slows everything down. Go busy yourself with chores."

"Birth takes too long," he complained, rubbing his ear.

"Think waiting is hard? Try giving birth. I will call when it's over." The crone shooed him away before reentering the hogan.

Big Bear fetched water, sharpened the hatchet, chopped wood, and paced outside. He pouted over the fact that the midwife did not grant him a bedside spot to watch. At first, the reason was his large body was crowding the limited space. He grumbled, "And now I'm too eager. Waiting is boring."

Before long, Moon Pebble's breathing changed into panting. Unable to deal with the intensity of the pain, she rolled onto her back and screamed.

"Head is crowning," Rabbit Tail said. "Moon Pebble, what do your insides feel like?"

"Urge to push," Moon Pebble said, holding her breath.

"Go ahead," instructed Rabbit Tail.

Moon Pebble's cheeks tightened, she gritted her teeth and bore down. Without further ado, she gave birth to a son. Her round face softened once the labor was over.

Orange embers in the fire pit emitted a soft light on the features of her newborn. His hands, feet, and ears appeared small, as did the body. The midwife commented on the easy delivery. Disbelief had Moon Pebble say, "You mean other women open and give birth to babies twice the size as mine? How do they do it?"

"Strength from the Great Mother," Rabbit Tail said.

"Now that the hard work is done, I have more strength. I want to show Big Bear his son," said Moon Pebble.

"You should name him Lizard; he's so little," Talking Bird said, admiring the glow of the new mother.

"Big Bear, you can come in now," the midwife yelled out the door.

No answer.

"I'll light a torch and find him," volunteered Talking Bird. "Surely he's not far away." She stepped outside into stark darkness. The evening clouds hid the stars, and the moonless sky made her thankful the light from the flames lit the way.

Rabbit Tail cut the cord and cleaned off the baby. The semi-darkness hindered her failing night vision. She saw ten toes and fingers. Nothing was abnormal. Deft hands swaddled and presented the newborn to the eager arms of the mother.

"Rabbit Tail, you could do that blindfolded. How many births have you attended?" Moon Pebble said, admiring her son.

"Too many to count. Maybe half our clan or more. This little warrior is the smallest I have ever seen."

Moon Pebble fretted, "He has not cried yet. My baby won't die, will he?"

"Worry not. You carried him nine moons. He's small boned, like you," the midwife reassured. A flash of doubt had Rabbit Tail reach inside the blanket for the miniature foot and firmly pinch a heel.

The baby began to fuss and broke into a cry.

"You are hurting him," Moon Pebble said, aghast.

Satisfied the lungs responded to pain, the old woman let go. "He sounds fine."

"What do I do to make him stop crying?" Moon Pebble worried.

"Feed him." Rabbit Tail stroked Moon Pebble's back. "First, lower your shoulders and take a breath. That's it."

Moon Pebble drew him to her breast. The baby failed to nurse. "What am I doing wrong?" she said nervously.

"Press your nipple on the roof of the mouth. Helps him latch on," Rabbit Tail instructed.

Her little one suckled feebly. "I am in love," cooed Moon Pebble, staring at the magnificent wonder in her arms. The Great Mother had cast the magic of the "feeding bliss"; the instinct to nourish and protect struck at the first letdown of milk.

"You need to rest and let your womb heal. As soon as he falls asleep, join him," advised Rabbit Tail. "I'll clean up and wait for Big Bear to return."

"Big Bear will wish to see his son," Moon Pebble said with a yawn.

"Plenty of time for that. Now rest," insisted Rabbit Tail.

❋ ❋

Moon Pebble awoke at dawn, curled around her new charge. She arose, squatted over a pee pot, and placed a lid on top. Rabbit Tail would be by later to examine the contents and determine blood loss.

Tradition had Big Bear outside, facing east and greeting the sun. Clothed in leather, his large frame stood erect like a monolith casting a long shadow on the ground. His disheveled hair was tied loosely into a ponytail. Normally, before breakfast, the patient hands of his wife would dress the ebony queue in wool straps and bone.

Moon Pebble carried her son outside into the growing light, excited to hold the first family sun honoring. She watched Big Bear give salutations with hand gestures.

Out of respect, Moon Pebble stood silently beside her husband. A long arm reached around her waist. She nestled into his embrace.

Big Bear said, "Grandfather Great Spirit, thank you for the gift of light you shine on Mother Earth. My wife and I present you with our newborn son. Bless him with your radiance. I am eager to mate soon."

Moon Pebble suppressed a giggle as she elbowed him in the ribs.

"To provide playmates for the firstborn," he faltered.

Moon Pebble took over. "On the first day of our son's life, I offer tiny feet to the fire of the east, to the water of the south, to the earth of the west, and to the air of the north. Let his first steps walk a path of wholeness among our people."

A mild morning breeze still carried the coolness of the night. She instinctively adjusted the blanket snug around her son. The little one awoke without a fuss.

"You were asleep when I returned last night. I wanted to see our son. There was no moon, no stars, no fire; nothing to give light. Rabbit Tail insisted I not disturb you. She warned me the Spirits were teaching me how to wait. If the Spirits did not twist off my ears for not obeying an elder, she'd take a go at it," Big Bear said with apprehension in his voice.

"You haven't seen him yet?" Moon Pebble rubbed a finger along the baby's cheek, enjoying the soft texture.

"Not yet," Big Bear cried. He reached for his son.

"Here, sweet one, go to Father." She handed over her precious bundle.

"A-a-agh! The eyes go in opposite directions," he said, alarmed. "They are too wide and slant like a sheep bladder."

"What? He's beautiful," Moon Pebble protested.

"Those ears look like they'd fit onto a mouse." Discarding the blanket, Big Bear said, "How can he be my son? He's no bigger than my hand."

"His smallness is cute. He's like me," exclaimed Moon Pebble.

"My mother gave birth to the markings of this kind, and she killed it. They are poor thrivers. Dumb as can be."

"He is a gift from the Mother. He already lives in my heart just like you do," she coaxed.

"He'll be a burden on us and the clan. Besides, it's custom to weed out the bad seed."

The baby began to whimper.

Moon Pebble stammered for the right words to save her child, but the panic that flowed through her made it hard to breathe.

"Great Spirits, thank you for the gift of life we received this day. We return it back to you to bless it into the world beyond," Big Bear intoned.

Her face screwed up with disgust at the hasty terms. Another tiny cry kindled an unforeseen strength that pushed Moon Pebble past her immobilizing terror. Drawing a great breath, she said urgently, "He's hungry. I need to feed him. Give him to me."

"Only right to end its life now. You will be thankful of my wisdom," Big Bear disagreed as he jerked away.

The baby cried louder. The very sound caused Moon Pebble's milk to let down, and her engorged breasts began to leak.

"It? We were blessed with a son!" Moon Pebble screamed. Streams of warm milk rolled down onto her stomach.

"This is not my son. Looks more like a half-breed sheep."

"How dare you imply I bedded with an animal," Moon Pebble said with a gasp. She scrunched her owl eyes into narrowed slits and took a swing at him.

Big Bear pivoted and dodged the blow. He appeared to enjoy the upper hand. Over the sound of the wailing baby, he bellowed, "Slaying a hairless sheep is no different from killing a woolly one."

"He's my son. Give him here," she spat.

In total disregard, Big Bear lifted the baby by the legs and dangled him upside down, challenging her to come and get him. Little lungs cried for mercy. Moon Pebble flared her nostrils and charged forward. Big Bear raised the newborn above his head, out of her reach. Overconfident that such a small woman was no match for his fighting skills, he laughed, "Give up. I won this match."

In one swift move, Moon Pebble took advantage of the carefree laughter and snatched the knife from her husband's belt. "Give him to me, or I'll gut you." She bared her teeth and growled like a puma.

Big Bear spat, "No. Drop the knife." His eyes warned her to heed.

"Give him to me," she threatened, swiping the knife at him and barely missing.

Big Bear took a few steps back. Like a wolf hunting prey, Moon Pebble circled, looking for an opportunity to strike.

In haste, Big Bear said, "Great Mother, the body of this child returns to you."

"No! Stop!" she bellowed.

The wailing of her son ceased abruptly at the sudden snap of his neck.

"Too late. What's done is done," he said, claiming victory over the dispute.

"How dare you!" Moon Pebble screamed. She drew back the knife and lunged.

Big Bear moved aside with the quickness of an agile hunter. He tossed the limp infant into the cold fire pit as if it were a carcass of a freshly eaten bird. A flurry of hands struggled over the knife. Moon Pebble fought like a wildcat avenging her cub. She bit, pulled hair, scratched, jabbed elbows, and twisted until Big Bear overtook her. He backed away, holding the knife over his head and out of her reach. A warm drop of liquid fell onto his forehead. With the back of his hand, he wiped the moisture off and saw red. The same hue darkened the collar of his wife's dress.

"Stop. You are bleeding," he commanded, calling a truce. A scarlet stream poured from his wife's neck. "The flow is too fast."

In the few seconds he paused to look, she charged at him and kicked him in the balls. While he bent forward, groaning in agony, she repeated the same blow from behind. "Teach you to kill my son," she snarled venomously.

"Ahh," he yelled until out of breath. Big Bear's giant form careened like a canoe in white water rapids before he tumbled to his side.

Moon Pebble turned to the baby. Her entire body shook. Desperate to revive the small lungs, she was unable to reach the fire pit, for she fell unconscious.

Rabbit Tail, who was on her way to visit the new parents, quickened her pace, causing the fur bangles attached to her belt to jostle. The salt-and-pepper braids tied with leather thongs swished in unison with each step.

"Come, Talking Bird, hurry. That scream is telling my bones something is wrong," exclaimed Rabbit Tail.

"Right behind you," said Talking Bird, shooing a gnat away as she passed a fresh sheep hide tied to a frame, drying in the sun.

The two women gasped as they scanned the scene at Moon Pebble's hearth. The entire family was sprawled on the ground as if struck by lightning. There were no scorch marks indicating this to be true. Rabbit Tail rushed to the baby, and Talking Bird went to the mother.

"What happened here?" Talking Bird said. "Moon Pebble lost much blood. Looks like a knife slice to the neck, fingers, and arms." She held a palm over the neck wound to stanch the bleeding.

"Not sure. Great Mother! Baby is dead." Rabbit Tail puckered her lips, deepening the wrinkles that lined her mouth. The morning sun enabled her old eyes to see what she had been unable to see the night before: the markings of a short-life baby. To find the little one naked in the fire pit, his wide eyes staring lifeless, filled her with pity. She closed the tiny lids and wrapped him in the blanket she found on the ground.

Talking Bird bowed her head, saying, "May the young spirit travel north to join his ancestors. All his relations."

"All his relations," Rabbit Tail repeated. She checked on Big Bear. His left cheek bore superficial claw marks; there was a bite mark on a forearm and several small gashes on one hand. A bloody knife lay near his feet. He was out cold. His body curled forward, and his hands clutched his man parts.

"Does he still breathe?" Talking Bird asked. She kept a firm grip over Moon Pebble's wound.

"Yes. See his hands, how they are protecting his sac? My best guess is that we heard one of his screams. A direct hit."

"Ouch. It had to be a powerful blow to knock him out. You think someone attacked them, or was this some type of accident?" Talking Bird questioned.

"Maybe they fought each other. Whatever happened, the entire family needs the medicine man." Rabbit Tail stood up and scurried off in the direction of Turtle's lean-to.

❋ ❋

Turtle and Cedar Claw arrived on Farwalker. The horse, pulling the travois, jibbed away at the smell of blood. As weathered and fragile as Turtle looked, he held the reins with incredible strength. Displaying an enormous amount of patience, he sang a soothing chant and petted the horse's muzzle.

"Cedar Claw, hold tight. Give no lead." Turtle handed over the rope and shuffled slowly to Moon Pebble, with a medicine bag hung across one shoulder and a bladder of water on the other.

Cedar Claw sat on an old broken drum covered with a folded woven mat.

"Deep cut," said Talking Bird, still holding the neck wound. "We need to stop the bleeding before she is moved."

Turtle smiled at his acolyte's knowledge. He reached into his bag for a small gourd and removed the antler cap. A steady hand sprinkled ground yarrow onto the wound, which immediately stanched the bleeding.

The women removed the stained dress and rinsed the blood from Moon Pebble's torso with the contents of the water bag.

"Rabbit Tail and Talking Bird, lift Moon Pebble onto the sled," Turtle instructed, knowing full well that the weight of the collapsed body was too much for Cedar Claw to manage with his lame foot and crutch.

Talking Bird took hold of the shoulders, and Rabbit Tail gripped the knees.

"Stop," Rabbit Tail insisted. "Set her down. She bleeds from the womb." The midwife rummaged in her bag and pulled out a handful of wool.

The horse let out a disturbed whinny.

"See if there's water in that urn," Cedar Claw said, keeping his grip firm on the rope.

Turtle nodded his head and then brought the clay vase next to the patient.

Once again, Rabbit Tail cleaned off more blood. She said, "Talking Bird, hold this wad of wool over the birth opening while I attach the afterbirth belt." The apparatus looked like scanty underwear tied on by leather thongs.

"Farwalker will be much happier if Moon Pebble is clean," said Talking Bird as the two women hoisted the unconscious body onto the travois.

Many days passed, one for each finger, and Moon Pebble's vitality increased to the point that she had energy to walk the short distance to the creek to bathe, escorted by Talking Bird. The two women sat on the bank, warming their clean bodies in the sun while sipping mugs of tea.

Brittle leaves of cottonwoods rustled together in symphony with the breeze; once green, then yellow, now tan, the leaves fluttered among the branches. The women watched random leaves dislodge from the lofty heights and drift aimlessly to the ground.

"What's in this tea?" Moon Pebble asked. The dark circles under her eyes were evidence that a full recovery was not yet complete. "The first taste is bitter, yet once I start drinking, I cannot put it down."

"Your body craves what it needs: yellowdock, nettle, and sheep sorrel. Uncle Turtle said it makes strong blood," Talking Bird said, finishing the herringbone braid in Moon Pebble's hair.

A strip of soft sheep leather riddled with holes covered Moon Pebble's neck wound. She pushed a finger under the bandage and scratched.

"Stop picking at that. You have spilled enough blood onto the earth," scolded Talking Bird.

"It itches," Moon Pebble whined.

"Leave it, or my uncle will bind your hand."

"Any worse than the scolding I got from Rabbit Tail? Ugh! The old woman pounded me like a drum because I exerted myself while my womb was still healing," Moon Pebble said in disbelief.

Talking Bird saw something move downstream. "Great Mother, look who's coming our way."

"Poor Big Bear! He walks bowlegged," Moon Pebble said sarcastically. "He deserves it." She picked up a rock and eyed his approach.

"Put that down. Big Bear soaks his blackened sac in the creek every day. I heard it swelled to the size of a gourd," said Talking Bird.

"Cedar Claw tell you that?" Moon Pebble wiped dirt off the underside of the rock.

"Yes. Big Bear suffers more than you know. Give me the stone," begged Talking Bird.

"Does he? Good." She tossed the rock into the air and caught it, looking at it with a calculating eye.

"His manhood does not rise with the sun anymore," Talking Bird added.

Moon Pebble broke into a sardonic grin. Through clenched teeth she uttered, "This stone could break one of Big Bear's bones." She tossed the rock up again.

Quick as a frog catches a fly, Talking Bird snatched the rock in midair.

"Clever move, friend," said Moon Pebble, frowning.

Big Bear stopped several arm lengths away. He slouched forward, and his face drooped with reluctance. As if rehearsed, he said, "The medicine man wants me to make peace. I wish to say that my heart is glad to see the life force has returned to your body."

"One Who Kills Babies now cares how I feel?" Moon Pebble snapped.

Wary of any sudden moves, Big Bear said, "Turtle spoke wise words into my ears. If I wish to live to be as old as he is, I must never act so hastily in front of a nursing woman."

"'Steal a cub from its mother, bid farewell to your brothers,'" Talking Bird cut in with the childhood quote.

He interrupted, "Does that mouth of yours ever shut? I'm speaking to my wife, not a meddling half-breed."

Talking Bird grunted disapprovingly. She knew her birth father was a Spaniard with blue eyes and a narrow nose, but she assumed the knowledge of her mixed blood was long forgotten. True, she was knife-trade conceived and raised by a Navajo father. It mattered not, for her mother gave up her maidenhood to honor her husband with such an esteemed gift. Most importantly, she knew the blood inside her own veins flowed from a heart that revered life in all things.

"You can no longer call me wife," Moon Pebble retorted. "Who wants a husband whose penis cannot rise? Great Mother curses you."

Her words stung. He took a step forward, as if to strike her, but retreated, growling angrily, "Woman, evil wind blows pass your lips. My spirit will not rest until it wins over yours."

❋ ❋

Moon Pebble wintered at a neighboring Navajo village and returned for the spring celebration. Her eyes were bright, and she walked with a content stride.

The entire clan gathered around the community hearth to share a meal. They feasted on venison that roasted all day in a pit lined with stones. Rabbit Tail had spiced the meat with juniper berries, dried currants, and mushrooms. This early in the season, the available greens that served as side dishes were dandelion leaves and prickly-pear stems.

Big Bear approached as Moon Pebble strode away from the pit, her bowl brimming with food. They had not seen each other all winter. Tension filled the air. He threw his shoulders back, towering over her, and found his nerve.

"Can we let there be peace between us and at least be friends?" he asked.

"Your face does not match your words," she said, glaring. "I suspect your manhood is as droopy as a soft strip of leather. I have a real man in my life now, older and mature." Without anything left to say, she turned and left him alone.

Big Bear's young face looked dejected as he filled his bowl. Between spoonfuls, he watched Moon Pebble sit next to a man as they fed each other from the same dish.

"Hawk Nose. That ugly wife stealer owns many horses," Big Bear fumed, attracting curious looks that volleyed from him to his former wife.

Hawk Nose, named after his prominent physical attribute, had a wiry, slight build. He spoke fluent Hopi, negotiated trades, and had a reputation as the village hoarder who had a second hogan that stored bartering supplies.

Big Bear locked into a stare with Hawk Nose. The crowd grew silent. The younger man's face dropped when the older man gave a kiss of ownership to Moon Pebble's cheek.

"Perhaps we should have named you Grazing Bear," said an old voice. "You eat such large plates."

"Yes, Turtle. Always hungry," said Big Bear. He glanced down, surprised at the amount of food in his bowl, gave a respectful nod to his elder, and sped off to escape the whispers.

Once out of earshot, Big Bear muttered, "They certainly shared each other's bed too. Why should I try to make amends?"

Big Bear vacillated, but he wanted to heal his man parts. Turtle advised that making peace with Moon Pebble was a good start. Big Bear found a pair of Moon Pebble's winter moccasins tucked away in the bottom of a basket. The fur lining would keep her warm and happy. The act of kindness may soften her bitter heart. More importantly, it might please the Spirits.

The waxing half-moon lit his way along the path to Hawk Nose's hogan, making it an easy journey. Big Bear had not the nerve to call at their door; he planned to leave the footwear at the threshold. The nearer he approached, the quieter he made each step, creeping along with the stealth of a hunter. As he set the moccasins on the ground, a noise startled him, and he froze. The groans of lovemaking filled his ears. Ever so slowly, he stood to his full height at the door. As much as he wished himself coupling with Moon Pebble, invading their privacy was unacceptable among the tribe. Instead of leaving, he stayed and witnessed the miracle of his penis engorging.

"Come on, let's return," coaxed Jack, squeezing Aster's hand.

"Sure." Aster followed, feeling as though they had just left a movie theater. Instead of retreating from tiered seats, they were on their backs, gazing at the off-white ceiling in Aster's bedroom.

Jack sat up on the bed, agitated. "Wow, I had a vision inside the journey. You won't believe it. I saw a rainbow connect the name of Big Bear to Peter Jansen. Peter is J. J.'s brother. Right?"

Aster nodded and remained lying on the bed.

"A rainbow? Is that another one of your interpretation tricks?" she said, surprised.

"Yeah, not a manly image, but that's my magic."

"Peter was J. J.'s first husband in the Navajo life," Aster said, digesting what Jack had related. "Remember, Big Bear made a vow that his spirit would not rest until it won over Moon Pebble's. Think that's why Peter never tried to stop the raping?"

"Without more research, I'm not sure what their destiny is," Jack said with a shrug. "Their entangled lives might be power plays of besting one another. No doubt, those two had appointments with each other and probably still do in the future."

"Wow, the saga continues. You know, the more I think about

it, the family feud is helping me understand J. J.'s situation. Unless you look deep, you might miss the hidden reasons for why things happen. It soothes the sting a bit," Aster mused.

"Good, let's go eat. 'You haven't had a bloody thing all day. We're so sorry, Uncle Albert. But the kettle's on the boil and we're so easily called away.'" Jack sang an impromptu version of the Paul McCartney tune.

❋ ❋

Grannyme stood in front of a blackboard, holding a rubber-tipped pointing stick. Her attire gave the appearance of an old-fashioned schoolmarm. The Victorian dress, cameo pin, and hair twisted into a bun all reeked of yesteryear. She placed both hands over her heart, saying, "I can sense your heart aches. Sorry about your loss. Cousin J. J. and you go way back."

Aster, whose hair was also in a bun, sat at an antique wooden school desk, the kind that had a book cubby below the seat and an ink-bottle hole on the desktop.

"Thanks," she said in a languid tone. "Another loved one gone. I regret I wasn't there to stop her. I think about how daunting it must have been for J. J. to revisit the barn where Uncle Marvin raped her. I could have swallowed my pride and told Leroy. He could have kept an eye on her. I feel stupid … responsible for not speaking up."

Grannyme interrupted, "You feel stupid that you aren't as omnipotent as God? Why do you do that?"

"Grieve?" Aster said, confused.

"No, blame yourself for other people's deaths."

"Ease up! My heart feels raw, as though it's been put through a meat grinder. I'm not in the mood to have you roast it over the coals."

Grannyme peered over reading glasses halfway down her nose. "We're not here to coddle ignorance. You're in my classroom, and I'm here to help."

"Great." Aster rolled her eyes. "Is this another lesson on the finding the grail? I finished reading *King Arthur and the Holy Grail.* Aside from feeling as lost and confused as the Knights of the Round Table, the only thing I gleaned from the story is that the quest is a personal journey unique to each individual. I doubt I'll ever find the damn thing."

Grannyme took a diversionary tactic and said, "In that case, let's call this class Self-Worth 101. The lesson for today centers around deserving to be loved. My job is to assist you in reframing your thought process, because love is exactly what you're looking for."

Aster sulked as she looked at the purple floor, pining to lounge on its plush surface. The oak desk seat proved unforgiving on her butt. "So, my goal has changed from the grail to love?"

"They are one and the same."

Aster perked up. "Really? That narrows it down. My therapist talked about reframing. I get it. You're talking about emotional wounds, aren't you?"

"Shush! I've said too much already," Grannyme's lips curled. "You have a hurdle to jump over, and there's no need to scrape your knees. Listen up."

"Can I have a pillow to sit on?" Aster interrupted.

"Zip it. I'm only saying this once, and I need your full attention. Now, where were we? Ah yes, blaming yourself for other people's deaths," Grannyme instructed.

She cleared her throat and, using the pointing stick, touched the blackboard. The word *denial* appeared on the board, written in a cursive font. Another tap, and the word *anger* appeared below it. *Depression* and *acceptance* followed in sequence.

Aster stood up and without a word pointed at her uncomfortable seat. A cushion instantly appeared, and she sat back down.

The old woman continued, "These are the typical stages of grief. My bumpkin, you have chosen to defy the norm by adding the word *responsible* to the list."

Grannyme snapped a sharp tap to the blackboard. *Responsible* appeared on the blackboard.

Aster flinched, giving Grannyme her full attention.

"You ignore the fact that people die because it's their time to go. You feel responsible for the death of family and friends. A bit odd, isn't it?" The crone pushed her glasses down further and glared with a ferocity that forced Aster to lean back.

"Dunno. It's only natural," Aster said feebly.

"You're too attached! You struggle with letting people go."

"So, I have abandonment issues," Aster said in her own defense.

"Yeah, but you're missing my point. Because you were born to broken parents, left a broken home, lived in a disarrayed home, and married a broken man, you have a deep desire to—" Grannyme stopped herself. She rolled her hand, signaling Aster to finish the sentence.

"Suffer, escape, avoid reruns?" Aster said hopefully.

"If something is broken, you—" Grannyme led.

"Fix it! Never occurred to me to go there," Aster said with a touch of sarcasm.

"A wounded fixer or caretaker, if you will. It's no mistake your career involves fixing people's health."

"The reason I chose to be a health coach was to help people live happier lives. My therapist used to say I was my mom's caretaker ... when I cooked for her as a little kid," Aster recalled. "So, what's wrong with that?"

"My darling bumpkin, let me be clear. Your soul made a contract to learn to caretake yourself. You were lost in the first half of your life. These golden years are supposed to be all about you. A big piece of that is giving up the idea that people die because of your actions."

"Stop beating a dead horse! I get it. My challenge is a cruel joke. I have to reprogram my caretaking conditioning from other to self. Breaking old habits is easier said than done," Aster complained.

"Then do a reframe and fix it."

"Right. Show me the light switch, and I'll flip it. I can program my feelings like a computer game," Aster said sarcastically.

"By the way, you are in the midst of a lesson right now. The head injury you are healing from forced you into self-nurture mode. Mishaps like that will keep happening until you get it right. If need be, the issue will spill over to your next life."

"It's too big. I can't do it alone," Aster moaned reluctantly.

"I'll be here. Jack too. Simply learn to allow," the old woman said.

Grannyme snapped her fingers, and the word *allow* appeared on the blackboard. She waved her hand, and the word reappeared in capital letters.

Chapter 18

Game Night

Hours later, Aster had another dream. Grannyme knelt on the purple cushion, before a large fireplace. With an iron poker, she wiggled a log, shaking the ash aside. The movement created an air pocket that fed the flames, sending sparks up the flue. A wooden box with the italicized words *Stumbling Block* carved into the side suddenly appeared in her lap. She opened the lid and took out a yellowed scroll.

Anticipation grew in Aster as she watched Grannyme blow powder off the parchment. Little particulates wafted in the air.

Aster sneezed. "Yuck! Smells like a musty old library."

"Mummy dust is the worst tickler of all," Grannyme snickered like a mischievous urchin.

"Not from a corpse?" Aster grimaced.

"No, silly, just ancient dust. I reckon you want to read this. It's written on papyrus," the old woman cajoled, examining the tube of paper.

Without further ado, she placed the scroll in Aster's hands.

Aster carefully unrolled the brittle scroll to find Egyptian symbols drawn across the page. The hieroglyphic art on the top of the page included a bird with tail feathers, a threaded bead, half a circle, a tailless bird, and a flattened oval. The remaining figures, all lined in neat rows, seemed to tell a story.

"What do these symbols say?" Aster said, partly annoyed but mostly distracted by the foreign script before her.

"It's Nimlot's vow."

"Who?"

"The person you were in your Egyptian life," Grannyme answered.

Grannyme snapped her fingers, turning the writing into English. The scroll read, "I vow to the gods, my soul does not deserve love, for I cast shame upon the afterlife of my king. Nimlot Meshbah."

"Obviously, he was very distraught to request life without love," Aster commented.

"Nimlot made a mistake in making such a vow. He placed an extraordinary amount of intention on self-punishment, as if praying through a megaphone with all his might. In doing so, he literally cursed lifetime after lifetime. Is it not true, Aster, that you suffered lack of love in your youth?" Grannyme explained.

"I did. It was horrible. What awful thing did Nimlot do to have such a profound effect on my life?" Aster asked, curious as ever.

"In a time when the king wore a gold headdress that fanned out at the top, you were a priest who conducted the mummification ceremony on a royal subject. You were nervous and forgot a very important step. No one but you knew of the blunder. Nevertheless, the error gave you enormous guilt for supposedly ruining your sovereign's afterlife." Grannyme paused and eyed her student, looking for signs of understanding.

"I went into self-destruct mode over my career," Aster declared.

Grannyme agreed. "True! You see, back then, Egyptians revered the afterlife more than everyday life. They considered it the highest honor to live forever among the gods of the dead. The mummifying process appeased the gods, encouraging them to open the gates and let the soul in. If the priest failed in his duties, he would suffer the worst social humiliation possible. He would be denied funerary rites and therefore be unable to enter an esteemed afterlife. There was also a possibility the surviving family might sentence the priest to a tragic death."

"What did Nimlot forget?" Aster longed to know the answer.

"You and Jack can explore that." Grannyme shrugged off the subject with a dismissive flick of her wrist.

"But how can I correct Nimlot's failure without knowing what he forgot?" Aster complained.

"My little bumpkin, now we are getting somewhere. Without all the frilly details, I'll get to the point. You need to forgive Nimlot for his outdated religious concepts. It never mattered if he hopped on the wrong foot or forgot a line in a prayer, because humans made up those so-called important rituals, not God. Forgiving is the first step toward sending this Stumbling Block into the flames." Grannyme directed her eyes toward the fireplace.

"Okay. Nimlot's beliefs were primitive. I can forgive his ignorance. Does that release the vow?" Aster glanced at the Stumbling Block. It did not budge.

"If you say, 'I release the loveless vow that I, Nimlot Meshbah made. I truly believe I, Nimlot Meshbah, deserve to be loved.' You might get better results."

Aster repeated the words verbatim. The box vibrated, as if a motor inside had switched on.

"My dear, you must emphasize your intention with passion, like you really mean it," Grannyme rasped with a slight chuckle.

Aster focused all her attention on her heart and spoke the words with intensity, as if she were pushing them out of her chest.

The box flew into the fireplace. Hungry flames crackled on contact, the outside blackened, and then—poof!—the box disintegrated into ash.

Grinning wide, Grannyme said, "Good job. This is what I mean when I say that thoughts are powerful. Congratulations on letting go of old crap."

"Thanks," Aster said proudly.

Grannyme said, "For the record, since we are cleaning house, I will tell you what Keith thought when he died. It was the most loving passing his soul ever had. He saw you as a doting wife who cared for him tenderly until the end. He thanks you for the gift."

Tears fell. "I had no idea he appreciated me so. I wanted him to. I did a good job. I actually did good," Aster said. She then repeated the last sentence in a jubilant shout.

Swoosh! Another Stumbling Block appeared and then flew into the fire.

"There ya go! Two for the price of one. One more thing before I go. In case you haven't noticed, your fiancé is a good man. He's worth keeping. If I were in your shoes, I'd do what I can to hold on to him."

"Why? You foresee him leaving me?" Aster knitted her brow.

"He treasures honesty. And you are withholding information from him, to the point of being dishonest."

"He knows more about me than any other person walking the planet," Aster retorted, wiping her cheek dry with the back of her hand.

"Not about the money."

"Ugh. I'm a little guarded in that area. It's just—I wanted him to love me for who I am, not for my pocketbook," Aster reasoned.

"Mission accomplished. It's time for full disclosure, or you will lose him. Withholding the truth will act like a snowball rolling down a hill. When it gets to the bottom, the enormous ball destroys everything in its path."

"Our love is strong enough to not let money matters get in the way. We adore each other completely," Aster protested, dreading the idea of being alone.

Grannyme clicked her well-manicured fingers once again. Where the fireplace had stood, a large-screen TV appeared. A remote control suddenly materialized in Grannyme's hand. She pressed the on button, and Aster appeared on the screen.

Aster was standing in the middle of an intersection surrounded by endless fields. Unclear if the location was Minnesota or, perhaps, Texas she asked, "Where am I?"

"At a crossroads," Grannyme's voice narrated.

A wooden sign, cut in the shape of an arrow and pointing to her left, read, "Without Jack." On the same post, another sign pointed in the opposite direction, reading, "With Jack." The Without Jack road had all sorts of potholes and numerous Stumbling Blocks scattered about, whereas the surface of the road With Jack proved to be a smooth and clear route.

The obvious choice was to take a right. Aster turned to head in that direction, but something prevented her foot from moving. Looking down, she saw a sturdy metal ring wrapped tight around her ankle. A thick-linked chain connected the ring to a heavy dollar sign as big as a basketball. She winced, for the metal dug into her flesh.

"How do I get this thing off?" Aster panicked, looking to see if she was bleeding.

"Voice activated," Grannyme chirped.

"A-a-agh! What do I need to say?"

"To Jack's ears, 'I'm a millionaire.'"

Fog clung to the top the foothills, bringing a bitter dampness to the air. Aster, Jack, and Galen stayed warm in Aster's kitchen, nibbling on gruyère cheese, cucumber slices, and olives.

"Galen, there's an important question I want to ask you," said Aster. She suppressed her regret that her cousin was no longer alive to do it. Lost in a vacant stare, she returned to the conversation at the sound of her name.

"Aster, is something wrong?" asked Galen.

"Oh no, not at all. On the contrary, I was trying to think of a clever way to ask if you will be my maid of honor at our wedding." The corners of Aster's fishhook mouth twitched from telling the white lie.

Liquid blue eyes darted back and forth between the future bride and groom. Galen blurted out, "I'm replacing J. J., aren't I?"

"Yep," Aster said, feigning happiness. "It won't happen until next spring, maybe later. We'll have ample time to plan for it."

Galen replied, "That's like calling me a best friend. Of course, I will. Never been a maid of honor before."

"A toast then," Jack insisted, raising his water glass. "To Galen, our tell-it-like-it-is good friend."

"Cheers," Aster added.

"Thanks. This means a lot." Galen grinned. Her impish smile warmed Aster's heart.

"We'll make it as stress-free as possible," Aster said, forgetting her cousin.

"How formal is it, and what should I wear?" asked Galen.

"Casual and simple. No frills. Something you can wear more than once. We can have fun shopping around for the perfect dress," Aster said.

Jack cut in, "Please, no polka dots or stripes."

"Tsk," Aster hissed.

Galen let out a gleeful "Nice. I love buying dresses. Baby blue is my best color."

Jack groaned, "Spare me. You girls can mull over what color you're wearing some other time. I'm more concerned about serving great food and wine. We'll whoop it up with Boulder's finest."

Aster cringed at his extravagant nature. She said, "I was thinking a potluck."

"I envisioned catering to keep you, Miss Busy, out of the kitchen," Jack said.

"You're thoughtful, but my way is cheaper," Aster insisted.

"This is my first wedding. Why not have a carefree day? I'll foot the bill. Don't fret about it," Jack insisted.

Aster winced over the conflicting viewpoints. "Let's sleep on it."

"Yeah. We'll decide later," Jack said, confident.

"How big ya thinking?" Galen asked.

"Small. I'd like enough people to sit around a large dinner table. Jack is pushing for fifty," Aster said.

"Good. Small is more intimate," Galen agreed.

Jack had a look as if he knew different. He said, "Aster, it's your turn to choose entertainment for tonight. What will it be?"

"Hold on," said Galen. "I want to savor the moment. It's not every day that I get this much adulation." She hugged herself and moaned a silly "Mm-hmm."

Aster picked her favorite game, Parcheesi. She played competitively and managed to move all four pawns from start to home before everyone else. "Yahoo!" she cried in victory.

"Okay. You don't have to gloat about winning," joked Jack.

"The kids and I used to chase each other around the board with a vengeance. Keith refused to play with me because I never let him use the lucky yellow pieces. He always lost," said Aster.

"You rarely talk about him. Keith Snowden," Jack commented.

"Keith Hendricks," she corrected. "I kept my family name when we married. I thought that if you wanted to know, you'd ask."

"So, your kids' last name is Hendricks?" Galen asked.

"No, it's Felman. Bill, my first hubby, fathered my children. While Bill and I were married, I was Aster Felman."

"What made you decide to not change your name the second time around?" Jack furrowed his brow.

"Bill was a spoiled rich kid who thought he was the center of the universe. My naïveté saw him as a misguided, wayward soul I could fix. In doing so, I suffered a major identity crisis being his wife. After the divorce, I clung to my birth name and vowed never to change it for another man," Aster said, looking Jack straight in the eye.

"But, sweetie, Aster McFadden has a nice ring to it," crooned Jack.

Aster quipped, "Ever consider Jack Snowden?"

"Never." He looked perplexed. "I'm the last male in the family line. I haven't sired any children, and my heritage feels rather important."

"Jack's got a thing about tradition," Galen said.

"Unless one of us changes our mind, we can keep our birth names," Aster reasoned, not willing to give in.

Peacekeeper Jack changed the subject. "Were there any bad things about your marriage to Keith?"

"Why?" Aster said.

"I'm looking for pointers to what makes you tick."

Aster read the sincerity in his eyes and said, "Our biggest issue was money. I'm frugal, and Keith was a spendthrift. He couldn't go a day without buying CDs, DVDs, clothes, books, or concert tickets—anything to self-gratify. It drove me nuts watching him. We each paid half the bills, and then he'd drain his checkbook down to twenty bucks. By some act of God, he never suffered an overdraft. Separate bank accounts held our marriage together."

"Explains a lot. Okay, then. Since exclusive his and hers checkbooks prevented you two from strangling each other, we'd best do the same. Compared to you, I'm a spender," Jack reasoned.

"Works for me. Separate accounts are what I had in mind. For the record, you are not a shopaholic getting a daily fix at the cash register," noted Aster.

"Overspending is a challenge. Got it," Jack said.

"Speaking of challenge, I forgot to tell you about a dream I had with Grannyme." Aster glanced at Galen, explaining," Grannyme is the old lady who frequents my dreams. Aster was in no mood to delve into money matters any further, nor did she intend to disclose her fortune in front of Galen.

"One of your predictive dreams?" asked Jack.

"Not exactly," Aster replied.

"Do tell," Galen encouraged.

"Grannyme mentioned an Egyptian past life of mine. I was a priest who conducted the mummification ceremony on a king. I forgot an important step. Out of shame, I made a vow that my soul does not deserve love. Apparently, that vow has affected me in every lifetime ever since," Aster explained.

"What a heavy-duty act, making a vow of lovelessness. Did Grannyme give a name?" Galen said.

"Nimlot Meshbah."

"What did Nimlot forget?" Jack asked.

"Dunno. You are supposed to help me find the answer," Aster said.

"Okay. I'll go on a journey by myself. It's quicker that way. Do I have your permission to visit your Egyptian life?" Jack said with great interest.

"Sure."

Jack took several deep breaths and then became very still. While he went back in time, Aster and Galen watched Jack's eyelids flicker. His round belly expanded slowly to the rhythm of his breathing. In what seemed a mere ten minutes, Jack returned.

Aster wasted no time asking, "Whatcha find out?"

"Yeah, tell us a story," Galen begged.

Jack said passionately, "I adore Egyptian history. I entered a temple-like building with stone walls. The room smelled heavily of cloves. All the holy men inside had shaved heads. A boy king lay dead on a stone bed. Nimlot was a lector priest, in charge of preparing the king for the afterlife. His job was to place jewels and carved stones on the corpse, while his minions wrapped the body with strips of linen. Once the lid of the coffin was sealed and carried out, the minions cleaned up. The lector lagged behind to chant a prayer to cleanse the room. When the lector lifted the funerary purse, he heard a clank. Upon inspecting the contents, he found the royal scepter inside. Not the jeweled scepter the queen kept, but a smaller one made of pure gold.

Struck with horror that the king would rest in his tomb without a scepter, Nimlot suffered regret not only for the king but also for his own fate. A blunder such as this would ruin his reputation, deny him access to the afterlife as well, and possibly ensure a tortured death. Riddled with fear, he made a decision. That evening, under a moonless sky, he flung the scepter into the Mediterranean Sea."

"Poor guy. He got himself in a hell of a bind," Galen said.

Wide-eyed, Aster said, "No wonder Nimlot made such a horrible vow." She began to stow the game pieces back in the box.

"No kidding," Jack agreed. "The scepter represents the ultimate power to govern; it's a gift from Osiris. Osiris is the god of the afterlife. Can you imagine Nimlot's anguish? His king showed up at the pearly gates, with no scepter. Such disgrace undoubtedly angered Osiris. The boy king would have been outraged when denied entrance. Poor Nimlot! His nerves must have been rattled, big time, with two powerful spirits against him."

"Major guilt factor," Galen said.

"Well, yeah. Back then, people were known to spend their entire fortunes preparing for the afterlife," Jack added.

"Jack, were you or Galen at the temple too?" asked Aster.

"Nope. Only priests could enter the temple. I sensed I was your wife, but I didn't stay long enough to find out the details. Perhaps some other time, when it's not so late, we'll venture there together," suggested Jack.

"That would be fun. Bet I'm in that life too," Galen said.

"Good chance we're all in it together. At first, checking out that life sounded fun. But, on second thought, entering a life full of anguish might not be so entertaining," Aster said, still wary of overstimulation.

Wanting a little private time to reevaluate Nimlot's tragedy, she carried the Parcheesi game down the hall to the linen closet. The gold-colored box showed its many years of use: clear packing tape held the edges together; grease from popcorn, chips, and nuts lived on the surface—all recording her personal history in a smudgy sort of way. Aster opened the closet door. As she slid the royal game of India into its rectangular slot on the shelf, she thought, *This game is a lot like me and Nimlot: a bit tattered yet functional.*

Chapter 19

Money Matters

Aster stood in the bathroom, fixing her hair. The huge wall mirror was as wide as the counter and reflected her every move. Trying to figure out a game plan for how to open up and talk about money with Jack, Aster moved her bangs off to the side, exposing parallel wrinkles on her forehead. Aghast at appearing older, she combed them straight down to her brow. She thought, *I don't want to look this old. And ... I don't want to tell Jack I have millions. The two big things we're planning cost money: traveling and a wedding. Good thing I pushed both events back. There's less pressure. It's not fair for him to pay for everything, while I keep my secret. I'm one big cheap SOB.*

Aster stared into the mirror until her eyes lost focus. Gertie had taught her that money was a lot like poker: keep your cards close to your chest, and no one will take advantage of you. Mulling over the conservative advice, Aster reasoned, *Avoidance has kept me safe, but now, with Jack in the picture, avoidance makes me a liar. Why does life have to be so complicated? Grandma Snowden had a bunch of money, and it all went to paying the retirement home. I want to be wise. I want financial security. And I want to grow old with Jack. He makes me happy. I want it all. Life without him would be lonely. I hate being lonely.*

The previous night's dream of measuring life with and without Jack haunted her.

"All right, all right! I'll make changes," Aster said. She parted her bangs in the middle, pushing the tresses aside, and exposed the lines on her forehead.

This is who I am, Aster thought, ready to confess to the world her actual age.

Ready to confess to Jack who she really was, she called Bernie Schneider and asked him to draw up a prenuptial agreement. She planned to expose herself completely on the day the papers arrived.

A week later, the prenuptial documents came in the mail.

Jack and Aster sat at the kitchen table, drinking afternoon tea. Jack nibbled on shortbread cookies, while Aster had apple slices and almond butter. The old blue-and-white plates, relics from their childhoods, put Jack in a sentimental mood.

Jack said, "It's synchronistic that you own the entire Currier and Ives set. I fell in love with food while eating off these puppies. Now, thanks to you, I can continue the affair. I get to double dip—a little love from my fiancée, topped with a huge scoop of good grub. These puppies are definitely a sign that you and I were meant to be."

"Jack, you're such a romantic foodie," Aster said. She adored his tender comments.

His dinnerware memories were far better than her own childhood recollections. Nurture was a rare commodity living with a mother who was physically present but emotionally unavailable. The only meat Regina knew how to cook was pot roast. Anything else ended up burned. At age five, Aster mastered the electric can opener and learned to heat up food. Without much effort, she surpassed her mother's culinary skills by simply following recipes out of cookbooks or following directions printed on food containers. Aster had served up plenty of meals on the blue-and-white plates.

"Maybe we should make flower arrangements in the soup bowls for decorations at our wedding," he quipped.

They shared a laugh.

Jack's comment about flowers reminded Aster of wedding costs, which led to thoughts of her secret fortune and the prenuptial agreement. Since Jack was in a great mood, now would be a good time to mention them.

"I keep thinking about Felix. My hero of the year. I hope he liked the case of mushroom supplements I gave him," Aster said, instead of what she knew she should say, and proceeded to spread almond butter on an apple slice.

Jack chimed in, "Our friendly neighborhood fireman. At least he accepted your gift. When I offered to give him a free soul journey, he refused, saying it wasn't his thing." Jack grimaced as he popped a piece of shortbread into his mouth.

"Do mushrooms seem like an appropriate gift? They are great health supports after cancer treatments." Aster scrunched her eyes.

Jack took a moment to chew. He said, "Tell ya what, dream weaver, use your nocturnal skills."

Aster frowned at him. "Tsk. What are you suggesting?"

"If Felix has an aversion to mushrooms, well, dream up the winning lottery numbers. Buy a ticket and give it to Felix." Jack toyed with her.

Unwilling to meet Jack's eyes, Aster studied the floor. Every muscle of her face tensed with worry. *Does he already know?* Tightness moved down her neck, all the way to her toes.

"Gambling and psychic abilities rarely mingle well," she said through a clenched jaw. *Yet it worked for me.*

"I'd sleep on it if I were you," he said with a chuckle as he reached for the last cookie.

The uncanny segue made her feel queasy. She placed a hand over her stomach in an attempt to settle it.

"You okay?"

"Indigestion." She paled.

"Make a run for the john if you're gonna hurl," advised Jack.

Aster tottered down the hallway to the bathroom. She knelt at the bowl. The food in her stomach churned while she fretted. *I need to tell Jack I'm worth millions. Putting it off will only make things worse. The sooner, the better.*

A glimmer of openness tugged at her reluctance to share her story. Yet Aster's fortune had been kept secret for so long, a fortress had built in her mind, secured in chains and covered in dust. She vacillated back and forth until the nausea reached an apex. She vomited.

"Yuck," she groaned, rinsing her mouth out at the sink.

"You okay in there?" Jack yelled down the hall.

"Yeah. Put some water on for tea. I'll be right out," Aster said, reaching for her toothbrush.

She returned to the kitchen, looking a bit less green.

Leery of smelling bile, Jack kept his distance. He said, "I'd hug you, but I have a weak stomach around puke vapors. Think ya had a bad apple?"

"No," Aster answered, rummaging through the tea cupboard.

"Touch of the flu?"

Mustering up courage, she said, "It's a nervous stomach. I need to tell ya something."

She chose a box of ginger-chamomile tea and removed a bag. Unceremoniously she plunked the bag into a mug and poured in boiling water.

"What's up? Should I be worried?"

"After Keith died, I had one of my predictive dreams."

"A scary one?" Jack interrupted.

"Not exactly. I dreamed up lottery numbers, and I won."

"That's my girl. See? You can do it. I knew it," Jack said admiringly.

"Yeah, but—" She stopped midsentence, letting out a tormented sigh.

"Winning money is upsetting?"

"No. I enjoyed buying the house, fixing it up, and replacing old furniture. Even gave money to charity—anonymously, of course."

"Jackpot must not have been small then." He looked perplexed.

Aster twisted her hair and said, "The thing is, I never told anybody I won. Felt safer not drawing attention to my luck. Too scared I'd pull in weirdos exploiting my special night visions."

"Or exploit you for your money? That's why you never told me?" Jack's brows raised up in his forehead.

"I had to make sure that you love me for who I am."

Jack said rapidly, "Thought that was obvious. I don't care how much money you have. I've loved you for lifetimes. It took me nearly half a century to find you. I feel a bit stung it took this long to earn your trust. Almost as if I love you more than you love me."

"Sweetie cakes, I'm sorry you feel that way. Our hearts are mutual. I've had trust issues since I was a kid," Aster apologized.

Jack softened. "I get the violent-dad stuff. It's just that you're more than frugal; you're an eccentric old miser."

"Old?" she huffed, tugging at her bangs to cover her forehead.

"Sorry. Figure of speech. I thought I knew everything about you."

Aster winced, picking up the tea bag from the mug. Scalding thumb and index finger, she dropped the steaming bag back in the cup. She said, "I'm a Scorpio; I expose myself slowly. My broker and lawyer don't even know my whole story. You are the only one who knows the winning numbers came in a dream."

Jack plucked a spoon from the dish strainer and handed it to Aster. Not having the customary tea-caddy saucer, she scooped out the bag and tossed the tiny satchel in the sink to cool.

"Thanks for letting me in. I'm not an ogre you need to fear.

We're getting married. You know, partners in life," Jack said, sounding bruised from the revelation.

The thought of mentioning the prenuptial agreement caused the muscles along her spine to tense. Aster balked. "I'm a scared rabbit to the core—a regular loco conejo who wants nothing more than to be your wife." Her stomach gurgled.

"I'm Jack who's got your back." He pointed his thumbs at himself. "It's rather impressive you whizzed up the numbers in a dream. Knew you could do it. I'm beyond intrigued; in fact, downright curious. How much did you win?"

"I'll let you in on my secret. After taxes, seven million. Burned through a million buying the house, fixing it up, and donating a wad to support battered women," she confessed in a shy voice. A sudden spasm in her leg had her envision the iron anklet unlatched. No longer tethered to the enormous dollar sign, she felt great satisfaction knowing that her future would include Jack.

"Real estate in Boulder is outrageous. The house alone must have been half a million."

"Five hundred fifty-five thousand, to be exact. Paid in full," said Aster.

"It's a bit daunting to know you have millions more than I do. Almost feels like I need to catch up. It's shocking to think I'm engaged to a multimillionaire. Until now, I was clueless. Never got why you were so evasive about money. You never flaunted a dime. My dear, you act as if every penny counts," Jack said, appearing bothered.

Aster tried to brush it off. "Aunt Gertie taught me well. She pinched pennies until Abe Lincoln cried 'uncle.'" She clutched the teacup in her hands, too stressed to drop the prenup bomb at this time.

"I'm in the mood to play piano. I need to work out a song before we play at the Boulder Theater next week," Jack said flatly. He walked over to the coatrack and started putting on his shoes.

Aster could tell Jack's urgent need to escape was caused by

anger. She wondered whether to ask him if he wanted to explore the Egypt life, to cheer him up, but changed her mind.

"How about if I cook chicken parmigiana tonight?" she suggested, tempting him with a favorite.

"Nah. I'll order a pizza."

Surprised at the refusal, Aster said, "Do you need a time-out?"

"Bingo," he said and left without another word.

Two days later, Jack showed up with lattes and almond croissants. He arrived early, at half past seven, and found Aster in the living room, twisted in a yoga pose. She wore a pink velour bathrobe over pajamas and had slippers on her feet; her hair was in pigtails. The sound of waves crashing onto the shore floated peacefully out of the CD player.

"Hello, Aster. How's it going?" Jack said, raising his voice above the sound of the waves.

Aster was sitting with her torso turned to the right. At the sound of his voice, she looked up. "Hiya, Jack. I wanted to call you, but that would break the time-out rules," she said and stood up. Her eyes scanned for signs of welcome.

"You ready for a coffee break? I stopped at the Java Joint on the way over," he said, giving no clue as to how he felt.

"Yeah, sure. I could use a pick-me-up. I didn't sleep well," Aster said.

No hug, no kiss, not even a smile from Jack. Aster started to worry that Jack intended to end the relationship. She turned off the CD player and went into the kitchen. Jack followed. At the sight of the croissants, she got two small plates out of the cabinet, hoping the Currier and Ives design would soften his mood.

They sat across from each other.

Jack stared into her eyes and said, "I'm working hard trying to sort out all the money stuff. I know you have your reasons, but the whole surprise threw me off. For one, I thought I knew who you were. The lying made me wonder what other secrets you're keeping. Are you some type of Dr. Jekyll and Mr. Hyde?"

"Jack, I was overly cautious; that's all. My grandmother lost all her savings to a retirement home. I don't wanna do that. There's nothing else. ... I'm not leading a double life," she said.

Jack struggled for a second and then blurted a seemingly memorized speech: "You had money issues with your late husband. And with me, you're so hung up on protecting your fortune, I fear the issues that will come between us. I don't know where I fit in, or if I should even try."

"Big deal—I'm quirky with money. I've got a simple solution that worked with Keith: We can stay separate but equal. We have separate bank accounts, and we split the bills," Aster said, as though it were the best solution in the world.

Jack frowned and then said solemnly, "There's more. I'm uncomfortable being an underdog financially. I know it's a guy thing, a pride bruiser, and it won't work for me."

"You're gonna let an ego trip get in the way of our relationship?" Aster said, taken aback.

"Nope, not gonna do that. I plan to even the score," Jack said, taking the lid off his coffee and dunking the croissant.

"Ask Grannyme for more lottery numbers?" Aster inquired. She impatiently waited for him to swallow the mouthful.

"Nope."

"What then?"

"Going on tour."

"Playing music?" Aster asked. Her tone implied there was little money potential for a garage-band keyboardist.

"Think again. Soul-journey seminars," Jack answered smugly.

"With Tasha Wingstrom?" Aster grimaced.

"Yep. She's a producer and has connections all over the place. She wants to do seminars once a month this winter and then a tour of major cities in the summer."

"I can't stand that woman." Aster's face turned three shades of sour.

"She's a handful, but I make big bucks at the seminars."

"Is it worth putting up with her?"

"Up to ten grand a pop." Jack enjoyed another soggy bite.

"Wow." Aster's eyes enlarged.

Jack said, "That's not all. I'm changing up a few things around here. I'm gonna rent my place out as an Airbnb. It's better income than signing a long-term lease. Rosita will do the cleaning."

"That's a smart idea," Aster mused. The change meant Jack needed to live elsewhere for it to work.

"It gives me flexibility if I want to use the townhome for any reason. I'm also renting out my office at night to Discovery Center graduates."

"You never use it at night. That's a brilliant idea. And you'll keep teaching as well?" she asked.

"Yes indeed. I can live off my teaching income and save the rest."

"Which means?" Aside from the financial improvements, Jack's flexibility plan concerning the townhome made her uneasy. For if he wanted out, he had an easy escape to end the relationship. And yet, she wanted a prenuptial agreement. Fearing she sounded silly questioning his money plans, she kept the thought to herself.

"On the drive over, I wasn't 100 percent convinced we could work it out, but the more I talk about the changes, the more practical it all seems."

"Building a nest egg is a great idea. It's self-empowering. You and I can save money living together too. I have no house payment," Aster said encouragingly.

"It's all good except for one snag. I know Tasha is not on your top-ten list. She is part of the package deal. Can you handle me working with her?"

"Not sure! I hate her, but I like her ability to offer you big bucks. Last thing I want is to give her the power to drive us apart," Aster said, gritting her teeth.

"Let me remind you, Tasha will never be anything but a business partner. I swear on my mother's grave." He raised a palm as if taking an oath.

Sensing the question was a challenge, a part of the quest to allow, Aster called upon Grannyme for help. In a flash, the image of standing at the crossroads and looking at the smooth road With Jack and the bumpy road Without Jack, had Aster say, "More than once Grannyme said you are a good guy and advised me to stick with you. So, yes, I will tolerate Tasha—as long as the relationship stays professional."

"No problem. You know, Grannyme is right. We are destined to be together, and why fight it?" Jack flashed an adorable smile.

"Yahoo! I was so worried that I pushed you away. These past few days have been lonely without you." Aster clutched his hands.

"Tell me about it. I was a perpetual bachelor until you came along. It blows my mind how much you mean to me. The old me would have avoided the confrontation at all costs and ended the relationship in a snap. The new me got worked up and processed every detail until I nearly exploded."

"I could tell you were angry with me," she said.

Seeming to contemplate before answering, Jack said, "At first, I was; and then I was angry at myself. My head spun from thinking too hard. When I realized I want to grow old with you, it pissed me off, because I don't have a retirement plan and you do. So, I called up my buddy Tony; he's a financial consultant."

"Your friend in California?"

"Yep. Tony gave me all these great ideas. He also advised me to hold on to you."

"Smart friend." She winked at him.

"Yeah. Providing we worked it all out, I asked Tony to be my best man."

Chapter 20

Fort Collins

Aster poured a cup of coffee. Wrapped in a pink velour bathrobe, she sat at the kitchen table, thankful Jack's and her relationship had returned to normal. Her phone rang, and she answered it.

"Hi, Mom," Iris said cheerfully.

"Hello, Iris. What's up?"

"I just got back from soaking at Saratoga Hot Springs in Wyoming. I was there with a friend. It's a mellow place. You and Jack ought to go there for your birthday. There's a bed-and-breakfast that you'd love."

"Mellow is about my speed. I dreamed about a hot spring last night," Aster admitted.

"Then it's bound to happen, isn't it? Listen, I gotta go, my neighbor is at the door. I'll call ya later. Love ya," Iris said.

"Love you. Later. Bye." Aster hung up.

Little quickies on the phone were common for them. She and Iris were very close. In fact, Iris was the only one in the Felman family who knew the story behind Aster's predictive dreams.

Aster stared out the kitchen window, watching leaves fall from the maple tree. Swirls of reddish foliage aimlessly rose and fell in the autumn wind. Pondering Iris's advice, she recalled the previous night's dream.

The scene started on the purple cushion. Like Alice in *Alice in Wonderland,* Aster had shrunk in size. A red maple leaf floated at her side. She sat upon it and flew around on a test-drive. Using the power of her mind, she steered it like a spaceship. Suddenly Jack appeared. The stem of his identical leaf attached to hers, and they soared north in tandem. Both wore gloves and scarves, as if intending to take a journey.

After a while, they met up with Iris.

Iris sat atop an oak leaf. Her legs dangled over the sculptured edge, fitting snugly at the indentations.

All three joined hands. A tabletop appeared, and plates of omelets sat in front of them.

"Would you like some butter?" Jack asked as he pulled a butter dish out of thin air.

Iris buttered a muffin. A piece fell onto her shirt, leaving a trail of crumbs. She glanced at the soiled top, gave a carefree shrug, and continued enjoying the food.

The scene changed abruptly, and Aster and Jack flew to Wyoming. They hovered over a small town in a large valley. Below them, twelve streets formed a community. A river swung a curved arm through the town. In the center, like a hole in a bagel, steam evaporated from hot springs. The smell of sulfur welcomed them as they landed at the water's edge.

Just as Aster stuck her foot in the water to test the temperature, she heard the words, "Hello, are you there?"

Full-sized Aster sat at the kitchen table. The leaves in the backyard swirled in the wind. She turned to focus on Jack. He stood at the kitchen counter, dressed in jeans and an olive-green Henley sweater, pouring himself a cup of coffee.

Aster admired how the color made his eyes pop. *Handsome sight,* she thought privately.

"Gathering wool?" said Jack, adding cream to the coffee.

"Oh gosh, remembering a traveling dream—a quasi-prediction. Iris called a few minutes ago and suggested we go to a hot spring. Last night, I dreamed about visiting a hot spring."

"Did you dream about the same hot spring Iris went to?" he asked.

"Yeah, Saratoga Hot Springs in Wyoming."

"Tell me the dream," asked Jack.

Aster described the entire dream sequence.

Jack was already working on a second cup of coffee when she finished the story. He snickered at the play on words, "Leaf on a trip to Wyoming. What a green way to travel. I'm ready to get out of town; go soak the old bones. Aren't you?"

"I'm thrilled the leaf ride took me on a virtual tour. I'm so relieved it's a small and quiet place. We can relax in the hot water. Iris said there's a bed-and-breakfast. Let's check it out," she said.

Aster picked up her cell phone and did a search. The Bill Cody House came on-screen.

"Great! You found it. See if they have any openings," Jack said enthusiastically.

"November 10 and 11," she answered, not mentioning that November 11 was her birthday.

"I know for a fact I'm free that weekend. Make reservations," Jack encouraged her.

"Okay." Her thumbs sped across the screen.

Jack picked up his phone to do a search. In a few moments, he said, "Look. Here's a photo of the Bill Cody B and B on their website. Isn't it charming?" He showed her a picture of a two-story Victorian house with a covered front porch.

"Cute."

Jack nodded. "Much more romantic than a hotel. Look. The blurb says the house is zoned a historical building. Maybe it was one of the first homes built when the community got settled."

Aster read a welcome note attached to the reservation confirmation. She said, "Apparently, the owner's name is Rosemary. She can probably fill you in on the details."

"Looking forward to it."

On November 10, Aster awoke with the sun. The house shone spotless as she made the last-minute preparations for the trip. Unsure what type of erratic fall weather Wyoming had in store, Aster packed as if she might earn a Girl Scout merit badge.

The kitchen door slammed shut.

"Gassed up the car," Jack said, taking inventory of the brimmed totes lined up along the washer and dryer.

"Good. I'm all packed and ready to go," Aster said.

"You realize we're staying two nights, not a week? I'd have to cancel clients if you changed our plans," he teased. A playful grin deepened his crows' feet.

"I like being prepared for whatever we might run into. Did ya wash the car?" she said expectantly.

"What for?"

She shot him a look of disbelief. "It's dirty."

He said, "Come on, loosen up, Aster. We're gonna be entering cowboy country. Dontcha think it's a bit rugged to bring Colorado dirt to Wyoming?"

Aster felt foolish complaining any further. "All right then. I'm fine as long as the windshield is clean."

"Already done."

"Let's get this stuff in the car," directed Aster.

Aster and Jack caught Highway 287 in Longmont and headed north. They reached Fort Collins, where they planned to have breakfast with Iris.

"I finally get to meet your daughter. I missed her by minutes when you were in the hospital," Jack said.

"I know. At least for today, she doesn't have any students to deal with. She's a people person. Real easy to talk to. I should call her and let her know we are almost there," Aster suggested.

Jack turned down the music and absently played the piano part on the steering wheel with one hand.

Aster talked on the phone, "Okay, Iris, we'll meet you at Marselle's. ... Yeah, I remember how to get there. See ya in a bit. ... Good-bye."

Aster stowed her cell phone in her purse. She said, "You're going to love Marselle's. It's a good thing we are getting there early. We'll beat the crowd. People will stand outside for an hour just to get a table."

"I'm starving. Can hardly wait to get there. What kind of food?" asked Jack.

"It's cajun food; you know, Louisiana style."

"Where is it?" Jack said, reading business signs on both sides of the street.

"We just passed Harmony Road. It's about eight traffic lights ahead."

"That's near the college. Why don't we just go to her house? Iris lives in that neighborhood, right?"

Hesitant to divulge the truth, she said, "Well ... ah ... how do I say this without sounding too crass? Okay, the short and sweet version. Iris is a slob. Ya need a shovel to find the floor. She has three cats. Anywhere ya sit, it's like being submerged in a hairbrush. The entire house reeks of eau de litter box. I can't handle being inside."

Jack suppressed a smile. "Wow, polar opposites. When she was little, I imagine you chasing Iris around the house with a vacuum nozzle. *Varoom!* Catching dirt as it hit the floor," he teased.

"I swear, the character Pig Pen from the *Peanuts* comic was her mentor."

"The battle to keep the house clean must have driven you mad." He gave a sideways glance as he chuckled.

Stung by the honesty, Aster confessed, "At age five, I was chief cook and bottle washer for my cosmetic-crazy mother. When I moved in with Gertie, I had daily farm chores. I grew up as Little Miss Responsible and didn't want Iris to suffer the same burdens. Besides, it was less stress for me to clean than to get her to do it. My lopsided reasoning backfired, for I created a bona fide slob."

"I'm a member of the Pig Pen club too. So far, you've put up with me. Is it pity or love that keeps you at my side?" inquired Jack.

"It helps that you come with a maid. My days as a helicopter mom are over."

"That's the kind of mom I grew up with. She did everything for me," Jack said.

"No doubt. At times, I do wish the messy little boy inside of you would grow up and pitch in," declared Aster.

They grew silent.

Jack spoke up, "Honestly I never got it until now that cleaning is more than a compulsion for you: it's a burden. You must resent me."

"Cleaning is an ingrained habit. What makes it less of a burden is when it stays clean. I admit picking up after you is not much different than living with Iris," she said, relieved to broach the subject.

"Really?" Jack made a disappointed face.

"Ideally, I was hoping for a liberated male, but with your financial makeover, I chose not to push it," Aster said.

"By 'liberated male,' you mean what exactly?" Jack asked.

"Equality. A liberated man steps out of the breadwinner-only paradigm. He becomes androgynous and does domestic chores in tandem with his partner. You could start by taking a cooking class or watching cooking shows on TV. Also doing the dishes every day," Aster explained with a touch of sharpness.

"Don't know which I hate worse: conflict or cleaning. I'm so unprepared with a comeback, I'm speechless."

"Savor the rare moment, and find a parking place. We just passed Marselle's," Aster snapped.

"I could get into cooking. I doubt I'll ever get as good as you," Jack offered.

"And dishes?"

"*Grr!* All right, already," said Jack, sounding as if he had just agreed to get a tooth pulled.

All the tables inside the restaurant were full. The lace cafe curtains, cloth napkins, and fleur-de-lis upholstery created a French ambience. Pleasant aromas wafting from the kitchen confirmed the feeling that you had come to the right place to eat.

Iris sat at a table, reading on her cell phone. Her brown curly hair practically reached the tabletop. When she stood to greet Aster with a hug, the family resemblance became apparent. The two women were the same height. Both had tall, slender body types, though Iris was a good ten pounds thinner. Their high cheekbones showed the same curves and angles.

"Missed ya. Now I gotta kiss ya," Aster said softly and gave Iris a peck on the cheek.

"Ditto," Iris whispered, returning a quick kiss. She turned to greet Jack with a hug as well.

Not until everyone sat down did Aster notice cat hair clinging to Iris's black cardigan. Immediately scanning the arms of her own purple fleece, Aster removed a stray hair. Acting as though it was a hot ember, she yanked the bottom of the jacket away from her body, inspecting it frantically for more clinging hairs. *Yuck,* Aster's internal voice complained, as she plucked three calico strands from her garment and flicked them to the floor.

From years of experience, Iris ignored her mother's fastidious behavior and engaged in conversation with Jack. "You two are on your way to Saratoga Hot Springs. It's a great place to chill. Normally I pitch a tent, hike in the Medicine Bow Mountains, and go soak. Last visit, I stayed at the B and B. Either way, the springs are one of my favorite places to gaze at the stars. Ya ever been there?" Iris asked.

"First time. Stargazing, ya say. I can handle that. My phone has an app that identifies constellations," Jack said.

"Cool. Astronomy 101. This week's homework for my class is to complete the dot-to-dot drawing of the constellation Orion. For extra credit, their parents sign the drawing, indicating they located Orion in the sky." Iris's smile matched Aster's.

"Right. You teach elementary-school urchins." Jack measured three feet from the floor with a splayed hand, depicting little people.

"Third-graders," Iris said, raising her hand to four feet.

"Hello, I'm Jessica," the waitress greeted them. She handed out menus and poured everyone coffee. "Special today is a shrimp-gumbo omelet with a dash of okra, a side of grits, and braised mustard greens. If you want—"

While the waitress explained the options, Jack doused his coffee with cream and took a sip. He interrupted the waitress's spiel, saying, "What's up with this coffee?"

"It's Louisiana-style French roast. Will it do, or do you care for something else?" Jessica inquired.

"Sweetie, it's blended with chicory. Good liver support," Aster said, joining the conversation.

Jack's face relaxed into approval. He said, "It's all good. I'll take some extra cream, though." He opened up the menu to peruse the entrees.

The waitress sped off toward the kitchen.

Iris, a frequent patron, already knew what she wanted. Nervous hands wrapped around her cup. Looking expectant, as if wondering how to approach the topic, she blurted out, "Mom, I'm seeing someone."

Aster, who only moments ago had delighted in her choice of a veggie omelet smothered in hollandaise sauce, feigned a polite, "Male or female?" Remembering the hours of consoling Iris's broken heart from one failed relationship after another, Aster suppressed the impulse to protect her daughter.

"A guy. Kenneth. He's a helicopter pilot. He's got a pair of chocolate-brown eyes that make me melt into a messy nougat. Real yummy!" said Iris.

"Nothing like romance to feed the soul. I'd like to meet Kenneth. We could double-date," Jack said, flashing a secret wink at Iris.

"That would be interesting," Aster said cautiously.

Jessica returned to the table, refilling the coffees. She asked, "Ready to order?"

Jack chose the special. Aster ordered the veggie omelet. Iris opted for *the medley,* a creamed-spinach plate with shrimp, poached egg, and bacon.

Full of concern, Iris said, "Oh it's dreadful! Patches's arthritis is so bad, she can't jump onto the bed anymore. Her belly's riddled with tumors. The vet advised to put her down."

"Ugh, what a tough turn. I take it Patches is a cat," Jack said consolingly.

Iris nodded. "A long-haired calico."

The mention of Patches made Aster think of Aunt Gertie, also known as Patch because of her penchant for mismatched items. The fact that the name implied a poor old ragamuffin had never bothered Gertie Olsen.

"I like cats, but not that fur ball. She never failed to use my legs as a clawing post. Drawing blood finished her off as far as I'm concerned," Aster said, sounding fierier than she was aware.

"Where's the love in that, Mom?" Iris reprimanded.

"Nowhere to be seen," Aster snorted. "That bloodletter needs to reincarnate as a mellower cat."

"Thanks," Iris said, sulking.

"The situation must be stressful for you. How long have you had her?" Jack said, kicking Aster's shoe.

Aster shot Jack a sideways glance followed by a slight nod to let him know she'd gotten his message to lighten up.

"Since freshman year of college. Got her at the pound when I broke up with my high-school sweetheart," Iris said sullenly.

"Yes. You and Patches have been through a lot. Perhaps you

and I will have to go shopping after it's all over. We both know you love that pesky feline, while I loathe it," Aster said consolingly, placing a hand on Iris's arm.

"Shopping therapy works for me," Iris said, her eyes welling with tears.

Jack made light of the situation. He flicked a thumb at Jessica, carrying a tray from the kitchen, and in a British accent said, "Ready to tuck in for a bit of nosh?"

"Reckon so. Cheers mate," Aster returned the lilt, lifting her coffee to a three-way toast.

After enjoying a delicious meal, they bid farewell at the cafe door.

Iris said, "Have a happy birthday, Mom." She gave Aster a light peck on the cheek.

"Thanks, love," Aster said with a smile.

Jack opened his arms for a bear hug. He met Iris's eyes with a covert glance and said, "See ya soon."

Iris fell into the embrace, saying, "Real soon."

"What's that smirk all about?" Aster asked.

"Nothin'. Just holding back a burp," Iris replied. She swallowed air only to let out an unladylike belch.

"That's my girl. She can burp whole sentences," Aster murmured into Jack's ear. She fled outside, away from potential disgusted onlookers.

"You're excused," Jack said, pointing at Iris. He then secretly flipped Iris an okay sign as he strode off to the car.

Chapter 21

Wyoming

Jack and Aster continued their journey north in Aster's Subaru Outback. Once out of Colorado, the mountains receded and were replaced by rolling prairie grass and a few rock outcroppings. Scattered herds of antelope grazed lazily on the foliage. The highway twisted along the uneven terrain. Aster sat behind the wheel, enjoying the varied course of the road. Full of caffeine, she and Jack chatted endlessly. Time seemed to zip by. Before they knew it, they had reached Laramie, Wyoming, where they stopped to gas up and switch drivers.

"Brr! That wind is icy." Aster blew air through her lips as she buckled her seat belt.

"It's snowing," Jack announced.

"Only flurries. Gotta be the first snow of the year. Everything here is bone-dry," Aster said.

Jack took the scenic route through the Medicine Bow Mountains. The winding road and pined forest reminded them of Colorado. They drove through a half a foot of snow at the summit and then found dry road on the western slope. Continuing north, they entered a wide valley that followed the Platte River. Huge ranches stocked cattle, horses, and sheep. Aster enjoyed comparing the cattle ranches to the milk farms in Minnesota. Farms where she grew up were smaller, green, and resembled patchwork quilts, whereas the arid Wyoming ranches looked like a tan endless carpet with a meandering river flowing through it.

The clock on the dashboard indicated it was almost noon. Feeling weary from the trip, Aster complained, "It's been three hours since breakfast. Can't wait to get out of the car. My butt is sore from sitting so long."

"Look at that rusty old sign: 'Saratoga Airport.' It's gotta be one of the smallest airports I've ever seen," Jack said, laughing.

A lone dirt runway cut a straight path through a field. No signs of life except for two buildings, an aluminum-sided hangar, and a shed no bigger than an ice shanty.

"The shed must be the control tower, 'cause there's a long antenna above the roof," Aster said, impressed with the compacted efficiency.

"Private planes and helicopters are the only things that could land here," Jack said.

"Yeah. Weather permitting," she added.

The road descended into Saratoga. Other amenities to sustain life, such as a gas station and a motel, prompted Jack to whoop, "Yee haw! Hope the Bear Motel serves burgers. In the mood for one, aren't you?"

"Not yet. Back there, we passed Walnut Street, which is the turnoff to the hot springs," Aster said confidently.

"How do you know?"

"My dream. Everything looks familiar. It feels like déjà vu, like I've been here before. This is Bridge Street. Go left. The bed-and-breakfast is down on Third Street."

"Vivid dream," Jack said, impressed at the accurate recall.

"Story of my life." Aster shrugged nonchalantly.

They pulled in front of the Bill Cody House, a red-brick two-story Victorian with gabled roofs and a screened-in front porch. A scalloped wrought-iron fence enclosed the tidy yard composed of manicured flowerbeds, flagstone walkways, and a small statue of Buffalo Bill Cody on horseback. The property was so quaint that it took little imagination to picture the home on the cover of *Bed-and-Breakfast Beautiful* magazine.

"Who needs a GPS when you're around!" Jack gave a wink. "Let's go inside. I need to take a leak." He hurried out of the car.

Aster got out and took a moment to stretch. The blowing wind smelled clean, but the cold penetrated deep into her bones. She hadn't experienced that in the dream. Wasting no time, she snagged her fleece coat and caught up to Jack.

Inside the closed-in porch, a sticky note attached to the window of the beveled glass door read, "Welcome, Jack and Aster. Please enter. Call me upon arrival. Phone is on the kitchen counter. Enjoy your stay! Rosemary."

A coiled radiator in the foyer blasted out delicious heat. Aster warmed her backside as she studied the multiple options of where to go. She could either take a right into the billiard room, a left into the living room, go forward down the hall, or go up a grand oak staircase, presumably to the bedrooms. She explored the downstairs and found the floor plan enabled her to walk in a complete circle, with the hallway cutting a path through the center of the circle. She lingered in the study filled with antique furniture and bookcases full of novels. Her attention was drawn to a maroon three-ringed binder atop a claw-foot table snug against the bay window. Its cover, typed in a calligraphy font, read, "Places to Eat in Saratoga and Location of Hot Springs." Inside, actual menus from local restaurants were inserted into plastic pages. The overview of the map resembled a waffle-iron grid with a river going through it, exactly like in her dream. Yellow highlights from a marker showed directions to the hot springs.

Aster ventured to the kitchen in the very back of the house. She heard the toilet flush and saw Jack leaving a small bathroom.

He sighed. "Much better. Suppose we should make our arrival known."

Next to the phone was a note: "Call Rosemary soon as you arrive," accompanied by a local number.

Aster called and heard a boisterous voice on the other end. "Welcome! Glad you made it. Make yourselves at home. I'll see you two in the morning. Just don't lock the door. My husband is spending the night in Cheyenne, and he's grabbed my keys."

"Rosemary, your home is lovely. You don't live here?" Aster inquired.

"Nah. I live way over on the other side of town."

Aster mused inwardly, *How far can it be? Maybe a few blocks*. She asked, "Are we the only ones staying here tonight?"

"Yep. Tomorrow, there'll be another couple."

"All right. We'll see ya in the morning," Aster said.

"Hold on. What do ya want for breakfast, and what time works for ya?" Rosemary asked.

They worked out the details.

As Aster hung up the phone, she said to Jack, "We've got the whole place to ourselves. Rosemary won't be here till breakfast. She's very trusting of strangers. That woman has a great setup here; place practically runs itself. Let's unpack."

"Okay. After that, let's go explore and scope out a place to eat. I'd love a burger and a cold beer. Let's see if there are any microbreweries."

"Then, afterward, we'll go soak," Aster added.

❋ ❋

The town was small indeed, just as Aster had dreamed. The community thrived year-round, with only one gas station, one grocery store, a post office, three bars, a handful of eateries, and various gift shops for tourists.

Aster and Jack ate burgers and salads at the local microbrewery. They played a game of pool afterward to allow the food to digest. At the hot-springs parking lot, they even parked in the very same spot where the flying leaf had landed in the dream. She led Jack down the sidewalk. A huge thermometer on the side of the changing room showed that it was thirty-two degrees

Fahrenheit. Back home in Boulder, where the elevation was a thousand feet lower, temperatures had not gotten that low yet. Aster's teeth chattered as she smelled sulfur. There was a flight of stairs, and steam rose from it, coming from the pool nestled inside three cinder-block walls. Apparently, the walls gave protection from the wind, for the steam wafted up in straight lines. The dressing rooms enclosed the perimeter to the south, fashioning a cozy courtyard ambience.

"The men's room is there. Women's is over here. See ya in a bit. Brr!" Aster directed Jack and then hurried inside.

Thankful for the heated building, she undressed down to her swimsuit and left her head covered in a knitted hat. Dreading to bare her legs to the cold, she stepped into a pair of flip-flops, wrapped a towel around her shoulders, and power walked to the pool.

Jack stood poolside, his full belly rounded over his swim trunks. He was chatting with a plump couple who seemed impervious to the cold.

Aster, who was thinner, wasted no time and slipped into the wet warmth. "Ah, nice," she said with a sigh. She squatted, since the water only reached hip level. Once again experiencing a déjà vu sensation, she found comfort in the surroundings.

"Hey, sweets, come meet Dottie and Wayne. They're from Cheyenne," Jack said, pulling Aster out of her reverie.

Aster duckwalked the short distance in order to keep her shoulders submersed.

Jack chuckled and said, "This is my waddling fiancée, Aster. Fell in love with my little ducky at first sight. Aster, meet Wayne and Dottie. Wayne is a rodeo coordinator; Dottie is a reporter for the *Wyoming Tribune Eagle*."

"Hello, pleased to meet ya," Aster said. Their chubby faces were so smooth, Aster could not tell how old they were.

Wayne tipped his rodeo-chief baseball cap in a friendly hello, exposing a bald scalp. "Same here," he said. His horse-tooth smile gave Aster the impression he was an adorable character.

"I suppose Jack already told ya we're from Boulder." Aster smiled back.

A middle-aged man in a cowboy hat cut into their conversation, saying, "Just what we need, a pool full of liberals. Ya oughta go back from where ya came. This here is a Republican water hole." The man gave them a vicious sneer. He was built solid like an out-of-shape football player. He cracked his knuckles, daring them to stay.

Aster sized up the cowboy as a redneck ready to fight. In his attempt to express dominance, he seemed small. She reminded herself that he was not her father, the huge monster who'd sent her to the hospital with a bleeding liver and a broken finger. She gave him a pitiful glance and said, "Whatever."

Jack, Dottie, Wayne, and Aster watched the cowboy shrink his inflated chest as he grabbed a metal hip flask at the pool's edge and took a large gulp.

The drink fueled the cowboy up again. He dug his fists into his hips, emulating the stance of a superhero, and began to mouth off. "Damn hippies. Can't ya keep that peace-and-love crap in Colorado? They ought to ban you fruit loops from coming here. Before ya know it, you'll try to grow alfalfa sprouts in the pool."

"Go home and sleep it off, buster," Aster said, having no patience to deal with an intoxicated man. For the first time in her life, she spoke back to a belligerent sot, for she was no longer a child—nor was she alone.

"Gotta sassy one here," the cowboy said, seeming to enjoy the interaction.

"Sheriff in these parts don't like drunks disturbing the peace," Jack said, quoted a line from a western movie, thinking the cowboy's pea brain might relate.

"Old Clifford Rainey. That codger don't know his ass from a hole in the ground," the cowboy growled.

"Sheriff's got a cot with your name on it." Wayne gave a forceful warning.

Wayne and Jack took a few steps forward.

"Look at all the air pollution that blew in here. Reckon I best leave so I don't get contaminated," the cowboy spat sarcastically.

He clambered out of the pool, exposing multiple scars along his arms and torso. Dripping wet, he put on his fringed leather coat. Without bothering to dress further, he snatched up an old-fashioned leather saddlebag, a pair of pointed cowboy boots, and the flask, and proceeded to shuffle toward the parking lot.

"How do you think he got all those scars?" Aster whispered.

"Those are wrangling scars from working the rodeo. Probably too injured to ride anything but an old nag now. I didn't recognize him until he got closer. He calls himself the Duke. All the folks in these parts know he's nothin' but a washed-up roper," Wayne said in a low voice.

"I'm glad he's gone. Nothing but trouble. My daddy was an angry drunk. Being around people like that gives me the willies," Dottie said, pulling a sour face.

Aster met a pair of gray eyes staring her down. Two beady orbs scanned for safety. Recognizing the fear instinct, Aster said, "That was one heck of an introduction. You two come here often?"

"We come here the first weekend of the month. Does wonders for the arthritis," Dottie said. Her red hair was twisted up in a bun to keep it dry.

Aster noted Dottie's professionally done nails and a sizable diamond ring, possibly a whole carat. Aster said, "Dottie, I assume by the gorgeous rock on your finger that you two are married."

"Oh yes, twenty-five years. We're soul mates," Dottie said, smiling.

"Which means we drive each other crazy day after day," Wayne said with a chuckle.

"We're mates too. We're on our first year, but it seems like lifetimes." Jack placed a hand on Aster's shoulder.

The two couples talked for more than an hour. They soaked,

got overheated, and climbed out of the pool to cool off countless times, repeating the cycle until their stiff muscles turned to mush.

Dottie, who out of habit brought extra water, gave a bottle to each of her newfound friends.

Dusk had fallen. Overcast skies blocked the opportunity to stargaze.

With wrinkly fingers and all, Aster felt waterlogged and simultaneously thirsty. Not in the mood to continue as a foursome over drinks or dinner, she avoided the subject. In a subdued tone along and with a suggestive wink, she said to Jack, "Let's go snuggle up."

"Only need to ask one time," Jack said.

Jack brought the cooler in from the car, carrying it to the porch of the B and B. "How about a nightcap, my dear? I brought a vintage Bordeaux."

"I packed brie, olives, grapes, and crackers," Aster said as she held the porch door open for Jack.

"Nice-sounding combo. Let's do it." He made his way back to the kitchen.

They found wineglasses hanging from a rack.

Aster arranged a platter of food, and they retreated to the dining area.

"I say we should make a toast," Jack said, smelling the wine.

"I'm delighted all the tension from traveling disappeared. To the relaxing hot springs," Aster said, raising her glass.

"To the hot springs," Jack echoed.

As Jack poured them each a second glass, Aster said, "Did you go into the billiard room at all?"

"No. Why?"

"There's an upright piano in there. You could play something for me." She was feeling a little tipsy.

"Only if it's tuned up," he said and strode into the next room.

Aster found the light switch and turned it on.

"Wow, such an oldie. I learned on a puppy like this." Jack sat on the bench and played a few chords. He gave an approving nod and said, "Darling, this one's for you."

Aster swayed to the melody, running her fingers through his hair. The music sent a dazzling sensation all the way down to her feet. When he stopped, she said, "Pretty song. Thanks." She hugged him from behind.

"It's a Marvin Gaye number called, 'Let's Get It On.' I thought I'd lure you in with a romantic song," Jack said. He then mimicked the motion of winding a spool on a fishing rod.

Jack reached around, took her hand and kissed it, planted another kiss on her forearm, and then stood and kissed her shoulder and her neck. Finally, he gave her a lingering kiss full on the mouth.

Aster said, "If this is what you've got for bait, I'm game." Despite the romantic moment, the taste of alcohol from the kiss reminded her of the Duke at the pool. The guy was nothing but a sottish cad.

"Let's grab our wine and go upstairs. I've got more tricks in my tackle box to show you," Jack said seductively.

Their room had a touch of yesteryear, filled with an impressive array of antiques. The set of leaf-carved oak furniture included a bed, dresser, freestanding oval mirror, washbasin, and nightstand. Wainscoting and floral wallpaper covered the walls. Pullback lace curtains dressed the windows.

Jack helped Aster out of her clothes and guided her to the canopy bed. He said, "Being in this bedroom is like going back in time. I bet we had a room like this in one of our past lives."

"Does it give you warm fuzzies?" she asked.

"Oh yeah."

"Me too. Brr! My feet are cold," Aster said and hopped into bed.

Jack picked up the coconut oil from the nightstand and

offered, "I'll warm them up for you." He oiled his hands and massaged every inch of her feet, taking care to get in between the toes. Then, he worked his way up her shins and thighs.

"Oh, babe, that feels marvelous." Aster let out a sigh.

"Good," Jack said softly. He brushed lightly over her pubic mound, a slight tease, and caressed her stomach and breasts. The nipples he did not oil; instead, he licked them until they stood erect.

Aster groaned.

Jack moved up and kissed her passionately on the mouth.

The taste of alcohol made Aster pull away. The Duke returned once again. Try as she might to push the thought away, the image the gruff man stayed. How dare he ruin the moment! Wanting to focus on Jack, she reached for the oil bottle, intending to rub some on him.

"What's wrong?" Jack asked as he witnessed a frown on her face.

"Our lovemaking feels real erotic, then—wham!—the alcohol on your breath makes me flash on Cowboy Duke. Probably reminds me of my dad. It's not fair to have Dad crap interrupting us," she said with a pout.

"I've got an idea: hypnosis."

"What?"

"It's another weird thing I know how to do." Jack shrugged.

"Okay." She set the oil bottle down.

Jack placed a palm on Aster's pubic mound. He talked in a slow, rhythmic tone, saying, "With every exhale, breathe into my hand. Send the breath down your spine. On your inhales, send the breath to the top of your head."

Aster followed the instructions.

Jack said, "There ya go; that's the ticket. Now, imagine a violet cloud enveloping you—a cleansing cloud that washes away thoughts of the Duke, cleansing away thoughts of your dad. ... Good job. Now, as the violet cloud goes away, a golden cloud envelops you. The golden cloud seals in the good; the golden cloud protects you from the unwanted. You are safe. Repeat after me: 'I am safe.'"

"I am safe."

Jack asked, "Are you willing to continue with the lovemaking?"

"Yes."

"Then, breathe again into my hand until you feel your body opening up," Jack instructed. He palmed her mound the entire time, and charged himself with energy by breathing up and down his own spine as well.

It took a few minutes, and then a surge of energy poured out of Aster. An erotic energy rushed in her loins. No longer trapped in her head, she uttered in excitement, "Jack, it worked. I'm ready—very ready."

She grabbed the coconut oil and lubed him up.

In no time, both Jack and Aster were hungry to renew their ancient vows. He worked his penis in slowly. Once fully inside, they melded into one—heart, body, and soul—flowing to the sacred dance, rising to the apex, until fireworks burst from within.

❋ ❋

The next morning, Aster awoke in the canopy bed. Jack lay on his side, facing away from her, in a peaceful slumber. The smaller bed—a full size, as opposed to the queen bed they at home—had their bodies snuggling close all night.

Today was her birthday, but she felt content not drawing any attention to getting older. Aster's mind drifted from appreciating the sex the night before, to being thankful she was no longer alone. The sound of the front door shutting and footsteps walking down the hallway made her guess Rosemary had just arrived. The clock on the nightstand showed that it was seven thirty; breakfast was in an hour.

Aster got up to use the restroom. The second she left the toasty covers, instant gooseflesh had her snatch a complimentary bathrobe and sprint into the tiniest bathroom ever. Shivering while sitting on the ice-cold toilet seat, she spotted a wall heater just out of reach. Praying the heater worked, she turned it on; much to her delight, the inner coils turned red. Cold feet hastened Aster back to the bed, where she crawled under the covers.

Newly awake, Jack watched her dash into the bed.

"Brr! Warm me up, sweetie cakes. I'm freezing." She clung to Jack, absorbing his heat. "Mm! The sheets smell like coconut," she added.

Jack remained on his back, content as a teddy bear. A brief smile graced his lips as he said sleepily, "Good morning, you sexy vixen. How'd ya sleep?"

"Like a rock," Aster said, rubbing her feet together.

"Hot sex is the best sleeping pill in the world. Nice, wasn't it?" Jack said, planting a quick kiss on the top of her head.

"More like delightful! It was yummy being on the same page. Thanks for getting me out of my head. Don't know what possessed me to mouth off to the drunk in the hot springs. It's something I'd ordinarily never do. Then, like magic, you put a hand on my yoni, and—whammo!—we were back on track." Aster gave a pleasant sigh.

"You felt a little far away, so I reeled you in."

"Where did you learn how to do that?"

"Years ago, at the Discovery Center. I modified it a bit to fit our scenario," Jack explained.

Aster said, "Nice move, Fisherman Jack. Keep that one in your tackle box. I'm beginning to think it's true what you said about repeating the same skills in subsequent lives. After a gazillion tries, you get masterful at it."

"Told ya from the get-go: I'm all about repeating history. How about s'more snugglin'?" Jack reached over and palmed her breast.

"Jack, you maniac. Rosemary's downstairs in the kitchen. We arranged to have breakfast at eight thirty. That's in less than an hour."

"All right. I'll go shower. Better yet, let's take one together," said Jack, rubbing the sleep out of his eyes.

Following the smell of bacon, Jack and Aster headed down the oak staircase. His still-wet white hair was slicked back; her hair, also wet, was twisted up in a bun. They both wore zippered sweatshirts over their street clothes. Aster held onto the ornate banister, for the stairway appeared steeper when descending than it had while ascending.

When they reached the hallway, Jack offered his arm and said in a French accent, "Shall we, my dear? Zee aroma has a nice bouquet of bacon."

She returned in the same accent, "But, of course, darling. I am famished."

Displayed on the dining room buffet was a coffee urn surrounded by cups, saucers, cream and sugar, along with a calligraphy sign reading, "Help Yourself."

They sat at the table next to the window, enjoying the fresh-brewed coffee.

The kitchen door burst open. A stout woman wearing a full apron and holding a tray with two small fruit salads approached. Her thick brown hair was pulled back in metal clamps. Frizzy ringlets too wild to be contained framed a freckled face. By the artistic arrangement of the fruit, Aster deduced that the woman must be a foodie.

"Hello, I'm Rosemary. Aster, Jack, make yourselves at home."

"Good morning, Rosemary," Jack said Aster in greeting.

"How was the drive up?" Rosemary asked.

"Beautiful. We took the scenic route through the mountains," Jack replied.

"I've driven it plenty of times and even flown that route. My father lived in Boulder. But he's gone now." Rosemary's eyes filled with tears.

"I'm sorry. Must have been recent. You must miss him," Aster consoled.

Rosemary wiped her eyes. She said, "Thanks. Story of my life. Only saw Dad a few days a month. I talked to him on the phone on the days he worked. He always called me from his office."

"Were your parents divorced?" Aster asked.

Rosemary said candidly, "I was his love child. Mom and Dad had a fling while he was married to his wife in Boulder. I remained hidden here in Saratoga until the reading of his will. Oh dear, what a fiasco that was!"

A timer went off in the kitchen.

"Oh shoot! I gotta go flip the bacon. Be back in a sec." Rosemary pushed a hip against the swinging door and disappeared into the kitchen.

"Poor thing. It's awful having an absentee parent," Aster whispered.

"Serious jawbone," Jack commented.

"I bet the dam must have burst now that the secret is out," Aster said in an understanding voice.

Jack shrugged, saying, "This fruit salad is colorful. It's fresh too."

"Probably not organic. Oh well, when in Rome, do as the Romans do." Aster scooped up blueberries, strawberries, and kiwis, set aside her concerns, and enjoyed the food.

Jack got them more coffee.

As soon as he sat down, Rosemary burst through the door with another tray of food. As she set a plate in front of Aster, she formally announced, "Spinach frittata and a side of bacon."

"I love frittatas. When I said just cook any type of egg, I had no idea we spoke the same language," Aster said approvingly.

"House specialty," Rosemary said with a slight curl of her lips.

"Hmm, delicious," Jack chimed in, chewing a small bite.

The telephone rang.

"Expecting a call. Be right back." Rosemary darted back into the kitchen.

Fully sated from the scrumptious meal, Aster and Jack were on their third cup of coffee, talking up a storm.

"Let's explore the town and do another soak today," Jack suggested.

Rosemary came back to collect the empty plates.

Aster changed the focus onto their host. "Rosemary, I love your place here. It's like a walk back in time."

"Thanks. The house is zoned historical. My mother and I spent my whole life restoring it. Buying the antiques was the best part."

"Sounds like a labor of love!" Aster said.

"More like blood, sweat, and tears," Rosemary admitted. "Say, you mind if I take a seat and join ya in a cup? I made poppy-seed muffins."

"We'd love that," Jack volunteered.

Aster shrugged. "We're on vacation. Might as well indulge a little."

Rosemary set off and returned with a basket covered in a floral napkin. She parted the napkin, saying, "Help yourselves. They're still warm."

Jack broke a muffin in half and buttered it. He said, "If you don't mind, I'm a bit of a history buff. You'll have to tell me when this house was built."

"The house still has radiators. It must be at least one hundred years old," Aster added.

Rosemary said enthusiastically, "This place was built in the early 1860s. Don't know exactly when, because a fire destroyed the town records back in the copper-mining days."

"Is that how the town got settled?" Jack inquired.

The muffin in Rosemary's hand remained uneaten; she was too busy talking. "The hot springs were a natural stopping point for anyone passing through. Before Saratoga became a town, fur trappers traveled along the North Platte and traded with the Ute and Cherokee Indians. The route the trappers took eventually became the Cherokee Trail for all the folks heading for the Gold Rush in California."

"That's right. Before the railroads were built, wagon trains had a much easier go of it crossing the Continental Divide in Wyoming or New Mexico because the elevations are lower than in Colorado. Can you imagine how tough it was for wooden wagon wheels to break trail on steep unpaved roads? Rugged hard cores or what?" Jack said, impressed.

"Or foolish," Rosemary chimed in.

At that moment, the kitchen door flung open and the tune of "Happy Birthday" filled the room. Iris walked in, carrying a pie with lit candles. Jack and Rosemary joined in singing.

Aster dropped her jaw as Iris and a strange man neared the table. She hoped Sam had made it too but saw no sign of her son. Iris set a green pie in front of her. An outer ring of rainbow candles and a smaller ring in the middle illuminated her pupils.

"What a surprise! Can't believe you came all this way," Aster said.

"Aw, shucks. Make a wish, Mom," Iris said, pecking her on the cheek.

"This is key lime. Yum, I can smell it!" Aster exclaimed, barely able to contain herself.

"Your favorite." Iris smiled.

"I'd better blow out the candles before they melt away," Aster said. She made a wish to grow old with Jack.

While everyone applauded Aster's ability to blow out all the candles in a single breath, she looked around at every person, and said, "You bunch of connivers! Ya had me fooled. I thought Jack forgot my birthday. He kept it zipped until you two came strolling in. Ya musta sneaked in the back door."

"Yep, we did." Iris gave a cunning smirk.

Aster beamed. "Thanks for such a marvelous surprise. Iris, I haven't met your friend."

"Mom, Jack, this is Kenneth Schneider," Iris said, introducing her new beau.

Kenneth was not much taller than Iris and wore aviator sunglasses on top of a military haircut. His black-leather bomber jacket with leather gloves hanging from the pockets gave the look of a worldly traveler.

Jack extended a hand out, and they shook.

"Hey, buddy, we finally meet. How's it going? We seemed to pull it off without a hitch," Jack said casually.

Kenneth said, "We did good. The birthday girl here is flying high without wings."

Aster said jovially, "Kenneth, that's so true. I'm totally stunned. So, Iris finagled you into this covert operation."

"My job was to get us here quickly," Kenneth said.

Aster noticed a tattoo of eagle wings on each of Kenneth's wrists. Remembering what Iris had told them, she said, "That's right, you're a helicopter pilot."

"I am, yeah. We flew up this morning. Tried to make it in time for breakfast, but the wind was against us," Kenneth said, removing his jacket and exposing a red thermal undershirt stretched over a muscular physique.

Aster's first impression had her thinking, *He's as handsome as Keanu Reeves. Hope he's good to her.*

"Military trained?" Aster inquired.

"Nah. Started flying with my grandpa when I was eight and spent every available opportunity as his copilot." Kenneth's chocolate-brown eyes filled with affection at the mention of his grandfather. "At seventeen, I got my license. Now I deliver people and medical supplies between Wyoming and Colorado."

"Kenneth has his own business," Iris chimed in proudly.

"Gramps died this past summer, and I inherited his chopper," Kenneth said.

"His grandpa was Lenny, my father," Rosemary said, giving Kenneth a hug.

Aster and Jack exchanged glances.

"I see. You two are related," Aster said, noticing the similar eye color of nephew and aunt.

Rosemary plunked a handful of spoons and forks on the table, along with a stack of dessert plates. She piped up matter-of-factly, "Yep. Kenneth and Dad were the only ones in Boulder who knew about me. Here's a knife to cut the pie."

"Interesting family tree," Jack said.

"Lenny must have been a busy man juggling both families," Aster said while cutting the pie.

"He was. Gramps was a heart surgeon in Boulder and rode horse in Cheyenne rodeos. He'd get sore from riding and fly here to go soak in the hot springs," Kenneth said.

"Dad sure got around," Rosemary said.

Looking at Aster, Iris widened her eyes, implying, "I'll say," and then passed around the plates of pie.

Jack, who was listening to every detail, asked, "I've got a hunch I may know of Lenny. Kenneth, did he share your last name?"

"Schneider, yes," said Kenneth.

Jack shot another glance at Aster and then asked, "By any chance, was he fond of Appaloosa horses?"

"Crazy about 'em. He boarded Appaloosas at a ranch up the road. He owned a stud that sired most of the herd," Rosemary replied.

Kenneth chuckled, saying, "Gramps was a serious cowboy dude. He put on a long wig, dressed up in fancy duds, and traipsed around as Buffalo Bill Cody. Sometimes he filled in for other roles too. He was always doing something. Never held still for too long."

"On the way here, Kenneth told me that Lenny was a silent partner in this bed-and-breakfast," Iris added.

"What a complicated man," Aster said, impressed. She could hardly wait to fill Galen in on all the details.

"Yes, he was. Dad left me this bed-and-breakfast. I thought the reading of the will would be quick and easy. That is, until

I met the Boulder family, who did not know who I was. What a fiasco! I brought my birth certificate, but no one believed me until I got a blood test," Rosemary said incredulously.

"My dad was the lawyer and executor of Gramps's estate. He blew a gasket discovering that Rosemary Cartwright is his half-sister," Kenneth said.

"Bernie called me a bastard daughter. Until this rascal here made him apologize." Rosemary pushed on Kenneth's arm affectionately.

Aster raised a brow at the amount of unfiltered information about Lenny Schneider, and Jack mouthed, "Wow." Strangely enough, neither had ever met Lenny, and yet his legacy kept spilling at their feet like a bag of marbles.

Rosemary Cartwright, his illegitimate daughter, continued to reveal volumes of information.

"How did you guys know Gramps?" Kenneth queried.

"Oh, well, I went to his estate sale and saw a woman try to steal a horse statue. I had to report it at the police station and then talk to your father. As fate would have it, Bernie is also my lawyer. Small world, huh?" Aster said.

"No shit! My dad is your lawyer?" Kenneth said.

"Well, there are only so many lawyers in Boulder," Iris said, wary of coincidences concerning her mother.

Aster nodded and said, "Amazing, isn't it?"

Jack and Aster set out on foot to the main street to buy souvenirs, while Iris and Kenneth ate breakfast and unpacked.

With the wind at their backs, Jack and Aster walked down Bridge Street until it turned into the downtown area. For a mere block and a half, an assortment of motels, bars, eateries, and gift shops served as a congregation site for tourists and locals alike.

"Jack, how did you get Iris's phone number?"

"Bulletin board in the kitchen," he answered.

"Right. Forgot it was there. Say, dontcha think it's weird, or at least ironic, how Lenny has come into our lives? We know his secrets. He was our daughter-in-law in our Navajo lives. Currently, his grandson is dating my daughter. And, if by chance, Iris and Kenneth marry, Kenneth will be our son-in-law," Aster mused.

"What a complicated twist of synchronicity," Jack said.

"It's incredible."

"You know, it was no accident you went to the estate sale at Lenny's. You were led to discover old family ties. Lenny is just one example, one thread of the tapestry of life. In your everyday life, you meet countless souls that share your heritage. Thank God, you don't recognize them all. It would be overstimulating," Jack explained.

"No kidding," Aster said.

The first store they entered, the Trading Post, sold all sorts of cowboy paraphernalia—from boots, to hats, to saddles. Jack gravitated to the Native American displays of jewelry, kachina dolls, tribal blankets, and sandpaintings. He bought a pair of place mats that looked like miniature Navajo blankets. "Gonna use these as seat covers in the car," he explained.

Aster bought a turtle carved out of obsidian as a Christmas gift for her son. "Sam collects turtles. Too bad he's not here too. He's always too busy to include me in his life," she said, leaving the shop.

Jack said, "I talked to him. He'll be sending you a text from Las Vegas. He's at an expo with Sally."

"You know more about my son than I do," Aster complained and then asked, "What type of expo?" She checked her phone. Much to her dismay, there was no message.

"Food expo. Sally started a spiced-chocolate business called Hot Coco."

"As in drinks?"

Jack shook his head, saying, "More like candy bars spiced with ginger, turmeric, garlic, cayenne, and black pepper."

"Really? You mean he's gone beyond a one-night stand? I

fear Sam thinks I'm an evil temptress for having an affair and therefore believes all woman are untrustworthy."

"Or perhaps Sam got it. Maybe dating Sally has started to clue him in to the fact that his self-serving father treated you like crap. Sweetie, from what you told me, Bill was no angel. He was a jerk who said the divorce was entirely your fault. A guy like that would blame you for the avocado pit being too big," Jack said.

"Actually, I think he did. But you know what? We're on vacation. I'm over feeling guilty about being the family wrecker. Hey, let's go into this place, Michelle's Boutique," Aster said, glad to change the subject.

"You're the birthday girl. I'm hoping to find your present today. Thought you might like a cool souvenir from Wyoming." Jack smoothed over the fact that he had forgotten a gift and gave her behind a sensual caress.

"How romantic can ya get? Let's go!" Aster beamed.

They toured among the racks of handmade clothes, scarves, and hats.

At a glass jewelry case, Aster exclaimed, "Oh, that lapis necklace is beautiful."

"The snowman-shaped one with the silver inlay?" Jack guessed.

"Yep."

The clerk, eager to make a sale during off-season, removed the necklace from the case and handed it to Aster. She said, "This piece was made by a new Navajo jeweler whose style is more modern than traditional. Try it on. Here's a mirror."

Jack commented enthusiastically, "Honey, turn this way, so I can see. Nice piece! It's Navajo. What do ya think?" He winked at her in response the Navajo connection.

"I love it. It symbolizes a loving bond between you and me," Aster said, beaming once again.

"We'll take it," Jack said.

On the walk back to the bed-and-breakfast, Aster had a

bounce in her step, and the brisk wind blowing madly at her bangs mattered not.

Iris and Kenneth were playing a game of pool when they arrived.

"Mom, got something to ask you," Iris said, leaning on her cue stick.

"Want to challenge us in a game?" Aster said as she watched Kenneth sink the seven ball.

"No, it's something else. Ya know, Kenneth has to fly to Seminoe Reservoir to scatter his grandpa's ashes. Since it's your birthday, we thought you might like to take a little journey in the helicopter. That is, if the ashes don't weird ya out," Iris stammered.

"Never been in as helicopter! I'd love to. Lenny's ashes won't bother me. I never met him. But wait. Rosemary will have to go too. It's her dad. How many seats are in the chopper?"

"Four," Kenneth answered.

"There's five of us, including Rosemary." Aster pointed to each person in the room.

"I'll stay and read a book," Jack offered.

"I've got lesson plans to do. I want to get them out of the way so that I can enjoy a good soak later. I confess the ash thing creeps me out," Iris said.

"All right then. Iris gets the short straw. Let's head out," Kenneth said. He stuck his head in the kitchen. "You ready, Rosemary?"

"I am," Rosemary answered, chewing on candied ginger that Aster had given her to settle her stomach.

❋ ❋

Aster sat in the copilot seat, wearing sunglasses and headphones. The sound of the blades spinning overhead was too noisy to be without ear protection, and the headphones enabled communication among the passengers. Lifting off the ground felt exhilarating. She turned around to Jack and signaled thumbs-up, grinning happily.

She spoke into the microphone attached to the headset. "Kenneth, what's the proper name of this valley?"

"North Platte River Valley," he answered.

"Looks like a scene from a western movie. It's awfully wide." Aster craned her neck, moving her head from side to side, taking it all in.

"It's about thirty miles wide from the Medicine Bow Mountains in the east to the Sierra Madres in the west." Kenneth's voice sounded like that of a well-seasoned tour guide.

"From up here, you can see the snowcaps. Does that little doohickey on the dashboard say we are going north?" Aster inquired.

"Yeah. The reservoir is about forty miles straight north," replied Kenneth.

They flew over Interstate 80. The vehicles looked like toys gliding along in endless double lanes.

"We're flying so much lower than a plane. What the heck is that? An eagle? Aster, look to your right—it's soaring over there," Jack said excitedly.

"It is a bald eagle. I'd try to fly nearer, but they shy away from the chopper. Gramps said sighting an eagle was good luck," noted Kenneth.

"Check out the wingspan. She's a big girl. Reminds me of Cedar Claw," Aster blurted out without thinking.

"Who?" asked Kenneth.

Unsure whether the subject of past lives would be an acceptable conversation topic, Jack responded quickly. "Cedar Claw is a Navajo we know. He's full of old sayings like, 'Witnessing the soaring eagle is the Spirit's way to bless the day with a good omen.'"

"I find it an endearing way to say good luck," Aster said, turning to smirk at Jack.

Minutes later, the Seminoe Reservoir came into view, a

squiggly finger of shimmering water abutting a mountain range in the northeast. A herd of prong-horned antelope frightened by the sound of the helicopter fled in a zigzag course to higher ground.

"The river seems to widen here, as if a dam created the reservoir," said Jack, observing the geography with interest.

"Yep. That is none other than the Seminoe Dam nestled next to the Shirley Mountains on the right and the Seminoe Mountains further away to the northwest. It's the best fishing in Wyoming. There are trout, walleye, and perch that literally race each other to swallow the baited hooks." Kenneth resumed his tour-guide delivery with a touch of mockery.

With not another soul around, Kenneth landed in an area free of sagebrush and cut the engine. He said, "Aster, can you fetch the gym bag from under your seat? It's Gramps. I can't do it. Holding him is too intense."

Aster recalled how she'd broken into tears simply being in close proximity to Keith's ashes. Compassion helped her hoist the bag onto her lap. From the weight and feel, she could tell the ashes were in a vase.

She said, "All right, Kenneth, how do I get out of here?"

"Turn the lever and pull back," Kenneth instructed.

Greeted by an endless wind, they all assembled at the shoreline.

Tightening his lips, Kenneth said, "Aster, will you get the instructions out of the bag? It's the only piece of paper in there. Please read it."

Aster set the urn on the ground. The pottery container looked similar to one of Jack's original Hopi vases. She removed a parchment scroll tied with a leather strap, which she untied.

"Let's form a circle around Lenny, and I'll read this," she instructed.

Opening the scroll, she exposed a sepia document, decorated with curly borders. Included in the header was a drawing of a medicine wheel. Aster cleared her throat and read:

Dear Beloved Family,

I had a rich life, a dual life full of adventure. I loved my Colorado family and my Wyoming family equally. Ironically, I did not have enough time for either. In my many visits to the hot spring, in Taos, I befriended a Pueblo Indian, Black Stone, who adopted me into his family. Of all the things in Black Stone's culture, I found the medicine wheel to be the most intriguing. So much so that I wish it to be part of my burial. Like my life, these steps follow passion, not tradition.

Sniffling and nose blowing came from both family members.

"The rest is the instructions about what to do while spreading the ashes," Aster said, skimming down the page. She looked back and forth, from Kenneth to Rosemary, at a loss for what to do next.

"You wanna do the honors?" Kenneth asked Rosemary. He pointed to his aunt, then slid his hand back into the warmth of the bomber jacket's pocket.

Rosemary had been silent the entire flight. Her hair was all tucked up in a navy beanie cap, its visor resting on the rim of large-framed, black sunglasses that gave the impression she was trying to hide. Her lips quivered, and she pressed them together to make them stop. Unable to speak, she shook her head no.

"I'm too creeped out to touch the urn. I'm the only one in my family willing to carry out Gramps's wishes. Can one of you spread the ashes?" Kenneth pleaded, his face tearstained and blotchy.

Aster cast a sideways glance at Jack. Seeing his reluctance, she volunteered. She had sobbed spreading Keith's ashes, but knowing her heart had no ties to Lenny would make the job easier. A vision of Cedar Claw popped into her head. Instantly, the idea of assuming the role as medicine man/woman seemed the appropriate thing to do.

She handed the parchment to Jack, saying, "Here, hold this. I may need your assistance. Rosemary, Kenneth, any last words?"

"Yes." Through tears, Rosemary gasped and said, "I was the love child ... a hidden secret. I suffered an absentee father ... endured shame. ... Today, I release it all. ... Love ya, Dad."

Kenneth worked his mouth, struggling with the rise of emotion. His cheeks streamed with tears as he said, "I spent more time with Gramps than anybody. We flew countless hours together. He told me stories, confessed many things. I was his secret keeper. I was his conscience. Gramps, you lovable scoundrel, expect you'll behave yourself in heaven. Thanks for teaching me to fly. Miss ya." His voice faltered as he covered his eyes with his hand.

While Kenneth spoke, Aster cleared her mind and grounded her energy using the same preparation she and Jack did for time travel. She set the intention to draw upon her old self, Cedar Claw, hoping to employ funerary wisdom in this moment of need.

Jack, who had scanned the instructions, volunteered a short good-bye, saying, "Until we meet again."

Aster squatted to pick up the urn, but before her hands reached the vase, foreign syllables came out of her mouth. She rambled on for some time, honoring spirits, and then finally stood up.

Jack, understanding what was happening, said, "I'd like to thank Cedar Claw for teaching you that Navajo prayer. Great recall. Sounded like he spoke right through ya." He then stated proudly, "I'll read the instructions while you pour."

"Are you fluent in Navajo?" Kenneth interjected.

"Oh no, just memorized the prayer. Isn't that right, Aster?" Jack made googly eyes at her, urging her to speak normally.

Aster thought she had spoken in English. On the spot, she caught on. Her intention had brought more than she asked for. How interesting to channel Cedar Claw in his native tongue! Exhilaration filled every fiber of her being over the emergence of two lives blending into one, as if connecting the dots. Not sure if the next words from her mouth would be English, she nodded.

Jack held the parchment at arm's length and addressed the task as a teacher in front of students. "Apparently, we are in the right place. For Lenny Schneider has requested Seminoe Reservoir as his burial site. To start things off, we are to draw a medicine wheel with the ashes." Jack showed Aster the diagram. "Aster, if you will."

The wind carried off the finer particles from the first pouring. From then on, Aster held the urn close to the ground and drew a three-foot circle. Next, she drew a straight line cutting the shape into equal halves and then made another straight line, as if dividing a pie into equal fourths. Still amazed by the clarity with which Cedar Claw spoke through her, the thought of self-meeting self had her suppress a gleeful giggle.

Jack cleared his throat. "Nice job. Now according to Lenny's instructions here, I will read a Native American–style prayer."

> Father Sun, Sister Moon, Mother Earth,
>
> We are humble at your feet. Each day, we honor the four directions. We bow to the fire of the east where the golden eagle spirit soars. We enter the water of the south where the red mouse stirs emotion. We kneel to the earth of the west where the bear embodies strength. We breathe the air of the north where the buffalo speaks wisdom. Today, we honor the spirit of Dr. Leonard Schneider, who joins

your world. As his spirit greets loving ancestors, as his ashes return to the earth, may his path follow peace. In reverence to all his relations, earthly and spirit, bless him in the wisdom of the sacred ways, Great Spirit.

He's paraphrasing what I just said, Aster thought elated. A giggle burst out of her mouth, and she disguised it by pretending to cry.

Jack, consumed by his love of Navajo heritage, experienced watery eyes over the beauty of the words he had spoken. A moment of silence ensued until he asked, "Aster, are there more ashes left?"

Unclear how to get her English voice back, Aster stalled, peering into the vase, knowing without a doubt that ash remained at the bottom. She nodded, staring at Jack expectantly.

Jack cleared his throat once again. "Let's see. It says here to pour the remainder into the reservoir. Apparently, this was his favorite fishing hole in the world."

"That's because he never left empty-handed. I used to call him Fish-Fry Daddy as a little girl," Rosemary reminisced. She took a picture of her father's remains with her phone.

Kenneth did the same and forwarded it to his parents.

Aster flung the remaining ashes into the water.

"That about does it," Jack said, rolling the scroll back up.

"Amen," Rosemary added. She unclasped fingers to make the sign of the cross, expressing her Catholic faith.

Aster pulled Jack aside and said softly, "Nod if this is English." She pointed at her mouth.

He nodded.

The foursome left the medicine wheel to the elements. The wind would surely erase it, and critters would nibble away at the circle. They boarded the chopper and returned to the bed-and-breakfast.

Iris sat at her laptop in the dining room, playing a game of Hearts. "How did it go?" she asked.

"Gramps can rest in peace. We followed his wishes to a tee. Aster drew the medicine wheel. Take a look." Kenneth showed Iris the picture on his cell.

"Definitely not synagogue material. Good thing you carried out his wishes. Bernie would have flipped his yarmulke over this. Now Lenny can rest in peace," Iris said. For some unknown reason, the picture of the medicine wheel made her feel less uneasy about the ashes.

"'Too eccentric' was Dad's politest comment. I sent him a picture anyway," Kenneth said.

"It was a thoughtful thing to do." Iris smiled at him and then asked, "Mom, did you like the 'copter ride?"

"Such a treat! Got an incredible bird's-eye view of the valley," Aster said.

"We even saw an eagle," Jack added.

"Sweet. Kenneth ain't called Birdman for nothing." Iris put a hand on his arm and flashed flirtatious eyes.

Iris, Kenneth, Jack, and Aster spent the rest of the day together, enjoying a soak in the hot springs, eating a steak dinner, gawking at the stars until they found the constellation Orion, and ending the day by playing a game of Liverpool Rummy, an old Schneider family favorite.

✻ ✻

The next day, Aster and Jack packed the car after breakfast and bid farewell to Iris and Kenneth. Eager to take an easier route, they planned to drive around the Medicine Bow Mountains this time, not over them.

Aster volunteered to drive until Laramie, where she would switch with Jack. They headed toward I-80 along the North Platte River Valley. Traveling on the ground compared to the air enabled a closer view of the toasted marshmallow grass swaying in the wind.

"Jack, I enjoyed the birthday getaway. Most unusual one I ever had. Nice to spend time with Iris. I liked Kenneth too. Thanks again for the great necklace. Right now, I'm looking forward to getting back home." Aster fingered the pendant with delight.

"My pleasure. Told ya! You needed a vacation. The sleepy town of Saratoga was a nice place to chill, but it's too remote to live there."

"Agreed."

Jack placed a Steve Winwood disk into the CD player, adjusted his seat to recline, and shut his eyes. Every song had piano or organ parts. Aster could tell he was picking out the notes, for every now and again his fingers played on his lap.

Traffic along I-80 flowed smoothly. Fully relaxed, they grew silent until a sign read, "Highway 287 Next Right."

"As soon as we turn off, I need to find a restroom," Aster announced. She exited south on the ramp and pulled in front of an antique store.

"Why are you stopping here?" Jack frowned.

"We can stretch our legs while looking at antiques."

"Good idea," Jack said, spotting a Native American blanket in the window.

From the outside, Bertha's Antiques looked like a huge old warehouse. Inside, quaint rows of consignment stalls seemed to go on for a half-mile. Methodically they perused up and down the aisles, reminiscing about merchandise they grew up with or that an older relative owned.

Aster stopped at a display of kitchenware near the register. "Wow! Currier and Ives salad plates in prime condition. Several of mine broke throughout the years. I should get them. They are hard to find." Seeing the price, she promptly set the plate down in disgust.

"You just said they're hard to find. Why don't you get them?" Jack said.

"At five dollars a pop, that'd be twenty-five for the whole stack."

"So?"

"My mom got the entire set for free!" Aster exclaimed.

"That was fifty years ago! Darling, they're antiques, just like we are." Jack rolled his eyes.

A clerk approached them and said, "Hello, I overheard you talking. This is my section. I'm marking everything half off to make room for a new truckload."

"Oh really? For $2.50 a piece, I'll take 'em!" Aster caught Jack's eyes and mouthed a victorious "Yeah."

They returned to the car, elated. As Jack drove out of the parking lot he said, "You got a great deal. Watching you go through the whole money ordeal just then made me realize, even though you have millions, you are the most frugal person I've ever met. This leads me to believe the reason you are balking over our wedding is money. My hunch says a prenuptial agreement would set you at ease."

"Oh my God," Aster said with a sigh. "I'm so glad you brought this up. I was afraid I'd sound like a nasty bitch at the slightest mention. But it's true: The entire issue is about safety. In fact, I already have the documents at home ready for you to sign. Bernie Schneider drew up the paperwork for me. I felt awkward approaching you about it."

"I'll gladly sign the papers. Hell, I've got my own little stash now. Those seminars are gonna build it up fast. I plan on having my first million in a year," Jack announced.

"You'd have to do one hundred seminars at ten grand a pop," Aster chimed in.

"Tony is gonna help me invest. He's a wizard at making money. Aster, what we have together resonates to my core. It's priceless. I want you to feel safe about money; be a happy wife who scratches my back when it itches," Jack said sincerely.

Very astounded, she said, "Thanks for understanding. I did not want to explain myself."

"I get you, my darling vixen. You're a bit quirky, but you're lovable," he admitted.

"Love how you speak your feelings so freely. Cleaning and cooking aside, you're a bona fide liberated male," Aster said, letting out a huge exhale.

"Soaking in those springs got me all mushy and gushy. And it's true, I'm not the macho type afraid of my feminine side. In fact, I'm looking forward to helping plan the wedding," Jack added.

"Let's keep the wedding small. Less stress for both of us. I'd love it if the entire wedding party fit around a dinner table."

"How about if we put a bunch of tables into a circle and have a round table? It worked for King Arthur," laughed Jack.

Aster and Jack made it to Boulder by early afternoon. The sight of the majestic Flatirons bordering the west end of the valley gave an immediate sense of home.

As they passed a group of cyclists and a lone jogger, Jack said, "Feels good to be back in the Boulder Bubble. Doesn't it?"

"I'll say."

Chapter 22

The Wedding

"Come join the fun. Here, put this on. It's the same as mine," Grannyme said, handing Aster a white stretchy headband.

The minute the band circled Aster's crown, both women were suddenly dressed in white spandex shorts, tank tops, and tennis shoes. Badminton rackets landed at their feet. The purple cushion expanded to accommodate the game, and a net divided the court in half.

"A bit sporty today, huh?" Aster checked out the new clothes.

"We love badminton, but we never play. Now, where the heck did I put that box? Oh. Here it is." The crone opened a Stumbling Block that appeared in front of her. She removed two files, and the wooden box vanished.

"Which ones are they?"

"In a minute, all will be revealed." Grannyme tucked the files under her arm.

"Why did you take them out of the box?"

"The little girl in you needs to play it out," replied Grannyme. "We are going to play badminton." Grannyme clicked her fingers, and the files turned into badminton birdies, one green and the other amber. You need to hit these past me for them to be completed."

"Okay. At your age, this ought to be easy. But can you at least tell me what one of the files is about?" Aster pleaded.

"You'll see." Grannyme tossed the green birdie to Aster. "Your serve."

Aster walked onto the court and faced her opponent. She threw the birdie in the air and swatted it. The serve flew too low, and the birdie got stuck in the net. Dollar signs oozed out of the birdie, and it dropped to the ground.

"Oops! Out of practice," Aster said, retrieving the birdie from the stringy web.

"Got a little stuck with your money at the antique shop," Grannyme taunted.

"Actually, I got a deal on the plates without any bartering. Turns out, Jack is fine with the prenup too." Aster gave a half-hearted chuckle, hitting a high flyer.

Grannyme floated up and easily knocked it back.

"So, you're playing with granny rules." Aster ran and hit it back.

"Yep. Because I can," Grannyme said as she returned the birdie, using a strong backhand.

Aster leapt to the net and spiked it past the crone's reach. As soon as the birdie hit the cushion, it melted below the surface. "All right!" she shouted, feeling smug at the easy win.

"Nice job. Don't you just feel like a kid?" Grannyme held the racket like a ukulele. She pretended to strum and sang in a high soprano, "Tiptoe through the tulips with me."

"Goofball." Aster giggled at the corny antics. She said, "Been ages since I've played. Does make me feel like a kid. Winning is not bad either."

"Good mojo. Destroying that birdie is a symbol that you completed another vow. You got honest. You talked about the prenuptial with Jack," Grannyme said, retrieving the gold birdie.

"Does that mean Jack and I are free and clear of vows? Will I find the grail when we are?"

"Not yet. You two made several contracts to help each other

grow. Your last vow might be on your deathbed. Starting a new game," Grannyme said abruptly as she made the first serve.

Deathbed had Aster brood over the possibility she might not graduate from the karma before then. A golden blur whizzed by and landed on the floor. She picked up the birdie and noticed a drawing of a beer mug on the bulbous end. Considering the markings a bit odd, she lobbed it over the net.

The women volleyed back and forth, for what seemed like forever. Aster worked up a sweat running every inch of the court. Her tank top was drenched. Grannyme, on the other side, appeared as if she had merely enjoyed a few yoga stretches.

During the challenge, Aster's eyes were playing tricks on her. Her father's name, Henry, replaced the mug, which made her cringe. She swore she smelled beer when the racket made contact with the bulbous end of the birdie. The odor alone triggered the memory of Henry breaking her pinkie finger. Instinctively, Aster switched into vigilant mode and scanned for danger. Next thing she knew, the birdie transformed into her father's fist coming at her. Acting quickly, she swung the racket with all her might, smashed the fist, and lobbed it over Grannyme's head. Upon contact to the floor, it burst into tiny particles.

"That's my girl!" Grannyme beamed in pride.

Full of adrenaline, Aster shouted, "Whoa! I always wanted to hit him back. I had fantasy paybacks of smashing him right in the kisser. This feels like a dream come true." She tossed aside the racket. With both fists clenched, she raised her arms in victory pumps above her head.

"My little bumpkin, after mouthing off to the Duke in the hot springs, you deserve your wish," Grannyme said, joining the excitement.

❋ ❋

The winter flew by, with mounds of snow in January, chinook winds in February, and signs of early spring in March. As planned, Jack held a seminar once a month: one in Sedona, Arizona; another in Miami, Florida; and the last in San Diego, California. Tasha Wingstrom's plan to draw people from the north to a nicer climate proved to be a wise strategy. All available seats had sold out.

During the time Jack spent at home, he and Aster planned their wedding. As promised, Jack took care of most of the arrangements. He rented space at the Chautauqua Community Center for the wedding and reception, ordered food from a caterer, and picked out a cake. At the florist, he learned a great deal about the meanings of flowers. He selected lavender roses, which struck a nostalgic chord, for they signify love at first sight. It seemed only fitting to use those flowers to decorate the lattice archway at the altar, the bridal bouquets for the women, and the boutonnieres for the men. Aster oversaw the paperwork, which included the invitations, the marriage license, and the prenuptial documents.

When Aster delivered the prenuptial papers to Bernie Schneider, she said, "Bernie, you know your son is dating my daughter."

"Yes. I've caught wind of that. Those two are flying down next week so that we can meet," Bernie said in a formal tone.

"They're a cute couple. I like Kenneth. He gave me a ride in his helicopter in Wyoming. What an incredible view from that height!" Aster said.

"Apparently, you got hoodwinked into spreading Father's ashes in my absence. Thank you," Bernie said a bit stiffly.

"No problem. I was glad to help out." Aster made light of the situation.

On the drive home Aster reflected on all the hoops she had jumped through in preparation for a third husband. Following the advice of Grannyme, she had agreed to Jack's wedding plans. With great effort, she ignored the price of everything to avoid bickering over the cost. As much as she disliked the head-in-the-sand approach, a response her mother had perfected, it helped her cope. Granted, all the effort Jack invested in wedding plans, seminars, teaching, and clients left them with little time to be together. Once again, a hint of loneliness seeped into Aster's heart. Because of her great fear of abandonment, she kept the peace by funneling resentment toward Regina Snowden, the mother she currently emulated. Ironic as it seemed, Aster loved Jack beyond measure. Thank God the wedding was a one-day event, not a lifetime of endurance.

Dressed in sweatpants and hoodie, Jack paced back and forth in the living room while talking on his cell phone. "Okay, you guys make sure you do some slow numbers and dance tunes. Great! See ya at practice." He returned to the kitchen to pour another cup of coffee, adding cream until the color turned tan.

Wrapped in a bathrobe and with wet hair tied up in a bun, Aster poked around in the pantry and refrigerator, making a grocery list.

"Hey, sweetie, I just hired the Retro Monkeys to play at our wedding," Jack said.

"Your band at our wedding? You understand this isn't a gig?" she said, absently placing the pencil behind one ear.

"'Course not. Helen Molsky is playing keyboards at the ceremony."

"Let me get this straight—Helen is the best man's wife. Sorry I'm slow on the uptake; damn brain injury has made me stupid. It's hard to connect the name until I see the face," Aster complained.

"Helen and Tony met in college. All my pictures are in storage, and I don't have any on my phone. I'll dig some photos out before the wedding," he offered.

"Good idea." On a sticky note she jotted, "Tony and Helen photos" and stuck the note on the refrigerator.

Jack said, "Since we've got roughly one month left, I need

to update ya on the last-minute details. I ordered a two-tiered carrot cake with cream-cheese frosting from Duchess Bakery. It's your favorite cake. The Chautauqua Dining Hall said they'll make tofu Wellington for the vegetarians. I'm so glad they're doing the catering. We're going to have one festive wedding with the best eats in town."

Reaching saturation point at the amount of money Jack was spending on the wedding, Aster clenched her jaw. She abruptly changed course when she heard Grannyme's raspy voice say, "Chautauqua is the first place you two kissed. Aster, if you value your relationship with Jack, pay attention to his enthusiasm. It's beyond romantic—it's priceless."

The message prompted Aster to resist suggesting a potluck reception in the backyard as a cheaper alternative. Feeling conked over the head, Aster stammered, "W-wow, Mr. Busy, when did you do all this?"

"While you showered," Jack answered.

❋ ❋

On June 5, the day before the wedding, Jack's best friend from college, Tony Molsky, and his wife, Helen, flew in from California. They stayed at Jack's townhome for the weekend. When his lanky pal knocked, Jack greeted him at the door with an affectionate bear hug. As skinny as ever, Tony still stood three inches taller than Jack. The men had not seen each other in two years. Jack noticed increased signs of age in Tony since their last visit. There were more wrinkles, brown spots on shaven cheeks, and less hair on the crown. The small space between Tony's front teeth and endearing gummy smile brought up fond memories.

"The best man made it. Good to see ya, ol' buddy." Jack beamed.

"Jackman, you haven't changed a bit," Tony said.

Jack rubbed his ample belly. "Added some girth here. Aster's a great cook." He turned to Helen. "Hello, gorgeous. Glad you could make it." He gave her a hug.

Helen, a heavyset woman with beautiful gray-blue eyes, scanned Jack's features, as if looking at him for the first time. She said, "Hi Jackman."

"I'm in charge of head count for the reception. To make things simple, I'll mark you down as Tony's plus-one," Jack chided, licking his finger and drawing a single tally in the air.

"I'll plus-one you right in the kisser, McFatOne," Helen replied, tucking a shoulder-length bleached-blond hair behind her ear.

Her comment reminded Jack of the "Fat Boys for Free Love" shirt he wore in freshmen year. "Oh boy, that shirt you gave me for my birthday. Got a lot of shits and grins at parties," said Jack, laughing at memories of his youth.

Tony chuckled. "You branded yourself McFatOne at the first keg party we went to. You got lucky with a girl and kept repeating 'fat boys for free love' over and over, all night long."

"We did a lot of kooky stuff back then," Jack said.

"Don't include me in kooky. I was an angel," Helen stated.

"Ha! Tell me, who stole a Helen of Troy toga from the drama department for a Halloween costume? Then used the toga to start a bonfire?" Jack challenged her.

"What's a poor student to do but make do with the resources at hand?" Helen bantered.

"And I was just going to ask Helen of Troy to come in for a drink. You must be thirsty from your trip. If it's too early for wine or beer, I've got coffee, lemonade, bubbly water, or iced tea," Jack offered.

They sat in the living room, drinking lemonade.

Jack sensed some awkwardness coming from his guests.

Tony looked troubled, but he managed to say, "Sorry, bud, but I won't be able to stand up at your wedding."

"Nor will I be able to play the piano at the ceremony," Helen said, disappointed.

"What? You pulling my chain?" Jack said, not sure whether to believe them.

"We don't have anything to wear is more like it," Tony said seriously.

"The airline lost our garment bag. Just our luck, his suit coat and my dress are in Minneapolis," Helen added.

"No problem. It's a causal wedding. Let's go to the mall," Jack suggested.

"I wear men's tall," Tony stated.

"I bet you do," Jack said looking up at him.

"Jack, I want to see what you are wearing, so we can coordinate," Helen said.

"A suit. I got it airing out in the backyard. I'll go get it. He returned, holding a navy-blue blazer on one hanger and matching slacks on another.

Helen took the pants off the hanger to get an idea of the style. Alarmed, she said, "You have a hole in your slacks."

"Yeah, right," Jack said, unwilling to fall for a fast one.

"I'm not joking. Look, moth holes. There's a bunch of them," Helen said.

"Oh shit! Those damn miller moths. I shouldn't have left these out overnight. This is my only suit." Jack was bummed. He scanned the jacket and found a small hole on the sleeve.

"Shopping, it is," Helen said, placing her purse strap on her shoulder.

Jack drove the three of them to the mall.

As they walked up to the main entrance, Helen said, "Tonight is the bachelor party, at Juanita's at six. We have a small window to find stuff that fits."

"No worries. Aster is all about being practical. If you wore a sundress, she'd be tickled you picked something you'd wear more than once," Jack assured her.

Tony stepped up onto the curb and said, "Hey, man, thanks for hooking me up with Rudra Patel. He made it possible to plan the bachelor party. He's a cool guy."

"Yeah, he is. Rudra and I started at the Discovery Center the same year. He teaches Hindu studies and meditation. Aster hasn't met him yet. For the past year, he's been teaching in Nepal. He just got back," Jack said.

"Are you aware your coworkers and students who are not invited to the wedding are joining us for the bachelor party?" Tony asked.

"I know. I invited my maid too," Jack said nonchalantly.

"Glad I won't be the only woman there," Helen said.

"Nah. It's a coed stag," Jack snickered at the contradictory term.

In lieu of a traditional bachelorette party, Aster, Galen, and Iris created a day of serenity. They took a yoga class, ate a gourmet brunch, and pampered themselves with facials and foot massages.

Galen and Iris stayed the night at Aster's house. All refreshed with a good night's sleep, the women arose early to get ready for the big day.

Galen fixed wedding braids in Aster's hair, swept back cornrows in Iris's locks, and set her own tresses set in huge rollers.

Iris applied a full array of makeup on her mom, Galen, and herself. She said, "Isn't this fun, us girls playing dress up?"

Aster looked in the mirror and said, "Oh my God! My mother would be so proud. She hosted cosmetic parties every Wednesday so that she could get free products."

"Glamour nut?" Galen asked.

"Yep. Funny thing is, she was a farmer's wife. I don't think the chickens ever saw her makeup-free," Aster said.

"If Grandma Regina were alive, would you have invited her to the wedding?" Iris asked.

"She wasn't at my first two weddings, and you kids never met her, so I doubt I'd have wasted a postage stamp on an invitation," Aster said in a flat tone.

Galen and Iris exchanged glances.

"All right then, we need to put the cake and the dresses in the car and get our buns to the community center so that we can be there for the flower delivery." Iris spoke as if she were giving instructions to her classroom of third-graders.

Even though she came off with a detached air about Regina Snowden, a buried piece of Aster wished she'd had a better relationship with her mom.

The Chautauqua Community Center, a stone-and-stucco building with a covered porch across the length of one side, had the appearance of a rather large house. Aster pondered the idea that the place carried an echo of the Navajo tradition, for a good portion of the exterior literally was made of mud, and the door faced east. This was a point worthy of sharing with Jack, so she took a picture of the venue with her phone.

Inside, the main room took on the ambience of an elongated den. On the far wall, a fireplace nestled between wood-paneled room dividers, and a second-story wooden balcony surrounded the entire room. When Aster stepped onto the hardwood flooring, she sensed a smidgen of elegance and a dash of warmth, similar to Cecil House in her and Jack's English past life. She snapped more pictures.

"Mom, where are the rooms where we can change?" Iris asked, with her dress slung over a shoulder.

"Gotta be the doors either on the left or right of the fireplace," Aster answered.

"I'll take the left," Galen said, clutching her dress.

"I'll go right," Iris stated.

Aster gave her dress to Iris and took pictures of the round tables draped in white linen near the entrance. She bit on her bottom lip and thought, *Everywhere I look, I see dollar signs. If it were up to me, we'd have a potluck wedding in my backyard. Why did I agree to all this extravagance?*

"Because I said so, you old cheapskate," Grannyme rasped as her wrinkly old face appeared on the phone screen.

Disturbed to see Grannyme in broad daylight, Aster whispered despondently, "Because Jack needs this more than I need to save money."

"He's working hard to catch up to your millions. He needs joy right now. This is his first wedding. If you suppress his expression of love, you might as well take him off your Christmas list now," Grannyme warned.

"Like you said, spending the money is an investment in our relationship," Aster scoffed, not wanting to repeat the same old argument.

"It's better than Jack thinking you are an oppressive mate who's too hard to please. It's better than him feeling marriage is too much of a battle. Aster, allow the joy to happen. Cast the miser aside, and celebrate love! You and he are worth it," Grannyme preached passionately.

"I'm trying."

"All right, repeat after me, 'Jack values me. He did well organizing the wedding,'" Grannyme insisted.

"Got it," Aster said. She heard footsteps and slid the phone into her back pocket.

Galen came from behind, saying, "Kitchen and bathroom are behind door number one."

"In here!" Iris shouted. She hung the dresses on hooks.

Aster gave a nod. Her phone rang. Grannyme's face was still on the screen, so Aster turned off the phone. "Jack did well organizing the wedding. This place is the perfect size to fit everybody," Aster said, scanning the room. The phone vibrated in her pocket.

"That man will do anything for you. I'm jealous," Galen said.

"Means a lot to have him value me," Aster replied. The phone stopped. She let out a sigh of relief at satisfying Grannyme's request.

"Hello. I'm Chad from Boulder Floral," a soft voice said from the entrance.

A skinny man dressed in spandex shorts and a tank top carried a white lattice archway into the hall. Aster noticed dangling gold earrings in each ear. Judging by the black crew cut and white sideburns, he seemed to be in his forties.

"Hiya," Galen said, waving the man in their direction.

"Hello. I'm Aster, the bride." She smiled.

Chad nodded. "And a beautiful one at that. You ready for the big day?" he asked in a rote sort of way.

"Getting there," Aster assured him.

He glanced at his watch, as if pressed for time. "Aster, where in tarnation you expect to put this? In front of the bay window or by the fireplace? Need to get this up before your guests come traipsing through the door." He sounded like a good ol' boy from Tennessee.

"The fireplace will do," noted Aster.

"Good choice. Reckon it's the best use of space. There's plenty of room for the bride and groom, and y'all guests can sit right yonder in them folding chairs." He glanced at the stack of chairs leaning against the wall.

Everything seemed to happen at once. The caterer set up the wet bar next to the kitchen. The band set up in front of the bay window. Iris and Galen set up chairs. Aster carried the wedding cake inside.

The girls watched Chad attach the roses to the archway.

Galen said, "Leave it to Jack to construct a past-life portal at his own wedding."

"I wonder if Mr. Nostalgia is half expecting Margaret Colton or Cedar Claw to come out from the other side and join us," Aster added cynically.

"I think it's sweet. I like the convenience of having the

ceremony and reception at the same place," Iris said, not understanding the private joke between Aster and Galen.

"It's handy," Aster said flatly. Beautiful as the archway was, her mind turned every flower into dollar signs. The phone buzzed once again. Sensing the nudge from Grannyme, one by one, the dollar signs turned into hearts.

Iris perused the checklist and said, "Besides getting dressed, all we need now is for the groom and best man to arrive. They're ten minutes late. Mom, it's time for your vanishing act."

"Come on! So what if Jack sees me?" Aster complained.

"It's tradition. Mr. History Buff will expect it." Galen urged Aster into the dressing room. As she passed the box of flowers, Galen snagged a fistful of baby's breath and two roses.

"Something borrowed," Iris giggled, trailing behind.

"Maybe we should call Jack," Aster said, reaching into her pocket.

"I will," Galen said, dialing. "Hey, it's Galen. Jack, you on your way? Great. See you in a bit. Aster, he's been calling you, but you don't answer."

"Oops," Aster said, thinking it was silly to assume Grannyme could make her phone ring. In a dream, she could.

"Okay, Mom, let's get you dressed," Iris insisted, checking off another item on the list.

"And these flowers are going in your hair," Galen said. "Aster, do you have anything that's old? I have a blue garter for you to wear. Here, put it on your thigh."

"Thanks. I do have something old. I brought the earrings J. J. gave me when I graduated high school," Aster said, digging out a pair of freshwater pearl earrings from her jeans pocket. She deeply regretted J. J.'s absence.

Galen glossed over the missing cousin and said, "Good taste. The pearls match your dress perfectly. In the old days, Hindu brides wore pearl necklaces as a symbol of sexual magic. My guess is, it gave virgin brides confidence on their first night in bed with their hubbies."

Iris laughed, saying, "I don't think that's an issue with Mom, since she ain't a virgin anymore."

All three dress styles were lacy vintage drapes that flowed down past the knee. Aster's was cream, while Iris and Galen wore baby blue.

"Nice call not wearing high heels," Iris said, slipping on wedged sandals.

"No point in torturing ourselves," Aster said.

While Galen fixed the flowers in Aster's hair, Iris left the room and returned with a bottle of champagne and glasses. She said, "A little bubbly while we wait."

"What is up with Jack? He's never late," Aster complained, suddenly feeling a bit jittery.

"Take a swig, and you'll be fine," Galen said, holding a glass while Iris poured.

Iris cracked the door open and peeked out. "People are arriving. I see Jack. He's setting up the keyboard."

"That man! I swear, I can't believe I'm going through all this rigmarole just to marry him." Aster sighed heavily.

"That's just nerves talking. If I ever saw a lid for a pot, it's you two. Come take a look. You look gorgeous." Galen chuckled, leading the bride to the mirror.

"Mom, you look like one of those ladies in the art nouveau calendar hanging in my kitchen," Iris commented.

Aster did a double take when looking at her refection in the mirror. For a moment, she swore Margaret Colton stared back at her and then gave an approving bow. The expression left a lingering sense that Aster was fulfilling her age-old destiny to renew the eternal lovers' vow. She smiled at her accomplishment.

"A regular historical period piece! Jack will love it!" Galen snickered.

The Retro Monkeys did an instrument check, strumming the acoustic guitar, plucking strings of the stand-up bass, and light brush strokes on the drums. Accommodating the request for a mellow atmosphere, they set up to play partially unplugged, only bringing amps for the keyboards and microphones. Ronnie Rodriguez, the guitar player with a 1970s shag haircut, gave a nod to Helen to begin. Sitting erect at the keyboard, she began the song "Color My World," by Chicago. Lloyd Higgins's ebony fingers added a soulful sound on the bass. Mike Simpson, with the sandy ponytail, kept tempo as he swished brushes across the drums. Ronnie wooed the room with his sweet voice.

A piano intro of the Beatles song "Something" cued the girls to grab bouquets out of the ice chest and exit. The minute Aster entered the room, the lyrics "Something in the way she moves attracts me like no other lover," filled the air, and she caught her breath.

Jack stood in front of the floral archway, dressed in a black suit coat. He beamed a gorgeous smile as he watched her approach.

Praying that her ankle would not twist in the raised shoes, she moved slowly. The last thing she needed was to repeat a historical setback and hobble like Cedar Claw all the way to the altar. Tuning out the fact that she was the center of attention, she set her sights on Jack. How handsome he looked in a black suit, not the navy blue he had intended. She was too preoccupied to notice that he and the best man wore black jeans under their coats. Jack's attire did not matter, for she had entered a sacred place. Each step felt like angels escorting her toward radiant love. She succumbed to the magnetism that drew their souls together millennia after millennia; it felt as though every cell in her body was blessed by the love of God. Aster practically floated the rest of the way to the altar. She passed her flowers to Galen and stood facing Jack, intoxicated by the smell of his sandalwood cologne. Obviously, under the same influence, Jack eyed Aster up and down and gave an approving wink. She beamed. They stood hand in hand.

Suddenly there appeared before her eyes an unworldly goblet that shimmered like the surface of a lake. Out of the cup a golden aura glowed and enveloped both her and Jack. It gave the sense of stepping into the other side of life, a place where angels bask in a vast amount of love. Aster's self-worth rose to a new level as abandonment issues with parents and grade-school classmates dissolved. She wiped away a tear.

"Congratulations! You found it!" Grannyme's voice cackled in her ear.

The grail? Aster thought, completely astonished to see it.

"It's filled with what you've been seeking," Grannyme added.

"Oh! Exalted love! It's delicious," Aster conversed silently.

Aster then inwardly thanked Grannyme for all the prodding that had led to this moment. Never in memory had Aster's heart been so full.

A little cough from the best man clued both bride and groom that the wedding party flanked them on each side. Tony, who towered inches over the others, resembled a charcoal pillar holding up the men's side. His sidekick, Rudra Patel, Jack's short and bald coworker from India, had a protruding belly that strained the buttons on his suit. Iris turned and smiled at Kenneth, who was seated in the audience. Galen dabbed her nose with a tissue.

Angelina Raphael, the ordained minister of no particular denomination, rang a tiny bell. She wore purple robes over a white shift. A pair of reading glass perched on the end of her nose while she read from an open book.

"We are all gathered together to witness the union of Jack Arthur McFadden and Aster Marian Snowden. Since this is a small group, and those in chairs are already in a semicircle, I think it appropriate for the entire wedding party to turn to face the congregation. The goal is to make a full circle. For a circle represents never-ending love ... the binding force that best joins a man and wife together. A circle describes the shape of the wedding ring ... a symbol of their vows."

While the minister preached on about circle metaphors, Aster scanned the attendees. One by one, she made eye contact with Irene, Felix, Kenneth, and the band members and their plus-ones, whose names she did not know. She lingered on one person longest. This man with curly ash-blond hair that nearly touched his ears, whose full cheeks wore a newly grown beard, looked happy. Her son aimed his phone at the wedding party and took a picture. Delighted that Sam had actually shown up, she gave a little wave.

"I told you he'd be here," Iris whispered, sweeping the cornrow braids behind her shoulder.

"To consecrate the union between Jack and Aster, the groom will now share his vows," Angelina said, giving a go-ahead nod to Jack.

Staring into lovely green eyes, Jack spoke to his bride. "Ever since I saw you by the creek talking to ducks, I knew you weren't crazy. I wondered if, perhaps, I was the loony bird falling in love at first sight. I was resolved to be a bachelor until I became lovestruck by you, my dear. Aster, you continue to dazzle my heart every day. And, beyond a doubt, you've enchanted me so, lifetime after lifetime. Humbly I bow in the honor of your presence, for you complete me. More than anything, I wish you to be my wife, because I vow to continue to love you throughout eternity."

Iris wept silently. Irene's arthritic hands wiped her nose with a hankie. Helen sniffled at the keyboard. Under bushy brows, Felix had blotchy red eyes.

Angelina paused to take a deep breath and said, "Well done. And now the vows from the bride."

Swallowing the lump in her throat, Aster wondered how many lifetimes she and Jack had married. Summoning up courage, she waited until a distinct tingly feeling inside inspired her to say, "Jack, when we met, I was an empty vessel. As time wore on, you filled me up. That romantic guy inside you had me envision us as two candles melted together. Our twin flames an everlasting light, a brilliant gift, impregnated by none other than Cupid's magic arrow. I cherish our bond deeply. Jack, my darling maniac, my friend, my lover, my piano-playing, soul-journey adventurer, you changed my life. You rekindled the fire, brought me joy, and made me believe in eternal love.

Because our relationship is blessed in this sacred way, I wish you to be my husband, and I vow to continue to love you forever."

Jack raised his hands to his heart and mimicked ripping open his chest, exposing his beating heart for all to see.

Thankful he did not beat his chest like an ape, Aster smiled at the antic.

Angelina suppressed a grin and concluded, "As we all bear witness before God, I pronounce you husband and wife. You may kiss the bride."

Electrical currents charged the air.

Jack whispered into Aster's ear, "Feel that rainbow connection?"

"I do."

The newlyweds kissed with such fervency that time disappeared.

About the Author

Holly Hunter writes fiction, nonfiction, and poetry. She is inspired to reach the hearts of readers who are attracted to transformation. Her areas of interest are psychology, herbs, nutrition, and spirituality. She lives in Colorado with a feral cat.

CPSIA information can be obtained
at www.ICGtesting.com
Printed in the USA
FFHW021919180919
55065051-60767FF

9 781480 881570